MIRACLE
An Exotic Wonder......

MIRACLE
An Exotic Wonder......

Aakash V Shivach

GenNext Publication

ISBN: 978-93-8022-280-6
Price: ₹ 290/-

First Published, 2016

Published by

GeNext Publications
5, Ansari Road, Daryaganj
Delhi - 110002
E-mail: gennext@hotmail.com Ph.: 9212142040

Printed at : G. Print Process, Delhi

Cataloging in Publication Data–DK

Courtesy: D.K. Agencies (P) Ltd. <docinfo@dkagencies.com>

Shivach, Aakash V, author.
Miracle : an exotic wonder...... / Aakash V Shivach.
pages cm
Novel.
ISBN 9789380222806

1. Adventure stories. 2. Indic fiction (English). I. Title.

DDC 823.92 23

A light glows to spread happiness and make us believe in it

Dedicated to

Varsha Shivach

My love, my life, open hearted kindly innocent, supportive my late sister

Contents

Acknowledgement

The Miracle is a new venture for me, seeing as it's the time to show a wonder land to everyone. A place which touches heart and sprays beauty all around with elegant evoking thoughts. Here we've followed the life of a group of guys with all twist of wonder never seen before. This will give standing to two buds of love and desperation. Then all climate is being set by them. It was an exciting project to work on, and I couldn't have done it without the support of many people. Thanks so much to my family and friends, particularly my close ones, for their constant love and cheer-leading. Many thanks are also due to the amazing publishing team who made this book possible.

Aakash V. Shivach

Prologue

I lost my sister. She left all of us three weeks back. Its have been a lot tough to club all sort of feelings in your heart and block your eyes from getting wet. All this is too harsh but I need to make my broken parents to stand by my grace. Burning pain in heart lingers on badly but pending rituals are there to be followed, so that my sister could rest in peace. Those weeked fingers of my parents struggling to pack things and align them, as we have to move to my *'Nani's'* place. At this time period these rituals are very tough to be followed. My eyes are just freezing up to save the other things that is left with me "Mother & Father". Now, we are ready to leave our home and I am struggling a lot to stop even a single drop of tear to be seen by my parents.

She is looking like an angle without any colour inbuilt as she always been, I said pointing towards my sister's sketch portrait which is being constantly starry-eyed by my mother.

'Yes she is an angel for all of us. So beautiful, as whichever colour she wears it adds into her beauty', Mother said with tears floating in her eyes.

'Let it be, we have to move on', I said.

'How can you handle all this so patiently', Mother said rolling her hand through my hairs and kiss me.

'See me, who is mine now apart from you both. You have to move on if not for yourself then for me', I said gracefully sucking my upcoming tears flowing out from my eyes.

'It is only you who said before that no one should try to go from this world before his time comes', I added.

'Hmmm....just see downstairs, I feel your father is ready or he may be still hearing those recordings of your sister', Mother said.

'Yes... wait I'll check', I said and moved towards the stair.

'How much more time will you both take and you don't need to worry about me, I am ok. But you just come and get into the car, I am waiting'. Father said coming out from room wiping his tears and removing out his phone leads from sister's his ears. The leeds he used these days to listen to sister's audio and video recordings.

'He's being fine and ready, come let us both get down and move for the place,' I said to Mother, who's still looking constantly at her cute doll...her friend....her protector...her supporter my sister..."Varsha".

This move of ours to my *'Nani's* place had started. This journey remained too good and exciting each time for me and my sister as we planned for it having immense fun. This time the ways becoming too tough for me to having handle while driving all four used to go together anywhere. My side seat being vacant, where my sweet, bubbly, smiley sister sat and talked to me and made me, happy every time. Driving car was becoming dangerous for me as it was becoming hard this time a lot for me to control my sensitivity and tears. My eyes just searching for her fragrance on her seat and getting more wet.

'I feel you both should sleep for the time being, as I feel we would take about 2 hours to reach there', I said.

'You know why he's saying all this, he feels we don't understand', Mother asked father.

'No, for what tell', Father asked.

'Same he's also the one who doesn't want to show tears to his parents, so that we are not going to break down more', Mother said.

'Ok...but this is also important for you both to have a bit of rest before we reach there. Isn't it', I asked.

'Don't worry my child, everything would be alright as I am alive still', Father said.

After driving for few hours, this is the time to get into the big giant gate of my *'Nani's'* estate. I horned loudly then the open. There was silence on every face with no expression, I stood out of the car to it make my Mother to get out easily and settled her at that area which was familiar to her childhood. I did so that my mother could think a bit about her infancy days and can be away from her pains.

'You stay with her papa, as whenever wants to come and meet you both was going to come here only', I said.

I had gone towards my *mama* (Mother's brother) and said, 'Look after her *mama* and see that he would stay away from any kind of infection. Tell everyone to console her not to let her weep more and more', I said to *mama*.

'I know that dear, we have to save any other cruel thing to happen now. Its a very hard time I know', *Mama* said.

There were all sort of elder people from my village who in our relation came meet my parents. They all start were going one after the other to give reliance and peace of my parent soul. This time there was no one to whom I could spray my internal evoking defeated desires which I had designed for my sister. I was just looking from a distance to my Mother as if I could't loose anything more now. She was kidney transplant person who needs special care.

A hand clubbed my shoulder from my back side and that too very tightly. I turned around and came to see that he was my childhood friend named "Kuldeep". He was the only one with whom I had done everything in my infancy days in this village. Whenever my summer vacation came we were here. I and Kuldeep did everything together. Kuldeep also treated my sister as his own sister and respect her a lot. That time we both were facing to each other but with no words. There were just tears coming out both our eyes and words vanished from our mind. I just hugged him. He made my deep breaths to get calm.

Breaking up the silence now he said 'Come lets go to the field. You need this change as you will feel better'.

'But mother.....'... I said.

"Don't worry dear many people are over here and everyone aware of mother's health. Each would be conscious about it, not to worry for that", Kuldeep said.

'Well...yes I think so', I said.

So, after this we moved towards the field where Kuldeep field need to water the sown seeds as it hadn't rained from a long period. He started doing his work and told me to stand a side and look towards him at what he does.

'*Hey* dear I feel that this could change your mood a bit and you feel relaxed in this open air and can think something else. But I was wrong I feel you were still lost and giving yourself pain', Kuldeep said.

'No dear.... don't worry I am ok', I said.

'Leave dear, I can see everything on your face. Seriously brother this thing on your face is killing me, you do know that she is my sister too, I also have that pain. So please bro.'.. Kuldeep said.

'Ok lets leave this place too we get back to my room where we do those adventurous stuffs.........Yes', Kuldeep added.

'Yes.'.. I said with a smile.

We left that place and reached at Kuldeep's home. His home was dark. I asked;

Then I feel there is no light at this place.

'Light is not functioning well these days I think supply is not there. Come carefully dear, look I am switching on my phone torch. Step forward slowly', Kuldeep said.

After that we entered in his house.

'Aakash, you just sit over here. There is no light and no one else at my home, so I need to arrange to light lamp on my own to go towards my room', Kuldeep said and moved away from me while letting me sit on a chair.

'I think Kuldeep would be over there, let me also go towards him', I thought and started stepping towards that room.

As I came closer to that place I hear voice of a person who seemed to be in pain. This person started shouting loudly now as I reached closer to the room. I stepped inside the room and found a Guy lying over there on the bed wearing just a trouser and nothing else over the top. His upper body part completely red and his muscles seemed to be bulging outwards. His body structure was a perfect muscled personality.

'Who's this person and why is he in pain', I said with intense confusion.

'Me......... ah...... my name is "Yash" you are right I am in no relation with Kuldeep but he had given me space over here to stay in humanity', He said.

'Huh... humanity...', I said and laughed.

'Why... you smiling like that for humanity. Is there something wrong in helping any person', Kuldeep said while in entering in the same room. He had gone holding the lamp this time for which he went off.

'Oh!... you came... yes humanity. I laughed on humanity. This is because it just give others and kills you', I said.

Yash was trying to make him sit comfortably on his bed which was becoming very tough for him. Kuldeep came forward and helped Yash to sit properly.

'Sorry... dear nothing being clear to me. How... is humanity going to kill you', Yash asked.

'Humanity is the only thing that killed my sister dear. I am also very humanitarian but when these kind of things happen to you then it becomes hard for you to believe in humanity', I said.

'Oh!... sorry for that I don't know about any such incident. But still something are not clear as such you said humanity took her away', Yash said.

'Dear, sorry for interrupting you more but really I want to know about her and how she left. Please brother if its ok for you', Yash asked.

'I don't want to talk too much and inform everybody about this incidence'. I said.

'Please like me your brother and elaborate your last line', Yash said with a pleasing face filled with sentiments.

'Ok listen then its my sister left me in an accident she met. This accident was because her car crashed to an electric pole. Then her car rolled two times on that road. You know that she was completely fine and she had came out of it without any injury. Driver was finished on the spot. There was one more girl with her in that car who collapsed the car and unable to came out of it. My sister left everything and ran on the highway forward and backward shouting for help but no one came. At last she called a person from 200 m distance and started pulling that girl, she saved her. Because of that car crash the high tension electric pole wire was hanging now just over her top and because of night darkness she was unable to look at it. So as she saved the girl and put her head up that wire touched her forehead and she left all of us'. I conveyed this story to Yash.

'So tell me now that how we can have a hope of building humanity inside our souls', I added.

A sense of numberness, confusion and distress captured both Yash and Kuldeep's face, who was standing on the door step still. Kuldeep this time seemed to brozen and provoked feels of both set my soul to be relax. As this time I felt that I was not the only one to be cut apart internally after thinking about these clumsy thoughts. Both of them who I had sprayed my feeting to with me on my way, so I was not wrong in conveying all what I felt to both.

'Ah.....bro if I can change all this by sacrificing any thing I do have, then this would be the foremost desire of my life', Kuldeep said while stepping towards me to put his hand on my shoulder.

'No Kuldeep...... I know this thing is so sensitive and all this grif had to be removed by Aakash only and we are only to make him to do so', Yash said.

'But for your wrong part I need to brush up some sort of beliefs that you had developed internally in your soul towards humanity', Yash said to me.

'Ha... trying to deliver same those sort of common repeated norms of humanity which being dispersed by everyone. Yash... don't you feel that all these humanitarian stanza's are just to said and don't have any valid example behind them', I said.

Yash stacked in silence.

He started moving his muscles upwards, seems like he was feeling uncomfortable to be seated in that posture for long.

'Wait dear let me help you', Kuldeep said.

'Yes... its not like, I am feeling uncomfortable now but the thing is I am trying for a more suitable posture in which I could sit', Yash said.

'Oh!.....I feel you were a lot afraid after what I said and that had disturbed your comfortability', I said so intensively.

'Ha...', Yash smiled.

'See my these unusual body maintenance is just because of all you said. Wait I'll convey all this to you just give me time to get a feasible sustainable posture', Yash said it to me while being adjusting his body and with a smile out-flowing from his face.

'Thanks... Kuldeep... I think this would be good, its been very much comfortable for me to sit like this. You can also take your seat now, as I feel conversation was going to continue for a long time', Yash said.

Oh!... dear could I ask what you want to converse now? Kuldeep asked Yash.

'All this is about Humanity...' Yash said with a smile overcoming on his face.

'Humanity... could you expand it and give a perfect outlook to your words... gentle guy', I said.

'Seems like you are in a move to go on with it rapidly. So my dear let me tell you that all this is just because of you. As such whatever I am going to convey to you I hadn't done to anyone and I don't either want to do so. These sort of things which I would convey this time are not been sprayed to Kuldeep either. Kuldeep, who is the person to help me', Yash said with peace coming on his face and his body pain moving apart.

'So... what is the need to tell me that then', I asked.

'Its because you changed your mind towards humanity and I can't let anyone do so. You know I had also become like you sometime before after getting continuously thrashed by natures killing attempts to my soul', Yash said pointing his face towards me and his eyes straight away digging in mine.

'I am still not getting your words clearly, till you are not going to clear this thing from the start and enlighten my eyes to the source factor', I insisted to Yash.

'I feel Aakash Yash wants to tell you about some thing, so you have to be patience dear. As such he is conveying something after a long time. He had not even told me anything still as he never wanted', Kuldeep putting his palms on my thighs and making me calm.

'So....this thing is about my life dear. As Aakash you talked about example of humanity and its source factor. So I felt that I got the right person to disperse my life event for whom I was waiting for as per God's guidance', Yash said pointing towords me again.

'Aakash.... my life was not very easy in my childhood days and never stayed easy thereafter till I hadn't been through "Heaven's Hell" ', Yash said.

'Heaven's Hell.....'.., Kuldeep interrupted as such I was trying to listen all that in brief first.

'Yes... its "Heaven's Hell", please I request you to not quest in between as it wouldn't allow me to convey and elaborate all those concerns that I need to enlighten with you', Yash said.

'Its been the story of "Heavens Hell" a unique beautiful place that was meant by God and governed to teach humanity', Yash added.

This last stanza of Yash had made both of us Kuldeep and me, Stuck in awe as these sort of things are out of bound from my memories.

Yash said, 'Please you both don't show such awkward reaction as it would make me difficult to proceed further. Let me tell you both first that I had seen a complete different world which named "Heavens Hell" and from there I had came. I had left that place not just all alone,' there were many guys and a girl with me at the time of my departure. So its been a story to give you a look how humanity brings Love, Peace and Power in your life', Yash said.

'So listen to all that you both have to be in peace as I go on from one stage to the other. Ha... so this is the reason for me to set myself that much comfort to sit dear Kuldeep', Yash said and smiled.

'Now I feel dear you don't make things much more curious and suspenseful', I said.

'Yes dear as I also don't want to keep you awaiting for that. As if I had met after a long time to a person whom I need to deliver the whole sort of my Journey to Heaven's Hell. As I told to inform, who could further deliver this to other beings and update them with this information', Yash replied.

'Ok........this is the reason why I hadn't cleared even a single doubt that I had in my soul regarding your past life. Which you had not discussed even after a lot of my effort', Kuldeep said.

'Yes... that is so...... dear', Yash replied.

'Ok... if in that sense of telling me your whole story you want me to write it down then I confess you I'll do so. But you need to be a little more elaborate in your context dear', I replied.

'Wait you start this, I just come back after taking tea and snacks for you', Kuldeep said.

'Kuldeep sit over here only with us from the start of it. *Hey* dear you just stay here and else nothing required', I said.

'*Hey*, how he got to know about your writing innovations, as its only me who know that'. Kuldeep replied.

'Ha.......now don't react like this dear', I said.

'For what my brother, I don't feel I am regretting anything', Kuldeep replied.

'Ok lets not make these small thing sound conspicious as I am not pointing you out. As you were thinking so', I said.

'Hahaha... what... what did you just say, I feel you are wrong somewhere or you were misleading in some manner', Kuldeep said.

'Dear listen... , I am all ok. So it is clear to you now', I said to Kuldeep this time while starring into his eyes which were trying to be hidden.

'And I feel you both shouldn't start all this now', Yash said.

Yash replied again, 'Yes Aakash, its like Kuldeep told me a lot about you before and we usually talk on your concerns. So now you can judge about all that yourself.'

My intimate gestures was just pointing towards Kuldeep now who was looking sideways.

Yash's eyes were so passionate to disperse some concern to me so deliberately which I could easily measure by his intensive eyes. Stress lines had started covering his head. Seems like there was something in him that becoming irresistible.

Yash stressed face, shuffling fingers and weak body now exciting a feel of help in my soul.

'Yash dear...... please...... I request...... dear sit easily, we are over here you don't need to worry about anything', I said holding right hand of Kuldeep and taking him back closer to Yash.

'Look we are just here and about to sit beside you. Neither you nor I are going anywhere now', Kuldeep said.

'Now I just want you to listen me...... those all things about my exotic wonders that I met. About all those heavenly touch that set my life on smooth shower. The love of mine which lets me to get closer to supernatural powers. At last the story of "Heaven's Hell" a place spread of heavenly beauty surrounds..."*A story of Miracle*"...' Yash said with the same still reaction attached on his face.

'*Miracle*.... whats that', Kuldeep asked with an intense desire on his face.

'I am really getting thrilled after hearing all this evoking wonders from your words', I said while putting my hand over his head, rolling his hair.

Yash insisted, 'look I am not alone in my ways as I have some supporting hands always safeguard me. So my story is about me and all those trackers with me. In which everyone is special as nothing would have happened just by me, if I had been left alone'.

'Wait... I feel all this should begin with a cup of tea', Kuldeep said.

'As you wish my dear...' Yash replied.

'So what are you waiting for go and arrange tea for all of us...' I said to Kuldeep.

'Yes I get back with hot cups of tea... just give me some time', Kuldeep replied and left the place.

'So Yash this short flame that you had burned inside me is not letting spare my single second. So I wish you should start with it dear as the tea would come thereafter', I insisted to Yash.

'Oh!... wow... look light has come', Yash said with sort of happiness on his face.

Yash replied, 'Now I can see you very clearly..... ah..... I mean physically'.

'Physically...'.. I said.

'Yes, its like after constantly hearing about you from the day I had came over here. All this had meant a kind of sketch of yours in my mind and now I can easily compare it to yours equally', Yash said.

'But I don't think it would be worthy for you', I said.

'Um...... don't get into my sort of thinking. It would be worthy for me, leave that you wouldn't understand', Yash replied.

'Let me start now to inform you about *Miracle*..... that is a humanitarian, peace loving, Lovely attached, inspirational story of sacrifice which tells you about the importance of humanity. It shows that humanity shouldn't be killed from your heart as God always respect every attempt of yours towards it. It praised me with my Love and which changed everything in my life beyond it...'.. Yash conveyed his whole sort of pleasures on his way towards *Miracle.*

'Go on dear I am listening to spray that marvellously to the outside world', I said.

"Miracle" An Exotic Wonder......

"Its hard to believe the extent power of love, sometimes it comes in a manner to help humanity and become a wonder of this world by making you free from your hassle. Sometimes it makes you realise that if the two natural powers as such the beauty of god's creation meet together to evoke auspicious love. They can give birth to new globe that can cure this world and save nature from ongoing cruelty and brutality of living being's. Sometimes these stories are meant to save our natures beauty, that smile's from these within dashing emotions that do encompass our mind for a peaceful sustainable growth. So hereby showing you this plus datum, I am going to set your mind to a majestic love story that is of mutiny, desperation and full of heaven's blue sky where you can see entire love spread apart "........Because Love do mutate a lot........:

- The only purpose of living that enlighten the spirit of happiness in our life.
- Love touch meant to make your breathless and to meet your soul auspicious desires.
- Love lighten up like a flame and involving persons attraction that includes sexual desires. A perceptional affection realised by people in there romantic life.
- Life attempts to sacrifice for there buds, for these loved ones beams on which there life dreams relies.
- The most unforgettable and mysterious game which stands still waiting for you to hold itself ....that's Love.

- Love is a force that can't be stopped and after its emergence tried to stopped it just destroys everything. It never allows anyone to understand it and enslaves us.
- The love you take is equal to the love you make.

A closed case that's of god, where love and humanity is the sole responsibility of every person that is set by the owner of this case before designing it with his golden stick........ Yes you all may be thinking of it in the rigorous direction and getting that all we are talking about is the "world". Which is meant for god over where the slaves. We the "Human being" that drives our car in it and starts driving it out too rough sometimes that even we don't realise that we are spoiling there own architecture, peace and prosperity. *Hey,* please don't feel that this whole nature is just studded with only these kind of people all around. Lets us talk about a group of guys abide at the place where God's presence being felt and as said by the holy scholar's the place where god's tone flows in the air and touches every heart, where along the line a drop of god fragrance persists evoke.

So let's not start to prove about those guys who were known said as criminal not because they were spoiling sober people's happiness nor doing any economic crime. It was all because they were prone to so much of violence and crime in theirs holistic place too. They had seen all those things that exist even a single per cent in there norms and values that were told to them since infancy. So I start my way with all that, Yash conveyed to me and I listen to him passing days and night in the same studded fashion. This story is all headed by the key role opting in all this mechanism a boy named "Yash" who had grown up in a Brahman's family and his father is an scholar and doctor for needy people. Yash's father used to deliver free treatment to all deficit people. Yash was always taught that moral of living to help needy and spread smile to others, but he never seen in his life the charity and devotion for others to do that he did it every time and others to follow too. So that none of the person faced wanted lack of happiness in their area and they can set a trend to the entire world from which other can see and realise the same.

Day by day he started getting depressed and frustrated by having a brief view of all these greedy faces of humanity that just wanted there task to be fulfilled any how.

Then at that time he opted for a step that was not difficult to follow. Which is because of the fact that he raised in his soul feeling for devoting his life for others. This step was a lot tricky which he took to tell the tale. It took a lot of guts to make it so.

The step that he opted was just to sacrifice himself for the sake of humanity by eradicating every single piece from this nation who was making a big wreck of nature's humanity.

He left his home, went through several harsh and stricky situation's and do you know what way he started this.

He had started killing to the persons who were being responsible for the degradation of all that he didn't want. He felt that this would be the only way to remedy all this and to heal up all vacant holes that the nation had by digging a big well and dumping all these small holes in it and when the holes of all this nation were terminated off then finishing that well too.

He was too smart in doing all this and slowly he met one by one some people that started to espouse him in his movement. So there were four more guys came in contact with him and took off his actions to the target by being a part of it. They all were named as:

Sunny, Soni, Ankit, Gaurav

Yash : He was a medium height guy with long light brown hair. He was fond of changing looks after he get abduct with his present posture and style. Yash wears loose hanging cloths as having an athletic body. Tight clothes didn't give him comfort. He was afraid of girls as he's not engaged in any phase of his life with them.

Sunny : A tall personality with small eyes and long black hair. Easy and cool person, relieved on his present to enhance his future, not worried about anything what he was going to face next. Childhood friend Soni, spent his childhood in Orphanage.

Soni: Short fat boy, with hanging pants, Delightful personality. He acts as supporter of Sunny whenever he gets low. As Soni was more confident than Sunny about life related facts. Childhood friend Sunny, spent his childhood in Orphanage.

Gaurav : He is a short guy ever smiling face and lighten eyes finding joy. He was the person who makes other amused and irritated by his innocent and careless acts. Fond of girls but it becomes hard for him to catch anyone.

All were being similar in there concepts and dreams as Yash and that's why Yash started to be with them and work accordingly towards as a savior of humanity.

By making some typical kinds of ethics and standard of survival.

I had mentioned in my first intro stanza about criminal, by this act. I want to tell you that doing all these things would be a crime in one's sense but this is not in the others. Some people intentions and thoughts don't even feel it so because according to them the person should be punished to that extent. While other people who follows the same way, don't scared.

"The story contains some stages each and every phase over here has its own natural colour and flavor mixed in it of its own.

Somewhere it is covered by love, other places by super natural power and at others it shows the shower of nature's beauty and wonder."

1

Heaven's Caught

"Life becomes elegant not by getting apart from your objectives but to design your impassioned and exciting way to reach that Goal".

Some thing get wrong in this market everything is just in a rush.

Happiness spread out at this place because it was the time of Diwali festival season and every one poised with there family. Market was looking too dashing because of the lightning and decoration by the big shop owners, which was looking extremely out of bound for people to visit for shopping and be a part of the glory and colourful happiness by spreading all this in their life too.

There were some people singing holy song's to make a mood for the crowd as God was visiting that place. So every body would be seeking to impress the God by greeting him with all that they have. It were conveniently measurable that how much pleasures they all had because of the forthcoming season.

Every shop was blaining with musical sound which also entertaining every single person.

But this is just the background phase of story on the other end:

Group of guys were running inside this market like someone had left man eater animal behind them and they were just running for survival by saving themselves from it. In that big crowd they was running like they have the last stage of marathon race and just seeking to be at the top.

But why they were running like that for what sake they so stressed and apprehensive that explicitly written on their face.

This would be a question that you all were thinking of and crowd at the market also think the same. Whoever comes in contact with all these?

Ah.....That's the thing they are running because of Cops, Who were following them and seeking to nail them. May be they had done certain mischief for which they are being reproached so.

But as per people who wandered at that place these guys were looking too decent with good personality and appeared to come from a good background. So what kind of crime they had done? This is also a thing that was coming into their mind.

The crime that they did was murder one of the richest man belongs to that place. But none of the people wanted to talk about that convicted person because he took lives of a lot of families just to use them as a stepping stone for being at the top.

The man who following them was not dress up in a peculiar police man posture, it looked like he dressed to show just the colour of Cops dress (*khaki*).

Cops that were following these guys listed three, from which two of them quite young enough. I think one of them senior, who's having inches of white moustache on his face and wearing a unique kind of hat having shiny colourful shades on eyes.

These guys were running here and there to safeguard themselves and not to be caught by them. You know this was not the first time they did a thing like this, they had done it before too but every time they did there work so cleverly that no chance was left for them to be caught by someone. But this is there first time they got caught and that's why they were running every where to rescue them. They all were also having innocence on there face because while doing all this they never feeling that they doing any crime.

Yash gets into a shopping mall.

He did not know where to hide himself at that place, so he got into washroom but that's of women.

Girl shouted.... Aw...

'Afraid miss', Yash said as soon as he saw her and realised that he's at wrong place, stepping out his foot towards the first floor.

Same girl again Ankit stood there after Yash.

'Afraid' Ankit said and ran away.

Sunny is still forth, not in the mall running in market here and there.

As he was in the market a small boy of around four years came in his way crying badly.

Sunny tried to move forward not listen to that boy's crying but he want to attached with spirit. So he did not walk forward and went towards the boy, buy a toy for him, and set him happy then again ran away.

'Gaurav', Yash shouted.

'Yes', Gaurav said

Yash said, 'come here soon where you were left behind'.

'I had seen there; a couple having romance at that place. I got the memories of 'Shruti' in my mind that's why I had halted there', Gaurav said.

'*Hey* my brother this is not the time for you to do all this. we were in a massive scrape now and we have to get rid of it as soon as feasible', Yash said.

'Afraid brother', Gaurav said lets go now, where others.

'Sunny and Ankit was with me, we had to move towards main city now. I think cops was no where around and we can conveniently step forward but where is Soni left, had you seen him', Yash asked Gaurav.

'No I didn't saw him, I think he entered in the cross sheet bar when I had seen him last', Gaurav said.

'Oh!...God what would I do for you all boys, I think you all were taking it too lightly', Yash said 'hey man we are criminals as per government.'

'We don't feel it so that's all about ours spirit not the spirit of the government. Why don't you all get my points, we have to save our self at every step and see you all are just not giving that much response to this concern as now. Soni is still in the bar. I know and what he's doing there god knows', Yash replied again to make things explicit to there wisdom.

'Ok, you all don't be tense I am just going to take Soni with me till then you all should go and reach the church, I and Soni going to reach there', Ankit replied.

Ankit soon left that place in pursuit of Soni.

He reached at bar and shouted Soni once but there was no response from any where, he got a bit apprehensive whether Soni being caught by the cops because he was not saw anywhere.

'Had you seen a tall, handsome person wearing pink shirt over here', Ankit asked to bar tender.

'Yes, a person came here in pink shirt he was tall too but he didn't sit here because as soon as he came he clicked up with a group of music club people sitting. here and went off with them', Bar tender said.

'Life... this music of Soni would going to take us to hell', Ankit said.

Soni was there sitting under the tree with guitar in his hand and the whole music club people sitting around him listing ecstatically to the auspicious beauty of his music.

Ankit walked closer to that group and said;

'What a melodious beat of strings, I think some solemn musician had came here from Rome'.

Soni smiled and said 'whoever be the musician but first he's your friend my dear'.

'Well...my brother let's get rid of this place, I think this is not the right place for us to stay for so long', Ankit said.

Ankit said, 'Soni we have to go for the wedding, so pack up and come soon with me'.

2

They both walked silently as if not talking to each other. But there was faint smile on the face of Soni because he again met with his first love that's his music. That is why Ankit too didn't say anything to him regarding this kind of activity today at a lot hazardous moment. Ankit was also quite happy as his friend smile blast had evoked at that time.

'Don't feel that I am not telling you anything about all this that you did here which is not to be done at this point of time, so it's all fine.

'Dear please get to know this thing that we have to direct our mental strategy as time suggest so be conscious about it in past', Ankit said.

'Yes brother' smiley and too conveniently Soni said. Let's go now.

The time when they were talking about all this Ankit felt someone following them. He turned back and saw that the Cop who is having white moustache is just standing a foot back and as soon as he saw that, the Cop smiled at him.

Ankit got too feared by that and just said 'run...run'.

They both raced towards the building, went to its second floor stair's but the man came there too behind them holding the gun in his hand. At that time due to fear Ankit stepped his foot a bit back and he fell from second floor stairs to the ground.

'Ankit...' Soni shouted.

Soni step down speedily roushed towards the ground to save his friends life. But as soon as he reached, he saw that Ankit stood profoundly fine, standing over there rubbing his clothes, nothing went wrong with him.

Soni took a deep breath.

'Thanks GOD', Soni said.

'God saved me', Ankit said.

But there is one standing at present over the second floor. Now the cops are no where to be seen, and that time they decided to straight away move towards church where all of that friend's are just waiting for there arrival.

'Chill and just walk towards the destination' Soni said.

Then both of them in an hour reached church this is because they didn't took any vehicle, any conveyance and went through the hazardous way inside forest to the church.

'Where have you been took so much time to come here. Can you even guess how much stressful it is to be waiting for you over here', Yash said screamingly.

'We all here are just being apprehensive of you both'. Sunny asked desperately 'say dear what happened to you'.

But he didn't tell them about the incident that happened with him at building and Soni also noticed this thing which Ankit didn't wants to tell them. He felt may be he did't want them to know it, because they could get more disturbed in this difficult time.

Soni said excitedly 'we saved our self from those cops just came here without thinking about anything'.

'Yes let's move from this area too, it's not easy to stay here for a long now, this is also getting unsecure as time passes', Yash said.

Then they all enter in the church, Sat down for a while on chairs lying there, prayed to god for adherence in their way. All this is because as I said before they all were good humanitarian people and there's way of solving problem apart but there soul denies or put it into bad category.

As they finished doing all this;

Those three Cops that were following them, just waiting to get out of church so that they can take all of them for punishment.

'Ah...what's this how come they got to know about us', Sunny said have been

'They have been waiting here as if they know that we are going to come at this place only', Yash said.

'Fucked up', Yash added .

The man with the white moustache came close and said 'now this is my turn to say something and you all just need to listen'.

He reminded all of them like a kid who had lost the way and be on a vague track which never finishes off because it did have no ends, as God is the only person to draw line on it.

'Sir do you know that person to whom we stained'. Yash said to make him realise that what they did is not a crime it's in favour of humanity. 'How much life's had he spoiled and taken away even the life hope from many families'.

'But crime is crime, we can't say a murder as the charity and every one being punished for it you too' Cop said.

The Cop that looked to be of old age but the two other cops that were with him not doing any action. They were just present over there for the sake of formality it looked so.

'The thing that you all were doing is not written in humanity. You meant it right yourself according to yours own desire', Cop said angrily.

'But sir you don't even know about us, we are not here to spread crime. We were just seeking to solve the tragic pyramid of our nature that gives wealth and glory to the person who just cheats and hurts others. This nature stands empty handed for those who follow the track of truthfulness and sacrifices. What nature does is make sacrifices to grow more and more without any act of kindness to them' Sunny said.

'I know everything about you all and just get in and come with me, we hadn't enough of conversation', the Cop said putting a way to their conversation.

The older Cop said to the two other cops who were with him to aid as he is going to take care of all them and take them with him.

The vehicle that they were having also a typical one and not a Jeep.

Neither a car it was nor a bullock cart having two horses at the front which are going to take it forward.

'What's this..., we have to go in this', Sunny asked.

'Oh!... Yes do you need any jet or a Ferrari to take you from here', the old Cop asked smilingly.

As they all got into it, the old cops tightened up the strings of horse and started to depart from that place.

'Sometimes the thing that you see actually too is not the case you should focus on the other part of life also', Yash said in need of help.

"Because whoever is spared of personal pain must feel himself *called* to help in diminishing the pain of others' this is what we had learn from life and applied in the sense to help others, Yash replied again.

'Yes... you were right in this context my child, but to fill a well, it's not required for you to jump into it and then start filling it because in that case you won't be able to finish your task you would also finish up soon', the old Cop replied.

'But don't you feel that we are sacrificing our life just for the sake of humanity'. Ankit said calmly to impact the mind of the Cop so that he can deliver a sense of realisation and the spirit and sacrifice behind all this that they were doing. 'Sir you should give us some more time for this phase, till then we can make this world that much better so that no one is scared of breathing freely'.

'You all should know that the act you were performing is not regarded as a sacrifice or a charity in "The solemn Bible" and judiciary'. The old Cop said. 'So you are not flawless in both God's and living being perspective'.

'Soni...do you think that your music school had been taken off from you and your all little students to whom you teaches on free basis. You both faced problem because of the single person', old Cop said.

'And Ankit you think that the people to whom your father delivered lessons on "*Adhyatama*" were only one's responsible. Your father to be slained and making your life to be ruined off', Old cop said dictating them all 'Now by killing those kind of people you feel that there is no one going to regenerate again like them. All this is not your work. This is just governed by that supernatural power who makes you move, feel and realise that's GOD'.

'How can you know all this', Soni asked in a big misconception of dilemma and shouted at the priest.

'It doesn't matter what do I know and how I came to know the whole ketchup stories about you all', old Cop said.

'What matters is that you all presented and performed for the tribe till now', old Cop replied.

'You don't even know what all I faced in my life. (When someone two held a hammer on the same place with the same pace. What is precious for you even if you plead in front of them for some sympathy. Apart from emulsifying broken legs of the person if he doesn't even listen. Then situation becomes a bit confusing in your mind whether the peace and prosperity track which you opt is of any use or not)', Soni replied with depth on his face.

3

Abruptly Gaurav saw in this four sided small bullock cart was shining like gold. As if spread with gold at the side corners of it.

There were two beam stands meant to hold your self to feel cosy inside but those two also looked of gold.

Now something was there that Gaurav couldn't digest this time started setting a mood for Gaurav as frightful things were coming across him.

'I don't feel that I need to explain anything to you Soni, for all that you told me because I know that every answer is inside your soul only'. Old cop replied after some break 'As you think for it and ask of it every day in the evening time when you settle in church'.

'How you know about this thing, as if I even didn't share with any of my friends either', Soni asked himself.

'And I don't feel there would be any reason with you Yash because being good is your trait, you can't enforce anyone to be the same in humanitarian functionality', old Cop asked Yash.

'Yes... you were right but...', Yash said it before getting silent with no words no thought's ahead, like he was asking the same question from himself.

"By just brutally ruining the garden full of Cactus doesn't aid those sort not going to grow at that place again", old Cop said. 'They had grown before going to grow again but the thing that you can do it just make a kind of atmosphere where they can't resist'.

'You are getting my point Yash', old Cop asked.

'Yes... I do', Yash replied.

'So why do you debate that by just killing the person who is accountable for a nuisance going to fill this gap of nature', old Cop said.

Now this time everyone had set a vacancy of words.

'Tell me how you were knowing that much about each one of us. As we don't have any past record also', Ankit said with cracking sound.

'I was wondering that why this boy is not conveying anything as these dilemma going in his mind', old Cop said to Ankit.

'Yes for sure...I was just measuring everything and acculturating your every work and the situation all around this place'. Yash replied anxiously.

'I see nothing is going natural over here from the time we met, can you please explain what all has been gone.'

'Good to listen and know about your skill of judgment and your intellectual six sense is working too fine over here too. But it would be a lot good if you helped your friends to not follow you in your way', Cop overpowered.

'But why I am telling you all this as you think that inventor of all this conspiracy', old Cop said smilingly.

Gaurav's confusion got much wired with time because of those suspicious things he saw last.

He wandered for a while whether he should disclose these things to Ankit because he was the only one who is going to listen and give regard to what he is seeking to say.

Gaurav took a coin from his wallet and threw it towards Ankit so that he could be attentive towards him and come close to him, so that he can share all this mysterious matter with him.

'What is this, and what do you want, 'Ankit said frustratingly.

'No....nothing I am just making my mind to get rid of these emulsifying stresses, Gaurav giggled.

'And this is how you are going to do so', Ankit said with striking stress on his face.

'Every time behaving like this, doesn't work be a bit decisive at least for some sort of period my brother'. Ankit replied again 'In a time like this hectic one you should just think of getting saved not to play around to refresh up your mind'.

'Uf..... I just crack to craft my words with him. I wandered if he could understand it and he also reacted like, I had burned up his cloth', Gaurav murmered to himself.

Soni was started murmuring a song that he usually does every time and no one over there reaction towards it because everyone know that he does it whenever the time is not working according to his needs.

Soni and Sunny were being infancy (childhood) friends who studied together in a convent and at that time they both daily share their food with those hungry and needy.

During childhood nights they both worked to collect there own and others unused cloths, for making them utilitarian for those needy people to wear. They bear this pain so that other children could feel better. On one hand, Sunny was being solemn rigorouser of poems, on the other hand, music was too melodious as every one just want to listen to make their day.

But no one aware the desire of nature. Cruelty of human being had stood so high up in the sky and affected the direction of air flow for them.

Some people make climate so friendly for themselves while others can't even feel the air to breath.

They both belong to the same town and their town with whole family was used up so brutally that just deadly fumes were spread around.

The track they were following and all they were facing kept them happy because they halted demanding anything from nature.

They were not even experience a little of discomfort as....the bullock cart on which they were travelling was move like an ice floating over water. No one could realise how a bullock cart could move so smoothly like a scrolling plane.

'*Hey* what's this something moved over here', Gaurav said in dilemma.

He was talking about the place where they sitting upon a white cloth.

Yash probed the place togather what he had seen there but he find nothing.

'There's nothing other there....be easy', Yash said.

But the curiosity of Gaurav had taken a flight. Which couldn't take a halt as yet his crazing sunder wanted to know that what is present there underneath.

'Do you all need some food to eat', the old Cop asked.

'No it's not required we just needed to get rid of all this if you can do so then do it', Yash said irritatingly.

'Ha... I think you are thinking that I am a tourist guide, who had just taken you all up to give a ride,' old Cop asked. 'Well my childrens I am going to make you get rid of it just wait and watch'.

'It's irritating me too, please would you tell me where you were taking all of us and where did your police station stand'. Sunny said curiously.

'It's been a long way, as we travelled so far now'.

'Which tracks you were taking us as every route is too empty. It settle that this whole track is owned by you for us...say', Sunny tried to speak up all his wanders.

'I didn't ask you anything and I don't think that you have to talk about it or think about it', old Cop said.

'Really.....this is not working now. You have to spray our mind with the answer of all sort of questions like where you shall taking us all because from your talk and your behaviour even I am also confused', Yash said.

'Ha...', Cops laughed.

'Seriously... first tell us how do you know our familiar things so profound that include our inside truths which we even didn't share with our own soul'. Ankit said profoundly judging the situation and breaking his silence.

'You all would had heard in your primary school classes that if a person does good think then it could be feasible for him to be not noticed by others. But when person does something bad then it doesn't take much time to spread like a virus', old Cop said. 'So I don't think if you are criminal's it could have take much time to me to know everything about you all'.

'*Hey* you please don't talk so philosophically with us and stop calling us criminals again and as you don't know anything', Yash said.

Old Cop giggled and said...

'This doesn't mean that if someone love, being slain then he can't love anymore. So after that he's going to opt a way of saving others love by being a killer of human being'...

Sunny got in gloomy silence after listening as him to he touched that part of his life which never permit him to stay happy. He had lost his family in childhood. When he grew up,

God had blessed him with a truly difficult world. His lover mate as luck would have it in his life to be with for long and he lost her.

'It settle to be a book', Gaurav said to himself.

He probed all over to see that.... and what he had grape was the Bible lying over there.

He removed the cloth over it, it's been covered with flowers all around as if someone kept it too precisely with a lot grace and a stick lying over it. Stick was shining like anything this time, its too deep that he just can't think anything else apart from seeking to see it more deeper, as if he started getting profoundly lost in it.

When he went through it, he saw that there was all blue everywhere in its depth as It's feel like it was profoundly full of blue ocean waves and they just used over it.

As much as he was seeking to look inside it, he felt more and more dissolved though and that too he wasn't able to think anything else apart from that Bible, he just kept seeing it till the time he looked off................

'*Hey* Gaurav what happened...........hey hello....Gaurav', Ankit said.

'I think has been tired and spirit sleepy too, let him sleep now', Yash said.

Slowly the climate of there's aura started drifting itself to make an abrupt change, now it looked like fog had covered them all around.

'*Hey* why this climate is being like this, it's not the season and time too for the climate to show its like this', Soni asked.

'Don't be apprehensive about what this climate is now as its not a exotica', old Cop asked. 'Just think about what would you all do in your future'.

'This doesn't matter, that much to us sir, if it does then we can also plan for a beautiful and secure life before doing all this', Yash said with confident eye'.

At this point Ankit felt shadow of something getting dark.

Abruptly climate was becoming worse and too dark now. It settle that dark clouds were started to bulge in black as they had covered them from all around.

That time Ankit was thinking about this thought that being sprayed to his mind by Gaurav, did not feet and he felt something underneath over there. Ankit moved a bit and came close to Gaurav in a way to probe those instincts he felt.

'*Hey* sir, tell me that...Where the hell is your prison or police station. Do you know from how long we have been travelling and not getting at any place a jest or what', Yash said after losing his patience.

Ankit stacked and came to observe the same thing that Bible lying over there which is being covered with flower's all around and a stick lying over it. The stick was shining like anything and when Ankit saw that he was just seeking to feel why all this is being kept over here.

As Ankit had a solemn wisdom about god's will and their character functionality. As all the holistic traditional books that are there in this world were familiar to him.

He was just seeking to encapsulate that why this Bible stuck there. He informed about this to Sunny and Soni both. The clothes that veiling the bible had been taken off by Ankit now...

As soon as they came to see Bible over there they just seems to be hypnotised and mixed in it.

Now all these three are just penetrating into it as the same have been seen by all them and just being lost in its depth.

This time Yash was sitting at the corner with his eyes closed and rubbing his head with one of his palm.

Now after all three being mixed in the same flavor, they got too sleepy same as Gaurav.

Yash shouted 'hey you all.....what happened to you, this is not the time to take rest, wake up'.

After all that he shouted on them with clumsy spirit but there too no one responded.

Yash then shouted facing towards the old Cop 'would you tell me, what happened to all my friends and what is going on here, tell me'.

'You are taking us to give punishment but this is not the time to do so. You are responsible for my friends to be in this condition'.

'This is not a way to take us, why are you bluffing it' Yash said pleasingly.

'You are not doing right and why you have not been responding to me', Yash said again to the old Cop.

At that time don't know from where like a big bundle lots of light just left the sky and started coming from the front side where Yash was facing the old Cop........and at that time the old Cop turned back having an extreme smile on his face and just looked at Yash.

Yash felt some shining impassioned two diamonds shining in old Cops eyes. He won't be able to resist that much shine that came from his eye's and he started to be fallen down by some sort of restlessness.

Now it's just the old Cop who is conscious at this point of time and was really blissful the way he took every one to their destination. The way being profoundly filled with natural wonders and why it wouldn't be, as it's been towards a place that being created by god. Everything that god does is fabulous because he's only the ultimate creator.

Old Cop was happy because he was getting back to his pre-existence place after a long time. Where all creatures obstructed to do things and he was one of the superiors in that place.

Nature dispersed and started becoming too dashing with its distributed s as time passed.

Birds started to sing melodious songs making that climate more and more ecstatic.

The ocean waves were rising as much higher as they could, feels like they want to go at the place where they all about to reach. So ocean was making a heavy sound through its waves rising and falling so it touch their vehicle which started floating up close to the sky.

The rainbow also came at the top and started showing its colour, like it is inviting all of them to the purest place of the galaxy.

The air also started flowing in the direction towards which they all were proceedings. It's also helping them to reach that place as soon as they could and air can also drop them at the gate of Glory (The Heaven).

This whole journey stays every time a precious moment for old Cop because the beauty all around just overwhelmed him and he's the only one who knew what's next phase was going to be.

Steadily.......steeply they surged towards their destination.

After some time Soni seemed to feel a bit of move and he craked to open his eye's and stood up. As Soni got up rubbing his head and making his hair aligned, what he got to see that they were in entire region deep inside the sky above clouds. He had seen his friends lying faint in the same position as before.

'What......, happened to all of them', Soni shouted.

He crack to wake them up by rubbing their face there hands. Then everyone body started surge upward settle responding too.

Old Cop was smiling that time to settle now he wanted them to awake up and start to face the new phase of life that was seeking to club them in its arms.

'Who are you.......why are you not revealing all this to us and why you doing all this', Yash shouted breaking the silence.

'There is no need to shout, all that is happening. Its all about what you did in your life', old Cop said.

'But this is not the way you should remedy us, you are taking us to the prison for our punishment as everyone does. So where dio you bring us, are you some magical person say.... who you are and what you want from us', Ankit asked.

'So childrens, this is the time to tell you everything, that what all is going on around you as per my dictates on every sort of thing to you on our way. I crack my best so that I can make you realise that the act you all were doing is not the way to follow and make the world to go on a wonderous track', old man approached to give them a brief wandered about the thing that he's going to tell them next.

The crime that you all did leverage life of those peoples who was a shame on humanity that's why you don't come in the area of harsh criminals but you did it and it's a crime'. Old man replied. 'You are not allowed to take lives of anyone, as this is just under God surveillance then who are you to decide and do that your way'.

'But please tell us first that who are you to say all this and what is your plan behind it', Yash asked from him.

'Who am I to plan anything about humanity and their future, I am just slave of god', old man replied.

'Oh!.......are you the priest', Ankit asked.

'Good Ankit...rigorously answered...yes I am the Aficionado of the solemn powerful man and the biggest creator of this world...........Our God'... Old priest said.

Everyone stood in shock.

'And I had come to take you all with me for a punishment by God, as you all had done a crime which comes in amidst of God and humanity correction. So God had decided to put you all in our (Heaven's Hell)', all this thing were being stated by the old priest.

'Heaven hell, what's this.....could you give a glimpses to us', Ankit asked with a shocking reaction on his face.

'I don't think that I need to reveal you all about it now', Old priest guided them all. 'Only the thing you all should know is that this time, you were not been punished in your world. You being punished in climate Heaven'.

What is next is not getting explicit in their mind even a single per cent.

Now after seeing all these implications, face and answer finding eye's of all of them, old priest without wasting any more time just stretched the strings of horse and moved towards the golden gate of God's glory...

...Those broken tone mixed with tearing pain.

Felt by our soul when we started looking deep into those eyes of world drain.

We crack to club them, enforced our feels to set calm and crack to breath in crawling overhauled suspicious human's desire.

We stepped towards it but everyone spread our land with spokes that were too bitter.

Those which meant to evade my underneath space of foot either.

We pledged to try till 'The last through' which could give us time to set reliance in this poisonous air.

Yash took a breath and spread— I never felt alone as every time being joined by some more.

Who do have the same itching towards the whole as I do...so I didn't feel alone.

I had never sown seeds as it is just the courage of the people to save the world. Which were dropped by our God on "Earth surface" and never shown.

I do have faith on other and know about my intentions to be felt inside people and God. As I just impassioned to adorn this world and rattle its cozy suburban dreams.

Lastly we all plucked, sizzle down and silenced some tones that make so much noise to just fill their own homes".

2

Arrival of Slaves

"More you bear knowingly or unknowingly is equal to the more you deserve....".

4

Something settled to come from far apart as all who wasstanding on the top cover of the cave which is the place called as Heaven's Hell.

There seemed to be a discussion going on amidst all of them about who is coming now and from which planet they belongs too. As it is the third time they were having a look at creatures like these.

'I think that all these belong to the planet where spirituality stays and breathes in the heart of people', said by the door keeper (watchman) of this large cave, 'because I am getting smell of god's flavour from his gesture and appearance'. This is the most I could gather from it, as being at a large distance from them'.

Yash with his friends and priest were on their way towards the golden gate of Glory. Behind which as conveyed, they were going to be punished.

After being known about the priest they all stood a bit amased about all these wonders.

Wandering that could also occur we are being deferent reproach by the god not by the judicial for a crime like this. They were just crinkling by some sort of relaxation from the god for whatever they did.

'What you all started thinking now, asking relaxation from god... hey listen let me make you all clear "This is your defying relaxation only as god asked for your punishment in the heaven's hell not over the 'Earth surface' by your judicial". 'Old priest replied to as if to explicit the theme that is dipping up in all their mind set round and round.

'*Hey* don't be shocked like this.........as per you all are knowing now that I am a person of god'. priest replied again 'So it's been too easy for me to discern what all had been going into your mind'.

'But one thing which I am not getting and I think my friends were also tensed for this why god wants to punish us in this note'. Ankit asked the priest after cracking that silence.

Yash provoked into speech after that 'If he feels that we were criminal then he could just leave us to be caught by our land force. Is it that he wants to give us a more harsh correction that's why God called us over here'.

'I hadn't expected such a reply from you Yash', Cop said.

'*Nah*......why do you think so. Think in a bit opposite manner god may have called you here because he felt that you all had been flying off at a tangent and misguided by some one', priest said to them informatively.' Also because you all are working towards making humanity to live conveniently'.

'Ok... I feel things were not getting clear to you. It's all that the crime you all did God counseled about this with me and we concluded that your crime is not for your own growth and wealth. All these you did, so that humanity could survive conveniently. That's why you were being spared from this ruthless and wasteful punishment of land and as per you all need to know a lot and want a right guidance. That is why God decided to put you all for punishment at Heaven's Hell', priest said to them informing about everything with his swift open eyes. As these are the only words he sprayed that conveyed he is a bit inclined toward our sentiments.

Excitement being grabbed in priest pocket and he will get them out one by one.

'There is a heavy shine over there. Did we come closer to sun. Wait... if this is so then please put us back and cover up, don't let us to get burnt like this', Sunny said as he wandered that because of our punishment may be the priest is going to throw us in this sun's heat so that our body got ruined up in this manner.

'This is not the sun's heat that you came across there. This is something else' priest replied.

'What then......it's producing an extreme light which is not bearable', Sunny asked.

'Child...this is the gate where I am going to let you in, where you are going to start other phase of life', priest answered.

'This is the gate where all living being from other planets were brought up, whom God wants and being punished', priest turned and said 'don't be tensed Sunny as you are not going to be burned inside'.

'Ok...we need to get in it', Soni said.

'Yes as you know about it now', priest smiled and replied.

Birds started crawling there in a heavy tone and some of them started singing song too making that climate everlasting musically auspicious.

'How birds came here at this place. I think it's been very much higher so how did they come here, as they do n't fly that much', Gaurav asked priest.

'You can't say like that', priest replied.

'Why..?'

'As it is so obvious and you could measure the same', Yash replied.

'And what if I am going to say the reverse of it. As if this place is very much deepest apart from highest', preist giggled and said.

'Ha....' Yash.

'Yes, you can say... as its your mouth and your decisive tongue inside it. Which is going to convey what you want', Yash smiled on his last words and tried to express himself 'So if you want to say and feel like that, we are not going to feel so'.

'Yes, perfectly right Yash as it had no features of earth's core had crust all is just space around', Ankit stood forward and added to Yash's words.

'Even I am not agree on giving you all the realization and wasting my precious time here', preist said 'Time is going to convey all that to you'.

'So how did living animals like birds being brought up at this place. As I asked this question from you first', Gaurav raised back his ques.

'So I do just tell you that, you all also don't stay here how did you all came here', priest asked.

'It aid you to make them to come here', Gaurav replied.

'Park this is not the thing that you need to know. These are all creatures that God meant over here to make environment familiar to them. Who comes here because the original place of God is land only in this sense', priest replied.

5

There is climate that remains in my perception that every time at this place above the clouds a foggy kind of environment, refreshing air to breathe, a sort of music going on.

They came a lot new to their destination now and the men standing there on the Gate of glory had seen them coming from far apart. He was also wondering that who all were coming from the God's favourite planet the land of mercy, the planet of human being. They being called from earth.

They all urged towards it so rapidly. With a smile on priest face and a sense of stress and discomfort on all of their face.... earth.

'Tell us how many period we have to tick fast over there......priest', Sunny asked to priest.

'*Hey* my boy you were going over there to be corrected, Scolded by god and not for any work or purpose of yours', priest said to them 'So don't accept the time limit nothing is in your hand everything is set for you all over there'.

They was reached at the gate of glory at peak time. This was the time when automatically they wanders what they see according to the priest. They wandered about all he said every word by the priest on the way. They all now uttered to be implicated and their presume everything that priest said to them and guided can be seen on their faces so explicitly now. All of them got to know about everything that priest discussed and said to them on their way was just a sort of guidance, which could make them feel and realise. They started feeling how much wrong they were in their wondering and expression. They felt that whatever they did at their place just being far from crime in our sense. In our eye's but the scene of this world doesn't go based on our belief, our judgment. These all things were being governed by the Supreme Power which is the creator of this auspicious beauty of nature our God.

They all the time were realising that the thing priest say them were simple from which they understand the actuality of life. Living being whom we are spoiling without any authority. They realised that every word the priest said to them were those from which they can take informative and guidance track also wash the mind of people with there's wanders. So that the seeds of new generation can follow them..... yes this track is a tricky one but it could give more power around us.

Everything was getting more explicit to them one by one all sort of dilemmas started getting abolished from their mind.

There are some beliefs that are prescribed for this Gate of Glory as:

So let me tell you that before entering it that all dilemmas, misunderstanding, confusion of every single living being was expolied wether it being human or even an animal.

All things were just happening in this sphere because the air all around was being too refreshing and pure. Which go into every beings circulation to make him realise the power of truthfulness and spirituality.

All this was done to make them pure and well defined before entering the God's creation Heaven Hell.

After realising all these things there are some among them who are liable and guilty about their part.

God is the one who responsible for all this makeover of every single person present with him over there.

Yash just rigorously hit his head heavily in anger with his palm. He couldn't let himself sit calmly now as he stood up at the place he was and start to look here and there in frustration and anger and all others were still silent and lost in wondering.

Priest said; 'Why are you fumbling to catch your past. It's has gone by child.......and I think you shouldn't be apprehensive about it just you should think about the new beginning ', priest said.

'Oh!... sorry what a blunder I assaulted with my and everyone's life over here...but seriously I didn't wandered it be in human in any way...' Yash said to priest in a way to consolidate himself.

'I think my child you should not think about it now............take my view and leave this wandering as soon as feasible', priest said to Yash ' because now it shows this air had made you too pure and well defined'.

'I think now you should see your friends in which thought they all are lost. Wake them up from it, we are just few steps away from pride "The Gate of Glory".

Yash with a depth of what he said in his eyes went towards his friends to get them away from their wander and talked to all of them. Convinced everything they did was because of him as he wasn't able to guide them from start and that's how they dug a wrong well.

Yash, 'You didn't crack to make our way clear, we all wandered and followed it. So how could you say like that for your own', Gaurav replied trust-worthily to cover up what he said.

'Yes the start was not just yours, it was started by everyone together. So please don't say like that dear as we all were a part of it'. Ankit said to make him realise that everything happen because all of us.

This time here as at one end all the discussion which is conducted by the priest, at the other end loud tone of instrumental sitar of playing music which was heard by all.

Priest knew that they reached at the place that he desires.

All others were a bit shocked, stubbed and seeking to find out that where this music was coming from and after some seconds tone of a hundreds of people speaking together started to come and pinched their ears. The whole lot of sound was just saying..............

'ARRIVAL OF SLAVES..........ARRIVAL OF SLAVES........ ARRIVAL OF SLAVES...'.

'Arrival of slaves...what's that 'Sunny asked from priest.

'Yes...slaves...Arrival of slaves....As per this we all are slaves of God so this word being used to inform everyone entering it. So that the thing becomes very explicit in the mind about what they did. Why they came here and who is the supreme power who rules this world', priest told it to everyone so that they could know how to be inside over there.

'The idea that god was far away. His distance from man was the measure of his majesty, man was called upon to conduct his life on earth with faith and fear. The fruit of such faith was to be reaped after death', priest replied again.

The golden gate appears (Gate of glory) behind the white clouds as if the cloud being torn off from amidst.

All the aura had filled up with whiteness giving them all the spirit of peacefulness and humanity there.

'Wow... what is this "A majestic golden gate with bunch of flower's spread all apart in its aura", with white sparrows never seen before are here sitting at the top of the Gate', Soni said after being amazed after seeing it.

'All this settle to you because it's the majestic creation of God with peace spread all apart. With a sense of bowling wonders inside that mutate immediately as per God mood.........well you come to know about it', priest said. That being a prisoner in the heaven's hell would mean that they are spare a lot in their crime as God finds them as his good slaves.

'Wait...why all these big bats are revolving around here at the top, it seems that they had covered the whole area in a sphere at the top. Why is it so as you said that this was a peaceful place of God', Sunny said as he got shocked by looking at all the bats revolving so rapidly here and there over the top.

'This thing comes to your mind because you all just debate that everything in this world should just go as you all want. But you don't even know that nothing is there in this world perfect. Each and every thing consists of some kind of flaws and God made this with everyone so that no one could feel much superior. But see in this nature the things are going apart from expectation', priest said again to guide to realise once more their destination door for punishment is in front of you.

'But how could we step down. There is nothing like where we can even put our foot as all is just covered with white fumes at below and our top', Gaurav asked the priest making his two eyes as much big as he could. Which shows how much shocked he is after listening to that all.

I think you want all of us to fallen down.

'Child...let me tell you that if you don't know, that you are now in a climate of zero gravity and here everything goes in a different manner 'priest said and halt, asking these silly questions now as per you all got to know that you are in a world where nothing goes like your world.

Now Sunny noticed the music was in the air over there and the spirit it created the heart was a lot amazing, he told about this to all his friends.

They all listened to this melodious music of ringing bells coming from all directions and when they face towards that way there was nothing to be seen till long distance.

They saw a river flowing from that place in a downward direction and where it ends it could not be measurable. It appeared to be a big river with stars twinkling kind of particles spread all over in it from one end to the other.

'Ha....what's this now have a look over it...', Gaurav said as he saw that river.

'What role that river plays over there' Yash asked.

Because such an enormous river covering a large area and that too not a normal one. They started to think about it that weather it was working towards any task to solve in that 'Heaven's Hell' or for what reason this elegant river was designed over there.

'Now again you are asking these illogical questions childrens. Let me tell you that I have not been present over here to answer you and solve every dilemma of yours. So don't expect anything more from me now', priest said.

'And you don't have to be concerned about it as it doesn't come under the premises where you are going to be kept for your surveillance', priest said again as soon as he finished his last stanza.

Soni was now suspecious about this thing because as from the commencing this priest answered every sort of question they asked and now he was profoundly neglecting to inform about even a single thing. It settle from his reaction and face that he didn't even want us to see this river and as he's being shocked too that how come it came to our view. His expressions on face described the same.

'Well....God knows whatever is going on priest mind. Let us don't think about it', Yash said to Soni.

'Yash....ok....lets go', Soni said after exhailing air from his mouth.

Ultimately they all reached the door, "Door of Glory" where priest wished them to walk through.

Priest standing too still admist this door with his eyes closed taking long breath again and again.

Priest turned his arms in both opposite ends and instantly crossed them. Then the wind storm from both sides came one by one and thrashed everyone. As if the priest told the air to slap us too hard so that we could realise that our bad time begins. But according to the climate in around they were not realising that evenone going to face something wrong.

Abruptly a loud tone came from inside "Arrival of Slaves".

'You listened to this tone, just to tell you that this universe. Its rule is the creation of only super natural power and no one should dare to make a change', priest distatced loudly to them.

'Now what... we have to get inside this gate', Sunny asked priest.

The gate opens up. One man with a big smile on his face was standing there to greet them. He had worn a typical kind of watchman dress with hat at the top with his eyes staring at us and smiling.

'You came here.... It's been good to see you all here from my "Earth surface". Hellooooo....my name is Sharif and I had been guarding this Golden place since many centuries. It's good to see that you are going to make this place with elegant colour of "Earth surface" now...

'Yes am I rigorous'... watchman over there said all of them.

'Well.....what happened to you all, I asked you something', watchman Sharif said to them.

'Ah.....wait, I think I need to tell them something more now, I know why did they shocked right now', priest said to watchman Sharif.

Priest started to speak in a heavy tone, 'So my children... let me tell you about this place. This place is created by God to do justice to built good concepts of humanity and well being. Here this is the place where punishment is given in sense to guide and to inform people about sacrifices for others happiness and to spread smiles on everyone face. This is the place where people like you are brought who had done crime which is not for their growth and wealth but for others better sustainability. The people who come here don't consist of any sort of poisonous thoughts in their mind that's why they are being selected and adored so that their act would not wreck the nation after being brutally punished for their act by the human on the land. So that as per they had done crime, surely deserve to get the punishment. They called here to face punishment in a better manner and taught here too, against whatever they did', priest said to all of them over there so that the last part of difficulty having in their mind get washed off...

Soni raised his tone and asked. 'Ok... we got to know about it...very apart and unbelievable things but one word that is still a lot striking in my mind is why this watchman talked about "Earth surface" to them "a too big thing that in a easy and smaller way" why is it so',

'Yes...even I am thinking that', Ankit said to priest.

'Oh!..... so you were thinking that, yes I should tell you about that too. As per what it told you that this place being designed to give away the punishment. So this punishment is not just for the people from "Earth surface." Here people comes from every other planet the whole universe to get familiar with God ethics. Then go back to work towards their planet development', priest replied to clear out there confusions.

Things were becoming a bit more hard to digest by all.

'And you know why this watchman is too excited to see you all here because you belongs to his planet', priest told them.

'Oh!....is that so...yes we are also very happy to see you here shake hand...', Yash said to watchman.

This watchman was a big man in ethics, humanity and morality. Watchman greet so humble then shake hand with them and give confident so that they can go on this way too solemnly.

Waiting to see that what kind of other planet creatures they are going to encover over there and which kind of living lifestyle do they persists. There was no fear that existed inside their soul now but these unuse things as were making them vibrant. The last stanza that priest said to them was going out of bound from their mind. The watchman of this new world for them came close to all and told them to put their right hand palm forward and open it up. All didn't wander as to why he was asking them so. They all did what he said and then he dropped two drops of water on each one's hand... After dropping it on their hand he turned back and abruptly as he turned again to see them all. As soon as he saw them all there was a burning fire emerging from everyone's hand. It felt as if somebody had burned up bricks over it.

Burning flame was seen on everyone hands and everyone was standing too comfortably and if the flame was not burning on their hand. There is a entire shock and surprise eye that we could see on all the faces' seeking to know to judge what happened immediately.

'What...what is this, why you had done this to us', Sunny asked watchman Sharif to know about what's been going on because one thing is also there that this flame and heat did not damage their hand if they are not spirit.

'Ah...... halt it are you in fear, this heat are burned up'... watchmen Sharif said to Sunny.

'*Nah*......no not spirit that way but tell me what's that', Sunny replied to him.

Watchman Sharif didn't answer to what Sunny said again as he was just looking towards Yash... because he's the only one over there whose hand on there that no burning flame was to be seen. This thing is what Sharif watchman wanted to probe and then he said to the priest.

'You also know that while staying here everyone needs to control their emotion and love so that they can deal with each and every circumstance as set by this place rule. I think that you came to know the thing that this person Yash had out of bound love and emotion fed inside his heart. It also seems that his heart is too pure and holistic that's why the thing doesn't pressurise his body to eject heat from his hand. You tell me what we have to do now, do I have to allow him to enter the premises or what I have to do now', watchman sharif asked priest.

"Is this boy Yash is going to abide Heaven's hall rule's"

'You have to do just what had been told, let them all go inside and start the punishment', priest said to Sharif.

They all entered the premises and just a look over it, seen two scenes or you can say phases of life both together like the one area of well defined climate, moisture, greenery as per everyone wanted to see. The other one with a whole lot of things that was making it to look like a dreamland that was conveniently seen by anyone in dreams.

On the other hand there was a cave made of mud. It looked to be a restricted area also where every person had to live in a specified region and they could not go beyond that and the auras is too striking that if you see it once you definitely want to go in it to have full joy of it. No one can go out of that particular restricted area that is full of all living creatures from all over different planets.

'So see child, this is the place where you all have to be, throughout your entire punishment and here only you got to learn that whatever you did was not in the part of good humanity', priest said to all of them.

'Here.... was we have to resist, just this is only the thing that I am waiting for you to say as soon as I have seen this place and I think I got this concept too in my mind that why... tell me...', Ankit asked priest.

'I think that's why you are calling this place as "Heaven's Hell" like while being everything over there in surrounding nothing internally and nothing for them', Yash replied again to priest.

'Yes...I think you are getting everything quickly and settle to be acting too smart too, but my child the time ahead is not that much good for you as you also know that the flame didn't burned on your hand. Something is there in you which is going to make you face tricky climate in your future, so my child be secured......that can be anything your emotion, anger or your love', priest said to Yash.

'Let's see sir what's going to happen next with me but I am just apprehensive about my time that how long I have to be here. I devoted my life to work for happiness of human being and don't know how long we have to be here, can you please tell us', Yash replied with a question in his mind to priest.

'My child over here you have to be for a short period of time. It's about some months only but the time is not easy for you and also the days are going to be very much bigger and else everything you are going to know inside when you are going to corelate with others', priest instructed.

'Now everything that you are going to face, is there for you and all going to know everything inside before you are going to start living over here because every place has some rules and this is your punishment. Rules would be somewhat difficult for you. There is no key to solve your problem inside and you are also not going to find that key anywhere even if you try now, just one thing remains for you here to deal with the situations and be friendly with them and to the Being that are brought from different planet's', priest replied last to them and after it he just got lost as if he didn't want to answer any question further.

'*Hey*...now nobody is here, watchman Sharif and priest both had flown off somewhere. I think we need to step forward our own towards the hall of this area, may be we are going to find someone there', Yash said to all of his friends.

Now everyone started to step there foot forward towards the hall. The atmosphere over there settled like a hill station of entire while the whiteness spread on ground that is because of the snow. This environment had its own trait, its own colour which had a fabulous fragrance spread everywhere. The place where they all are going (hall) is the place which is curved muddy area having some mud meant seats in both sides of it for someone to come and sit. As soon as they reach in hall, they saw that no one was over there. It was empty. Soon a sound came to listen by them all who said that....

'Feel the air and come along it. I am waiting for you at its end', this is the sound that came to be heard by them. Soon at that time a big blow of air came and flow them all with it. This blow of air halted at the boundary of this cave and where a person is standing in entire white facing forth the boundary of cave.

'My name is Siffy and I am the one who control all management and organisation work of this cave and the person who stays here. So I tell you about the rules and regulation of this place and else all you need to know, but I think it would be not required now, all had been told about this place a lot before'.

'What we need to do here...how long we are going to live over here', Gaurav asked to Siffy.

'Yes I should inform you that over here will you going to stay just for 65 days but as per tell to you before also these days are not going to be that much easy and short because a day over here takes a very long duration to be entire up', Siffy told to them.

'Ah... amazing that's too good. I love to be in this kind of climate', Sunny said to Soni slowly facing him.

'But not for a longer period of time, I feel so...' Siffy said as he listen to what Sunny is saying to Soni.

Everyone of them apart from Yash got dreaded up. They all are seeking to imagine picture in their mind that what's all is going to happen. After seeing all such type of fears on everyone face Siffy started to tell them everything in brief now so that they can continue. Siffy said...

'There are certain norms over here you need to follow, some boundation you need to carry faces lessons you need to learn. When you came, you have seen that boundary separating that creative auspicious heaven from this area because that is the purest and well defined place. The person who kept here is been close to this beauty but can't go and feel it. One of the pressure he have to bear on him while staying here. Then you have to stay here with whole lot of apart planets who are being carrying on their punishment over here and you need to adjust with them and uphold a peaceful environment over here. Third and a emphasise thing that you have to follow is to take classes of lesson's that are being meant to make parts of your mind to be in the direction which is being set by the god', Siffy said to all and adopt.

'Hm...so that the tough thing to do', Sunny replied instantly.

'How can you say now, all will going to be known, as you go on with your first day over here', Siffy said this.

'Where is Gaurav, and he gone', Yash asked to everyone but no one knew about him.

Everyone went out to search Gaurav. They were seeking to find him in all directions, they all were thinking that this is a kind of prank facing on their arrival.

While in search of Gaurav, abruptly Sunny saw Gaurav roaming around in search of something. He shouted to call Gaurav.

"Gaurav.....What are you doing there, come here everyone is worried about you and searching you", Sunny shouted on Gaurav.

Gaurav said to himself 'Uf.... why these all unusual things happens every time with me only and why I am the first one to face them. Now what would I am going to tell them again. They are going to feel that I am not serious now too'.

'Coming...'. Gaurav replied to Sunny.

'Where had you gone, do you know how much we got scared about you. Everyone is still searching you. Let, tell everyone that you are safe', Sunny said this and they moved together.

He didn't told them about what he had seen over there because he thinks that may be that all would be his illusion.

Everyone started to move towards the same place where Siffy was present but they came to see that Siffy was nowhere to be seen around the coverage area. Suddenly they listened a elegant pray of god was going somewhere around that place. The song was too melodious and that's why Soni urged everyone that before surge they should measure that where it's been going on.

The room where this prayer was going on, just at the backyard of that hall. They reached there, seen that some girls wearing dashing white dress full of stars in it, and there dress is being glowing and shinning they all were sit facing towards God and singing devotional song simultaneously in single tone. All this is too fabulous aid and a salient stand of this heaven to make it a dashing one.

But all of them won't be able to take full pleasure of that aura because as everyone is spirit bit dreaded that in all this Yash had left something due to which he's perceptional looking at it with a smile catty face.

'*Hey* what happened to you Yash, where you were lost' Ankit asked to Yash.

'My dear brother see that girl sitting in the first row having in her hand a small cup shape oil lamp made of baked clay, I'd just seen her when she turned back to pick it and I don't know why I am not able to move my eyes from it', Yash tell to Ankit.

'Ok....my dear brother see it, let us we move from here first and find our way as all other things we can carry on later', Ankit said to Yash.

'*Hey*....you all come with me, I had seen Siffy over there let's talk to him'. Sunny shouted to call everyone.

'Where you all went that time when I was revealing you the most emphasise thing of this place and about its auras, you all even didn't wait until I finish my words', Siffy asked them all when they reached to him back.

'Sir...That like our one friend in way missing at that time and we all warried about him. I feel you knew about this thing. I said this in your presence only', Yash replied to Siffy.

'So where's your friend now. I don't know that what are you apprehensive for about your friend.' God's Siffy said to all of them.

'Afraid for that sir...'. Yash said.

'I am not going to tell you everything in brief, this is your failure that you are not able to grasp details in one assault but I'll tell you about the person who resists over here as I told you that from every planet living being comes here to work them as per God guidance. But you should face structured people as everyone is not like you from "Earth surface". So you all have to stay here with them, they would be of so apart personalities in terms of looks, appearance and there food standard. That's why the food standard of "Heaven's Hell" being meant in such a peculiar sense so that everyone is going to take a specified food as per granted and it doesn't matter whether the food is being favour of you or not. You have to go on with that only', Siffy said to them.

6

Everyone was dreaded about this datum now but Sunny's reaction was too exasperating as he's too fond of having good food every time. But he had to compromise a lot here regarding food facilities and that's the thing which is making him more embarrassed as time passes off.

As soon Siffy finished telling them all about this datum. Gaurav instantly realised that it's best time to tell all about what he had seen there.

'Yes...I too had seen a typical kind of person walking forth the door at that time. I just followed him to know about it. He is having a big trunk nose like an elephant and tail meant like a crocodile very heavy being', Gaurav said to Siffy.

'Oh!.... then, I feel you had seen Pee who is from the farthest and coolest planet a funny kind of person my boy. He makes everyone happy every time. But because of too over weigh it's been difficult for him to do usual things on daily. You all should get in touch with him surely will bliss his company', Siffy said to everyone.

Everything was fine and nothing over there going against them. Siffy was also summing up them that concern which were going helpful to them. All others were just looking both of them with curiacity as such what all they are talking about. As the description of the person given by Gaurav settle to be a very apart structured hard to dictate creature. There was a suspense in their mind that how much more terrible personalities they are going to meet now.

'Where did you all lost this time now, you all go to your place and follow routine and lifestyle of this place', Siffy said to everyone.

'But sir where we go', Soni asked.

'You have to reach at room No. 11 that is the place decided for all of you. Just face towards south and walk until you get that place', Siffy told it to them and left that place.

They started to move towards that place, nothing is to be seen as far as they can see but they were walking harder so that they can find that, soon. In their way they had seen firstly a green ground but without flowers and no other obstacle it's just an empty one. They had came to a place over where there was all empty land which looks like a barren land. When they had seen at back it settle that they were standing in the mid of it, they abruptly shocked.

'Just now we left a green garden behind us and where did that gone. It's been nowhere to be seen at our back, its all settle to be infertile land all around, looks like we are standing in the middle of it', Soni said.

'Yah...when we were going to reach that place it's not too be seen still in our front row as we are being walking from hours', Gaurav said.

'Don't be worried about it if they had said that its going to lie in this direction. We should not get apprehensive about anything else apart from just walking in this direction, relax...you all are going to find that place soon', Yash said everyone.

That place was objected to them so instantly as it is not to be seen to them from a far long distance and now they were just standing in front of it. They took a big breath and then step forward to walk into it.

The residences were made of wood and small ground floor residence connected to one another. They then started to find there room No. 11.

As they find room, everyone gone inside it and settle from their face that how much tired they were at that time. They just cure themselves as they can, by way of lying down or by rinse their face by water.

Soni was standing near the window because the breeze that is coming from forth is so cool and stress free as he wants to feel. So he had gone close towards the window.

'Oh!.....what's this place is near to us see.....I can see it conveniently and we had drawn many kilometers to reach here, what this I don't know', Soni said this as he had seen that place from where they came to residence so close to it. As he can conveniently see that place profoundly, explicitly close.

'Yes......you were rigorous, this is not even a little far from this place, it settle to be a close neighbour part of it', Ankit replied to what Soni said.

Then all of them get out from the room and run to see it more explicitly from forth. As they came out had seen that really that place are neighbour of each other but then the wander which is perceptional striking there mind that the places they had seen while coming to the residence where they way.

'Search someone around here who can tell us about Pee', Ankit said.

'There is no one to be seen here all around, I think everyone is in their room', Gauarv said.

'I think some one is there at the backside of the residence garden....let me see that', Yash said.

'Yes I think he is the gardener working over there. There is a person too standing at the far back side of that gardener holding weapons in his hand and I think he's a soldier with his full costum', Sunny said.

Everyone gone towards that gardener for his help so that he could guide them.

'Hello.....sir can I ask you a question', Yash asked to Gardener.

'Yes my boy ask what do you want', Gardener said.

'Sir we are new here and we want to meet Pee, can you please guide us where he would be available now', Yash asked from Gardener.

'Oh!...Pee that all heart devotion guy. He is a too fabulous child of this place and assaults to be funny. Ah... sorry... you were asking me about place of existence. I started to tell you whole sort of his activity and nature. Yes... his room No. 12, you can go and meet Pee now', Gardener said to them with a smile.

'Thanks... Thanks a lot sir', Yash said.

'God bless you my child', Gardener said.

'*Hey* this is just next to our room, exciting and very difficult. So I think if Pee is going to help us about here day to day difficultty to out', Gaurav said with a great enthusiasm and excitement on his face.

'Firstly...go and meet to Pee then we'll talk next', Soni said.

They moved towards residence housing where Pee room No. 12 as just next to their room. As they reached there;

'I think door is not lock, it open we need to knock it or just we would go straight in it and talk to Pee', Gaurav said.

'*Hey* why did you say every time these innocence kinds of things. We had come here to ask someone for help and the person whom we are asking for help. We should have a lot of respect for him in our eyes. So how can you say that without knocking the door', Yash instructed with anger.

Gaurav said to himself 'I didn't said something that much wrong then why he was start firing on me'.

'You can't even pressurise anyone to help you or to give you adherence. You have to first ask for it with need in your eyes, now don't make faces please, knock the door dear', Yash said to Gaurav again'. I'll see to you afterwards'.

Gaurav knocked the door.

'Who's there', Pee asked sitting inside.

'It's been Gaurav here', Gaurav replied to Pee.

'Who.......ok whomever it is come inside', Pee called them all inside and as they stood at this time not just Gaurav had seen him otherwise he came in everyone's notice. His structure which is like having a big trunk nose, a elephant and tail meant like a crocodile very heavy weighted he looks so. His body colour was all in green and he is lying on a chair in which he is not been able to manage himself properly.

'Who are you all, weather you are also from some planet and came for the punishment over here', Pee asked from them.

'Yes you said it right, we had came from planet "Earth surface" to continue our punishment here', Ankit said to Pee.

'Ok....please have a seat in my room.... please feel easy and don't think much about my room. My room been messy a lot and say had you met others person and creatures before coming to me...hm', Pee asked to Yash.

'No... we didn't... but frankly speaking it would be too difficult for us to adjust ourselves with all people that we will come to meet in future... I think', Yash said to Pee.

'But why are you saying this, it's not just the problem of yours. It's a problem that everyone faces over here when they came in the beginning to adjust and mix up in the environment and staying happy. You can also think like it's a part of punishment and you have to prove yourselves as being the best in this perspective from others. In the other manner you can think this as an opportunity for you all to be with those living creature that are present in this galaxy. These all are whom you don't even feel and resist. This is the time you are staying with them', Pee said to all of them so that he can make everyone cosy over here.

Soni said to himself, 'This cartoon type looking being is saying such a big things to make all of us feel good. But his structure and personality says he doesn't settle to be that much minded one'.

'*Hey* tell me about yourself my dear friends, how you all reached here.What all you did', Pee asked from them.

'Nothing......we all just having this thing because of our a bit lack of wisdom. As we think at that time when we were staying on "Earth surface" by killing all those who were involved in destroying humanity, who all had a key role in plucking away the happiness of others. Destruction of those people are a good thing to do and by that we can make the whole world so peaceful. But lastly I think as I heard about the words said by priest there is somewhat ours mistake. Mistake could be in terms of our wisdom or in our wanders but ultimately frankly speaking', I think that it's our fault to do that. The thing that we did was not having a single point of concern about our benefit and reliance so might that's why priest brought up all of us over here. So that we can think about these thing and gain wisdom accordingly', Yash said all this to Pee and as he said all this he makes everyone to be still at that present time because no one expected this from him.

Now it seems like the all Yash had listen from priest in our way had impected his soul.

Breaking his silence Ankit said;

'Hello... my dear I think your mind is thinking something in wrong direction and let me tell you something very explicitly that you are not only responsible for anything we did. We all totally contributed to dug this well all together', Ankit said to Yash.

'Hm... good dear you all have a fortified bonding build in you all towards each other. Your kind and helpful nature is shown by your words. I am going to ask more. These all thing are very much enough for me to know you all', Pee said to all of them.

Sunny was quite amazed to see that there are gadgets lying everywhere in the room of Pee and each gadget have some trait in itself. These were not normal electron gadgets to be seen and environment over there that he meant is to techy.

'Yes...well Pee can you tell us about yourself and why did you came over here, which fault you did', Sunny asked to Pee.

'My case is also quite like yours only, I am Scientist of my planet and I had done a lot more for my people development', Pee said.

'But tell us that what' was the reason you faced and brought over here', Ankit asked from Pee.

'Ah....My reason....My reason was that I used to live alone in my house. I didn't even married because of my work dedication and I truly devoted towards my country's progress. There was a time come when my ongoing research was set for live roll out mechanism so that everyone can take benefit from it. It's all about the food availability by a faster aid to all my country people and to those also who don't have money to buy it but this bucks of nature people doesn't allowed me to do so. They pressurised government and the whole environment to walk according to them and my dream to serve my people failed and broken up into many pieces.

Then I took a sailent step to give relief to my soul by killing every person and dumping them all in well and after that my case is same as yours they came and picked me up', Pee told everyone about his story.

After revealing those about him Pee said.

'Uf....leave now let us don't talk about the past because whatever we all did, for happiness of peoples and to make a mutation in our world towards a positive direction. So I think now that we just need to talk about our present and focus whatever we are having over here', Pee said this to all to set their mind to face forward.

Yash facing forth from the room of Pee standing close to window said;

'It's been darkening now....and feel of stars from here is somewhat like kids are playing hide and seek inside this open sky. Seems like whole world saying something about his glory which can be realised just by seeing natures behaviour', Yash said this facing towards the blinking dark night forth.

'Yes its seems like an exotic start of life the began', Sunny said to Yash while coming closer to him and putting his hand over his shoulder.

'Hope for the best dear... my finger are crossed and I have full faith to my god. Whatever he's going to do will be somewhat in the sense to give me relief and not to break my broken life more with hammer again', Yash said to Sunny. They both together look window with their blank eyes facing towards the aura which says a lot, If you can listen.

'Ok...dear I think it's too late now and you all are in a mood to have ease now. So you can go to your room if you feel so. Yes you told me that you all hadn't met anyone over here then I am going to introduce you all tomorrow morning to every person from apart chances who are also being brought up over here', Pee said to them.

Soni asked instantly that how can we meet all of them together tomorrow, there any place where everyone accumulate all together.

'Yes...my dear we all gather two times a day firstly in the morning pray. Then in the night at the time of dinner. This is a kind of schedule that is being followed over here you can think like that also. Well, I am not saying to meet all persons at these two place's tomorrow. As you all are new to this place, so you don't know about the sports match that being flirt over here after every ten days. The winner of the game is going to decide the chart that is going to be followed by every person staying here for a week. So that this game becomes more emphasis also. You all are new to this place so might not you going to participate in sports tomorrow but I am going to introduce you to them tomorrow only', Pee told to them.

Sunny is a national athletics player and was member in sports team at his studies and everyone know about this thing so well because Sunny is a big lover of sports. So it can be saw by Sunny happiness.

'So......Sunny, you are inclined ...to be the best in all sports over here, if you should not be so that it could help us too in living conveniently at this place', Soni said this while smile towards Sunny.

'Oh!..... you know that how this sport is close to me', Sunny said to Soni.

While these conversations are going on Yash said to Pee 'Do you know ours room No., it's been just next to your room No. 11......'

'Oh!....is it so then that's too good, I have a fabulous company of you all', Soni said to Pee.

'Ok.....lets we go now Pee and wake up tomorrow morning to see sleaves of the most sophisticated place of God meant world', Yash said it to Pee.

And then they stepped forth the room of Pee and moved towards there room by saying happily...GOOD NIGHT Pee............

"Started our way towards spirituality & humanity,

A deep and silent depth is there in devastating peoples locality.

We stepped our foot to gaze undercover,

So that we would be able to know about all these hidden secret thrillers...

Depressed and stressed awaken our titter breaths.

We assaulted to conceptualise our smiles,

Soon our breath started to lessen up for the sake of human sovereignty...

To impart them a cave of hospitality with the flowering fraternity...

Which could bloom the light of overwhelming spirits and delight?

That could make everyone very much sagacious to be self dependent and survive with full pride.

We opt a route to balance the imbalanced nature

In a way to pluck those unwanted selfish, greedy smiles from the face of heartless people...

and extend this happiness like a fever to those weak poor people which carry light and hope as they were also happiness believer.

We move for a place where those bars of extension were not stacked in anyone's heart,

Everyone eyes should just blink with sleaveling love which could make the mutation and make the sky to touch the "Earth surface".

We leg that............enthusiastic, magnetic

Humanity that we dreamed to plough on our "Earth surface" shadow without any devastating blunder,

But see that came in our gloves as per meant by the Supreme of this Universe in 'Heavens Hell' Shearing specter."

3

Realm's Wonder

"We should love the knowledge delivered to us everyday by our rising pain. Making our life more costlier".

7

Today everything is like silence spread all over and nothing is precept to move till something happen. Yash woke up early in the morning and he started perceiving his surrounding nature. Yash felt that it been quite apart morning over here, as everything here is even ten times more beauty present in the nature comparison to their place but it settle that all were bounded for some sort of instruction for them to spread their fragrances and auspicious beauty in the environment all around. They need to call and look at all this, Yash said while standing near foot of the door.

'Till now we have observed and beard everything in upfront, encouraging but what's this. Why the nature is not drifting in its own way. I hadn't seen nature following rules anywhere', Yash said.

Abruptly there was a tone of ringing bells started in the air, a big collective group of bird started to flow from one zone to the other in a peculiar manner. It looks like they all are unfolding peace and smile all around. Then next group of birds started and it happened one after the other group like they were giving some message from one side to the other.

'Oh!......so I think this nature being just waiting for a call to start and see how everything changes to be majestic as time passes. Ok....I think my friends need to wake up now' Yash said.

After it there was an extreme mutation of classy extruct of nature's wonder all together, free started to be greener. Leaves were becoming Shiny as the light ray's touches the top like twinkling leave. Like they want to say that nothing much elegant than nature's architecture. It was becoming glorious to a fairy that now Yash can't be able to digest this beauty all alone, he want his friends to be a part of it.

Gaurav fallen down from the bed saying "Earth quake... "Earth quake"... Waked up instantly and started running at every corner of the room.

"*Ha*..............."Earth surface"quakes...Dear do you know where we are now, it's a place where no earthquake can occur so how you got stacked with "Earth surface" quake....Ok, leaves come in that case and see what a wonder game of nature was happening forth" Yash said.

'Ah!......what I am saying, am I fool, I know that we are nowhere on land now.... brother it's my dream I feel', Gaurav said.

'Yash....I know that and even if it's not your dream then too this thing done by you not new to me, you did these kind of activity usually. If you want your heart to be infancy let it be adolescence from your mind as soon as possible because this place. I don't know how it would be for us at the next door. We have to move towards "Earth surface" soon as we all devoted towards helping humanity which is being slained day by day. Ok just make everyone to be in consciousness, so that they all can realise that a new day new life had standing up', Yash said to Gaurav.

Each one from them left their bed came close to the door. Soon they seen that Pee is walking up from the ground towards the residence and came close to their back yard and rang their bell.

'Very good morning Pee, what's up...all is ok'... Sunny wrist door and said to Pee standing on the backyard.

'Yash all is well here, you all say that how your last night was, and I came here to tell'.

"What happen Pee, where did you come', Sunny asked.

'Nothing, I had gone for morning walk early then, I realised that I hadn't told you time to reach at field today. So I came to inform you that today because here you have to be too time conscious in everything', Pee said.

'Thanks...Pee to be concerned. It is grateful for us that we met you first here and got to know all bucks soon for the day. Otherwise no one came to us to tell anything. I don't think that everyone concerned about anyone over here', Soni said.

'It's not like that but you have to spread that this place is not the same where you lived previous because your place consists of a locality that you prefer. With all those food and lifestyle that you do opt. Here you have to face everything in reverse, nothing matching, nothing same. So some sort of compromising attitude everyone need to carry over every time with them. So crack to understand others and go on with them', Pee said.

'Ya... Pee all you said is rigorously right and don't tensed we know that', Yash said.

'Oh!......the main purpose for which I come hadn't said yet. It's like the timing of the game to start off when the light going to be dim in environment because every activities over here performed in night time only', Pee said.

'But it's been morning time now, so it would take longer for game to start off', Gaurav said.

'No you can't say that because even a day over here takes much longer to be finished off and in that day only you face no time climate mutate in the nature. So we can't say when would forth illumination gets mold and we need to reach at the field for that, so be conscious about it', Pee said.

'Is it like that, this also happens over here', Yash said.

'Ok...I have to leave now. You told the whole shebang about it, now you should be aware of it and attain there on time', Pee said and gone towards his room door.' Don't wait for me because may be I have some work and reach only anytime'.

'*Hm*.....guys so I think you all have become aware about it now', Yash said this to all as Pee left that place. 'So be updated but this time climate not with Cops....Because time passes concerned over here......ha'.

Everything is going in its usual way...but that usually stayed for a bit of hour and after that nature again shown its colour. It is waver like someone had commanded it to be in apart look now. The nature is dress up in a look that suits the climate which Pee said before leaving. So they wander that the time for them also to go and coincide with everyone came from all over the universe and resides here.

All creatures were poised in very unique code of dress and even theirs external appearance is too exotic that to see all together at one time. There mind having a feel that can't be measured by any meter. Now this time they are just waiting to see what would happen when these all are going to collect at a specific place. Big sound of nonstop horn and all creatures around started to step speedily towards the place where everyone need to assemble.

'Don't know what is all this going on as firstly this place is too apart for us and now everything is remarks in this manner', Soni said.

'That's true and there is no one to inform and guide us about what all being happening over here'. Sunny said, 'Where is Pee, he also had gone. If he would be with us then he can at least tell us that what all is this happening up'.

'I think you both should talking halt like this and we should all concentrate on the scene that being happening over here. I think we do also run now as every other one is doing because they all had gone far from us. Lets first reach over there and then sort out your questions there', Yash said as this is not the time for all of them to say all this.

'This is an inevitable thing.....so you all should know that', Ankit said.

As all reached the place, they came to see that it's a garden across a big green ground. This garden is so elegantly designed with red, green, yellow roses pots spread all around its corner and around the benches that were lying at the middle of it, seems like these benches are meant for them.

'*Hey* see......Pee is coming from the back side towards the garden area', Gaurav said.

'Pee...' Soni crack to call Pee.

'You all came on time that's good. How you all were realising now', Pee said.

'What you were spirit dear. Everything is too isolated that's all happening over here and nobody is still allotted and conveying about what is this going on', Yash asked Pee.

'Don't be afraid of what all you are facing here. It's an assembly point for all of us and after this a short speech by priest Malton deliver before game starts in the field', Pee said.

Pee replied again 'Dear just stop and watch what is going to happen...because like me your time has also started. So just see, bliss and learn from every jiffy over here'.

'Let us see which game would be going to be flirt over here... Ah!... I think they are going to play volleyball, see that Humpty Dumpy thick person is holding volleyball in his coffers and surge towards the beach', Sunny said facing towards Yash.

'Could you please be quite for some time?' Yash said that after getting irritated by reciting to all his friends talk that settle to him without any tensed.

'Listen you all we are to be a part of it. Interact with several apart personality and looks people over here, so please think about that and be brew for it' Yash said to them. They started to move towards all others with Pee.

'Ok... firstly let me give you all, a sort of interaction with people staying over here. This may happen that they don't know English and won't be able to get you, so here rules says and we also perform that all you need to talk them by gestures, but you have to entire thing you want to say', Pee told them all.

'Ok... I think goodish of conversation', Yash said to all.

Now Pee started to instruct them about all around there 'can you see those three big persons standing over there behind the net. These people are not our team and in opposition team. The main thing to know about them is that the person standing at the middle named Barrack. He is the ruler of a planet and had been brought up over here.....but why that just God knew. Other two were his follower whatever he spade they does, even both find out the whole secrecy of tribe and fill in his ears so that they can make further conspiracy regarding it. The thing is that Barrack was a big ruler and a heavy strengthened man as he was having immense power and mysterious magic with him before he came over here. When he came here his all sort of energy was being pull up by god so that now here. He is going to live without them. This is why because of without power he can't make people's to be in front of him that he wants to be and then he uses other tactics', Pee told this thing about the Barrack and took a exhaled air of stress.

'But what this three creature's were weave now, while standing over there', Ankit asked.

'My friend you know the game is about to begin so they are making strategies to win the game'. Pee said. 'But Barrack doesn't plays the game he just instruct his players'.

'Never mind lets see what all packets he is going to flow off in the sky. But frankly speaking a person who can't even show his face also in his surround. I don't think that he's a man to be admired by others', Soni said.

Instantly Pee replied they...who instructed you, that he's being admired by others, I didn't said you that. Yes that's the only thing which you all had also observed for creatures. You had seen around him and be like in favour of him. This is because they stood away from him after knowing about his stacked previous history. As he has the supreme power of his planet because of his unbeatable power over there nothing else'.

'I conceive without concerning about this entire thing. We should go on for our event which is just going to occur', Yash said as he excited for that event even though he is not having that much qusiacity in sports.

'What had happen to you, Yash, much pleasure and excitement for sports never seen before', Ankit said.

'Dear you know that I have big anxiety of girls and my six sense being making me realise that something good will happening is waiting for me next. You know that too, as my six sense never says erroneous things', Yash said to Ankit.

Ankit starred, Yash with his flirty eyes.

Abruptly a heavy tone came from one side, when they group that side. They come to see that a guy being slapped by a girl liveried in white gown and as soon as pee came to gather all this, he laughed and said Figo... again.

They all feel that may be this would be the name of that guy but now did Pee knew him so well. The guy is wearing shorts at his bottom and nothing else, but he is a person with unique physique. He is a bit funny too because as he slapped by a girl after that he had seen everywhere in his surroundings. If somebody had seen him while getting slap. So, as he got to know that no one familiar to him over there then he smiled like a child rubbed his head by his palm and came close to them as Pee called him.

The texture of Figo is also quite unique, as he is having big ears three times more than them with pointed nose but his physique to be tough build with good pack of abs on his base.

Pee introduced, 'See he's Pojo a solemn sportsman came two month before you and he had attended this sports meet two times before. Yash and you all should know that he's a laugh players and can necklace a team on his own because he's too crazy about girls. The thing that you just seen is because of that only. So Figo say what conversation you did with priest girl this time' Pee said all this and asked Figo about the happening.

Figo replied, 'Nothing friend,' I was just interrogated her that after close time of match which drink they are going to serve us and I asked her to serve my drink herself to me'. Pee asked Figo 'That's been ok too but then I asked her why didn't she wore that pink clip in her hair and said you look too lovable. I think my last line went wrong and she did what she felt'.

'And you blissed it as always'. Pee said.

'Why were you saying like that dear as I am not a punching bag which could be punched or slapped by anyone whomever wants to' Figo said.

Pee replied, 'But that's not for everyone' your statement just goes for girls. Why you say every time those comments to a girl whom you just met first time and you knew that they are priest girls and no one is going to listen to your words'.

'Ok... Pee leave this and say who are these new creatures and from where did they came, Figo asked.

'Oh!... really they are from "Earth surface"...and dear let me inform you that I like a lot people from your land. *Hey* Pee see what a good thing for them *na*...as the priest girls also belong to your place only', Figo said to all of them.

Pee replied, 'Oh! I see that why you prefer there land. Dear please turn yourself, this is not going to worth you. If you are going to think like and work like that'.

Then Figo said, 'Again....again you took me in erroneous way my dear. Yes, this is true that I like priest girls and they all too belong to the "Earth surface" but I didn't said my words in that manner. I do love to see the style of speech these people do consist, there way of living and there love, emotion all together makes living too awesome that's why I mean that. Even if I get chance, I want to go there land. I feel, now, Pee you can judge my wanders and emotions by my words'.

'Ok... don't get tensed dear, I am not taking you in erroneous way now I am just seeking to set your mind towards rigorous track to be followed', Pee said to Figo.

Last thing that Figo exclaimed which conclude his wish to visit "Earth surface" whenever he get chance. Yash can't halt himself and conveyed 'If this is like that, it's been your wish to come to our land then I promise you to take you once to our land. I will show you its entire beauty that it has and I am sure that you will be a lot amazed to see all that we have over there'.

'Oh!.....that's so good of you dear...thanks', Figo said to Yash.

Pee said, 'I feel now we have to move towards the court, time of match is just going to start and I think Figo you are in opposite team of Barrack, I am rigorous', Pee asked Figo.

'Yes dear your inferenced is right and you know that I don't like Barrack for even a single per cent then there is no reason to play for his benefit' Figo said.

'And today I am going to drop every ball in these court and they would not be able to handle even single of mine' Figo replied again.

Sunny who is to a solemn sports man said 'ok....Figo then it would be a solemn thing to see your game today. I think that excitement is waiting for everyone at the time of game by you'.

Then small pieces of ribbon started to fall from upward like a colourful snowfall. Each and everyone from them after having a view of it wanted to know the reason behind it.

Soon Pee said '*Hey*, now you all come with me the game has started Figo you go and join your team see you later'.

'Yes this is the big thing that is going in the mind of everyone from us'. Soni said 'but as we met you and then Figo we came to realise that we have to see a lot uniqueness over here and that's why I didn't asked'. Game started.

'*Hey*...see what a splash had given by Figo to Barrack team...it that Figo is going to carry his said words all along the match and entertain us through that', Sunny again insisted.

'So I think that you all are really pleasureful here.... This period of your punishment is going to be favourable and wisdom-able for you all', Pee said.

'Don't know what all would going to happen or we are going to face but yes this is true that we are not happy because the track we started to follow on "Earth surface" is not a easy one. We left everything of ours behind and every sort of our pleasure to make peace and reliance in the world'. 'If we had not reached at its final then it would be hard to live for us'. Ankit said to Pee.

'You should not find that now as you all were doing a lot for others. So God wants you to be happy the same', Pee said 'You must feel like that such'.

Sunny shouted on the next splash that is done by Figo for their opponent team had been directly gone and hit the nose of player who been jumping a lot from long time and doing nothing.

Sunny said 'Ah!..... really now I am also going to say what a solemn player Figo is and it's been too appetiser to play with him whenever I get chance. Before that sure all that tonight, I am going to take a glass of wine with Figo'.

'Pee said that we have wine over here and how can we get that', Sunny asked.

Pee replied, 'ya... sure you can have that. There are a bit of restriction and boundation for us over here but we all were given a royal kind of remedy. The thing to be delivered to us and taken off from us being decided by god. God gives the requirement of ours which makes us to think in the wrong direction of humanity, So don't get tensed about wine, you will get that', Pee said to Sunny.

Yash senses was revealing him about something dashing. Something for which he is waiting to occur at that span. As his life wants that and waiting for it to happen.

'My dear Yash why you are much anxious as at the start of this match, do you want something,' Gaurav asked Yash.

'I conceive that Yash is again gone in his past foreground of life which he won't be able to live to his expectation', Soni said.

'*Huh*....You all, why would you feel like that, it is not that so. I am not unhappy or lost somewhere. I am just expecting that what's going to be next', Yash graced to his friends.

Yash murmured 'Do this time my senses are working in rigorous direction or do they are just making me cure by giving a prediction of quite happiness in my life. Well, I think, I need to give more time for it'.

Sudden mutation has stated in Gaurav health. He start feeling uncomfortable over there. It settle like long travel and he won't be able to sleep because of that. He is feeling ceaseless and weakness.

'You must go back and take rest because without that you can't be able to backup for everyday work', Pee said to Gaurav.

'Yes that's right dear and I would say Gaurav that you should take along Soni and Ankit also with you. They will take proper care of you' Yash said to them as he know that nobody is going to leave this place unless its as said to them.

'Ok... we all should depart now and bliss this match as most so that if something exciting happens you can interpret it to us well', Gaurav, Ankit, Soni said this and left the place.

'Yes, sure we'll inform you about all live updates. You take good care of Gaurav please', Yash said.

8

As they left the place at time for break after first game over. The two team players get back to their accrediting area. Everyone over there had come close to Figo as he became the hero of this match. The splashes that he meant in first close are flawless. This time Figo is also receiving fine remedy at his place so that he can go on with this spirit and flow in the second close too. On the other side Barrack is not able to digest whatever he had just measured in this match as his teammate work is nowhere to be seen in this whole case. Barrack team is walking side of necklace. So Barrack is conspiring something else to win this match. It could be conveniently attained by his movements while guiding his teammates.

Soon a light sweet music started over there touching the floor. What peer that the court is now being covered by the priest girls to whom Pee told to all of them before the game started.

When this happened its usual for all of the surrounding people over there except Yash. Everything is becoming more dashing by their beauty. So everything is acting in more fantastic way as these priest girls were kept by God over here. So that because of their devotion towards god and there wonderful wanders can make this environment more holistic and pleasures. They had come to the field for the purpose of cheering both the team who are doing a tough combat for win. They were wearing a entire and shiny white gown which settle to be very precious as it is shining like diamonds are attached to it.

Pee whispered slowly, 'Yash do you know that, as at this place girls are not allowed to be punished previously. So God from the beginning allotted this work of upholding to them and making the place to look like meant of with hybrid of both God creations men and women. From that past time generation they were serving this heaven's hell and making its environment more prosperous and delight. This drink is a nutritious liquid which is going to boost with power and make them more energetic. These all girls are going towards everyone and serving them at their own place. It was a kind of royal remedy that they were giving to them', Pee asked Yash to not make an stubborn face now while looking towards them.

This time when all this is going on, Yash was still perceptionally looking to these girls and recapitulating his retentions. This is because all of them who came in the row last to the field was similar in her looks to the girl that Yash had seen in the prayer room. This thing is two fold conceiving Yash implication after and after as he wants to know that girl is the same as he had seen before.

'Yash where were you gone astray', Pee insisted Yash.

There is something that also exalted in that girl because as she came last in the row and looks like she is coordinating everything. Other priest girls that are over there surge around in every part of the field with a never ending overtightened flow of music. These all girls were dancing in this flow too as such making the environment as much better as it can be. That time when all this was happening nature too settle to join its hand with them to make everything much delightful.

At last Yash asked Pee, 'Pee I have a annoyance and I want you to sort it out'.

'Yes say...or wait, I will answer your question if you have any but don't talk now. You are new to this place that's why you don't know that these priest girls are a lot respected over here because they are too pure by internal spirit. There features that do they posses being inbuilt in them by god since there birth. So I just want to say you that this time as they are performing for us. We are not allowed to utter a single piece of word', Pee informed Yash. 'This is the reason and you should also know that's why I told you'.

'Ok.... I registered your words, This is not the time to indulge in any sort of conversation. Now I am rigorous Na...?'.

'Yes that's good...' Pee replied.

Yash didn't asked anything to Pee over there but this storm of confusion is still going in his mind and soon after serving drinks to others these girls came close to Yash and Pee's place to serve them too. Drinks are carried by all of those girls but being served by that girl only for whom, Yash is a in dilemma. While serving drinks she is passing a healthy smile to everyone over there and Yash said 'Wow... she looks when she smiles, settle like the world happiness came all together'.

'Yash again I told you, that you are doing the same', Pee replied to Yash.

'Ops...afraid I am not going to speak up now', Yash said.

Now this is the time when these girls are just next to Pee and Yash, its time for them to be served. Yash is holding his breath to see the entire face of that girl so that he could judge that the one whom he saw before. Yash is also implication this time from his wanders. He is asking himself that why...as he is not penchant to know about other girls. No matter how much beautiful they were but this time why he is to conscious to know about this girl. This all that too when he hasn't met her even once personally. This girl came close and asked for drink to Pee first. This is because they were having different flavour drinks and asked for Pee appetite.

'White lemon soda', Pee answered.

She asked for drink to Yash took some second Yash replied 'The same'. She served white lemon soda to Yash and moved forward but she had also measured from Yash eyes and her gestures that something is there which he is seeking to know. But these girls doesn't bother about all this much because they don't even waste a single piece of time in thinking about such things that doesn't consist God praise.

These priest girls left that area.

Yash face settle to have some relaxation.

'Yes...she is that girl only whom I had seen before...but why I am so happy now', Yash said to himself while still holding drink in his hand and he hasn't taken a sip of his drink.

Soon the bell rung to start the left second part of the game...........

BIZZARE................................!!

Everyone be too excited to see this left part of game and there is a solemn excitement on Pee face.

'Now you just see what Barrack team is going to do because Barrack never allowed things to go against his wish' Pee said to Yash.

Both teams after break, left there zone came out of it with their manager with them guiding all fronts of match ahead. But some words being heard in the crowd for Barrack and we can realise that every person was waiting to see what act Barrack is going to perform now. Barrack is also out of his zone with his teammates and they were not talking, not discussing anything now. They all know what to do the next.

Figo to be much happy and confident about whatever he is going to perform as the source blood of all his teammates. The next bell rung and match started up.

BIZARE..............!!

Match is going smoothly as Figo not assaulting any hard splash now towards the opponent team. Seems like he is taking time to set himself on the field and then show itS colour to everyone.

Game touched now its peak and Figo also settle to be back in screen and on a short ball he raised and assault a hard splash towards opponent team and what being seen is a hard and pumped source reply from Barrack teams.

As hard he meant, the short and much slower speed ball attains to reach towards Barrack team court. In other sense the action of Figo which he meant seems to come back towards their team with the same force which they can't handle. This being happening again and again, scores of team become same and they both are on same level. Everyone in the field amazed by looking all this abrupt changes and can't realise the force that is governing the match.

Pee said 'are you watching this, all this that going in the match, is it digestible to you'.

'Yes...even I realised that how did the face of match is been mutationed and no..... This is not even digestible to the surrounding crowd', Yash said to Pee.

Wisttle for Figo had slowed down. The twist of the match which is just showing its result in front of them as failure of Figo team.

'Figo is realising that much pressure and efforts he make to drop down the ball in his opponent team the more his team have to face the same pressure from other side'. Yash said to Pee. 'Why Figo is not centralising himself and making any other strategy to win the game. This thing is going to make his team to sacrifice'.

Suddenly Yash see that Barrack being sitting at the place which is out of reach of the people in the field for everyone is just lost at the court. No one is appetite to see anything else apart from that. But Yash seen that mysterious Barrack being sitting forth and not varifing the match. He set himself to perceptional look that's why he sit there. Yash came to capture that whenever the Figo team cross to a point towards Barrack team. He open up his hand wider and pull up a force in the sky.

Yash started conveying things to himself 'Oh!.... the reason behind all this, Barrack is the one who that is responsible to bring a lot twist in this match. But as he is sitting out of bound of this court then how he able to see what's all going in this match to react accordingly'.

Yash still didn't came profoundly out of that thought which he's dealing with before. So he don't want to get inside all this whatever being happening. As he still can't separate himself from wander of that priest girl. This is the reason, why he didn't intertwine all that he had seen about Barrack with anyone. He hadn't told that to Pee. Yash just smiled and didn't shared anything to anyone.

Match is just going to be finished now and the situation is profoundly mutate from what it is before break time. Figo team demoralised and there is no hope of playing now in their gestures. Barrack team necklaced Figo team with a solemn margin. Everyone in the field at last started to act like the audience that whoever wins is the king and other are the looser. After the match, apart from uploading and congratulating Barrack teammates everyone briefed a explicit view of the game that being flirt by Figo and for that they were becoming fan of Figo. They started veiling him and very happy for the game he flirt and entertained the audience.

'See... you are looking all this, it aid you the assault to make never goes waste. It is uploaded and respected every time', Pee said to Yash.

'Yes I had realised it and seen today', Yash said.

Sunny said, 'Now the game has been over but the game that being flirt by Figo is out of bound. So today I am going to spend my night while allotted some thoughts with him, if he will get agree for it'.

'Oh!... sure Sunny but what you are going to do with him in the night. What is so secret about it. Why wouldn't in the day time', Pee said to Sunny.

'*Hey* don't make it funny and there is nothing required to think in other way. I am not that type of boy and it's simple that as I informed you before dear at the time when match stood going on. I said you that today, I am going to share my tonight drink with him twining some good thoughts', Sunny replied to Pee.

'Yes dear I don't meant that only. Doesn't matters, you can do anything asits your life', Pee said to Sunny.

Yash replied to Sunny. Something sure that Figo have in him as a sports man for which you are making him so solemn full. I prefer to think you to as a solemn sportsman dear because as much of my wisdom.'

'But I think you should not just talk on over here, if you want to be with him you should go and talk to him. Listen he's a nice person too by heart', Pee told to Sunny.

So everything is finish and everybody started leaving the field as match came to its end and started to go towards there room.

'*Hey*..... Yash lets move now towards our room. The sports meet had been over now', Pee said to Yash.

Yash replied 'Pee I want to be here for a bit more time, so am I allowed to sit over here. I don't know but I desire to be here and need to talk myself'.

'Yes dear...you can sit here as much you want but before 6 in the evening you need to go back towards your room as per rule. So before that you can be sit at this place and no one is going to disturb you', Pee said to Yash.

9

All sort of noise becoming calm now as everyone left this field now but Yash is still sitting on the corner stair in the field facing towards court. He is still wandering about that moment when priest girl which he had seen before came close to them and served drinks. He had seen her and recaptulated that both these girls were same. This thing is also not the sort of tension that being going on in his mind because of some hassle. But the thing that is going on is — "why he not be able to oversighten that girl and can't erase her memories from his mind as he's not crazy about girls not even a per cent and apart from that also he won't be able to cancel her memories from his mind. This is only the confusion he got".

All this is going in the field with Yash. But what is going on with Sunny and Figo. Sunny had moved from there to talk to him reached in dressing room. He find Figo dress up himself like a Rock star because he's wearing silver circular ear rings in his both ears and in his bottom he wears black tight jeans with long leather boots adherence them, a silver chain noose in front of his jeans. At his top he had wear a funky looking T-shirt which is too black in colour and it's true that he being looking difficult in that.

Sunny said 'Wow....it aid as being a solemn sports man. You are appetite in making your looks more rigorous by giving them variety looks', Sunny said this to Figo in dressing room where just they both present.

'Oh!... whose there...can I know what is your name..', Figo asked.

'Yes sure......my name is Sunny', Sunny replied.

'You came over here for what and stay at heaven's hell. I didn't seen you before....?', Figo asked Sunny.

'Hm...Yes I stay over here as me and my friend all together brought up for our punishment', Sunny said.

'So what crime you did.....?', Figo asked.

'*Hey* we are playing certain kind of game here like "coffee with Figo" in which you are going to ask questions from me and I am going to answer every sort of your questions'. Sunny said to Figo. '*Hey* dear I just see your fabulous match forth and as a sport man I leg some trait in you and came to share them, is it ok...now'.

'I interrogate one more thing that what crime I did so that I am being punished. As per my wisdom here every person had done similar kind of crime and that's why they are brought here. So my dear I think it would be the waste of time to talk on this context', Sunny answered Figo.

'Oh!....if this is the context of this question & answer session, then I am afraid that if you feel anything wrong about my words'. Sunny said to Figo 'But apart from all this let leave this conversation and come to the point for which I came'.

'Yes say what you want to, feel free about it', Figo said to Sunny.

'My name is Sunny I came with my friends over here from "Earth surface". But today when I had seen you playing then a bit solemn about you and wanted to intertwine my views. I feel as you are being liveried up. You are going somewhere after this...?' Sunny asked to Figo.

'It's good to know about you and to listen from you applanding words about me. My dear I am not going for any celebration. This is just a dressing style of mine to be rigorous every time and look rocking dude. This style stays with me so that I can impress girls in my surrounds', Figo said to Sunny.

'Ok....this is the case, yup...I know that then I had listened rigorous from him about you', Sunny said to Figo.

'What....what had you said two fold once more say........?', Figo asked Sunny.

'*Hey* leave it now, lets go to have a drink if you are agreed for it', Sunny asked Figo.

'Yes...we will go for that even I am fond of having drink sometimes in the evening before going to bed', Figo said to Sunny.

'Halt I will take you to that place, come lets go there and spare some good time today', Figo replied again to Sunny.

The area which been covered with forest kind of environment all around. As they reached there, Figo said' this is the place where we drinks'.

Sunny is watching this place wonderly, green fleshes as the place is like a forest which covered with big green trees in all its surrounds. There is a cake space in amidst where there some round tables lying with benches and fire burns at both of its end.

Sunny said, 'This location to be in apart but exciting too'.

Figo has gone towards one corner of this place, there is the whole counter being made up for alcoholic drink item. Where you could see a number of collection of drinks available. He took one of them and came close to the bench where Sunny is killing its fatigue. Sunny wanted to know about Figo and his sports star, so he asked Figo 'what makes you to fit and fortified with a lot active mind while playing the game'.

Figo, 'The thing is that, the planet from which I had came is a place where there is no plane surface area and everywhere you just leg steep slopes. That is a big decorated reason about my fitness and not just me but it said for every person of our planet in terms of fitness. So for even a small reason we need to go through that track to solve our tasks and that's makes our planet people more fit and perfect', Figo said to Sunny.

'Oh!.... this is like that and because of it, I think this had make you extremely perfect in every game you play, am I right,' Sunny asked Figo.

'But what about your sports and how did you began that', Figo asked Sunny.

'My sport is not that much tougher as you're because I am having things with me and platform for me to grow in. My sport craze started in my early period of infancy and after that I am just flowing in the direction of the blow', Sunny replied to Figo.

Time passed so rapidly for both of them as they are blissful toward each other company.

As its been too late Figo said to Sunny 'you must go now, its been too late and we are not allow to stay out in the night, so from here you are directly been going towards your room not anywhere else'.

Sunny a bit not cosy as before drink but can walk conveniently so he waved his hand towards Figo, left that place to move towards his room. Figo after it went towards his room.

This is happen at one side but Yash is sitting on the stairs still wants to know about that girl. He had seen something in her eyes that he seen it no one else and that sort of attraction making him more attracted towards her. Yash started to feel helpless and all alone to solve this thing. There only one thing that going on in his mind, who that girl is.

He wants to know about her for that. When nothing looks to be in his bound, Yash said 'Now this time only Pee can help me out to solve my problem' he think and ran towards Pee room.

Yash knocked and Pee door. Pee swing of his cloths as he came to listen someone is there on the door. He left his work and moved towards the door to see who come. He came togather that Yash is standing forth his door and looking a bit tensed. He is taking deep breath because he had covered a long distance while running.

Pee wrist his door and asked 'what happened to you Yash say something is serious and from where did you came'.

Yash replied 'nothing is wrong but you need to help me out in some sort of thing...?'.

Pee—'Yes…yes dear I am going to help you out in whatever that you want but first you should come inside, sit cure and then we proceed. Say from where did you came just, you were not in your room', Pee asked.

'No I was there only where you left me last', Yash said.

'What were you doing over there for so long', Pee asked.

'Pee I am in some annoyance, please don't take me in other way understand me first and then guide me the thing that I ask you', Yash said.

'Ok….as you affinity', Pee replied.

Yash conveyed all sort of thoughts till now. He received for priest girls to know about it when that girl came close to us to serve drinks. I recapitulated her face and she is the one whom I had seen when I just entered Heaven's hell finding 'my room to that time. I had seen her performing prayer', Yash said.

'So…all this is ok now, told me what the thing that is making you in annoyance? Tell me about that specifically', Pee asked.

Yash—'Yes all this happened but I don't know why I couldn't erase her wandered from my mind. As much I don't want to debate of it the much the wandered irritates me and again comes to strike my mind. This is about that single girl who served us drinks. As I don't ever think about girls and not even penchant too, then why this time after having a look into her eyes, I won't allow myself to think anything else. As if my desperation desires to know more about her. Please Pee help me out in this manner and tell me about her as who's she', Yash asked to Pee.

Pee replied 'Dear make yourself more cool and don't get into these sort of things. From all of us as no one is allowed to disturb even of these priest girl. Private life so don't get into it my dear. As I told you before also that these girls are too pure and being developed and nourished by god'.

Pee dictated—'ok....she is being staying here since birth and she is also the controller of all the priest girl that are over here. These responsibilities being given to her as she consists of immense strength in her but she never uses that power as she does not new about it correctly. It can be understood like this that God had given power in her infancy to combat with those who destroy others and humanity. But all stamina that she poses never use that or it can be said like she doesn't even know how to use them but it is said that her power aid a lot towards this nature protection and wrecking', Pee answered Yash.

'Ok.......and what is her name Pee', Yash asked Pee.

'Her name is... Adrita, Pee said.

'Adrita.......' Yash said.

'Aid......aid........*Yah* don't see like that toward me. I don't know the meaning but whatever... it would be something a lot elegant and hopeful. As she comes in touch of aura environment each and everything around gets more shiny and graceful due to her presence', Yash said to Pee.

'Oh!... so you grasped senses gained a lot about her in a single day face off as you even didn't talked to her', Pee replied to Yash after listen to all.

Pee said to Yash 'Ok I tell you the meaning behind her name, as the name is pronounced Adrita....it aid loved by others.

A person which is so sweet, so humble and so humanitarian because of it the person loved by everyone in it's surrounds. This word Adrita makes environment also marvellous and when friendly, it's been spoken by someone. Adrita is staying over here since her infancy, following rules of this heaven's hell and being known to its atmospheric aura more than others'.

Yash pleasure can be measured conveniently by his step by step provoking smile even Pee also realised it. As Pee is noticing those sparking excitement and happiness on Yash face. He is a little apprehensive too because this kind of emotion and reaction of Yash towards Adrita were not a good instinctive. Pee realised that he should tell something more to Yash that is going to be helpful to him before letting himself into any annoyance.

Pee instructed 'Yash you should know that about Adrita and other priest girls as these all being favourite of God and he remedy them over here as his daughter. There are some rules which are meant very strictly by God in the favour of protecting even a small smile of them.

'But it settle that these girls are bounded too. As they don't looks like living a normal and happy life and were following certain kind of rules there', Yash said.

'I don't think you have good wisdom about them', Pee said to Yash.

'Ok...I got your point that you want convey to me. Yash said to Pee.

'Ok... Pee thanks.... thanks for revealing me about it as now. I am spirit too light and normal after being known about the beliefs that's raising my intention to know about them more and more', Yash said.

Pee said, leave them and don't oversighten togather at the dinner table as it's your first day over here so come and follow the rule of dinner and interact with peoples around there. This would be good exposer for all of you soon only to mug up soon with people around and make a safer and favourable zone around you which will be a lot helpful to you for staying here', Pee said to Yash.

'No....I don't feel I would require anyone else company to stay here as my friends are enough for me to stay happily', Yash said.

'Oh!.... that's solemn then ok, go and have company of your friends', Pee said to Yash.

Yash stepped towards his room as that was just near to Pee room. He came to capture that there is a tough conversation is going on amidst three of his friends Ankit, Gaurav and Soni. Sunny was not their as he was veiling his time with Figo. The conversation is going on about typical kind of creatures that were collected all together in the field.

'Soni what you are doing with the creature, sit at the last bench all covered. He would have covered his every organ like it's been too cold over there and he being present in snowfall', Gaurav asked Soni.

Soni replied 'Oh!....that guy, ok You all were curious to know about him even I am too a lot curious to know about him before. That's why I had gone close to his coverage in the sense to know about him. I came to know that he is totally meant of mud from top to bottom. He was sitting at the back side because as much being going near the shore and he afraid of water. As in their planet there is no water because that is damaging part of their body like if as soon as they come in contact with it makes them weaker and eradicate them slowly'.

'Oh! is it like that.....very unique personality', Ankit said.

'Yes...Soni if that person is of mud then he would have to be very conscious in all affinity because as much I know about him. Every person from us being dependent on water and if we are not going to get it we can even die but the scene of him is totally opposite', Yash said this while stepping to be a part of their conversation.

Yash don't want his friends to ask him anything regarding late.

Yash stood stepping inside the room, everyone is just looking at his face. They are waiting for him and now he come.

'Yes Yash you were correct in your context that is only the reason he being sitting far away from water's reach at the last bench in the corner with me all covered'. Soni answered.

'Ok.....let's leave all this and you say Yash where were you been, from long time we being waiting for you', Ankit asked.

'Oh!... I am just...Ah', Yash said.

'Ok... it's all right, nothing went wrong in your absence but you should inform all of us once', Ankit said to make Yash feel easy.

Yash getting cure and asked everyone.

'Yes say...you all why are waiting over here, let's go for dinner. I think Pee told us all that we need to get together with every persons of Heaven's hell at the time of dinner. My dear friends if you all are overtightened this thing let me tell you all this is compulsory for all here', Yash said to all his friends.

'*Hey* don't say like that we don't retain this but the things we all are felling a lot tired today. You also know that we are not able to sleep last night', Soni said to Yash.

'I think Soni is saying right this time, we all are not in this condition to go over there greet and meet everyone for just sake of dinner as we are not in the condition to stand also', Gaurav said.

'*Hey* Gaurav, I am afraid of your talking like this, don't be arrogant if you are tired still', Yash said to Gaurav.

Ankit, 'Listen dear, yes me too think like that. we are not in condition to go now for dinner so I think we should leave this thing over here only, as we have to go there every day and whatever else happen we'll see that in morning', Ankit said to Yash.

'Ok...you also feel like that Ankit as you were also aware that it's been a protocol for all of us to go there that can't be violated. I can faces this when Soni said but not from you dear', Yash said to Ankit.

'But I didn't say anything harsh my dear, it's just a wandered and need all of us together. You want to reveal it'. Ankit said.

Yash with a sad spirit and dull face said 'Ok... as you all want'.

But Yash didn't realised that Pee said these words for executive gathering takes place over there not for everyday gathering which occurs there like dinner.

'Why everyone is denying to go there Please anyone from them adherences me and remove this envoy to say yes for going over there. I Want to see Adrita once again as soon as I can don't know why this spirit is bulging so rapidly in me', Yash said to himself.

'Yash.... Ankit called Yash three times.

'*Hey* Yash where did you lost again...I am talking to you, are you listening', Ankit said.

'Yes.........say Ankit what you want to ask', Yash said to Ankit.

'Nothing I am just saying you that if we had decided not to go there. So we must have ease now I am going to my bed, there anyone who wants to come with me', Ankit said to all his friends.

Sunny also arrived soon inside the room and as everyone is exhaustion enough so no one asked anything from Sunny too.

They all with Sunny and Yash set to got on their bed and had a nice long sleep. After some time it settle that Yash friends gone into deep sleeping mode but still Yash was not spirit ease of sleep. He peering two fold forth from the opened window, which was very much close to his bed. After some time when Yash is also got to sleep then a new phase, a new thrill started to occur in their story as moon started to shine much brighter. The showering delight of that moon light was touching the green tree all around over there. It settle that tree were proud to receive that shine from moon. In response to those tree leaves which do sleaveled like they being energised. The climate was becoming too awesome and fragrance spread around of that place.

As moon light was enlighten the surface, its effect when touching sea surface were unpredictable. As it touches sneezed sea surface it settle like pearl were spread all over the sea surface and being twinkling like stars. Everything was becomes majestic over there as time passes but one person there who was too familiar with this entire climate and blissful everything.

She was a girl who seated on one corner of sea shore under a big giant tree with folded legs adherence. Her curling hand and head which she kept on it. As she was perceptional peering towards the moon looks like she being talking to it without words. Her dress shines and sleaveles as of being white and her hair was also wrist up. Moon was also increasing its rigorousness and seeking to fill some colours in her life to make her happier. She was consisting a bit of smile on her face while looking perceptional towards moon and also a lot legacy.

Yash was now to spirit normal. He sensed some irritation on his face while sleeping. The reason for this irritation that Yash was facing because the moon light directly falling on his face crossing that open window because of which he's having problem while sleeping. After facing this sort of discomfort for a while he woke up speedily from his sleeping mode and got to sit on his place. He tried to find the reason that troubling him from a long time and not allowing him to ease and peace. He came to see that as this sun light is directly falling on to his bed from this window only the reason of discomfort. He gone more close towards the window and profoundly amazed to see the all beauty that present forth in the environment there at that time. Yash was not able to remove his eyes to see all the beauty that being present there at that particular time. At last Yash won't allow himself to move out from his room and see what all this was going on and how this climates was becoming too much prettier. As Yash stepped out he crossed the garden in front of his residence and seek that at one corner of sea shore. There was a girl sitting over there and watching towards the moon.

Yash got still at that place just looking towards her. It looks like he was seeking to gather info regarding her unusual behaviour at that time.

'Why she is perceptional looking towards the sky. Oh!... she is looking towards moon. Is it like moon also being shinning more and more because of her attraction towards him', Yash said to himself.

Yash was looking towards her with a big question in his eyes too. While walking towards her Yash also felt that if this chemistry was going amidst moon and her then why he involved in this entire scene.

As he came more closer to that part where she as covered sitting ignorant from all her auras. She didn't even know that somebody was standing on her back side and noticing her actions.

Yash also wanted to know that did she having some annoyance or dieheartburn. So that Yash can help her in any way.

At last Yash said, '*Hey*...... listen.'

No reply came from the other side.

Yash replied again 'Hello.....can you listen me, I am talking to you'.

'Oh!..... it been you, afraid...afraid I really didn't know about it', Yash said to her as he came to know that she is a priest girl.

This time she didn't said anything and just looking towards him with a fire of burning anger increasing inside her, but other end Yash settle to be happy as he got a chance to meet that girl whom he saw at the court. This time Yash has forgotten what Pee told him about priest girls.

'*Hey* you......you were there who served us drinks at the volleyball court and if I am not wrong your name is Adrita...yes', Yash said to her.

She shocked now after listen to these words that Yash said because this was the first time anyone call like this to her and she's wondering that how he got to know her name. One thing which makes her uncomfortable most was that from where this person came to know my name. Then after breaking silence and in a loud tone she replied.

'What all you are doing and saying to me, do you know what all this can cost you. You have no rigorous to disturb us and if I am going to say about all this to priest. Then you need to bear a lot pain', Adrita said to Yash.

With a solemn forceful tone full of anger Adrita replied again, 'How come you got to know about my name as no one over here knows it and to say about you all prisoners here no one can dare to call me by name'.

'Prisoners...why are you talking like this. I think you are very much aware of why we being brought up here. If god is not finding us defaulter then how can you say us Prisoners', Yash said to Adrita.

'Yes...Prisoners, this is right thing, I said you were not free over here to do anything that you want at this place. This time also you are violating protocol which says that you can't interfere in our life, which you are doing now', Adrita replied.

'Ok... yes I am afraid for that to interfere you but this was not my fault', Yash said to Adrita 'I just wanted to know if you are in some annoyance or other as you were peering towards moon from a long time'.

'Its like that you were not in reliance, this is also the reason I asked you' Yash replied again.

'I feel this is not your business you just need to do what is instructed to you. This is our time to visit at this place', Adrita instructed this sober person' You had broken one more rule of this place of going to dinner with everyone, which being going on at present time'.

'Yes I knew that but I and my friends are new to this place we had come recently only and are unaware about all these. We are spirit a lot fatigue tonight that's why it's not been able for us to collect at dinner place', Yash said to Adrita 'We just wandered to have some cure which we had not done from a long time'.

'This is not a weep which you can give when they were going to ask you about your absence at the dinner place. Then you can't say that may be you are going to be tightly punished for this', Adrita greeds.

'I am decisive, I know all this and don't want to listen it from you', Yash said.

'Ok....even, I don't tensed to instruct you about all this', Adrita shouted with her big eyes peering Yash 'But I just desire to ask you that how can you dare to disturb me when no one is allowed to do so'.

'I told you before that I don't know you being over here and seriously if I do knew, then I didn't had disturbed you', Yash said to Adrita.

Adrita settle to be quite stood in awe. She was thinking at that time if anyone would see her with a man then it would become too tough for her to manage everything. This thought was going in her mind but she was still standing there to make Yash realise of his mistake that he did.

There was peace all around in that place but still she knews that nothing hides over here because everything was consisting life weather it was living or non living. Yash seen her too scary in her mood, he wants to know about the reason why she was not able to talk normally with him.

'You are not allowed to come here this time as per rule because at this time whole area becomes our place where we can live our life and be a part of nature. This time you are required to go for your dinner that being done by you slaves all together and no one is allowed to roam around after it and that what I told you. I think now all this stuff being explicit to you', Adrita informed Yash.

'Afraid, but I have two questions from you and I hope as you had given me so much information about the place', Yash asked Adrita.

'But these all guidance settle to me like milk without sugar. So could you please tell me about that this is the time when you all priest girl turn up this place or you come here usually', Yash added.

Adrita said, 'Why you are asking all this and who are you so that I am going to answer these things to you, be in your limits and don't cross that'.

'Ok...If you don't want to answer whatever I asked then don't tell me', Yash asked Adrita.

'I got to know that you consist a big respectful position over here which no one other does. Then why from the commencing of our conversation it have seen a big stress on your face. Can you tell me reason for that', Yash prompted again.

'*Hey*... why are you asking such things that I won't be able to answer you. First of all I should inform you that I am not appetite to answer any single question of yours. As you are so appetite to know about my personal and vital things this would led you in a big trouble, I am warning you', Adrita said and reminded Yash.

'So this means that you don't even wants to talk me, but, this thing I don't facet from a girl who is so sacred and belongs to heart of "Earth surface" (India)', Yash said to Adrita.

Adrita started to stared on his face settle he doesn't know what he said. Adrita had born here at this place only, she don't even know about her parent's that much. She is grown and developed under priest guidance and contains a supreme strength in all priest girls. Still she is unaware of all that Yash said because Yash had said those things which she never realised and wandered anytime. Yash told about her origination place. This he said because Adrita's features, gestures, body language and appearance were 100 per cent like a person from "Earth surface" which Adrita didn't realised before Yash told her.

Adrita asked, 'How can you say like that and why is it so'.

'*Hey* I am afraid now that I am not speaking anything too out of bound or upfront as I just said you that we both belongs to the same planet nothing else', Yash said Adrita.

Adrita reaction were becoming unaware and shocking more and more. A strong girl like her is loosing herself now.

Yash replied again, 'Oh!... don't tell that you are shocked on my words regarding planet from which you belongs to or it is like that you don't even know from which planet do you belongs too'.

'No... I didn't wandered about it as this doesn't matter. Here from the beginning that we discriminate amidst all on be close of their planet and way of living. So this doesn't matters here from where you belongs too', Adrita said but there are confusion lines on her forehead as the last stanza she said. Yash explicitly shows that she is too disappointed.

'Ok... now, I think you got to know about everything. So now at least you can be a bit turned towards me. I think I can expect that from you, may I......' Yash asked from Adrita.

She confused now because of which there entire innocence came on her face like a child.

'Oh!... afraid if I had said anything wrong to you, I didn't mean that', Yash said.

Slow and sweet tone 'No...there is none of your fault, I am just thinking of myself', Adrita replied.

'*Hey*.... does not say like that as much I had known about you priest girl. I knew that you all were jolly and passionate to deal with every kind of mishap whether it is of emotion, spirit and happiness too', Yash said this to Adrita as he had seen her in vain and which is the thing he won't be able to look in her eyes.

'Afraid...for this but you...whoever you are, now please go from here, I need some time to spare alone with myself', Adrita said to Yash.

'If there is any trouble going in your mind then please.......please dear tell it to me because frankly speaking I am not able to see sadness on your face. I want to see you as I just said about you', Yash said to Adrita in a pleasing manner.

Adrita said, 'You please for now, only don't get into this, please leave me and let me be with myself for some time. I won't be able to speak even a single word to you now and I can facet this much favour from your side'.

This time there conversation was going much deeper after knowing certain exotic thing from Yash that Adrita don't know about her and even no one told her till now, she was having combat of wandered in her sole. She wants to deal this thing on her own in peace. This time Yash was still standing there because he was not spirit ease after seeing Adrita in this kind of mood and stress. Yash is also unaware that why this thing was happening with me for this girl as nothing happens in my heart for any other person till now, I didn't felt these sorts of emotions for others.

'Adrita why are you being so low now and stress can be seen on your face conveniently, Yash said to Adrita.

'Listen...how can you call me by my name and from where did you got to know about it', Adrita said to Yash waver her reaction as soon as she listened her name from Yash with hears in her eyes.

'Your name........ah!... afraid but I got to know this in the field when the match was going on, someone called it from my backside when you with your other priest girl came to the field', Yash said a lie this time to Adrita. As such he didn't want to disclose the name of Pee in all this.

'You got to know my name in field. I don't feel that anyone from all slaves in Heaven's hell knows my name. Then who is the one who said that', Adrita said this while thinking for that person.

'Park all this, but I am happy now that you came back in that rock fortified attitude that I said you to be in', Yash said this to Adrita with smiling face.

As they were talking from a long time Adrita couldn't even realise that this was the time for her to go for prayer. Her presence in all holy activities over there was mandatory as she need to reach their first before others. Soon heavy sound of bells started to be heard at that place and everything surrounds started to mutation its colour looks like now this is the time for something else to start but what Yash was ignorant about all. As sound of bells reached Adrita's ears she started to look here and there as this time she got late for her prayer just started.

Adrita said, 'Oh!.... God prayer started now how could I reach out there early, this time I would have to use it as I am helpless'. She whispered slowly to her.

So she turned backward so much heavily as if her wrist hair fallen on Yash till that time. Yash remove those from his face she is nowhere to be seen. She don't want to use it in front of this vague guy Yash but for to do so because if she didn't used it and reached their normally. Then she would be standing in the part of norms breaker which no one expect from her side. After Adrita left that place and disappeared, Yash is the only one who being present over there that time watching this whole waver environment and its beauty all alone. Yash friend were sleeping in their residence room as before and no one knows that what Yash has observed and faced this night. Yash was also having various thoughts and questions collapsing his mind this time as he wants to meet Adrita again. So he taken a deep breath, folded his hands and prayed God, so that God can help him to meet Adrita again because the positive powers he is getting when he meet her. He never felt like this before.

Yash said, 'Sometimes...something becomes so exalted and exciting that you need no other bless apart from getting those things, I had never felt these words are rigorous but yes these words work'.

Yash is worried because he doesn't want that his friends to ask anything about what he had faced this night. Yash reached his room and see the door of his room which is still wrist in the same way as he left it. Yash stepped inside his room. He had seen that nothing is to be apprehensive here as his all friends were sleeping like anything rid of all anxiety.

Yash smiled, 'It seems like they were not going to wake up for many days and I am tenseded worthlessly'.

Yash—'Now let me too have some hours of sleep, as I don't knew about the hard work and stress is waiting for us on the next door. What would be the atmosphere of tomorrow's climate for us that is also not confirmed', Yash said to himself.

This time as Yash get on his bed, he slept within few minutes. This time Yash is now sleeping with smiling mug without anxiety.

So... This is how first day of all had been gone in Heaven's hell now, Night is becoming darker as time passes. As such time over there passes off as God wants that's why there is no watch to be seen in Heaven's hell. You can judge time by the climate around you and as per said before by priest who brought Yash. priest had conveyed to Yash and his friends before that in Heaven's hell that even a single day over here took a lot solemn time to pass off. You need to do number of work over here in a single day and to prove yourself. There are so many thing to be seen by them all in near forthcoming time but this time they all together spirit cure and tensed less.

10

Next morning, start with Sunny, who wake up too early as it's been his habit to do the same. He first gone towards the door to see that today morning is as elegant as yesterday or it's been something more new news to be heard today. He leg this morning same as yesterday with birds blissful in their full mood, as if they are profoundly free to live in their habitat. Sunny noticed that door is wrist up before he tried to open it as if someone had came inside yesterday to probe them. He doesn't knows that this door being wrist by Yash last night and what all had happened yesterday, he is profoundly unknown about that all till now. After this he tried to wake Gaurav and Ankit, as he want them to realise that new day has come and there is a start for new journey of the day. Now all of them wake up to see and realise the dashing start of the day. Ankit saw out from the window see that there is someone in the field who is running all around in the field on the track meant there.

'Look it's Figo in the field this time whom we met yesterday. I feel, he is having his morning jogging there see...', Ankit said to his friends.

'Really...I must say he is a man of accurate physique and willpower because as we both had took fortified drink last night and after that too he wake up early and gone for work out, this shows about his dedication', Sunny informed to Ankit.

'Yes if it is like that then he must be a solemn sportsman all over', Ankit said to Sunny.

Sunny insisted—'You know this is because one motivation also as at there planet they were not having plain surfaces anywhere. He told me that and just you have over there is up and down as slopes through which they suffice every day. This would be one reason for his fine fitness in all affinity. I feel that I want be able to win from Figo. Sunny said to Ankit.

'But this is a wrong attitude of living dear. If you don't want to have a competition then it's ok but you don't have to think about your necklace before any assault. I would suggest you to don't get in all these things as we came here not to do all these'. Ankit replied Sunny.

Gaurav realised that Soni is not present on his bed. He wanted to know where he had gone now so he asked 'Do you know where Soni had gone', Gaurav asked from Ankit.

'Look here he is, over there at field himself', Sunny said.

'Oh! my god...what I must wrangle with this guy, he doesn't anxious that without informing anyone from us if he go anywhere in this vague place then it would be difficult for all of us', Ankit said to all.

'Wait don't tensed, I call him', Sunny said.

'Before calling him tell me what he is doing over there and he is with Figo this time or busy in some other stuff', Ankit asked. While having a cup of tea in his hand.

Gaurav replied, '*Hey* Ankit don't be apprehensive that much about him, as we all knows that he is a little child from his mentality but you also know that he had done nothing like we were going to get any annoyance. Wait I see and probe out what is going there'.

'Oh!... see nothing to tensed about Soni being playing there with a dog as we all know that he is too fond of them', Gaurav said.

'Oh!... really but I just know that he is fond of one thing only which is food..food..and food'.... Sunny giggled.

'Sunny shut your mouth for now, this is not the time to laugh', Ankit said to Sunny.

'Ok... Gaurav but what are you waiting for call him now', Ankit said to Gaurav.

'Ok... ill call him.........Soni...' Gaurav shouted.

'Wait why are you shouting like this time. As this is your home or what as shouting would make others to listen your tone and I don't want any blunder to occur here in our commencing period. Please go and call him personally', Ankit said to Gaurav and he started to step towards field to call him.

'Sometimes I feel you all are same, no one cares that we are at a place that is not for us to bliss over here. We had came for our punishment', Ankit said to Sunny as Gaurav left the room and gone to call Soni.

'But I even don't know that why are you caring that much for everything here as we are not been given any sort of pressure and pain up till now and I think God doesn't wants to give that also. As you had also listened when priest told us all that over here. God just want to guide us certain norms and rules only and nothing else I feel', Sunny instructed Ankit.

'Now please you keep quiet for a while, problem is this only with you all that you just see what's been happening but you don't see the other face what can happen', Ankit said this to Sunny and after this Sunny also didn't replied to Ankit as his mood doesn't settle to be good enough.

Gaurav reached field and see Soni being too happy while playing with dog. Gaurav see that this dog devotion for Soni like anything as he is jumping over Soni again and after as he wants to curl him in his arms. Soni devotion to him a lot. As Gaurav came close to Soni and called him. Soni responded 'Yes...Gaurav good morning you wake up, come here see how sober and cute this dog like he is also from "Earth surface". He can feel we are from the same and that's why he is not even letting me to go from here and to just play with him', Soni said to Gaurav.

As Soni is speaking to Gaurav the dog ran away and when Soni looked back towards him he is nowhere to be seen. So Soni called him...but he doesn't know his name and Gaurav replied 'ok....lets go dear he had gone now and you too come with me'.

'Wait I think Figo had also completed his entire workout, let's take him along with us', Soni said Gaurav.

Soni and Gaurav moved towards Figo said, 'Figo come with us it's been long time from which you were having work out here, come lets go towards residence', Soni said to Figo.

Figo said, 'yes I think today I had worked a lot and I need ease now, ok lets go'.

11

As they reached Ankit see that Soni was coming and he said 'why didn't you even cared of revealing anyone from us before being leaving from here, this is not the way to remedy your friends my dear'.

Soni replied, 'Its not that I didn't cared to tell you about this but the thing is that today I wake up earlier as this dog with which I am playing come forth and started to bark forth our door. After listening to him two to three times I waked up and seen that our door is wrist up and as I had seen forth I came to see that dog is standing over there. He came along with those all girls that we had seen yesterday evening. As I looked forward I seen that these girls were surge towards backside of our residence. These all were carrying in their hand big plates filled with food and its acrid too good as I can even smell that from a long distance. This is the reason after which I won't be able to halt myself from walking towards them. After some time these all get disappeared, how come I don't know. But the best part is I left out with this sober dog with which I started playing in the field and there only I met Figo', Soni said this to his friends.

Sunny replied instantly, 'I was saying you Ankit that Soni is fond of just one thing food... food and food but you didn't even hear say to me...ha'.

'Sunny you started again, could you please be in silence mode', Ankit said and giggled.

Gaurav impeded in amidst said, '*Hey* leave all this thing amidst you and just see who had come with us, it's Figo whom we saw jogging.

'Oh!.... afraid Figo I didn't realised that you were over here and started to go away with my sort of tread on. Say Figo how is your morning today', Ankit said.

Figo replied, 'I think my morning meant to be quite warm after being listening to your words full of heat'.

'Why are you all been talking while standing on the door. We can sit inside and talk', Sunny said to all of them.

'Your friend doesn't wake up still, say him to wake up and get inclined as sleep till this time is against rule here. So you must ask him to wake up and get inclined soon', Figo said to all.

Sunny asked, 'Get inclined... inclined for what'.

'Soon it would be the time for Morning Prayer and hope you do know that all of your appearance over there is must. This I am saying as I didn't have seen you all present in our last dinner. You all don't know about it or you know but set you loose last night', Figo replied again.

Gaurav said to Ankit, 'Yes we don't know about it'.

Figo replied, 'Pee hadn't told you about all these things'.

Ankit asked, 'Why were you calling name of Pee to tell all this to us. He is not the member of this place and assigned person to inform us about every things.

Figo said, 'No I think Pee didn't had conveyed about him. He is the allotted responsible member whom God had given some responsibilities. I think you don't even know that Pee is living here since a past long time'.

Everyone moved and stressed now, as if why didn't Pee told them all about these.

Figo replied again, 'I think you all don't need to get apprehensive about it because Pee is the only person who tell rules to everyone new comer to this place. If Pee hadn't told you all then don't tensed about it and its been your pleasure that Pee's room is just next to yours. These are some emphasis that Pee can't say to everyone so if he hadn't told you these things before please don't inform him that I told you about all this'.

After listen to Figo words Ankit replied, 'No... my dear Figo we are not going to say even a single word to Pee, you don't tensed about it. We are just thinking that Pee told us about some rules but he didn't said about it anything that he is responsible to tell this to everyone. This is because as we met to Pee incidentally not any reason'.

'But I must tell you that everyone when comes up here they meet Pee incidentally and I would say that don't think about all these things much', Figo said all of them.

As Sunny was seeking to wake Yash from his sleep by calling his name and rubbing his hand. Yash settle not to listening his voice and was sleeping in his perception mood and abruptly what happened no one knows. Yash wake up from his bed and become still for a while.

Everybody being on there place looking Yash perceptional and seeking togather what had happened to Yash this time. Yash start to rub his eyes by his palm and looked upwards, everyone is looking towards him at that time. Yash just makes himself cool by taking again a deep breath and he turned back, gone towards the table to have a glass of water. Ankit came close to Yash and asked him 'What did happen to you. Yash is there anything to be apprehensive off'.

'No...nothing to be worried of, I am all ok', Yash said to them.

'But it do n't seems like that you are been ok this time, as you never reacted like this', Ankit said to Yash.

Yash was very happy and overwhelmed with smile on his face but those things that was making him to think about her again and again.

'Ok....Yash if everything is ok... so dear wash your face and as Figo is saying that we all need to gathered for morning prayer', Ankit said to Yash.

Yash that time trying to get back into actual world and leave his wandered mechanism. As Yash heard about Morning Prayer from Ankit, he replied 'Ah... we need to go for Morning Prayer I know that and I had told you also all, but what you said who told you', Yash said.

Ankit said 'yes... This is said by Figo. You didn't noticed he is over here only', Ankit said to Yash.

'Oh!... afraid Figo, welcome, it's been too grateful to see you over here. With us after seeing you're very much enhancing and powerful screening yesterday in the court. Ok you all just wait for me. I get inclined soon and then we'll go for the prayer', Yash said to Figo.

Yash rinse his face but still there, a lot discomfort which Yash is facing with his spirits. So he decided to share all this with his friends as he always does only when he have a combat with his spirits. Yash came out of wash room gone toward his friends and said.

'I need to tell certain thing to you all that occurred with me last night and for that only my attitude and reaction were not normal before. You were right there. Ankit is spirits combat going on in my heart', Yash said to all.

Ankit said, 'Yes my dear tell me I had not seen your remarks like this ever in the morning. Come here Yash, sit conveniently and tell us what is going on with you now'.

'Nothing dear I am just having some words, some pictures and spirit of last night going in my mind', Yash said to Ankit.

'What exalted or executive you faced last night as much I know we all faced the same', Ankit said to Yash.

Yash attempted conveying—'No...dear this is not the true thing when you all decided not to go for dinner last night and decided to sleep early. Last night when I am seeking to sleep on my bed which is to close towards the window. Abruptly moon light started to strike on my face too heavily that I won't be able to sleep. As this light is creating a kind of irritation which is not allowing me to have sleep, so I wake up and gone forth to see what is been the reason for moon be shining like this. I came to notice that there is one girl sitting near the sea shore forth. I impeded her and came know that she is priest girl and I am not aware about this before otherwise I had never assault or disturb priest girl. Then I came to know that she is from our planet "Earth surface" but the thing to be noticed is that she didn't knows that she is from "Earth surface". Then I had some sort of conversation with her and now the problem is that those words that she said and all her innocence is just clipped on my mind and two fold coming in my thoughts. These all are last night thing that are disturbing me', Yash said this whole story in front them of all.

'This is it', ... Ankit said to Yash.

'But this story is going in some other direction I think', Gaurav said to all.

'I know that what you all were thinking about me. I think you all know that I don't even get weaker towards any girl because I don't think that this is our requirement in any sense. Yash said.

As he compelled Figo replied soon, 'Could you tell me what her name is', Figo asked Yash.

Yash replied, 'Her name.......her name is Adrita', Yash said to Figo.

'Adrita... are you sure her name is Adrita only and no one else because I think I had heard this name somewhere', Figo said.

Figo said, "No, dear you were wrong. She knows about this but never excepts.

'Where...where did you have listened for this word', Yash asked to Figo.

'I don't know exactly about it but I had heard about this word when I was practicing with Barrack Team member even Barrack is also present over there and they were chat about this name. What all they were saying that time I didn't given that much emphasis to know that as my concentration was towards my practice that time', Figo said to Yash.

'What would they were chanting her name as even you too don't know about her name but Barrack knows that', Yash replied to Figo.

Figo said, 'My dear what did you know about Barrack....? I think nothing but when you come to know about him, you will know that what a powerful person he is'.

'Ok.....I don't want to get into that now, as I just wanted to know about Adrita and nothing else', Yash said to Figo.

'But, I can help you out to inform about their place of occurrence for the whole day. These are also some things that only I can tell you over here. This thing is because I am also a bit choosy for priest girls and love their style a lot', Figo said and smiled

'I think now he is going to tell something utilitarian', Yash said to himself.

'Ok listen then after prayer you can see and meet, if you can dare to do that in music session room. This is just behind prayer room in which we are just going for our prayer. There you can conveniently go and meet anyone from the priest girl because that is the place where you can find all of them together', Figo said to Yash and his friends.

Figo replied again, 'I think this could be utilitarian to you'.

'*Ya*...sure Figo, and thanks for revealing me these all sort of things. They would be helpful to me, I inference'. Yash said.

Ankit said, 'I think apart from just been stand and talking here only, we must now get poised to go for the prayer otherwise it would be more difficult for us'. Ankit said to Gaurav.

Gaurav replied, 'yes that's to sure if we missed this one also then there is nothing for us to be spared off. Ok......Soni and Sunny you both please just get inclined and hand over to me my clothes that have kept inside. I am going to wear something white today to go for the prayer'.

Ankit said to Sunny 'Now see how happy Gaurav is to do all these, I told him because I wandered that he is going to take this thing in a well organised way and say you all exactly but see how his reaction'.

'Leave dear Ankit... leave all this...', Sunny smiled and said to Ankit leave these things and don't think about them now.

After all these conversation Ankit and Figo started waiting in the room for the others to be inclined off soon. This time Ankit is taking wisdom of this place from Figo and in his description about the place. Figo raise this name Barrack many times. Ankit halted Figo and asked him 'Figo could you please tell me about this person Barrack in brief'.

'Yes you want to know about him, I am certainly going to tell you about him but how this appetite to know about him rose inside you', Figo asked Ankit.

'This is obvious that If you are two fold going to call a name in your context. Then other person wants to know that what the trait in that name is', Ankit said to Figo.

Figo with a deep heavy gone—'Yes there is a lot trait in this person 'Barrack' but his uniqueness is not helpful to even one per cent for good persons. Because to say about him, I can just say that, 'he is the master of black powers with his mysterious magical styles. Yes, he is having a lot wisdom too as he had gained all these powers by his concentration and devotion'. This is just I would like to convey about him. He is the person who brought over here not for the reason as we all being brought up but his description is something else. He is a cousin of superior king of his planet but because greediness and conspiracy towards his brother, Barrack slained him. Barrack crack to conquer the whole planet himself. When he did that he started spoiling life of sober and peace devotion people in his planet a lot more. So this all sort of stuffs I do know about him.

I don't think that I am able to instruct everything now. So let's talk about it in our spare time and you don't need to be apprehensive about Barrack here. As God had denied and destroyed his power strength to be used over here. Now here he is living his life like a normal and power less but yet his mentality never mutate and want to annulled every person here too. You were not there that time in morning with me, if you would be there, I had shown you at the corner of that field. Barrack is also present there and he on frequent base does meditation and practices to increase his Black power. The good thing for all of us here is that, he is not able to invoked or use his power on us and can't achieve anything here from them'. As Figo finishes telling all this to him soon there is instincts of somone arrival.

They come to see that he is no one else than Sunny who had gone forth washroom to refreshing up himself.

'What had happened here, Ankit everything is ok. Figo you say what happened here as I don't feel look to Ankit seems that everything is normal', Sunny said to Figo.

So as Sunny asked Figo about what being going on over there Ankit got a bit stressed because he doesn't want Figo to say anything regarding their conversation. Ankit faced towards Figo and pinched him as if no one can see that. He tried to say something to Figo quietly. Figo saw towards Ankit and from his gesture and expressions, Figo understood this thing exactly that Ankit don't want him to say anything to Sunny now and as he didn't informed about anything to Sunny before. Ankit replied;

'Nothing we are just talking about the waver climate over here', Ankit said this and change the topic.

Figo replied, 'Yes...this is a datum over here that climatic mutation occur after certain interval of time periodically. All this happens here because dear as you also know that here everyone from apart planet brought up and kept here. So god keeps a rigorous record of everyone's favourable climate and meant so dashing atmosphere which no one can see anywhere else. This climate is meant for beautiful hybrid of colours and breeze everywhere. Now, I think this sort of thing is explicit in your mind'.

'Solemn its like you know about everything that is going in our surrounding over here. How long you were staying over this place', Ankit asked Figo.

I am staying over here from three months', Figo replied to Ankit.

'In just this short span of time you had known that much about this place, it's amazing', Ankit said.

'This is not a short span of time dear over here three month aid a lot and see as you all were over here for just one day. Because of that many thing you had known about this place', Figo said.

'Yes... many things.... you were rigorous and with your help I came to know a lot more', Ankit said with a smile on his face.

Sunny replied, 'Pee also said us this thing but we came to know about him something else. Hope you were revealing about your period accurately', Sunny said this and everyone laughed on his context.

Figo said, 'No dear don't tensed this time. I am revealing you the rigorous interval of mine that I spared over here. Pee also does not say lie to anyone but he had to say that just because it's been his work.

'We know that Pee is a genuine person by heart and I feel that's why God had given him all these responsibilities', Sunny said to Figo.

Abruptly Yash came there and said in a hurry 'Get inclined boys what are you all waiting for, let's move towards the prayer room'.

'We are just waiting for you to come. Ok...lets we all move towards prayer room, come my friends but Figo you have to tell us where it is. I forget that you are coming with us only', Ankit said.

'Afraid dear as you all were inclined to go there but see, I am not inclined still. I need some time to get inclined. So for that I have to go in my room and be dressed off', Figo said to everyone.

'I can understand, ok take your time dear and reach at prayer room. We are leaving now but don't know the way and you need to guide us for that', Yash said Figo.

Figo guide them the way to go towards Prayer room. Which is very far from their residence but no one reaction in unusual manner.

Reaction of all were normal as they know about this place a bit as when came in the start; they have to travel a lot to reach their room. So after listen to Figo they all started to walk towards the way he told them.

While walking Sunny seems to be quite implication everyone looked and ignored him as they wandered that this time again something nuisance being going in his mind.

After thinking for a long time Sunny said, '*Hey* I was thinking same like Figo, Pee also said us all to go to the field yesterday where match was going on. So is it like as he didn't came with us for field, same is being done by Figo. Figo whatever said to us about Pee, I hope he is not like that and said us everything that is core hearted truth'.

Ankit said again, 'Now can I expect from you that you were not going to think like in this manner more and just move quietly with us'.

'I don't know why you just crack to make me to be quite as if I just speak truth', Sunny said this to Ankit and make exotic face towards it.

Yash said, 'Look there it is our prayer room......wow....it's too fabulous and made of black-white marble and a track in front of it which gives a appearance like God had wrist there arms to invite his children's towards him'.

'Dear seriously this place is just a auspicious even you can realise it. Do one thing just close your eyes without thinking anything else you will get that', Yash instructed to Gaurav.

Ankit said, 'So truely said about this place Yash. The spirit, God presence and attachment that I had felt over here nowhere else I got this. You all know too that I had visited every holistic place in our country but this is something very much solemner than those all', Ankit said to his friends.

Gaurav said, 'Yes that's rigorous now I can also feel the same'.

Soni said, 'I know that you all are very holistic but if you all are just going to talk over here, then how can we reach close to it. I can't see anyone else going towards it this time which aid we are late. So if you all step forward quickly we can get in soon'.

They reached at the gate from where they have to get in and start praying as others were going through. As they reached their someone came from back and put his hand on Yash shoulder, he turned back and said, 'Figo.....you come, difficult to meet you here as if I am thinking that there is no one standing at this door what is going inside'.

Figo said relaxing his body as he came there after running for that whole distance rapidly 'you don't need to think anything now just get in prayer being started off, come with me you all'.

As they stepped into with Figo, they came to gather a wonder inside as if this place is filled with holistic rituals and customs air all around. Everyone is present inside and a pin drop silence is uphold there. All creatures over there are standing by joining there both hands and spreading peace and wreck all around. There is place mean for everyone to stand on and above each place there is a bell on everyone head which is designed so well like that no one from them seen it before. A perception flow of flowers from where no one knows but they were falling down over everyone. Yash come to see that all priest girls are also over there in front of them facing towards all slaves. They also folded their hands and were praying with them all. Yash saw Adrita in front of him playing violin and standing in amidst of all these girls. She is so desperately busy in playing this violin that she is not even looking at anyone around her and just lost in her tunes but now Yash is looking at her perceptional and said;

'Oh! my God how anyone can look so enhancing to me', this time Yash started questions his God for all this as he wants to know that why is this happening to him and why couldn't this time also he won't be able to remove his eyes from her.

This is true that she was looking too in passionate beautiful that time. So Yash concentration is deviating from the prayer towards Adrita. As everyone is standing on white glass pamphlet below them at the time of prayer.

So Gaurav said by opening his one eye and facing towards Ankit, 'What is this below why I can't feel anything inside my body, it's all waked', As they were standing at the back so he felt no one is noticing him.

Ankit replied, 'I am also spirit like that, now you please keep quite, everyone is observing the same here and just concentrate on pray'.

As they both feel that no one is looking towards them and they could pass words to each other but they were wrong in this affinity. As soon as they finished passing there words multiple bells started ringing over both head. which rang once to inform them that everything being noticed over here. So they both realised the same seen towards each other got to know about their mistake and started praying again. This time also Yash with his joined hands and open eyes is being looking at Adrita perceptional. He is not even caring if somebody had seen him doing all this, then what would happen. So as the song that those girls were singing being finished, Adrita removed her concentration from that music and looked upward slowly. This time her friends had taken up a bowl filled up of milk in their coffers and started pouring it in front of them with a huge sound all together as if they were requesting something from God that time. This time Adrita is standing still in amidst and looking towards all creatures who were praying in front of her. Abruptly she came to gather Yash standing at the back side and is looking at her perception-ally which she felt not good at that time. As such no one can think anything else apart from God at present. She have this power in her control that she could scold anyone here whoever is not confined to their pray. But she won't be able to do this with him this time. She crack to call his name but not able to do as Yash told about her occurrence planet in their last talk. So she don't want him to be reproach now in front of everyone. As Yash is looking towards her still because of this she is also not spirit cosy while standing on her place and looking distracted from what she is doing. She don't want anyone else to see this sort of behaviour from Yash towards her as it could be hazardous for Yash afterward. So she started looking side wise like from one side to the other. Now it is the work of Adrita as of everyday she script certain humanitarian statements that would going to enhance humanity and prosperity in this universe. Everybody is just waiting for Adrita to speak up those statements so that they all can two fold after her and finish today Prayer session. As everyone is waiting for Adrita but she settle to thinking something and just spirit uneasy over there. As Yash is in front of her and looking her perception.

While as her friends from priest girls insisted her to hold two candles in her coffers and start performing the last action of their pray. This last section of them is about speaking certain humanitarian norms which God facets from them to follow. So after a while Adrita started and said;

1. I am going to spread pleasure on everyone face.
2. I never try to do a thing that would indirectly wreck anyone.
3. I every time work towards tribe development and growth.
4. I will never be greedy and selfish in my life and just try to build friendly relation amidst me and others.
5. My resources were every time available for each needy person whenever required.
6. I never allow anyone to sacrifice and bear stress of not getting required things for his life satisfaction.

So after Adrita said all these lines simultaneously everyone there is required to two fold after her these same lines. So everyone started to do so and reply after every line when she finishes off. As she finished her last line and others responded to this. These girls started to move out from the north side of prayer room and others started to move from the south side of the prayer room. slowly steadily this prayer room started to become vacant as everybody is leaving this room now.

As everyone is surge out from prayer room, Sunny came to see that Pee is also over there so he called him close to them by saying '*Hey...* Pee please come up'.

Then all of them started there discussion regarding the first day. As Pee is also anxious to know about what all they revealed up today's morning...

In this belief Pee stayed with Yash friends and tried to receive that mysterious thing which Yash whispered.

4

Love and Aspiration

"Some times ignorance of your presence by only one person makes your soul invisible for everyone in that aura".

A theme derived from Gods played Game

"When you make your attraction towards your beloved things to be diminished..........

your beloved increases attraction towards you after an interval of time and you never knows that's applied to everything".

12

Soon after listening to all his friends, Yash took Figo with him towards the corner to say him something personally. Then Yash said;

'Listen dear let's do one thing now, just you and me both together will go at the music room, where all the priest girls do instrumental practices'.

'Ok....wait for a while let they all finish their conversation and then we are going to ask them to go from here', Figo replied to Yash.

'Don't wait for their conversation to get over. I think they will not let me to go now with you because reaction of Ankit which was not good when I told you all about Adrita at our room', Yash said to Figo.

Figo replied, 'See dear it is not like that. He don't mind if we are going to ask them to go...............wait I'll ask them'.

Figo asked Ankit, 'Ok.....I and Yash are just surge for a while towards place. So wait here, we are just going to come back soon. You all go on with your conversation'.

'Ok....yes don't tensed if you want to go now, Yash go this time but don't do this like before as you didn't prefer time', Gaurav instantly replied to what Figo asked as he is also in dilemma that may be Ankit would get annoyed on all this.

Yash replied soon 'Thanks dear it's something emphasise for which I need to go there otherwise I don't and I'll get back to you all soon'.

Yash turned to see the surrounding place of this area and he realised that this Music place is close to the sea where he met first time with Adrita and conversed with her.

Figo said, '*Hey* what you are trying to musmerise. What do you need to know because your eye settle to be questionable this time'?

'I don't need to know anything, I am just looking at this place because this is the only place where I met Adrita and I told you all about it. This place is near sea shore where we were standing as that time becomes too precious for me', Yash said to Figo.

'And I would suggest you to please not to think all these things rigorous now because this place is not that much safe as we all are not allowed to come over here', Figo reminded to Yash fearously.

'Why is this any restricted place'?, Yash asked.

'Yes this is a restricted place for all of slaves like us over here, as if we are not members of Heaven's hell', Figo answered Yash.

'This is why I am thinking that why no one settle over here all around as much as I can see......ok now say where we need to go', Yash said to Figo.

Figo 'Ok listen that there are various class room in this building and different section perform role of music. You would be happy to know that all this is also governed by Adrita. She is the one who administrate and systemise this music and instrumental work for Heaven's hell even she does help girls here to dance on devotional songs toward God', Figo told to Yash.

'Figo now tell me about her where could we can go and meet her......', Yash asked in excitement.

'Please....dear don't say like this otherwise I and you both will get into a big annoyance that I don't want to be in now. So please be known about this datum that we are presently illegal over here and there are many of God meant saints which God had spread over all this place. Which notices whatever activities we perform against rule here', Figo requested to Yash.

Understanding what Figo seeking to say Yash.

Yash replied, 'No...dear I had never done anything which can make any other person in annoyance and those who helps me like you, I'll take excess care of them. Look now we will be quicker and let's move towards the place where she is, I am just going to see her and we'll go back as circumstances say that time'.

'Come...come with me so', Figo said to Yash.

They started to move inside this monument type building which is meant in an antique manner so that it would look like a collaboration of all cultures all together. There is small sweet sound which being heard by them when they started climbing stairs, this sound is of instrument 'sitar' flirt by someone over there.

Figo said, 'This looks like 'sitar' is being flirt by Adrita only because last time when we had our Heaven's hell ceremony she flirt this in same tone, but still I am not sure yet'.

At this time they reached first floor of this monument. Front of them there is dance class going on in which small girls are dancing in their full mood and there is no one to guide them. After looking towards that Yash said;

'Ok.... Figo that's ok...but see, who are these small girls practicing here and dancing so well on rhythm. Yash asked Figo.

'No...dear it's not about that, these are those girls that just stay in this monument and nourished up here itself. These girls were brought up from the entire universe that do God want to treat specially and be an everlasting member of Heaven's hell.

These all girls show you the childhood of priest girls', Figo said to Yash.

'So this is the childhood of Adrita too? She had also grown up here only as Pee told me about this', Yash asked Figo.

'No my dear friend, this is not where she had grown as her parent were from your planet named "Earth". She was the only child of them. Her parent are very kind and humanoid that they stay close to God heart every time. Adrita is not a normal priest girl. You should know that', Figo excite to tell something about Adrita life to Yash.

Yash said, 'I know......thanks for revealing me all this Figo'.

Figo said, 'Yes we'll go but before that let me instruct you more about her past life as much as I knew because I know you are going to ask about this further'.

Figo just thought that this time Yash is saying all this because he just wants to meet her and don't want to know anything else. There are certain features for which she being felt executive over here. She is having those strengths which no one else has over here.

Yash said, 'Figo, listen I got to know about her from you as much I needed to know and now can we proceed......'.

'Yash this is emphasise for you to know but ok...if you don't want then, let's go....I feel that they were in ground floor only, let's get back to the base and probe them out', Figo said.

This time what did Figo wants to say him. He oversighten that all as Yash don't want to listen and Figo also came back in his flirty mood because of his alignment towards priest girls. They both gone to the base again and searched that from where this tone of musical instrument is coming from. Figo realised that it's been coming from the room in which sunlight reaches first in morning period and that place is also very holistic. So he thought that this time also they were doing something which would be devoted towards God. He said to Yash then;

'Yash come I want to know where they all are right now. They were in that room which is profoundly free from others and is at the extreme corner the base of this whole monument. We need to go there safely as if its entire darkness in the way and as we come close to that room we will come in the bound of sunlight then that time we can see each other explicitly', Figo said to Yash.

They started surge towards the room now. Yash asked Figo while walking steepidly 'Figo are you able to see me because in this entire dark over here I can't see you'.

Figo replied, 'No... dear, I am not able to see you properly I said about this to you before, and you please don't talk here because God saints that keep watch on this place can look at us conveniently even we can't see them too'.

Getting close to that room its look like an auspicious kind of aura has wrist his coffers in the sense to greet them. All this is because a shower of pure and fine sunlight is making their way to get rigorous as they move closer to it. Ultimately they reached at the door step of that room and this time they can listen to the tones of 'Sitar' very much explicitly which being flirt dashingly. This sound is directly mixing up in Yash soul and making in realise that nature can be as wonderful as if now. Yash tried to open the door of this room and as he wrist the door, he came to see that all alone over there, Adrita is only present. She is sitting in the central zone of that room with her 'Sitar' in her hand in which she is lost profoundly and even didn't realised that someone had wrist the door. After looking at sugaring on her face while playing 'Sitar' and her devotion for music. Yash settle too stuck up there only and can't even think anything else apart from just looking at her perception with a smile on his face.

Figo said to Yash, '*Hey*... man doesn't feel that this place is our's we need to leave it as soon as possible before anyone could see us. I think now I had make my commitment and you are just wanting that, now let's go back'.

Yash, not in his consciousness this time as he had lost somewhere. After Figo called him three to four times he realised that they have to go now and said to Figo 'Yes afraid dear for remarks like that, I don't know that why this thing is becoming my weakness day by day. Ok.... let's go back wait before that I close this door, see how cute she is looking while playing with it'.

'Yes, I had seen that now please close that door and come with me back', Figo said.

So as Yash closed the door and looked towards Figo turning backward. He came to see that a lady is standing on his back side which Figo hadn't realised yet. This lady is wearing something like a long chiton that reached all the way to the ankles. Over the Chiton another garment which looks like a coat pointed towards the ground from both side and was carrying a sword in her hand. Yash is profoundly shocked this time not because they being caught by someone. But because he won't be able to uphold his commitment he had done to Figo regarding no wreck is going to occur him over here.

Yash said to Figo, 'Figo look backward there is someone'.

Figo peered back as if he got to know that they were caught now.

Figo said 'Afraid...we had just come here after losing our way'.

Yash asked, Figo inclined toward him whispered in his ear 'Who is she and why there immense stress on your face'.

Figo is in fear this time but seeking to bring a smile on his face so that everything looks like too normal and no one can point out their fault from their fear and said, 'This guy didn't know about you let me tell him. Yash she is 'Ray' one of the saint whom I told you about and they are responsible for rules and regulation to be uphold at this place'.

Yash said, 'Nice to meet you Ray'.

Ray said, '*Hey* listen....There is no need for all this affinity'.

This time Adrita is profoundly lost in her music and she didn't even realised that something is happening just on her door step. As this time both Yash and Figo were shocked to see the saint named 'Ray' who is being over there for shelter and maintenance purpose of that monument. It also looks like Figo is a lot familiar with Ray, looks like he visited this place many times before too.

Yash said to Ray, 'Afraid... but we didn't assault anything wrong here'.

Soon Figo replied to cover Yash words and save them from this circumstances, 'I just want to inform you that Yash had seen a hazardous animal coming and entering this place and we were just following him and reached here. Our aim is to protect all beings over here so that nobody gets wreck from that'.

Ray replied, 'I didn't seen anyone in surroundings and don't feel so that what all you being saying is true. I think you know about me and rules of this place Figo,' Ray said a bit of anger on her face.

Figo said the thing with a confident in his eyes that is only the positive point for which Ray need to believe them. But there is a lot discomfort over the face of Yash that can be a sort of annoyance. Yash wants to attention her mind to other concern because he doesn't want Figo to bear anything because of all this. So Yash thought that if she is a saint then takes regard of other rules also. Yash said.

'Please listen there is one thing for that also why we came over this place and seen animal which can wreck others', Yash said. As Ray come to hear this from Yash her appetite-diverted to know the other thing for which they came here as she knows that the first explanation and review that they had given is simply illogical.

Ray asked Yash, 'Yes you say what is that much emphasis thing for you to come here, which is not a place you all to visit'.

Yash said, 'This thing is because of me only as I didn't joined everyone in the last dinner as everyone need to do so here. So Figo informed me to ask all rules and regulation of this place from 'Eelly' who is the person here who knows about rules over this place the most. This is the reason just I came over this place and Figo just helped me to guide this place'.

Ray said, 'It mean you are the soul responsible person for all this mishap and the thing that you did last night that is too a crime. I think you should have to get some harsh remedy for that as you are breaking rules after and after'. Ray said this and Figo replied soon as he sensed that Yash is making him all responsible for this incidence.

'No.... Lets me tell you what is going.........'.

Yash blocked Figo words and said, 'don't say wrong things now. Figo I told her the right thing and I feel it's ok to say this now. You don't need to give any specification about these things.

'Look I am not over here to listen to you both and your rubbish thing. So if this person had done these mistakes. This being need to punish him for those as everyone do. *Hey*, you need to come along with me as this is the time to remedy you with prisoner homes'.

Figo said, 'means he need to go with you at the prison where everyone is kept for crimes they did. But I don't think so that he had done any big crime like that for which he needs to be punished'.

Ray replied in a loud tone 'And now who are you to tell all this things. This person need to go prison now as a *'Desmoids'* and need to be there so that he can understand the aid of Heaven's Hell'.

('Desmoids is the word which is used in ancient time to describe prisoners and here it's describing the same')

Yash was not spirit about the pressure and pain that he need to bear after saying all this. He is still thinking that if Adrita had listened to all this conversation then what she is going to think. All this he is thinking because they are just standing on the doorstep still. Yash want to go from this place as soon as feasible. So he replied.

'Ok.... Figo leave don't talk about this more and you say where we need to go now. I am inclined to go', after listening to these words of Yash, Figo just stuck up and looked Yash with blinking eyes.

Ray said, Figo to go back to his place and never to be seen over here again and she took Yash with him to the prison.

Ray said, 'Settle like you are taking everything too lightly over here, this is not the place as it's not your home land. You are brought here to learn and not to break norms' she hold his hand tightly and dragged him towards the new phase of this Heaven's Hell.

Yash being dragged by her 'But.......but nobody told me all these rules before' Yash asked for relief.

Ray said to Yash while dragging him towards the actual prison; 'Here no one tells you the rules as you are not a free bird over here to do anything you want. It's just you who need to realise this and work accordingly. If you are holistic then these things should be there in you, which doesn't seems so and for all this God had meant a place in Heaven's Hell to remedy all those who are like you with a harsh treatment. By this God shows that if he loves his children's then he also knows how to punish them. The last thing that I want to say you is that, this is your good luck as you being called to Heaven's Hell and keep this in mind ever'.

They reached the place where everyone who violate rule and regulation of Heaven's Hell is kept to cover a particular time period as per decided by priest. This place looks to be developed on ground only, veiling a large area where many other creatures like Yash and others were staying previously over there. Yash doesn't looks to be afraid of that place to stay there. But the thought going in his mind is about his friends that how could they came to know about him. So they don't be much apprehensive of him of not getting back to them. As they reached there, this place doesn't seem to be very apart from their residence where they all stay.

Ray with a laud voice instructed—'Look this is the place where you are going to stay and don't feel this place as other portion of Heaven's Hell. You will got to know about it as you get inside into it. Here you are going to be captivate and bear everything that others were facing inside. This would be your last chance from a more harsh remedy waiting for you if you are going to do anything illegal inside or forth of this prison from now onwards. You just pray to God that after today we don't meet in this kind of situation because this is your first break down which is took by me. Now till you being staying in this place, your custody is in my hold. So be careful of that and after having your punishment, I feel that these things going to be clear accordingly. This is the time for you to get inside before the time goes beyond 12:00, because after this your day in prison as a Desmoids will not be counted. So go to that person and he will guide you about everything', Ray as being a saint and a punishment driver to Yash. Told him all sort of thing that she supposed to inform him about. This time Yash is not having any sort of reaction of tension or discomfort on his face. It settle like he is not apprehensive about all that had happened with him and is going to happen.

Yash said to himself, 'I think I would be going to handle all this, but the thing that is making me tensed is my friend who is going to tell them about me and my being'. Because of thinking going in his mind that time he had not even queried anything from Ray, before being sending him to prison she is delivering lecture regarding his wisdom about life ahead. As Yash crack to make his wandered focus on the things that is going in present with him and not to be worried about others. Yash then crack to probe out and ask something from Ray about the same.

Yash raised and said, 'Is this the way used by everyone staying in this place to get disappear and that too so rapidly without the entire conversation. This thing that Adrita did first and when I crack to enter her and mine conversation. I get to stuck with another problem where I met Ray who also left conversation in unentered manner. I think this is also one of the rules over here to finish off the conversation like this and leave other one confused. Ok what could I do now I need to follow these rules let's get inside now as she told one thing more that to be in before 12:00'.

13

Yash gone towards the person to whom Ray pointed and asked to talk. Yash asked him 'Sir I being reproach and I need to stay here as that Lady.... No sorry afraid saint Ray said'.

Person said, 'ok let me tell you my name first. My name is 'Eugene' my child and the thing that you were saying Ray explained that all to me previously'.

Yash asked with curiosity, 'So sir......afraid again it's Eugene. Eugene please tell me that what would I need to do here and where I am going to stay'.

'My child here you are not going to get a climate that you have seen in all auras of this place, but you need to face certain problems here which I meant physically', Eugene is a person of old age.

He is working here since a long time. So as Yash asked him with his sober tone by giving him a lot respect. He also responded him with a kind heart and crack to explain him everything in a nice manner, so that whole sort of picture get clear in his mind.

Yash replied with his whole body being acting questionable and he said a bit loudly 'Physically... what did this mean'.

'Don't get sick that much child. This just mean the same as you have to bear pressure and pain over your physique due to mutation in your environment inside. This is the thing that everyone inside is also bearing till the date complete their period of being as a Desmoids over here', Eugene cure Yash so that he don't get tensed too much.

Eugene replied with a calmness, 'These sort of pressure were given so that to acknowledge the case of life "that everything is not that much easy to gain as you all feel ears burning". If you can't tackle tragic situation then you are not allowed to say you as a winner. So my suggestion to you is to face everything inside and give your best out of it. The shine I can see on your face says that all this will be nothing for you to deal with'.

Yash asked 'thanks for all this upliftment and knowledge but Eugene you can just inform me about the mutate I need to face here so that I get poised for that.

Yash seems to be a little weird after listening to all these things by Eugene and he asked him, 'I understood all this but before leaving this place you please drop me or inform me about the place where I need to stay. As Ray said I need to be inside it before 12:00, otherwise it could be more difficult for me'.

'Wait I'll drop you till that place first', Eugene said to Yash.

Eugene took Yash along with him as they were going to the place where Yash need to captivate. In amidst Yash being looking towards the other captivate cages in which other creatures like him were going on with their punishment. The look of these cages is like from the sides they were separated by big heavy multiple wood pamphlet. In their front they were having a glass, which is a transparent glass from which you can conveniently look inside to every piece and part of cage and from inside you can look forth the much you can see. These cages were meant both the sides parallel and in amidst there is a left space for anyone to cross it from one end to the other. There are all facility of furniture being there inside to sit and sleep with well designed and with a carpet underneath.

Eugene and Yash reached at the place. Eugene pointed his finger towards it and said 'have a look, this is your place where you need to stay and now you should go'.

Yash asked, 'But there is someone previously in it, Is it like that I need to share this room'? Yash asked this to Eugene.

'Yes he is your comrade now Cage (room)', Eugene replied to Yash.

So Yash left Eugene now as he need to enter this Cage (room) as it's been getting too late now. Yash entered into it and seen that a creature also reside inside it but he was sleeping that time, so Yash didn't disturbed him and let him sleep. This time Eugene had also gone back to his place and now there is some more curiosity which was emerging in Yash mind about this barred place. Yash wandered that he didn't asked Eugene about the time period to stay at this prison. So with this and some other confusion, Yash stood seated inside the Cage now with his back touching wall and he being sitting on floor facing towards the creature who is present over there before his arrival. Yash was looking towards him with needy eyes of help. So that he can wake up and answer some question that are going in Yash mind rigorous now. While looking towards him Yash talked to himself.

Yash said to himself;

'I don't think that he is from our land, our planet. He would be from any other planet as he doesn't have any resemblance to our planet people, but from which planet he would be. His height is also too small as he would be just 1/3rd height of mine. Look they had given him a bed that would be just fit for him to sleep and his equipments are also too small. I am sure they had only provided these to him and if they had impart these to him they are going to do so same with me too. Ok....then that's cool', Yash is talking to himself as no one around is there to discuss all this new.

Yash started looking towards the terrace of his Cage. Abruptly the other creature in his room waked up slowly from his bed and sat on it. He rubbed his eyes and looked all around him. He leg Yash sitting at one corner of the Cage and looking towards the terrace. He shouted;

'*Hey* who are you and what are you doing here who allowed you to enter my space, my room'? Small creature asked furiously from Yash.

Yash replied, 'Hello......*Hey* listen...listen if you are going to ask all these question all together then it would be a lot difficult for me to answer them. Ok don't tensed about anything, I am like you who is been brought up over here and due to protocol breakage I am thrown in this prison. It is a simple as that and I think after revealing all this to you, the picture being explicit in your mind that what I am doing here', Yash spoke in a very calm and sweet manner even if he asked everything from him in a arrogant manner, Yash wants to maintain his mind coolness to stay here.

Yash again, 'Before you are going to ask my name in that same arrogant manner let me tell you my name also it's been Yash. I told you my name because I don't like anyone asking my name arrogantly and roughly'.

Small creature replied, 'Listen I am not that much rough and my name is Pojo'.

Yash said slowly 'Yes you settle like that only and your name just suits you as Pojo... Tojo… and somewhat', Yash said this not to be heard by him that's why he said slowly.

'What….What all you are saying... tell me and say again', Pojo said this to Yash with a dilemma of listening something wrong about him.

'Nothing……nothing dear it was nothing solemn and also not for you, I was just stressed thinking about my way to reach here', He can't make him annoyed anyhow.

'Pojo from how long time you being over here'? Yash asked Pojo.

Pojo replied, 'from three days'.

'What for three days only, so I think you don't know much about this prison too...?' Yash asked.

Pojo said, 'What do you think that three days over here at this place for a small period of time. Have you seen how time passes here, when you lived forth this prison in this Heaven's Hell'?

'Yes I had seen. Time over here passes to late', Yash replied.

'So that period of passing time if you had noticed then just four times that period of a day forth you passed and that would be the time one day takes here to cross on. This is the place where you brought to be punished in the prison, so I think these all thing that you have to bear here as being a Desmoids', Pojo replied to Yash point and made him realise that this is not as much easy as he is mesmerizing.

Pojo in silent grief, 'But some times this journey never ends too'.

'Ok…..please tell me this thing more, that from how long period you are going to be captivated in this cage'? Yash asked Pojo.

'My time period is of five days and I'll be free on my sixth day', Pojo said to Yash.

'Oh! just this much is your prison time, that's good but how come I will be knowing my time over here..?', Yash asked Pojo.

Pojo replied, 'I think you don't need to be worried about all this over here because almost time of everyone is equal as five days or extreme six days'.

'You sorted out most of my doubts. Short in height but in mind you are...' Yash said this and halted in amidst.

Pojo laughed on his words and said, 'Ha... Small dear don't feel that so. Ya I know that I am very much smaller than you but it's genetic in our planet. This is the extreme height we attain but you don't feel us smaller in any other affinity as our planet and we are much solemner in technology than your planet. There are many examples for this and our planet people even researched that so', Pojo took words of Yash lightly and he didn't reacted in any other manner.

'Don't go into it that much. I am not going to argue about our technology and yours because this combat would be worthless. You leave all this and inform me something more about this place as Eugene told me after insisting him to tell me. Yash asked to Pojo.

Pojo started unwanted description—'As I had told you before also that this is our prison and we have to suffer from certain kind of mutate that we hadn't seen before like sudden mutate felt in climate which become extreme and intolerable but we need to sustain it and wait for that period to go. This picture would be explicit to you as this mutation would occur over here and you can see that time the reaction and stress of people in all around cages. This is the predicament with me also even it is too difficult for me to tackle and sustain myself in that climate. Need to face unwanted and idle tones that are so irritating can make anyone mad too if he is not competent to deal with those and what to tell you more, others you are also going to know while staying here', Pojo instructed.

Yash legged this close picture harder to digest. Now the case is that he had to face all this. So because of this thing there are no emotions and expression was coming on his face. As Yash settle to be profoundly numb.

14

Yash friend were there in the residence waiting for his arrival. Ankit, Gaurav were seated over the long hanging antique benches in there room and Sunny was standing on the window while Soni is there on the door. Everyone eyes were just waiting for Yash to come at the room as it's a lot late and this time much solemner delay than before he did yesterday.

Ankit said, 'Why every time after being reminding him also, Yash does the same thing every day'; Ankit said this while looking to the floor in a solemn annoyed manner.

Gaurav said, 'Ankit why are you burning your blood as you also knows that this is not the first time, Yash did that usually. The thing is that he doesn't listen as we all also trust him a lot and shows dependency'.

He is a master piece in various things but the sober and infancy activities he does sometimes that makes everyone to be apprehensive of like today. Who knows where he is', Ankit replied to Gaurav.

Sunny facing towards the window and looking forth said, 'I had said you don't allow him to go now, he's is surely going to make some mess'; Sunny said this and laughed as he is spirit all this thing very funny.

Ankit shouted on 'Sunny how you can take this matter so lightly as you do also know that we don't know about this place a 10 per cent'.

'Ok... when Yash is going to come ask him about this place I am sure that till now he had covered 80 per cent of it'. Sunny replied.

'You are not going to listen me, you are going to be as you are in this critical period of ours too, apart from Exaltation moral of everyone', Ankit said to Sunny.

Figo came to their doorstep all alone. Everyone is thinking about Yash as his absent. Now they had seen Figo all alone and Yash is no where to be seen.

As Figo reached after being running hard from that monument to the residence. Gaurav brought a glass of chocolate shake for him which is meant by him yesterday and not taken by any one yet. After that they waited so that Figo can be easy and tell us that he is seeking to say. No change in moods occurred yet.

We had gone to that place where music classes took place, it's been a monument type structured building. This place is not allowed for all of us slaves to be there, but we assault to get inside it as Yash was too desperate that time to meet Adrita. Figo instructed the whole story of Yash in front of everyone to tell that how much kind heart Yash is as he didn't allowed Figo to get into annoyance and taken all fault on his own.

Ankit said, 'This kindness of my dear Yash... why you took those colours to be so sweet every time to us and do sacrifices without even a clue from your side'. Ankit got tears in his eyes when he said those words and this shows how much he love Yash.

Sunny said, '*Hey* I was thinking that he would be going to come with a annoyance, but see he saved us again by his assaults and all alone bearing every pressure over there. If not going to the dinner is a crime we all did that why he is the only one who punished for that. We should go and adherence there'.

Gaurav said, 'Please you all guys understand the critical of this thing'.

'Ok... Let's think over it a bit. Figo today you stay with us only please as we can need any help of yours', Ankit said to everyone and Figo.

Now in the Prison

As Yash came to know everything about that he needs to face at this chance and every sort of discomfort too. So he is mentally poised now to cover up with this situation in future as it is going to strike this. Now after all this Pojo and Yash were settle to get friendly with each other. They were talking now in a manner that there is nothing difference amidst them.

Yash asked Pojo, "Dear tell me that, as over here no of people came from apart planets and staying all together. So tell me now is it like that we are all understand or knows a particular type of language having over here one common language with which we are communicating with one another...?', Yash asked this because he is in a big dilemma still.

Pojo again instructed —'I think you are in some confusion because as this place is meant by God and everything belongs to him over here. So apart from thinking to keep all of us over here, he also felt this thing that if everyone is from some other planet then how can they interpret with one another. So keeping all this in mind God meant a rule in this air that whenever there are two or more person involved in dialogues. One person speaks up then every one of them should receive those words in his native language to their ears after getting converted by air. In all this regard of conveying everything and helping other person to understand, this is air which plays all these roles', Pojo told these big things to Yash.

Yash said, 'I am going to tell these all things to my friend they would be surprised for the first time. I would love to see there wrist mouths at first but shock'.

Yash replied again, 'Dear Pojo this shows that you are seriously an awesome personality and you must be solemner in technology from our planet too. Tell me that do you having any additional powers too with you'.

'No....But why you are asking all these', Pojo said.

'Looks like you were a lot afraid to tell me about your powers if any. It's just that I felt and asked you because your food and ours is apart source of energy than emergence of energy. I also asked as my six sense said me ask you', Yash said to Pojo.

Pojo replied, 'I must say that your six senses is too fortified, it's saying accurate about me as I consist my exclusive powers over here beyond my intelligence. Those powers are of attraction, distraction, knowing about others by just looking, sky up your body in the sky by making it weightless etc. These are the stamina's that me have but my bad day started when I stated adherence 'Barrack' here. He had taken my powers but he don't know that the salient power that do I consist with me only but that is the problem. I won't be able to use that so it settle like I am powerless now. You should also stay far away from 'Barrack'. He is not the person to trust on as he is just greedy of Powers and wants togather more and more power from everywhere. God did one thing that is too solemn and according to which he is not allowed to use his any powers at this place. That's why he is taking others power shafted them with him so that he can use them when he leaves Heaven's Hell".

Yash replied, 'really.... He is a too slugged man. I don't even want to see face of these powerfull greedy people. "If you have certain powers and with those not solving problems of needy people then it is worthless"'.

Pojo said, 'Datum is that also everyone knows about this thing he does but then too trusts them why I don't know'.

Soon drastic mutation in environment over there. Increasing temperature of this place by one degree periodically after every second. Yash was looking to the waver reaction of Pojo in the cage as it seems. He started spirit uneasy now and because of which he being surge from one place to the other. Pojo started finding place inside the Cage that is not impacted still. So that he can be cure for the time being till that place also get heated up. Yash also seen that creatures in other Cages are also not cosy this present time, compressing there face as if they are not able to deal with the climate. One person in Cage, that is directly in front of their Cage started to remove his clothes one by one without even caring of saint over there could see him. Now that person become profoundly naked and still no saint came so, seems like this is ok to be undelivered over here and this doesn't violets any rule. Still that person is unstable. This is the position of every living being that were all residing at that incidence and particular period of time. Everyone is just seeking to get rid of this climatic exotic evolution for certain time period and don't want to face it for even a second.

Everything is surge as told to Yash before and listening and realising in real differs a lot which Yash has observed this time but someone is not going in the flow of it that is Yash only.

Yash is not still being touched as he didn't observed even a degree mismatch in the temperature of his body is bearing before. After this drastic climatic mutation occurred and started affecting one by one every person over there but till this time it hadn't touched Yash. These things started coming to the notice of Pojo who is in same Cage with Yash.

Yash said to Pojo, 'What is this climatic pressure too much higher, that it's be cut out to be too hard for you to bear it. Everyone from you is spirit this same but I am spirit equally fine here'.

Pojo get still on one place and contributed all his energy to speak up and reply Yash 'even I am really in a big dilemma about the datum because I haven't seen this happening with anyone over here', while delivering these words to Yash Pojo have to put his ultimate power as the pressure is so much that Pojo face had become entire Red.

This climatic flow goes on for a period of time as everyone knows but Yash standing safe in this period is a big question mark for both Yash and Pojo. It took some time before getting halted at this place and coming back to its actual temperature.

First thing that happened after it is Pojo jumped towards Yash like a child to ask him about the whole concern.

Pojo asked Yash, '*Hey* boy.......you are something......how come you did all these. Tell this to me also even I want to be get cure from this pain'.

Yash said, 'This is not as you thinking dear; even I am in this wandered and asking myself the same question. Why did this mutation didn't even effected me and make me crucial, superior and separate from you all really I don't know anything about this concern'.

Pojo said with dilemma in his eyes, 'Really is this so because I don't feel you were saying rigorous this time. As a big and executive thing is happening to you and that too in your favour which you even don't know about. Frankly speaking dear it's hard to digest. If you don't want to liberate out this stuff to me then you can explicitly say but don't feel that I am fool here'.

'Why are you just thinking by your perspectives and not regarding mine. You must think it in both way and I feel you know how to judge body gesture and physical moves of person in case of lie or truth as you said that you consists of those power', Yash replied to Pojo.

'You were rigorous. I can do so and yes by all these its looks like you are sober about this datum but still dilemma should be explicit', Pojo said.

'Now I am not going to give any kind of explanation to you. You can feel whatever you want. If you can't even feel this thing by my blank behaviour to this context', Yash replied last arrogantly and wanted to halt this here only.

Lunch came for them. They both left out with their conversation and moved to their respective places where they took their food without conversing even a single word with one another. After meal second stage of this place settle to start which is another climatic effect.

Pojo captured from his senses that now temperature will be going to reach in negative, as it started declining degree after degree.

Pojo is comfortable in this position of cold but he anxiety when temperature decreases to a solemner extent. So for being safe from this entire, he started wearing more and more cloths over him and making himself poised to be normal this time.

All this again is not affecting Yash. This time too after looking towards activities of Pojo. Yash looked to other beings and same he leg everywhere around him. Yash said;

'What is it; this is not happening with me again as everyone around scrambling and veiling their body with loads of cloths. It's good for me but I need to ask somebody about it. This time there is no one forth too whom I can ask all these things and confirm about why all this is remarks with me executive', Yash talked to himself as he is also flicking implication to see all these.

Pojo is quite a bit frequent with this environment as his planet being too coldest than everyone else. So after making him cosy from this mutation of surrounding weather by wearing cloths and veiling his body more with blankets so that he can feel everything normal. Then Pojo said to Yash, 'Dear again this coldly aura is also not impacting you, what is there all going on could you know anything about'.

Yash replied, 'Really dear, you need to believe me because this is the thing that is new to me also. As much executive this thing is making me; I didn't felt that much executive before'.

'Ok.... I think you were saying it right . Your eyes were saying everything with a sick face that you have with it. Both these things of yours speak a lot so I can understand. But yes, this is good dear because this cage is just meant to make we all slaves face exotic environment. So you are saved from this', Pojo said to Yash.

This time fog has came inside to their room and started to increase and make the whole space inside the cage full of it. As fog is veiling every corner of their room so it started tough for them to see each other too in this foggy interior.

Yash asked Pojo immediately, '*Hey* what is this, now I can't even see you correctly because of this fumes here, could you tell me why is all this happening now'.

Pojo said 'You don't need to scared now this is just fog came into as if you had seen warmed and cold coming up the same way it is. You just have to wait for a while everything would be visible to you'.

Pojo said, 'I think You don't need to be tensed, here sometimes such things happens that are extra ordinary because everything is governed by god and what all god wants just that happens and nothing else'.

Yash said, with low tone, 'Yes...you were saying it equally well but why God is doing like this that's too a big question.... Now I feel lets me not think about all this, if this is not affecting me then its good for me and I should be cure about it'.

Some time later auras get back to be normal again. Now Pojo and Yash stayed at that place like good room partner and as days over there were too long to be covered. They both started to have a good company of each other as when Pojo needs to bear pressure because of this extreme waver environment, Yash helps his partner Pojo to be cure and sustainable anyhow he could do so. So slowly they both uphold-ed a good bond of friendship amidst them.

15

Two days passed and affiliation and kinship between both has been increased.

Yash while sleeping heard tone of a dog Barking there, he firstly felt as his eyes being closed that this tone is coming from his dream or its just because any illusion he spirit all. As tone didn't got halted, Yash wake up his lazy manner to find out from where this tone is coming. He saw Pojo standing stuck to the glass putting his hand over it and facing forth. It looks like he is watching something or observing someone's activities. Yash is now just standing at the back side of Pojo seeking to accured by what Pojo is too happy all about and Yash see a scene which makes him to smile like Pojo.

Yash seen a dog that is combating with a portrait over there on the walls of this prison forth everyone Cage. This dog is spirit that portrait a real one and combating with him as that portrait also consist anger on its face. This portrait is of animal which looks like dog but we can't say that it's of dog because there is several dissimilarity among both.

Yash also laughed when he peered towards him as he is profoundly busy that time in combating with wall meant portrait. Yash asked instantly to Pojo '*Hey* what a nice German Shepherd he is, and see his texture, his body full of long hairs. The cutest thing is his face that is profoundly sober', Yash said.

Yash replied again to divert Pojo attention towards him by extending his last stanza as 'Yes the cutest thing is about his face that is profoundly sober just like yours...'.

Pojo too became active distracted his attention and said 'what................What you seeking to say'.

Yash replied while smiling, 'Dear don't feel in other way. You are not listening to what I said, so I'd make you attentive just that's it'.

'Ok......that's cool don't do this again......because I don't allow anyone to talk about my physique as I love my body', Pojo said this with a solemn attitude face.

Yash asked Pojo, '*Hey* leave now, tell me about this nice dog and do you know about him'.

Pojo while turning back towards this dog after looking Yash said, 'He is very nice dear to me also. When I am forth of this prison I used to play with him and in response he gives the same lovely response to me. His name is 'Ronu' and brilliant in every concern, look what a kind of fitness he has'.

Yash was looking towards the corner of this room if he could find any hole from where he can call Ronu towards him and can touch him to give love. Yash and Soni both loves animals. So with German Shepherd he have a executive attraction as also have one the same with him on 'Earth'. Yash pet name is 'Nikky' which he has at his home on "Earth surface" and here when he saw 'Ronu' Yash got a fortified spirit of his 'Nikky' because 'Ronu' looks just similar to him. So as Yash leg a corner of his Cage that has some space from which he can put his hand out. Yash gone towards that corner bend himself and moved his hand out from that space and called 'Ronu' as he knows this breed a lot.

Pojo said, 'Look be careful, don't make any harm to him. 'Ronu' will not going to hold you as he know to everything, it's just you to take care so that you don't wreck him knowingly or unknowingly'. Yash called Ronu close to him by making certain sounds.

Pojo said, '*Hey* he just came on your one call that's fantastic. You know he don't like this with anyone but did with you'.

Yash while rolling his hand over the forehead of Ronu said, 'Pojo tell me that it like he is not kept free over here. There is some boundation for him or like that because as much I can notice from his excitement and his crazy nature, is it like that Pojo'.

Pojo replied, 'Wow... you know about them and their spirits a lot. Yes dear Ronu is not allowed to move freely as not every person over here knows him. It is like only the members of this place knows him well and you also know that number of persons from apart planet stay here and have unique functionality. This is why Ronu stays with boundation and over this place too he is not allowed to come. I don't know how he came here', Pojo told Yash in brief about Ronu and his life.

Yash said, '*Hey* he is too deliberately cute just like my Nikky. I don't told you about it and calling his name. 'Nikky' is my pet at home, I love the most on "Earth surface". He knows everything about me and I know about him. Ronu is also just like him, can you tell me something about him as I am very much appetited to know about him'.

'I had told you whatever I know about him. There are just something more that I can tell you about him. Like Ronu over here is not a simple creature. He have various powers with him but doesn't uses them as God doesn't wants. Ronu here stays with the priest girls'.

Yash said, 'Ok........I see, so it's like he also involves in activities that they did'.

'I don't know that much about this thing but I feel so that may be he does that', Pojo replied.

Yash is also apprehensive that if it's not allowed for him to be here, then nobody could see him here. Yash was thinking like this because he's being scared this time for Ronu that if someone saw him here then he can harm him. There unknown sound came to be heard.

Yash said to Pojo, 'I think someone is calling him but it's the tone of a girl, maybe she would be one from priest girls as you said before'.

Pojo said, 'Yes its seems like that only.'

Yash was sitting at this time like previous rolling his hand still on Ronu's head with devotion a lot. Ronu is also seeking to touch Yash but he won't be able to do so as there is not much space there for them both to meet freely. Ronu's legs are just touching the glass seperation.

Yash see an instinct by looking at which he won't be able to halt his emotions now. Yash see from a far distance, there is a girl coming with saint (Eugene). She is the only one who calling name of Ronu this time as her face came in focus to Yash. Yash said with a blank face as he doesn't have any emotions left on his face; Adrita 'she is the one......', Yash said this and his eyes were just pointed towards her. There is a sense of relaxation also can see on his face. Adrita was moving slowly and a lot stressed on face. It settle like Ronu has big space in her life and this time apart from finding where Ronu is, she don't need anything else, that's seen conveniently by her face. Eugene is following her and both were coming close to them.

Adrita came to see that Ronu is inside there only and was playing with Yash. She ran speedily to get him into her arms.This time as Adrita is sitting close to Yash with just a glass difference amidst them, holding Ronu in her arms and putting her head over Ronu with her eyes wet with water.

Adrita said to Yash, 'Thanks...thanks a lot to you, as you not allowed him to go anywhere else apart from this place otherwise it could be very tough for me to find him.' Adrita said this while crying still.

Yash replied, 'No...you don't need to be thankful because I think after seeing Ronu he made my demoralising and weakening happiness power to flue off from my intern. He blessed me with a boost of nourishing my declining moral. So because of this I would be thankful to you', Yash smiled and said.

Adrita said to all people around there in this prison, 'I would like to request you all present in this prison and whoever had seen my Ronu over here. Please you all don't make complaint regarding that or don't inform anyone about it, this is my humble request from all you.' Adrita requested everyone by joining her hand and closed eyes facing towards everyone.

Yash is also implication that why these all spirit are striking his heart again and again. Yash was in a big dilemma and want to know the background of the whole scene.

Adrita with tears in her eyes, 'It's been just Eugene *Baba*, who adherence's me and helped me today too in finding my dear Ronu. He never complaints also if Ronu did something wrong in this aura area. He is always there for me and from heart I want to thanks this time to you Eugene *Baba*', Adrita said, holding Ronu tightly in her arms and wanted to thanks Eugene.

Yash got to know that Adrita call Eugene as Eugene *Baba*. May be this is because she feels him like her father and respect him like that, in response to this. Eugene also remedy her like daughter and saves her from every discomfort.

Adrita replied again, 'I am also afraid to get into prison like this because even I am not allowed to come here and disturb you all. So please spare me for all this'.

Yash as from long time he spirit uneasy to see her like this and becoming more and more polite person to others.

Yash said, 'I think everyone had listened to what she said and they all are going to adherence you in whatever you want. No one is so harsh. I think they can't do that much. So it's my request now to you please be normal and cure', after listening to Yash, Adrita just wake up from her position and took Ronu along.

It looks like Adrita didn't noticed Yash at this place still. He hadn't noticed Yash then too after been allotted some words with him. This is because her total concern at that time is to Ronu and no one else.

Adrita went and stood far from this place but her fragrance, and presence is not overtightened to Yash still after long time had been passed off. Yash is lost thinking about the datum that why did she reaction in that manner for just a small thing. She could have done all this in other manner also.

Yash asked Pojo, 'Do you know her who came here.' Yash asked this when he layed down on the bed and his legs are being folded. This time he is thinking.

Pojo said, 'Whom are you talking about......'...

Yash replied, 'I am talking about the girl who came sometime before. What a short retentions you have I am asking about priest girl that came here', Yash said.

Pojo replied, '.....you are still thinking of it. My dear for your wisdom let me tell you that the incident you are talking about we passed many hours. Where are you and as your queried, so let me tell you, I don't know that girl and haven't seen her before'.

Yash mumered, 'I think to talk with him in this concern, would not be ok. So I should ask and talk to someone who know about her because this would be a big question that would confuse me a lot that why she is so pleasing for Ronu. There is something bigger that I don't know and should be known too'.

Yash replied, 'Thanks... thank to swift my wisdom dear about time but I didn't wanted that from you and I think somehow you also know that. You must have this much intelligence I feel so'.

'*Hey* dear you had taken it in a wrong way, I didn't mean that. I just want you to not to think about it much as it's not going to worth you', Pojo replied.

'Ok let's finish this here only', Yash said.

'Ok... as you wish I am not going to say anything now', Pojo replied.

This question that what pain did she have and why those tear came in her eyes for just a small concern. Yash had seen that Eugene is forth their cage and bending down and finding something over that place. Yash called Eugene and said 'Hello...sir, can I ask you what you were finding here as I don't feel that something yours is being lost here'.

Eugene replied, 'Dear child the thing I am finding is not mine and that's of Adrita's concern', Eugene replied as he can't deny answering anyone.

'Afraid I said a name that you don't know. Ok, let me tell you that the girl which came here before to take her Ronu. You got my point, I am talking about her, she said me that there is a nod in her Ronu's neck where her mother tied an 'amulet' for some shelter of Ronu but it is been missing from his neck. This is why she asked me to probe it over here and that I am doing so', Eugene replied to Yash.

'Wow... you love her a lot as your child because I had seen your eyes that time which are profoundly in favour of Adrita and wanted to keep her smile. Am I rigorous sir', Yash asked Eugene.

'You seem to be a open spirit man. Tell me from where you came', Eugene asked Yash.

'I think from the same planet of yours. It's been 'Earth' the beauty of whole universe', Yash said.

Eugene in efficacy by words of Yash and said, 'You told my place of occurrence also thanks my boy because living here since a long time I had even forget my place because here we can't talk about our place. This is regarded as dominating nature which is a crime here. So you should also don't do it again.

Yash asked Eugene, 'Ok... sir could you please answer my certain questions that are striking my mind again and again'.

Eugene replied, 'ask my child what is troubling you so much'.

'Sir... I feel you are very much familiar with Adrita and you too know her well. Could you please tell me about the thing that happened today', Yash asked from Eugene and his eyes were too pleasing as it is very emphasise for him to know.

Eugene asked Yash, 'Yes I can tell you, but tell me before that why are your reaction to know about this thing are so instance'.

Yash said, 'just for kinship towards humanity, nothing else'.

Eugene said, 'you were saying nothing else but it seems to be in your eyes but leave all this. Ok you were asking about what ask now'.

'Sir I need to ask about the thing that happened with Adrita and Ronu. Sir, that time she settle to be too helpless and her reaction in this way. I don't feel this much required over here. Why did she plead and requested so much for just a small concern', Yash asked Eugene.

Eugene said, 'Look my boy, you are just looking at those things that you had seen from your eyes. You have not giving your concern to the other part of life that of every person. Firstly you tell me truly, Did you meet Adrita before....Ok I got my answer by your face. It aid that you had met Adrita before also and you would have seen her everlasting glory and attitude on her face. This time when you had seen her pleading and asking afraid from others this was the thing that makes you in doubt. Am rigorous I think so', as Eugene asked at last Yash.

So Yash replied, 'I am not confused about her, it's just like I won't be able to see tears in her eyes and she could have said all that she want to say without tears also', Yash clarified himself.

Eugene replied 'These tears which you are talking about not new to her because the loneliness of a person is the biggest rivalry of their life. The same is applied for Adrita too. She is a girl that consists most respect that none of the other girl have over here but it is not everything for a person to be happy. She spares her time with small girls at the monument of music', Yash impeded Eugene in amidst and said yes I know about that monument, as because of it only I am over here.

Eugene asked, ' and could I ask what you were being doing in the monument...?'.

Eugene said, 'You forget your place but I have very swift sense of humour. I think I am getting everything', this is like what all he don't want him to know Eugene is under standing on its own.

Yash said, 'Afraid to hamper you in between sir you please continue with it'; Yash pleased Eugene as he wants to get into the depth of the story.

Eugene said, 'So where we were talking about where she spares her time and feel happy. It's like she loves to teach those small girls at music and dancing classes as whole music monument is under her hold.

Everything works there according to her need and she knows it a lot well that how to care of others need and keeps everyone happy. She spares his salient time with Ronu which being given to her by her parent when she was of few years and too small. They said her to be with him every time and from that day Ronu and Adrita were together. Now with a bond that can't be broken because she loves him the most in this whole world after her Mother and Father left her',

Yash impeded, 'What had happened to them, are they not with her now...?', Yash asked with questionable eyes.

Eugene replied, 'No they are not with her now as there is a story behind this concern also. As Adrita's mother belongs to this place and was serving in this place like Adrita is doing these days. Saints over here send her mother on land for some specific purpose but she done one erroneous thing there'.

Yash asked, 'what...?'.

Eugene said, 'nothing illegal that's a normal thing but not normal for priest girls. The person whom Saints had send her to teach lesson she started devotion that guy and yes that person is also very gentle and humanitarian with good records. This is why Saints also given her consent to be with him after tying a knot of marriage for whole life. Then Saints had asked for her first child to be devoted to them which they all know would going to be a girl. They asked for her first child and also not allowed her to come back to Heaven's hell after marriage because it's against rules. They had lastly took all her powers that she have and let her to live her life on "Earth". They make her profoundly in apart from Heaven's Hell in every way. Then after all this when she gave birth to first child that was a cute, little angel covering all the beauty desires in her both little fist. This girl is named 'Adrita' which aid 'Love and Spread Love all around'.

Yash again disturbed and said, 'I know this meaning too difficult...' Eugene being seeing that shine coming on Yash face as he listens her name and he also being listening to what Eugene said so intensively, as he is going to have a test of questions about this regard after listening to all about them.

Yash insisted to Eugene, '*Hey* Eugene why had you halted revealing the entire story. Dear sir I think it's not been finished yet', there is an increasing curiosity too that can be seen in Yash eyes.

Eugene continued again and said 'Yes...as Adrita took birth, there came a call from our place to them for sending Adrita at Heaven's Hell. Then her parents need to do that as they committed about it. So they send Adrita to Heaven's Hell but there is one more thing they send with her it's been Ronu, whom you had just seen with her. There is one letter also send with both of them in which written that it is only for Adrita. So nobody is allowed to read it until Adrita become that much competent of understanding all these things. As Adrita shares everything with me, so she told me that in letter it was written that you need to take full care of Ronu every time not let him go away from you. There is also written the thing which we are finding today. Its about the 'amulet' that stays in Ronu's neck since he was small and this band over which 'amulet' is tied also adjusted himself accurately in Ronu's neck as year passed off'. So this is the whole story I told you just now and you listened too dedicated. I think if I am going to conduct a test now regarding all that I told you then you will be going to secure full marks.

Yash said to Eugene, 'Why are you saying like that....?' It's not that now. I had known everything regarding Adrita', Yash was thankful to Eugene for revealing all this to him but last line that Eugene said by that Yash need to explain himself.

Eugene replied, 'Why are you talking about Adrita. I didn't said those line to mean her', this time even Eugene had realised that Yash have a solemn attraction towards Adrita but he didn't want to interject him in this because Eugene was spirit something good this time about it as Yash is a good and funny guy. He wandered that if Yash is going to assault by being her friend then he can make her life a bit greenish.

Yash asked Eugene 'Where did you got lost in your thoughts after revealing all this story. I need to thanks you for all this'.

Yash asked Eugene 'Did Adrita knows about all these things and about her mother and father and if she knows about them does she miss them all'.

Eugene replied, 'Wow... good question I accept that from you. Yes Adrita knows about all these things and something being told by me only. The last and the emphasise thing that does she miss her Parent. Yes she memorised her parent but till now just there is one person who knows it all and now you too know this. She memorised her parent and wants to meet them'.

Eugene Replied again, 'Ok...look Yash you need to promise me that you are not going to talk about it with anyone or tell this thing to anyone'.

Yash replied, 'You have to be cure about it because I am not going to say anything to anyone and if it's about Adrita then never to me also. Yash ended up this conversation with a positive impact on Eugene.

Eugene said, 'Ok....Let me go now...don't know when other phase of this place starts of...ok see you dear'.

Yash dealing with all sort of mutate that being faced over here, but even Yash doesn't knows. At residence everyone is implication there about Yash and it's been three days were passed by them all like this without Yash only. Figo is also staying over there with them to consolidate and then they all did went to Pee's room to ask him the period of staying in the Prison for prisoners. They all reached at Pee's room and then.

Gaurav asked, 'can we come in'.

Pee replied, 'Yes who is there... please come in'.

Pee said, '.....it's been you all. Nice to see you all here. I want to ask you that can't you all meet me as you just stay next to my room. I think we all met after three days, am I rigorous'.

Sunny said, 'Yes you were absolutely right, but there were some salient issues over here that we faced and because of which we are not able to do anything else'.

Pee said to them, 'Please tell every problem I would like to hear them all and if feasible sort them out. *Hey* firstly tell me where is my that chocolate boy Yash, he didn't seem to come with you'.

'That is the only issue Pee, which we had come to discuss with you. It's like Yash because of some reason is not with us from three days and he is captivated in the prison. As nobody is with Yash that time when he is caught by saint. It's just Figo who is with him that time and Figo is going to tell you all that' Ankit said. After this Figo told everything happened there to Pee and they asked Pee regarding conclusion.

Pee replied, Its depressing for me as if 'all this had happened days before and you being revealing this to me now. Ok as you were saying that three days had passed away now its just two days may be left and you don't need to be tensed, he will come back soon'.

Ankit said 'Ok...dear thanks Pee for all this information as we are apprehensive as Yash is not coming and we are not even getting any information from other side about it', Pee, everybody just moved out of the room and as they inside their room.

Sunny said, 'I know that Pee is not going to do anything in this and how he is saying to us that three days passed and we are revealing this thing to him now. He would have done a lot if we had told him before'.

Ankit said, 'Dear Sunny chill, you also know that he is the man of rules and regulations and follow the same. Why don't you feel that at least he had told us the time when Yash is going to come'.

Today, is the fourth day in the prison and everybody tired after bearing heavy pressure for previous three days. All of them started there day too slowly but Yash wake up soon in the morning gone to take bath and then he came back from bathroom started his daily morning prayer and finished it. Then he see that there are creatures who had wake up now so he felt that now. He can does his prayer, so that nobody get disturbed from it. If someone wants to join him while praying can join him conveniently. So as soon as he finished his prayer nobody else he had seen with his own roommate for the first time in these whole four days came this time with folded hand like him and prayed to God. There is dedication and spiritualist in Pojo that can be conveniently seen in his body that time. May he could have seen the power of devotion empowering him.

As Pojo turn his eyes Yash come to notice that today is the day for Pojo to leave this place as soon as Pojo had wrist his eyes Yash slapped him and said;

'Why you hadn't gone out from here yet. Ok if you not gone up till now you have to go now. So get inclined and go my dear', Yash said to Pojo as today's his six days were completed over here which are assigned to him.

Pojo said, 'I don't feel to leave you now, so because of that I didn't gone till now and dear I want to stay with you and if I have to stay here also I can Please.........', he requested him as they both had came too close to each other while allotted their wandered.

Yash said, 'No dear you have to go now from here. Please understand that if you are going to stay here then you have to bear a lot physical and mental pressure that is hard for me to see you. So that's why I would just want you to leave today. Dear if I have to stay more here then I can stay conveniently as these changes doesn't affect me, not even a single per cent but with you, it becomes sometime hard for you to resist as I had seen that. So the last and final thing is that you go and just now ok'.

'Yes dear I ok. Then where would you meet me when you come out day after tomorrow', Pojo replied to Yash.

Yash said 'I will catch you don't tensed at your residence, just tell me the no of you room there'.

'My room is 220 over there. Surely come as you get free from here because as I am getting out Barrack will going to meet me, I feel so. As he will try again to indulge me with him so that the mechanism of tempting things towards you is in complete. He can complete it by the formulas that do I have', Pojo said this to Yash as he need to face Barrack forth.

Yash asked to Pojo, 'Why you don't avoid Barrack and straight forword say to him that he will not hamper you in your life'.

Pojo replied, 'This is not that much easier as you feel so dear. This is over here that he can't uses his power, otherwise he can make many things come under him very conveniently. I also know that he wants me this time because he need those formulas and tricks that I do have after learning those he will kill me. This is the thing he wants'.

Pojo replied again, 'Yash I would like to say something to you that I had seen in your eyes some love and devotion for Adrita, that is not good as per rules. The thing that I want to tell you is about no one else but Adrita. Yash you don't know something about Adrita. I don't know by her name that's why I said you that time as priest girl, but when I had seen her face I came to gather certain things that no one might be knows but you need to know that. When I was with Barrack I heard something about Adrita what she have in herself and she also doesn't even know about those but Barrack had felt those. As he knows about her powers and he had also said that those powers are not that everyone has. These powers being given to some executive peoples by god and she contains those. So Barrack was planning to curve Adrita like me whenever his rigorous time comes and with that immense power he could be the king of not his planet only but of whole universe. He is thinking in a lot disastrous way and I think you are the person that can halt him from doing all this or can mutation all this scene. Do you even felt that why you are not bearing stress and pain regarding this climatic turnover. This is because you are something executive here who can help us. So please think about it when you get out from the prison and save Adrita and all others too from Barrack brutality', this is all I wanted to inform you about before leaving from here.

Yash got profoundly burned up with anger as he came to hear this because a girl who is crying here. It is becoming too difficult for him to stabilise himself. When Barrack is going to wreck her then he will not be going to leave him and remedy him in the much harsh way he can.

Yash said, 'You don't need to worried as I don't know about Barrack. I even don't know how much power he contains but yes if even crack to hamper in my happiness then he would be the one who can't relax in his life ahead'.

Pojo said, 'Solemn.... solemn dear I just want this to be listened by you, as I had seen that sleave in you that can combat against him. You can make the mutation I feel so but you need to know everything about Barrack too before being doing so. You can't even judge that how much happy I am spirit today to meet a too daring human being like you'.

Yash said, 'Ok....Pojo lets finish off here only Yash that he can't listen a lot good about him.

'I leave now and you don't forget to meet me as you get free from here. I think you have it for five days and this is your fourth day so on sixth day you must meet me', Pojo said to Yash.

'My dear, you don't need to worried about it even I need your adherence now after I come out of this prison. Let's see now, who is this Barrack over here', Yash said to Pojo.

As Pojo left this place and now Yash is meant alone over here in that room. Yash need to stay like this for one day here. As Pojo left the Cage, he is just seeking to pass on his day by just looking around. To find any assault to deal. Yash over here is not impacted by the climatic drifts but he have to listen here sounds that's comes from all around. These sounds are disturbing the most every time but some time's their reaches such tones that are in the sense to guide everyone at that place and make them a rigorous human being by the realization they give.

Now four days of Yash had gone off.

'It's been long time, I won't be able to meet my friends and I don't even know that they know about me or not. I feel Figo would have told all of them about me and they were easy alive at residence. Now I would be able to know about them only when I am going to get free from here', Yash said this time to himself.

Settle like Yash had seen something over there that is a piece of cloth he felt lying over there. So Yash felt whose cloth being lying over here as apart from Adrita and Eugene no one had came over this place. This cloth is lying just close to the glass from which corner he made his hand to move out and give love to Ronu. So he is in dilemma that it could be of Adrita or Eugene. Yash gone towards that corner bend himself and put his hand out from that space and uplifted it up. He leg that this was not a cloth but it is an 'amulet' for which Eugene is talking about.

Yash murmured, 'So this is it that he won't be able to find that time and Adrita was asking about it from him.

Yash is too happy like he got immense of gold dug inside his home garden.

Yash said loudly 'Eugene sir... Please come here once. I need to show you something'.

'Look sir... here I got something. I feel that this is the only thing that you were seeking to find here that time and you didn't got it. This is the thing 'amulet' that you were finding here and unable to find that. I think that time this is hidden by something else or won't be visible to our eyes', Yash said.

Eugene said, 'That's solemn dear... you find that. You know Adrita was so stressed still when I told her that I am unable to find her 'amulet' over here. She didn't said me anything but I can feel her pain by looking at her dull face after that'. After this there is a sense of happiness to be seen on Yash face.

'It's been so difficult of you to find it out. Ok dear give it to me, because as much early it could reach to Adrita that would be good because she is really in stress rigorous now', Yash felt a bit low and falling happiness can be seen conveniently. Soon a buzzer ranged up over there.

Yash felt that 'May be this could be a call for someone, but over here who can call whom because everyone is in their Cages', Eugene seems to be lost somewhere after listening to it.

Yash asked from Eugene, 'What had happened sir, may I know what are you thinking for'?

Eugene said, 'I didn't realise that they will be going to call me so soon. I knew about it that they will call me but just now. Ok dear I need to go just now'.

Yash asked, 'Where sir........., you were going where so instantly and what about this 'amulet' that you were asking from me'.

'I can't tell but I need to go for it, this is something about this place and don't need to know about it. Ok and for this 'amulet' can you do me a favour now', Eugene asked.

'Yes... sir for sure and I think you don't need to ask about this from me. You can Command me also to do anything', Yash replied as Eugene consists of a lot respect in Yash heart.

He is very much devoted towards him now because he had shared that thing with Yash knowingly or unknowingly about Adrita. Whom after knowing he felt himself more close to her. The salient thing for Yash devotion towards Eugene is also that from the start time to the end Eugene remedied Yash with a cup full of hot coffee towards him.

Eugene asked Yash, 'Child could you please give this 'amulet' to Adrita as I know her a lot. If you could message him or give her this 'amulet' as soon as possible. She could relax and can feel easy.'

Yash said, 'What you are saying sir...........me, how could I as being the slave of Heaven's Hell can go and meet priest girls. I had been told strictly that we are not allowed to meet them. Sir if there is any solution for this then please inform me', Yash is a lot happy after being listening to words said by Eugene.

Eugene smiled and replied, 'No.... dear who said you all this as I can read out all question arising on your face. I think any priest girl said that to you. Dear if this thing occurred, so you don't need to tensed then. I'll tell you one intern thing but you should not tell that to anyone else..ok'.

'Ok... sir I'll promise for that please say', Yash asked with excitement.

Eugene—'My dear child all priest girl are being scared of all slaves that comes up over here and this is also because of the education and information they were taught about slaves coming here from apart planets. This is told to them so that they do not get friendly with anyone from all slaves and no misbalance occur in Heaven's Hell policies', Eugene said this to Yash only because he knows that Yash is not a ordinary person.

Yash asked Eugene with a heavy tone 'Really...'

'I want to tell you about this so that you won't feel scared in future about all this', Eugene said to Yash.

Yash replied, 'Thank you sir........ Thanks a lot you don't know that you helped me a lot after revealing that'.

Eugene replied, 'I knew it all my child.' So as Yash listened it from Eugene he got a little scared and apprehensive as he don't know what Eugene knows about all this. Yash was implication but apart from thinking about this much he just want to leave this place.

So after all this Yash feel that he is getting late now as his friends were waiting for him. This time he didn't even know that his friends knows about him or not because no one told him anything about all this and Figo also hadn't informed about this thing as he is not allowed to come here. Yash moved towards the door from where he came as he faced towards that side he leg that it's been entire dark on that way.

Yash asked to Eugene;

'Sir, tell me how could I go from this way towards the out going door'.

Eugene replied, 'You don't need to tensed about this thing as its my duty to drop you forth. You just hold my hand and come away with me'.

Eugene laughed and said 'My child this darkness is just for the prisoner like you who come over here in prison. This is for the shelter purpose as you can see that there is no one around over this place to take care of all you prisoner over here apart from me. Even I am not keeping a watch over you all. So this is not just darkness but it's a guided mechanism of God which doesn't allowed anyone to pass it through and for your information this place is dark just for you all and not for me. Hold my hand and come along with me'.

Yash, 'Ok is it like this. Same shelter question is going on in my mind too and you sort out that.'

Yash was walking towards the door holding hand of Eugene. There settle to be a smile on his face that explicitly shows his happiness because of the place he got with Eugene to meet Adrita once again without any effort. Soon Yash saw several firelight's noose on walls as he reached the door. All this settle like a confusing thing to him.

Eugene said, 'I know what you are thinking off. You are thinking that only ....What these firelight's are doing here as whole the way we came was entire dark enough. So I tell you that this is the next stage of shelter which doesn't allow any unauthorised person to exit his door'.

Yash said, 'Wow... what a use of natural resources God had shown over here. Really amazing...'

Eugene said, they both had come out, 'Now you should go back to your place. Be secured from any punishment over here because that could be too harsh and for that don't disturb rules here and if you don't know the exact rules here then ask Pee'.

Eugene replied, 'I think you know Pee..?'

Yash with low tone 'Yes, I do know him'.

Yash doesn't knows about case of Pee still so he asked to himself, 'Why he is saying Pee as a member of this place. I think Eugene is talking about some other Pee and I am thinking of someone else'.

Yash said to himself, 'Eugene doesn't know still that the climatic mutate occurred inside didn't touched me for one per cent, but I am also not going to tell him about it. Let it be like this only as now. I am too happy as if I am going to meet Adrita after just I leave this place'.

Eugene said 'ok....Child I go back and you go your way, but for sure give this to Adrita because she is still apprehensive about it'.

16

Yash seen on his way a waterfall. He started to move towards the way of residence. On his way Yash see a waterfall from a big hill nearby that place. This waterfall is veiling a big area and falling down after being riding on the rocks for a long way from top to bottom and getting dispersed in the valley underneath that flow. Water of this waterfall was so clean and looks like milk is mixed in it. There is no noise of falling water to be heard nearby it as still this time Yash had came too close to see and feel this wonder beauty of nature. Abruptly with flow of air towards North-east way opposite to which Yash is facing a small bird having all beauty of colours in her feather's come and sit on one of Yash shoulder after taking a spiral round of him. Yash felt something on his arms he faced towards that bird and smiled as if he is asking her from where you came.

Bird replied, 'You are wondering about me that who am I and why I came sat on your arms', Yash listened to her felt amazed that she knows to speak like all of us being, so he asked her.

'*Hey*... yes really tell me who are you and speak up like us, that's awe full', Yash said to bird.

Bird said 'Yes as you don't know about me. I am not going to tell you much about myself because I am not here to tell you about my being but the thing is that it's been you for whom do I came'.

'Me.....what ??...what you saying? I am literally not getting anything could you please guide me a bit', Yash asked Bird.

'Ok....I just tell you that I am the ease and finest creation of God over here, you should not go to my size as if I am the only one who can mutation people's life and can tell about their future exactly', Bird said to Yash.

Yash laughed and said, 'Ok....then you are the scholar over here and teaches people about their future being. Yes, that really funny'.

'Really funny, you fucking man is talking like this to me. You don't know what a kind of pride I do consist over here. My name is Piano and you can ask anyone over here about me', Bird said.

Bird Piano replied, 'Why I am talking to you as I don't want to, if a person thinks like that for me. I just tell you the thing for which I came and sure that this thing is a bit hard for you to digest', Yash was laughing still.

Yash asked with a big smile on his face, 'Thanks for making my mood more refreshing after getting bored in that prison but really I want to listen to your words. So tell me what cheesy thing you want to tell me....'

After listening to Yash Piano is just burning with anger. She shouted on Yash and replied;

'Silent.... You slave listen I had bared everything you said because you are not a common creature over here as if you didn't came here because of your fault. To start a new era of humanity and love God itself called you being called here. I am not going to spare my one more second over here', Piano said all this in anger and fly off up more deeper in the sky.

Yash said, 'Why she came here, firstly I felt that I would be going to have a nice time with her but she just meant me in annoyance of wandered again and just fly off after dropping me in boiling water'.

Yash was sitting near that valley now holding his head and just seeking to relax himself by making himself to forget whatever he had listened from that Piano. Noise of people around came to his ears and he didn't even reached to that, till then he didn't realised that these noises are of some girls in his surrounds. Yash was facing downwards that time as if he is being still thinking about Piano and whatever she said. Abruptly he responded towards the tone he heard. Noticed that this is flowing from the backside of shallow wall meant of green leaves spread from top to bottom and separating those two place's apart. One place is where Yash seeking to feel normal and happy. Other where someone so executive for Yash is present with her friends. They were having there evening party with light music and cool drinks including. So Yash get up so rapidly and crack to make him normal as if he wants to see what's been going on over there without their approval. He gone close to that shallow wall leg difficult to cross it and then he said.

'I think this would be not easy for me to cross it and see what's been happening there and whose presence is exciting me so much. I think that it would not good also for me to directly cover this wall. As I couldn't disturb anyone over here in their privacy because it's denied in rules over here'.

Yash replied again, 'Ok… I know all this but still I want to be there and see whose present and what's going on because these tone that I am listening making me lewd'.

So after it, he decided to climb the tree nearby him and go as much higher as he can so that he could see the scene behind the wall. Yash then did what he felt, he had gone upwards while climbing the tree and sat over there to see everything and he saw that 'these all were priest girls but I don't think so that this is any restricted place for us and they are also present over here' Yash murmured.

There is no crime to talk to them, it's just they are afraid of all slaves over this place that's why they do make a difference from all of them and nothing else.

Yash seen them all so happy and blissful with each other settle like they don't want any adherence or anything else apart from each other Yash said;

Adrita is also there, now I see… why my stomach is making annoyance after listening her tone. My inference and emotion were started to make her a big part of my way'. Yash said this and he is just looking at Adrita in a perception flow with dumping and periodically evoking smile on his face.

This time no one from the priest girls noticed Yash till that time but he is being noticed by any of them then it critically bad time could start up. This is the time when Yash not even worried about his health and body also as he is being at the top of the tree with not much adherence which could be blurring Danger for him. Yash with just single adherence that is of a trunk that being captured by his hands and curled profoundly by them. This time after looking at the activities and the girl named Adrita. He become entire still as if he didn't even bother that if the adherence trunk of the tree broken up by his weight then what would happen. After sparing small time noose over the tree, till this time also no one realised that someone is there on the top who is watching every activity that priest girls are performing. priest girls didn't noticed him still because the height where he is been noose is too high and no one can even think to see that much upwards. This is why Yash is saved still now. Yash is spirit too good after bearing pain also while noose on that trunk because this time his attention is not at the pressure. He was bearing to hold that trunk tightly but his attention was profoundly towards watching every cute smile and spontaneous actions that Adrita being performing over there. This was the time and spirit that Yash devotion the most for which he don't have any reason. priest girls were going on too fine and there a lot collection of music that also introduced by some priest girls to this party. After listening music and songs from other priest girl Yash wants Adrita to take a part in this act because Yash was too desperate to listen from Adrita.

Yash said being at the top of tree to him, 'Yes.....solemn now everyone did whatever they want to and now it's been time for Adrita to come, hope so'.

Adrita came to the stage and a girl handed over mike to her.

Adrita, 'It was being too solemn and relaxing to listen all yours cool, shafts and delightful songs over here today's eve. I feel grateful for being a guider of you all amazing girls that did exactly what I taught and expected from you', Adrita said this and after listening to her Yash face didn't settle like he was happy to listen all this from Adrita. He loves to listen even a single word from her side now. Yash said, 'I had been thinking that she is going to perform now and the climate is going to be awesome for me but it like she is just going to have a speech and close this eve with it'.

Adrita did the same for which Yash is thinking off, she said all this to her fellow priest girls and started to leave the stage. There is no erotic reaction on Yash face now because he had meant his heart to realise this, as he come to notice before only that this is going to happen. As Yash was a fun devotion person and he never make himself dishearten any time. He meant himself cure by memorising that all nice he listened from other priest girls was the part of Adrita's creation.

As Adrita started to move out of the stage and stepping downward from the stairs of stage. She felt tone of some birds crawling and she looked upwards. She is being harrowing up after looking at a guys noose like a balloon on the tree. She doesn't felt good to react in an unusual manner and disturb everyone happiness around the place. She firstly tried to realise that who's actually the person is over there and for what reason he is being present over there like this.

This time Yash reactions were dissolved because he also realised that he came in notice of Adrita now so Yash said 'Oh! my god...please do save me now because last time I met her she shouted on me so heavily that I can't even justify myself explicitly. I wish this thing about my presence over here she would not say it to anyone over here'.

Stepping down from the stairs of stage, Adrita talked to herself in a big dilemma 'this settle to be the same person I met that night. Yes...I am right he is the one from "Earth surface", who is revealing me that I too belongs to his planet. But why this person is present over here'.

Adrita stepped down from the stage gone towards a corner where other girls are now bust gut in having food at the food court. She said 'the thing he is doing is not a legal one but then too why my heart is not remarks in a way I should react to him. Why I am not informing others about his illegal action'.

Yash is also too distressed that what would be the next as Adrita had seen him and not saying a word to anyone now. Adrita just remember Yash because of some days before night they met together. This time, she don't know that Yash was the only person who present in the prison that time when she came to find her Ronu over there and thank him too for holding Ronu at that place. This is because that time she didn't even saw anything else than Ronu as in an intention to just find out where Ronu had gone and nothing else. Yash was thinking that she was not revealing that to anyone and saving him because to the act he did at the prison and helped her but he don't know that Adrita doesn't even knows that he's that person. She just knows about that night when they met accidentally.

Ronu is also present at this music concert as Adrita brought him with her as she usually does. After being thinking a lot about Yash, her internal spirit were not allowing her to tell about Yash to anyone over there. She don't want Yash to get punished for this. After that Adrita has gone close to one of her fellow priest girl and said, 'You please keep a watch over Ronu, don't let him to go anywhere. I am handling Ronu to you so take care of him......ok, I am just handover a work to do and get back to this place soon', Adrita said this and gone out of this place as she want to inform and scold this guy who is being noose on the tree (Yash).

Yash couldn't also gather whatever she said to her fellow and why she moved out of this place. He wants to know that would she is seeking to take any action and that's why Yash got entire numb now and not even seeking to get down from the tree.

Now there is no one over the stage as everyone is in the food court and having their food. Yash is being still noose at that trunk and bearing pressure too just because he had seen Adrita there and he wants to see her as much as he can. This time nor Adrita is there neither function has been going on but then too he is over there and not seeking to get down from it because he felt bad and was wondering to see Adrita back at that place of function.

Climate is very calm in the aura now as no tones and sound is coming from any side and it looks like everything finished at that place.

A sound come from Yash downwards, 'Who is this over there, don't you know about the datum of being at this place', this sound is of some girl who settle to annoyed.

Yash firstly get shocked and scared of being caught and he looked downwards towards the part from where he listened the tone.

Yash said, 'You are here, but I thought that you would be going to come back at the place of concern', Yash said this with his profoundly wrist eyes and mouth.

Adrita replied, 'Ok.....so you thought off.....can I ask you How can you think that much about me and do you know the thing that you did now if someone else would have seen then it would be worse for you', Adrita replied in a sense to guide him.

Yash said, 'Please give me a minute I won't be able to converse with you and tell you everything while being hanging like this. Let me come down and I'll inform you about the entire scene'.

Adrita listened to what Yash said and with an anger she replied 'again you are speaking like that, who you are tell me as if you are going to give me explanations and I would listen to you. Wait just I need to inform you not to violet the rules here otherwise it could be much wrecking for you', Adrita said it all and started to go away from this place.

Yash after looking that Adrita is being going from that place without regarding his request. Yash without caring of anything else took a jump from that much height directly to the ground. This is a hazardous and apprehensive thing he did that time but it's just about his desperation to talk to her. Yash wake up from the ground after being fell from that much height and it seems that nothing got happened to him. Adrita who became still after seeing all this broken her silence and said, 'Oh!... thank God you are all ok... nothing happened to you'.

Yash slowly seeking to stand on his feet and making himself normal said, 'Yes it's solemn even I don't know that I would be safe after being falling from that much height......thanks God from my side too'.

'This is not a joke I think and if you know that this thing can wreck you a lot than why did you assault that. This is just because God have some executive hand on you he saved you otherwise anything could happen', Adrita replied irritating from the act Yash performed. 'Can you tell me what's that much urgent and executive for which you didn't cared about your life'.

Yash replied 'So there is your fault also for not caring about anyone's spirit. I have a habit of doing the thing that I say to myself and I had said that time to myself that I am going to talk with you and you started leaving so I jumped up'.

Adrita said, 'My fault in this. Do you know with whom you are being talking all this? Let me make one thing explicit to you that for the entire priest girl are just here to serve you and help you all slaves and not to be apprehensive about your spirit. Could you get my point'?

Yash replied, 'Yes I do get your point miss.....but you would have to listen to me to be aware of the whole datum', Yash this time also wondering that why she remarks so arrogantly with him as if she is thanking him inside prison so deliberately. So she doesn't know that the person who helped her in prison is Yash only.

As Yash is being lost in wondering all this Adrita said '*Hey*...you where were you lost I said you something'.

Yash said, 'Yes I just request you listen to me first and then I'll finish off you can continue what you want to say'. Adrita doesn't need to follow whatever he is saying but she doesn't know why he is tolerating him from a long time as she never did this before.

Adrita said to Yash, 'Ok...what you want to say I am listening'.

Yash started to tell his story 'I had been in prison from last five days it's just today I was set free from it. After getting free from the prison I was surge towards our residence and I listened to some tones being coming from this place and as its been musical sounds too, so as being a music lover I had climbed the tree to see that all. After I reached at the place from where I can see everything explicitly. I had seen you and that's why I spared that much time noose like this over there. I have no other intentions'. Yash said these to be safe from that all and move to the next step that Eugene asked him to do.

Adrita replied, 'you said that after looking me you spared that much time over there. What do you mean by that'?

Yash said, 'I mean just that the 'amulet' that Ronu had wore over his neck is left out in the prison and after you and Ronu left that place. I leg that lying forth my cage and for that when my time period is over and I am leaving my cage. Eugene asked me to give this 'amulet' to you as you are being a lot worried about it and in need of it.

Adrita started to feel about what he said. She also realised that if he is the person who is there in the prison then he is the only one who helped her and how can she talk like that to him.

Adrita seeking to make explicit picture about that all and realise the face of that person who had helped her that time by making her past picture a bit more expliciter in mind. She won't be able to got any picture of that person that time as she is so tensed that time and didn't even bother to look at the face of that person who is Yash only.

Adrita lost in her thoughts for a while replied to Yash.

'Afraid, That kind of behaviour by you as for me by you it's not the rule of humanity to remedy someone like this who helped you in past. I am really very afraid for this... please spare me', Adrita asked for afraid from Yash.

Yash said, '*Hey,* you please don't get low for anything like that I am known about the identity and respect you all priest girls have and upholds that with well defined rules. It's just that I want to talk to you, share some words with you and nothing else, I want from your side. You please don't say afraid because I really don't want you to lessen up your attitude as it is a plus datum in your beauty'.

Adrita said, 'Thank you for that. Yash now you can say anything to me I am over here and not going anywhere. You can say whatever you wish to', This time there is a sense of respect in her eye towards Yash with no wrong fdeelings about him.

Yash said, 'firstly I would like to hand over to you this 'amulet' for which you are being apprehensive about since last day when we met at the prison'.

She said, 'Thank, but say where did you get this 'amulet' over there as if Eugene *Dada* failed to find it out over there', Adrita said and was extremely happy after knowing all this.

Yash replied, 'Yes he didn't get this over there before when he crack to find it out but then I saw something lying just forth my front glass of cage and then I told it to Eugene'.

Adrita said 'It's been so nice of you. Ok...give it to me I'll put this in Ronu's neck as it would be good for him to put it as soon as feasible',

Adrita said this to Yash and he hand over 'amulet' to her.

Happiness of Adrita is too high apart from her being halting her happiness to be disclosed then to we can conveniently measure her meter of happiness.

Yash asked Adrita, '*Hey* why you said this, like it's been so emphasise for Ronu to wear this 'amulet' is there something serious'.

Adrita replied, 'No you don't need to tensed, this 'amulet' being in Ronu's neck since my infancy and there is a long story behind all this'.

Yash asked, 'Story can you please tell me that, I don't know why but my appetite is being growing to know about it if you can tell that'.

Adrita replied with a smile 'what you are going to do after knowing all this', but this time she couldn't be able to deny any words of Yash as he is now the person who came close after helping her.

Adrita replied again, 'This is being given to Ronu by my mother. She said that this should remain in Ronu's neck every time and this would be essential and good for both of us', Adrita said it and she started to move towards the place where she left her fellow girls and Ronu. So she asked Yash 'Now I think I should go as I am getting late for other things and my fellow girls were being waiting for me'.

Adrita asked, 'Yes...you can say to me conveniently'.

Yash said, 'As over here there is no one from our planet and that's why the gesture and look of every single person is apart. It's been just you here who is from our planet "Earth" so I want to share some spirit and facets with you as you can only understand them better than anyone else', Yash said all this because he wants to spare more time with Adrita and without any valid reason she would not going to stay over there much he feel.

Adrita said, 'I can't give you time now, can you do one thing, wait for me here only and I'll came back at this place after finishing off my work and informing others of my late arrival', Yash listen to all this said by Adrita.

Yash happily waiting for her at that place till she came back after finishing up her left work.

Adrita reached at the place where her fellow girls were present and Ronu is too over there. Adrita said, 'Thanks my dear Jaify for showing your care towards Ronu in my absence. I would be grateful to you if you could be with Ronu for a bit more time because I had some work to do and for which I have to leave just now. So I feel you could understand'.

Jaify is a fast friend of Adrita and also student of her at that time. So Jaify replied, '*Hey* mam you don't need to say all this to me even if you say me to be with this nice cute Ronu for many years I can do so that too. As you and your every word towards me consists a lot respect by my side'.

Adrita said, 'thanks I would be grateful to have your kind of girl close to me and my good friend. Ok you just take care of him and don't allow him to go anywhere or rome around in garden. You give me a minute with Ronu let me just put this thing in his neck as you also knows this 'amulet' stays every time on neck but he fell this thing somewhere. So I have to put it back in his neck'.

Jaify said, 'Ok me too just come up after having a glass of juice from the stall in front and you take your time with Ronu as he is just yours and understand your languages only. Ok mam, 'I just come you to continue.'

Adrita took Ronu with her towards a corner of the ground. She bend on her knees and started to love Ronu. She took out the 'amulet' and put it over Ronu's neck and after that she took a relaxation breath as she is too scary about the 'amulet' before.

Adrita while hand over Ronu to Jaify said I'll see you back, Adrita said this and moved towards the same place where he said Yash to met back.

When she reached at that same place, she had seen that Yash is still standing at the same posture in which she left him last. It settle like he didn't even moved a foot from that place.

Adrita came close to Yash and asked, 'You....you are standing in the same place and same mood as I left you. This aid you didn't care to do anything else this mean time apart from just waiting for me', Yash was not known about the datum this time that Adrita is back to this place.

Yash replied getting back from whatever he is been thinking that time 'No....that's not the thing. I was just thinking about my friends over this place who came with me. They would be apprehensive about me as I didn't met them from last five days'.

Adrita said, 'Yes this is right too. You should first go and meet your friend as they came with you over here and are unaware about everything. They would feel a lot better to see you with them so you should go'.

Yash said, 'No...this is not the thing that I mean. I am going to meet them and we do stay together only. One slave with us named Figo would have told them about everything I faced because he is a previous one and know everything about here. So there is no need to be tensed. This time the much emphasis thing for me is to be with you and share wanders with you. Which is really a big wish of mine'?

Adrita smiled and said 'What....wish...but just to talk with me....why'?

Yash said, '*Hey* please don't take me in wrong way. It's just that something is striking again and again in my throat and wanting me to know about you whenever I see you and apart from this thing I don't know anything'.

Yash replied again, 'You please give a good concern to me about this wish'.

Adrita smiled again and said, 'yes I do going to give concern on that. How can I deny from your wish as you helped me to get out of a critical condition and feel happy again'.

Yash replied, 'I done a favour for you then you would be wrong as I did it for myself'.

'Yourself......how come you can say like that', Adrita replied.

'Yes myself because the smile I can see now on your face it settle to awesome to me. So you can feel that to make me feel good. I had make this happen and put this smile on your face', Yash replied he now realise that Adrita started to care about his spirit now. She is spreading her true colour this time that's of humanity and love.

Adrita said, 'Ok....don't say much, now otherwise I would feel that there is someone who cares for me a lot. Which I am not supposed to think off', she said this so softly as if Yash couldn't be able to listen to her. So Yash asked what did you said please two fold.

Adrita mutate her words and said 'nothing I was just saying you to not to waste time while being talking non utilitarian. You say what you want to say and ask from me'.

Yash said 'Don't you feel that this place is not a single per cent good for two people to communicate freely'.

'So, what do you want', Adrita asked Yash and smiled.

Yash said, 'I don't want anything, I just want to say that can we move on to some other place and talk over there'; Adrita listened to his wish and said where you want to go.

Yash said, 'I think that place where we met first is the peaceful and sacred space with a majestic climate. We should be over there. So can us'.

Adrita replied, 'I couldn't say no to this as I had accepted your request first. So come soon lets go there as you wish', Yash feel different because this time the last line said by Adrita and her reaction he hadn't seen before.

Yash is also happy to hear this last line that she said in a frank and bold manner. This is the trait Yash wants every girl should have.

Yash said, 'There is one problem that I don't know the way to opt from here to reach that place. So you need to guide me for reaching their'.

Adrita said, 'settle like you were too intelligent but don't feel if the other person is not remarks to what you say anything, person is not under standing your wanders', Yash listened to her and as he is not saying anything with any sort of intention, he asked himself 'what intention I am having to say all this, I couldn't realise'.

Yash asked to Adrita, 'Can you please tell me about my intention behind saying all this because I don't have any thought regarding it in my mind'.

Adrita said, 'I think you don't need to think that much and you are just wasting time both of us while just talking over here. Come I'll show you the way to the sea shore'.

They both started to walk together towards the place where Yash wants to be and it settle like this time climate also looking towards them and listening to their conversation. This is because when they started to move nature too covered them with his shelter of love by making specific kind of lovable climate. Yash didn't realised this climatic mutation because he is just lost in Adrita this time and wants to share with her a lot but Adrita is very close to climate of Heaven's Hell. This look and feel of so dashing becoming climate over here, she never seen before.

So she said, 'See what a glamorous and cheesy climate meant this time. I think this was the rigorous climate I want in my life to be seen over here and it's been today'.

Yash without even bothering about climate and just to reply her said 'Yes... good it's good', the confusion can be conveniently seen in the words of Yash and Adrita got to know about it through his reaction.

Adrita said while walking, 'Ok I think we can talk now too. So you tell me what you want to say and want to ask me'.

Yash said, 'It's not like that I want to ask you anything as I just said that I want to share some words with you. Ok I request you to please answer me truly one thing'.

Adrita said, 'This is though I am a priest girl and once we regard someone we can't yes anything wrong to him in any manner. I think you must know that priest girl also doesn't say lie any time'.

Yash asked, 'Ok then tell me a thing which goes in my mind periodically whenever I see you that you don't know that your planet is "Earth surface" and about your origin from that place'.

Adrita, 'I know that all thing as my mother is from "Earth surface" only', Yash is profoundly shocked.

Yash said, 'So why did you reaction in a manner of dilemma and ignorance when I asked you about your planet in our first meet'.

Adrita replied, 'I did said that to you because no one over here told me about my planet and my origination as no one from members of this place wants me to know about it. This is because the position I do consists over here is too respectful and governing for which I have to uphold a bond amidst every person from apart planet over here. This is why I pledged before taking responsibility over here to give one platform of happiness to everyone over here'.

Yash said, 'Ok if it is like this then I regard you for that but tell me do you know about your parent and where were they what happened to them'.

Adrita said, 'My parent......I don't know about them but yes they both are from your planet and nothing else. I do know about them because this much being told to me. This is also told by Eugene Baba and nobody else even appetite to tell me about them', Adrita with some pain in her eyes as they explicitly shows she wants to know about her parent.

Yash said, '*Hey* you please don't feel low for all this'.

Adrita replied, 'Who said you that I am spirit low and depressed about it. How can you say like that'?

Yash asked again, 'Ok....If it is not like that then good......You know you are the one from my planet and as I had been with lot of girls at our planet but I hadn't gone close to anyone as I didn't like them. This is not the case with you because you have something stored inside in you for which I won't be able to make myself away from your though'.

Yash replied again 'Please understand my thoughts. I just said that because I never hide my emotion, my feel and say it conveniently'.

Adrita said, 'don't tensed I am not going to care about what you said because this is the spirit which is not embeded in my life and I am not allowed to do so', Adrita said all this with a severely dull face as if she wants to be a part of this feel and emotion.

Adrita said again to move away from this conversation, 'Look your place came where you want to be and now what'.

Yash said, 'now nothing....Firstly lets be seated somewhere it doesn't settle good to stand and talk, I think as I got tired and you too I feel so'.

Adrita said, '.....come we do sit under tree shade over there...'.

After being seated at that place they were not talking to each other settle like they don't have any words to share now. After a while Yash broken up silence and said;

Yash asked her, 'Ok tell me something more about you..?'

Adrita said, '*Hey* don't you feel that you are asking a lot about my life and get to personal to me'.

Yash feel that she is saying rigorous as if he had asked a bundle of things from her in a single through without revealing anything about himself to her. So in this affinity Yash felt that he would first tell about his life to her then only he could be more personal.

Yash replied, 'Actually I don't share anything of mine with anyone and if it belongs to girls I don't say anything to them. But this time in front of you my heart wants to tell you everything about my past and this is my wish to share with you all. Why I am spirit like that I don't know'.

Adrita laughed loudly this time as Yash said all this in a deliberate sober manner as if he is requesting her to listen what he wants to say.

Adrita said, 'Ok.... now after this I am also excited to listen about your life. Yes say now I am waiting'.

Yash set happy to listen this from her and then he said 'My life....My life is a life that is not easy any day any time. I was too small when I lost my father. That time I was just two year old and not aware about the cruelty of our nation. My father was a police officer. He is too loyal towards his work and was a rigorous person with well defined goals and morals towards his duty. He just feels good when he serve people and make them rid of their problems. I got to know all about him when I become a bit older of eight year. I came to know everything from others and my mother about my father role, responsibilities and his actions towards people growth. He was a solemn opponent of corruption and this was what makes him to die', as Yash was revealing about all this to Adrita he came to mixed in all that and after entire his stanza he looked towards Adrita who is also lost in Yash words and asked;

'Does this is the rule of living that you have to be bad and corrupted like your surroundings and if you were not like that. Assaulted for a mutation you don't deserve to live at that place', Yash asked Adrita and she also don't have any answer to it so she didn't replied.

Yash continued and said, 'My mother was too adherence to my father and loves him a lot. Other people says that before my birth in every tragic situation my mother was the only person who come forward and face very annoyance which attacks my father. My mother with my father even helped a lot of families in making their living cosy in the aura. My father fought for many people's rights and assault his best to make people get what they deserve, but you know after death of my father no one even cared of my *mom* (mother) and we are not even having proper food to eat those days. My father slained because he denied being a part of ongoing corruption as he just adherence people to get their right and work for their happiness. Corruption took away my father and those people for whom he died didn't even step forward and asked about his family after him. I and my mother whom I loved the most in the whole world had to wipe tears from each other face. As sometimes my mother also becomes helpless when she can't impart proper food to me but she doesn't know that I don't want food to be happy as my mother one smile is enough for me those days', Yash speaking all this to Adrita and tears can be seen in his eyes conveniently that time and now after hearing all this Adrita is also getting her eyes filled of water.

Yash continued speaking now as he was in entire flow this time and wants to eject some sadness from his heart by revealing it all to Adrita.

Yash, 'You know I didn't even go to school those days. This is not because my mother didn't assaulted to do so. She do cries also in front of me to send me to school and I have to go that time but to send me there she had to work day and night without any ease and that's why I denied from going to school. We are not having any sort of money those days because the person who makes my father to die had also destroyed everything that we have next. After that it's just me and my *mom* (mother) who left with hopes in our eyes. I had been grown up a lot in my small age and just love my *mom* (mother) like anything. I can't see my *mom* (mother) in sane and pain but then too I have to see and bear it all because that time, I am not having any way to make my mothers feel cure. This is because she doesn't even allows me to do work as if she just wants me to study and gain wisdom but all that wisdom is just a waste for me that time. I am unable to remove my mother harsh day by it. No one came forward and asked about our being and my mother was too good that she didn't even complaint about that even ones. I remember each and every day of that time. That time I had to just cry and save myself so that my mother doesn't look at my tears. I pretend to be very much fortified in front of my mother but practically I am not that those days. My mother worked for my well being whole day and night and one day... One day she left me too', Yash said this and cried. He won't be able to halt his tears this time and so the Adrita too dropped water from her eyes as she listen to Yash last line.

Yash continued, 'I lost that time a person after whom I couldn't even think to live in my life. I am profoundly broken apart after this and can't see anything in life now. This time I was of fourteen age and after losing my mother who is my god I lost my all hopes. All this I faced is just because of this corruption spread apart in all of our auras. So I pledge that in my next birth I will just going to kill all those who were a part of this corruption and killing humanity. This thing I said to be done in my next birth because I won't be able to do this in my going generation because I lost my hopes to live now too. So I had decided that I am going to die for that. I had gone near Ganga (a holy river of Hindus) and tried to jump into it. But someone from my back pulled my hand towards himself as he got to know about my intention of dying. This is my new Parent a *Brahman* from Haridwar. He is that person who responsible for taking care of all *'Aarti'* that is being done over there. He also teaches as a head-master in school. He took me from there to his home and cared me like his child. I studied in the same school in which he was head-master. After some years I finished my entire studies and crossed 22 years but still the wandered to eradicate corruption was going inside. One day few person came to my place and dropped the school which was dream of Head-master by saying that this land is illegal. They said it wrong. The land is not illegal but they want to build their own resort over there that's why they did it. I am a lot annoyed because all this happened but no one from official took action against them. This is the face of corruption I met again. After this I won't be able to halt myself to killing all those persons of the land who kills other spirit and emotions illegally. Lastly I want to tell you that this is not good in God perspective and that's why I had been called up over here in this Heaven's Hell', Yash completed, it all, what he wanted to say and took a breath as all this that he faced was not easy for him. After this he looked towards Adrita who had came too close to Yash while being listening to all this that Yash is revealing her.

Adrita profoundly lost and was just looking towards Yash spirit and pain he beard in his past life and told everything to her. Adrita was speechless at this time and Yash also just staring towards her now. Adrita said to herself 'why this person trusts me so much and how could he had beard all this pain of his close ones'.

Yash asked, Adrita 'Hello.....where was you lost. Are you ok...'

Adrita getting back from her thought said, 'I am profoundly ok...you say you are all rigorous'.

Yash replied, 'Yes...I am all right ......you say now do I am a trustful person or not'.

Adrita replied, 'What....How can I say that? What are you asking me?'

Yash, 'Ok....leave this now it's your turn now you tell me. about yourself'. Yash wiped his tears.

Adrita replied, '*Hey* what are you saying we are not playing turn wise and this is not a game going on over here'.

Yash said, 'I am also not saying it a game. I am appetited to know about you a bit that's why I am asking'.

Adrita smiled again for Yash as they had a very emotional conversation just now and Yash came out of it very soon. This shows the problem dealing capability of Yash that's settle to be very high.

Adrita replied to Yash, 'If you want to know about me then you must know that I am not like other priest girls. As I have some sole responsibilities and some powers to manage peace at Heaven's Hell. I don't know much about me and this is all that I do know about myself'.

Yash said, 'Just this you must know about yourself. I didn't expected that from you as you looks too intelligent, gentle so would you haven't crack to know about your past or your origination from somewhere'.

Adrita said, 'What past....I had been over here since my childhood and before whatever had I think don't need to know that. I had also said you before that no one told me about anything. Except Eugene baba there is no one over here who really knows also about my past and whoever knows doesn't wants to tell me. Eugene *dada* had told me that I have some crucial powers to save humanity and need to realise myself. This is the only gift of my mother to me after my birth. *Dada* said, I am not going to realise them. I won't be able to help humanity and save them from forthcoming harsh brutality. I even don't know where my parent present or they do alive or dead'.

Yash said, 'It's like that afraid to insist you a lot to say all this to me as if you felt bad to memorise all this. You said about powers, so do you know any valid reason together it all'.

in colour. This shows about some black power empowering itself and gaining energy'.

'What...what you are saying', Yash said looked upwards in the sky and leg the same that she is saying.

Yash replied, 'You were correet but how can you say that black power is empowering and gaining energy through it. Are you familiar with all this before'?

'Yes this being done once more time by Barrack. This happens when he start his meditation and calls his other comrades from his planet. Who all comes over here and join their energy to adherence Barrack. He keeps them all safe in black sculpture, which looks exactly like him with covered face. This is meant for him which helps his planet people soul kept inside it to be spared from the pure effect of Heaven's Hell. They effecting them as are not being called by God to this place' Adrita replied to Yash frustratingly.

'So as this is God place why don't God punish him and block him while doing all this', Yash asked Adrita.

'God don't keep watch on everyone's activity every time and if he get to know also about anything he don't do something to solve it as if a rule of Heaven's Hell that 'You are the builder and saviour of your own', Adrita said.

Barrack is called back here because he was making his Planet people in annoyance every day and he meant there living very much difficult by his acts. So God called him at Heaven's Hell in the sense to let his Planet people live conveniently. Over here Barrack can't make any wreck to anyone as his energies don't work to peak. If he does want to use them then he can use a little and nothing else', Adrita replied to Yash.

Yash said, 'I think this need some action to be taken against him as if no one is liable here to bear all this. Barrack also doesn't have any rigorous to force you or to govern you. He is nothing; I am surely going to take any step'.

Adrita said, 'It's not going to be worked out by you as you are just a mango and simple man and Barrack is a man with experience, and power with judgmental tactics to govern others mind. What he does over here as you can see a lot people over here are scared from him and his activity.

Adrita was very much stressful because of Barrack activities as he crack to block her freedom also over here then she said again 'He made wreck to those people who come to assault him and react to others as he is just upholding rule's of Heaven's Hell'.

Yash replied in grief, 'No... he can't do like that to you and why did he says that he's upholding rules of Heaven's hell........what rules'.

Adrita said, 'Oh! afraid... I think this much conversation we did is enough and I'd been afraid for revealing you more about it'.

Adrita replied again, 'feel like we should go back now to both, place otherwise this could be perilous for me a lot more than you'.

'*Hey* I think we were talking on the safe place and we didn't seen anyone coming over here until now. I can't drop this conversation like this', Yash said but his anticipation is increasing as a volcano.

He wants to proceed further and know a bit more about the whole thing for which Adrita burned a sleave in him.

Yash replied again with full anxiety, 'what rules.....you have to tell me now please. I want to listen it all as I know that you priest girls are not blocked from talking to the slaves. This is just you all priest girls do to make a little difference every time amidst we slaves and you'.

Adrita listened to all this and got shocked. So she asked furiously 'Who told you these sorts of things about us because without any terrace no one can talk like this with confident in his eyes. I want answer.

There is desperation to know the name of person who knows all this because this is being done by priest girls which is known by them only. Yash is in dilemma to tell her the name of Eugene sir as they told him all because he feared that she annoyed for the person who told all this.

Yash wandered this and said to Adrita, whose face is having a big question mark to know the name 'Adrita the person who told me a little about these thing is Eugene sir and no one else when I am in prison'.

Yash got stuck after saying all this to Adrita as he is just looking at her next reaction and emotion. Yash take a relaxing breath as he saw that after listening name of Eugene sir Adrita reaction are getting back to normal as she is not annoyed now.

Adrita replied, 'Ok... if it is like this, that Eugene *Dada* told you all this then I am sure he would had some specific good reasons behind revealing you all this. He wouldn't talk like this to anyone may be he would had seen something in you apart from others and he told you'.

This has been conveniently shown by her words that how much she respects and loves her Eugene *dada*.

They were talking all this even when water was falling from the sky and there cloths had been profoundly wet. Instantly there was a heavy storm started at that place and Adrita started to be more worried now.

Adrita said, 'Now I can't wait for a single minute over here as I need to go back to my place. This time everyone would be going to come out of their place and they could see us'.

Adrita started to move towards her place. As she faced backward to go. Yash said her, 'Wait tell me just that because of Barrack only this is happening or what'.

Adrita said to Yash, 'Climate mutate occur at this place and such sort of climatic effect is also be seen but my judgment is not wrong because today it's just merger of black power. I am sure this is because of Barrack'.

'If this is the thing then I am just going to find his place and won't allow him to do any wreck to humanity', Yash said to Adrita.

Adrita while running and facing backward said the last dictating stanza to Yash that 'You should not try to do because he is ten times solemner than your age and all he does it. Because of his immense power generated by meditation. This is the power that even God can't deny, so you shouldn't try any sort of assault as it would wreck you only'.

Adrita said this and in a minute got lost from Yash eyes. Now there are many questions emerging in Yash mind and this place becoming very critical to be known by him with this in complete information about every task. After thinking for a while Yash slapped himself and said, 'I didn't even asked about the last thing she said. We were getting on the point and she just left everything.'

After this Yash also realised that he should also move towards his residence where friends will be waiting for him. Yash wandered to reach over there and discuss regarding Barrack to all them. The climate of this place was becoming unusual as time passes and soon storm started blowing with a much higher speed as rainfall halted.

17

Yash ran on the way towards residence and it's been close to the sea shore as Yash came here before too. So he know the way very well. Yash was running this time and after some time he saw that his friends were out of the residence and looking towards the sky.

Yash came closer to them put his hand from back on Ankit shoulder 'Who is this', Ankit asked.

As Ankit came to see that it is none other than Yash at its backside, he replied '*Hey* man where were you lost, you know everyone is just wishing for your goodness and shelter from last many days'.

Ankit said again when Yash is not getting any words to tell him about the entire scene he face. He said 'why you do things like that, which make everyone in a lot grief and stress and because of it our other work to get spoiled off'.

Yash asked himself, 'If Figo hadn't told them about me then not the anger on Ankit face is not obvious, anyone can react like that on this situation'.

Yash with his bowed head because of shame said, 'I am a lot afraid for all this too as I believed on Figo that he would go to inform you all'.

Ankit, 'what you are wandering. We all know that you are captivated in prison for these days as Figo only had told us on the same day you were missing, but we don't know that you are going to be set free today only', Ankit said.

Yash with a smile on his face 'So its aid that Figo informed you all about me. Now I can be cure'.

'Yes he told this entire thing to us and the case behind the whole act of yours. Tell me what is that much emphasis to you, while being going on a place that's being restricted for us...?', Ankit asked,

Yash, 'Don't you all feel that the aura had changed so rapidly and do you know this is not because of climatic mutation at this place but it do have some other reason', Yash said this to his friends.

'I know that you are seeking to change the topic and divert our attention towards something else. Firstly you have to tell us that why...for what reason you had gone over there and till then I am not going to leave you', Ankit said to Yash as he is not in favour of this kind of unusual things that Yash does every time and make things go wrong.

Yash replied 'Wait.....dear we can talk about this afterward. This time you just tell me do you all know anything about this'.

Ankit said, 'I think we all know that if we failed to ask you the reason about all the datum happened with you. Then no other time is going to come again as you are not going to give chance to anyone to ask you about it in future'. Yash smiled.

Sunny favours Yash in his spirit and mentality so Sunny though there could be a valid reason behind all these datums and that's why Yash is not revealing Ankit about it.

Sunny said, 'Ankit why are you forcing him. Let it be like that if he wants to tell everything afterwards then let him do that'.

'I think we must concentrate on present situation that is going on', Sunny replied again.

Ankit said, 'So it means that you are not going to tell about anything to us'.

Yash smiled and replied, 'No my dear it's not like that but my concern is to the thing that is happening and I asked you all that do you know about this'.

Ankit replied '....Yes we know about this, when we moved out of the residence. Pee informed about all this to us'.

'Pee where is he. I can't see him with you', Yash said.

Soni said, 'He is at the back, see...'

Yash saw that Pee is coming from the back side towards them and shouted '.... So Pee you told them about this thing can I also know what had you told them about all this'. Yash asked Pee as this time again he succeeded in waver the topic of everyone concern.

Pee laughed and said, 'My dear come came back...you know your friends are worried a lot as they don't have enough information about you'.

Yash while looking towards Ankit said, 'Yes I know they all love me a lot'.

Ankit said, 'That's why Pee, he informs everything in brief to us', Ankit taunted Yash.

Pee said, 'Yes you all have a solemn bond and that's explicitly shown by you all of your love towards each other'.

Pee replied again, 'Yash don't get depressed. I didn't told them much but just I said them that all this is being happening because of Barrack. This is the same person whom I shown you when the volleyball match being going on. I think you know about him a little'.

Yash said, 'No you were wrong Pee, I don't know about him a little but I know about him the most now as while staying in prison I listen about him a lot'.

'Ok...that's solemn then so you could share your wisdom of Barrack with your friends also', Pee replied to Yash.

Ankit replied, 'But I don't feel so that Yash is going to share his wisdom about him with us'.

Yash said, '*Hey* my dear...why do you say like that. You all know that how much I love you all. I am surely going to tell you about him'.

Ankit said, 'Hope so'.

Yash said to Pee, 'Pee could you help us to go at the chance where Barrack carries out his all these unusual activities that disturb the auras.'

'What.......but for what reason you are asking Pee to take all of us over there? Why we all are going to take appetite in that', Ankit replied.

Yash added, 'No.....you don't have to take appetite in that but I am truly very much interested to go towards that place and you have to come along with me for adherence'.

Pee said, 'But I don't think that you should go over there'.

Yash said, 'Pee don't be scary about anything dear. I know very much about him. I think nothing and no one can harm anyone over here as this place belongs to God'.

Pee, 'You were deliberately right and I could take you all to that place also but still I find this thing not rigorous to do'.

Ankit replied, 'What.......and why....What you both are being talking about I am not getting and Yash why we need to go there'.

Yash said, 'Brother doesn't think that much just come along with me. Pee you are going to take us over there'.

Pee said 'Yes I do, I don't have any query regarding it but you all are going to go there. This would be not ok'.

Yash said, 'Ok...let's do that me and Ankit would be going there and you all my friends ease at the residence nothing to tensed about'.

Sunny replied instantly, '*Hey*...I am also ready to go. I too want to see that place whatever it is'.

Yash said, 'ok...then Sunny you too come with us'.

Ankit said, 'But...'

Yash said, 'Ankit now let's don't waste time as this weather is also not favourable. See how it's been waver itself before it get worse. Let's move towards that place see it and come back'.

Ankit saw that they all started to go there. He felt that if they had set their mind then he won't be able to say anything.

Yash, Ankit and Sunny reached the place which is reserved for Barrack. Pee brought them all over there.

Pee instructed them, 'This place Barrack demanded from God when God asked him to stay at this place. He demanded that if they are forcing him to leave his place then God listen to his needs also. Otherwise this act of God comes under violence and place deficit effect. He pressurised God to do what he received from them a place which he calls 'Holey'. This is the place where he doesn't even allow anyone to see this and get noticed about it. His power's are submerged by him in this land those he generated by his concerned— power of his soul'.

Everyone standing still on their position no one even wants to dare of stepping forward towards Barrack place of living but Yash stepped forward as there is no pressure of anything on his face.

Pee said to Yash, 'No...don't move forward. As we know this is God's place and over here no one being sealded unless and until person does any crime but this place is a bit apart over here. This place is owned by Barrack only and this was his wish from God that he would not going to be disturbed by any person coming over here and residing at this place. This is the thing he asked to God when they said him to stay here and continue his living over this place'.

Pee replied pressurising to Yash, 'My dear this is not the place where you can enter without his approval and you can't even disturb him in his possessive work'. Yash set back for a while in just a sense to give good response to what pee said him. But his intention working the same as before.

Ankit and Sunny were also scare about Yash as it doesn't settle like he cared about what Pee said because this time too as they both were tensed, he was having no reaction on his face.

Sunny said to Ankit, 'There seems to be a dedication on his face to do something or maybe it's been just to know about Barrack more. Ankit you had also seen that how he is saying about him to you'.

Ankit said to Pee, 'If all this is true then it would be very perilous for us to disturb him. Ok........lets go back.......Yash. Yash.....come with us'.

Ankit realised that Yash is not even giving any concern to all what we are saying to him now. Ankit don't want Yash to go against words of Pee that he told us for our goodness but it doesn't looks that Yash is conscious about it.

Ankit said to Pee, 'Ok....Pee thanks a lot for bringing us to this place and yes we all are going to secure full over here and don't dare to do anything for which you reminded us. I think Yash wants to stay here for a while and we'll go after-wards. I think you Pee must go now, as the weather is also not that much supportive as its getting viral. So you don't tensed and go back to residence and have ease, we all come soon'.

Pee replied 'Don't tensed about this weather and all as I told you this is not a natural one. Everything will go to be normal soon when Barrack work finishes off. He send back his comrades back inside the Black Sculpture he meant'.

Ankit knows that Pee is the member of Heaven's Hell and it doesn't matter that how much he have soft corner for us. He would be going to inform authorities about whatever wrong we does against rules. Ankit felt this because Yash as he is in dilemma the some nuisance again Yash is going to spread out.

After listening to Ankit Pee started surge back towards the residence saying, 'Ok...dear as you wish but you are caring so much about me as I am not that much tired but I am going to keep your care up and go back but you all also come soon ok. I will be waiting for you all.........ok Yash Ankit Sunny...see you back'. Pee said it all and left that place.

Ankit shouted on Yash as he was still lost somewhere '.....where were you lost and what mishap is going in your mind now, do you even are a little about your friends'.

Yash said, 'What....happened Dear......is there something wrong'?

Ankit replied, 'Wrong.........is going to happen now as I can catch every sort of feelings that are going in your mind. *Hey* dear let me tell you that I had just send Pee away from his place. So that he is not going to inform about your breaking action that you perform after these reaction of yours. I know that you are going to try that thing for which Pee strictly denied to be done over here. Park.......what Pee is going to inform anyone but yes this's true that he said all this for our wellness only and nothing else'.

Yash getting out of his thoughts and replied to Ankit, 'Pee is going to inform whom......what are you saying'.

Yash replied while rubbing his head as he is swiftening his retentions '....I know that why you said this for Pee....Pee is a member of Heaven's Hell. I had been told about Pee when I was in Prison by Eugene for which you being concerned about him...I am rigorous'.

Ankit listened by Yash but this time he was not shocked about this datum that Yash also knows the case about Pee. This is because Ankit is being scared of the act that is going in mind of Yash this time. So he asked Yash now;

'You just leave all this now and tell me that you are going to come with us now or not. Tell me about the furious concern going into your mind this time'.

Yash laughed and said, 'My dear friend how could you realise things that goes in my mind. How...could you understand everything', by all this Yash just want to turn the scene and mind of Ankit which doesn't settle good towards Yash.

Yash said again, 'Dear Ankit......*Hey* why you are being so worried about all these thing, just chill my brother and if someone said something then how can we change our curiosity of mind'.

Ankit took a break of word and relaxed.

Ankit said, 'Ok so...everything is just because of your curiosity. No one like that Yash, it's been just you who do that only which you want. You should think about other phases also'.

Yash said, 'Dear just realises that what I am saying. We are just going to inside and don't make any wreck to anything. We enter into this place just gathered some things about Barrack'.

Sunny said, 'Ok...all this is alright......whatever Pee said we also listened it. Your desperation to go inside I can understand but it is not digestible to me that for just this reason you want to go inside as you are not that much adventurous. Say....what is the reason behind it', Sunny adherenced Yash in what he said but the thing for which Yash wants to take this risk is not valid reason. He think so, as he also knows a lot about Yash appetite.

Yash said to himself, 'Yes he is rigorous that I want to get in this place and know about Barrack as he is connected to Adrita somehow but I don't want to tell them about it'.

Ankit shouted in between and said, 'Can you both please halt talking and thinking about all these nonsense, it settle like you both have decided to probe out this place'.

Sunny said, '*Hey*....Ankit what's this leave scary attitude. You know that we all had never feared from big things to be done and did whatever we feel rigorous and good for others. I am sure this time, Yash is not doing it for his appetite to know or being adventurous but he is doing all this just for the sake of someone else only. I inference.....but the thing is that he is not going to tell also about it. So leave everything and just come with us let's see what there inside it'.

Ankit replied, 'I can't even think anything now or going to say anything to you all, as you all had set your mind to go'.

After all these conversation all three of them left every else wandered in their mind and gone inside that place for which Pee said no to them. While surge inside that place Yash said.

Yash said, 'See..... what a dashing place is this,...see greenery spread all over this place.......it looks like the place where Barrack reside, there in amidst I think so. A large white tomb and I think this is having highest peak over here'.

Ankit replied again as if he got something that should be known to everyone, 'This place is having everything which can feel us. Look at the trees over here. They didn't settle happy for us and this grass for which greenish behaviour you are talking, see it took waver colour'.

Sunny reaction was not good when he listened to all that and he replied, '*Hey* you Ankit, every time why you do like that, by thinking about everything in a wrong way. Transform yourself a bit like Yash so that you can also feel the same and be happy as he does.'

This time Yash had given his full concern on every sort of thing that Ankit said, so he didn't favoured Sunny whatever he said and replied '*Hey* Sunny don't say like that for Ankit. You know him well that whatever he say everything consists of a fact behind that'.

Yash replied again, 'Ankit tell me about your realisation, why you said all this as I had too felt the same after giving realization to your words.....yes tell me that so'.

Ankit replied, 'Yash I had warned you before also that this place is beyond our understanding and if we are going to indulge in all this then it would be difficult for all of us to get out of all it. I don't understand that why are we getting into this place if it is of no concern to us'.

Yash said, 'I think you were rigorous in all these thing, as I am also spirit that all this aura is staring us like it don't want us over here. As much I know nature is not cruel to anybody. It greet always and not differentiate as its doing with us. This attitude of nature is not its own but being meant by someone and governed by him that's why this started remarks according to his mood'.

Ankit said to Yash, 'Sometime I feel a lot glad to be with you because you make others feel happy by doing silly things but instead you know everything'.

Sunny said, 'Yash if you had said that much then do you know that who is responsible for all that or you are just adherence Ankit as he did what you want'.

'Don't talk like a silly boy Sunny and this thing is also obvious that Barrack place and everything whatever is going on just because of him only and no one else', Yash guided Sunny and then said to Ankit that;

'.....Ankit lets go inside and watch out what is so.......scary over there. Come...with me.........hey Sunny you too come', Yash said this to them and started walking towards that white 'Tomb' the place where Barrack reside with all his aura working according to his wish and spirit.

As Yash started walking towards the Tomb being courious about everything that he could face inside. He felt that his friends are following him. Ankit shouted and called him from back... Yash listen and Ankit said;

'Afraid dear but I am not going to allow anyone to go there as if we both are not going and you should also come back.' This time Ankit and Sunny were standing at the back without surge from their place where they are standing.

So Yash said, 'Ok...my dear brothers I can't put your words down'.

There is smile to be seen on both face Ankit and Sunny as they both felt that Yash responded to what they said in a positive way.

Soon Yash replied; 'Ok....let us do one thing, you just help me out while being over here only. I will go inside and probe out what kind of things he does inside. *Hey*.....don't get scared dear, I am going to stay far away from any kind of annoyance as I come to notice it', Yash said this and started walking alone towards the tomb.

Yash looked backward again to the dull and feared face of his friends and said;

'*Hey* now what... why you are remarks like that, wait I just come back in some minutes ok....', Yash said so conveniently as he is going for a play he loves most.

Ankit shouted, 'Dear we are just over here waiting for you, come soon as much feasible and take care of you'. Yash heard this from Ankit felt happy about his care towards him and he replied loudly 'Yes brother.......I will...'.

Yash pointed through his finger towards the tomb and said to Ankit 'Dear I am now going inside this and you keep a watch in this aura while standing over here. I'll be back soon'.

Now Yash left everyone and had gone too far from his friends reach and not even seen also by them. So as they are not able to see Yash, Sunny seems to be apprehensive about him. So he said to Ankit '*Hey* now Yash is not visible to our eyes too. I think he would have gone too far or maybe he would have gone inside that long building white Tomb'.

Ankit said, '*Hey* don't be so scary and make me too, nothing would happen wrong over here even when this place is of Barrack because this whole comes under Heaven's Hell and I am sure about it'.

Sunny said, 'hope so...'.

Yash came inside that place profoundly and now he is unable to find out the door to get inside of Tomb. As he came close to this tomb after veiling the green grass garden over where peace was profoundly spread apart. There he came to notice that as he was coming close to the tomb, he was being in contact with various perilous and poisonous animals. These all he leg hiding behind the green bushes in the garden.

When he came too close just at the foot of Barrak's white Tomb Yash said, 'What is this, I hadn't seen anyone at this as this garden is also too empty. Is it like that Barrack stay alone at this place'?

'Let me get into it now and see what a mesh he had created there. How come Adrita is too stressed about him and his powers that hampers in her life', Yash said all this and started to find a door anywhere around that place through which he can get into it.

Yash said, 'what a tragic place it is, I am unable to find any way or door to get into it and bull shit........what are these insects were doing at its walls. Are they over here for protection, But I don't feel that they can protect this place'.

'I think whatever Ankit said would be rigorous and no one is being present at this place. So that Barrack can carry out with his mysterious work inside', Yash said this to himself as no one was over there apart from empty land and big poisonous insects crawling on the wall of Barrack residing place.

Yash was getting late now. Ultimately after seeking a lot and going round the Tomb many times Yash came to see a small space on the wall which shows lining over it and was covered with dried twigs. This was the thing that makes him in dilemma about it as the whole place all around so rich in greenish behaviour, so then why here he leg all this. Yash made his steps move faster towards that wall and immediately those crawling insects on wall came altogether close to that specific place in the sense they were not going to allow him to get inside. This time Yash was profoundly sure of the datum that there could be a way behind these dried twigs.

Yash said, 'I think it would be difficult for me to get in as these insects are too viral and are kept here to halt. I need to find a way to get in soon. For this I need to betray these all or do any other mechanism because I need to go today inside anyhow.'

Yash said while being in vein that 'I think I can enter it from back side as I had seen the same scene like this over there too, but there is pond attached to it in which all black big fishes are present. I think it would be much difficult for me to get inside from that side. I have to try from this chance only'.

These perilous insects doesn't settle to allow him to go in at any cost. After searching a lot Yash felt that he can only govern all these with one of natural power because over here every natural power is too pure and well nourished as it directly comes from God Grievance. So he started to look around by which natural force would be able to make them leave that way for him to get in.

Yash saw some rocks with dry mosses lying nearby that place as the wall was also cover with dried twigs. So Yash smiled and said; 'My god solved my problem and shown me a way.'

Yash said, 'I am going to use these banging rocks and mosses to make a fire and I think fire is going to solve out my problem'.

Yash did what he said and when he was unable to burn those mosses by the rocks sleave that he was creating again and again.

Yash said, '*Hey* let me do now something more erotic. I am going to try to burn these loose twigs which would also help me to get rid of from all these insects. Now I am going to get into it and see who is Barrack.......and all that. Let's see whose he....'

Yash felt, 'Now what's this, why this heavy tone of drum striking inside, settle like many person were there inside who were striking drums'.

'But firstly I need to get in then only I could see what is been happening there', Yash said. This time Yash came to smell a stinking air at that place which also becoming unresistible for him. So that's why he's seeking his best to get in as soon as possible.

Yash crack to burn up those twigs and as he came close to it. Insect over there started shouting and falling down from that wall in the sense to halt him coming closer to the wall. Yash tried a bit harder to make him safe from these poisonous insects. As he knows that if no one can wreck any other person in this Heaven's Hell but these are insects and they could wreck anyone as there is no restriction to them.

Yash said, 'I think this is only the reason why Barrack is having only animals and insects at this place for protection purpose. I have to deal safely with this'.

I have to make my pattern more sophiscated and precise.

18

At last, after assaulting a lot to burn those twigs and making himself safe from those insects he ultimately got succeed in burning all those terraces and twigs over the wall. All this had given an explosion of fire all around that wall and it helped Yash in a way that all insects moved away from that place as they couldn't resist the heat and smoke of that fire. Yash wrist that door which is being too heavy for him to open also but he wrist it and gone inside.

Yash moved inside and there was smile on his face while getting in, which settle like he is very fearless of whatever he is doing this time.

Yash looked upward and said, 'Adrita…stay with me…help me'. Yash saw that this whole space inside is profoundly covered with dark shelter and there is no lightening seen inside no way to go so explicit to be seen.

The center space is profoundly vacant and some light is falling downwards at that place only. This settle like light is focusing that central space which being surrounded by the pillars in a circle from all side. There is a small space that left by these pillars on its outer ends which is the way for anyone to move around and reach to the stairs. These stairs are present inside the Tomb at its four sided corners. The atmosphere over this place is making Yash scared as the tone of striking drums he had listened when he was forth the tomb, now this tone is becoming heavier and difficult to listen. The indigestible thing this time for Yash is that there is no one present at this place who would strike drums as he felt forth. Drums are also not seen inside this place which is making him more implication about it. Breeze of air is flowing inside this space and that too with so heavy speed because of which Yash can conveniently listen to the tone of flowing thrashes of air inside. This is also uncertain to understand that from where this breeze is coming as if this is a closed space in a curve from each side.

Yash is still standing at the door and watching all these unusual things happening inside. As much he is asking about all these things from himself, he is unable to get any answer as all this things he had seen were deliberately new to his life.

Yash started spirit scary now as he couldn't gather datum behind anything that is being happening over there. This is because the reason too that no one is present all around in his aura and he couldn't even see Barrack anywhere around for whom he came at this mysterious place. Yash crack to a quaise all those thing inside that he had listened about Barrack from others. Yash moved towards his left side from where he could be able to see the entire circular track behind the pillars all around. Yash realised whatever he had listened about Barrack from others is rigorous as he came to see number of sculptures covered with cloth were being spread on this circular corridor.

Yash said, 'ok.....these are the all comrades of Barrack and inside these he keeps them. May be they would look me over here or could realise presence of any vague person at this place', Yash felt all this and bend on his knees, curled his body and hide himself behind a small short wall connecting every pillar. After bending down he realised that these are spiritless sculptures and can't see anything as per said by them. Barrack just uses them to keep his comrades here which could not get into anyone else notice.

Yash said, 'What I am doing....... is acting like dumb. These are just sculptures not beings who can look at my acts'.

Yash came to hear tone of someone from his opposite side as he can feel the tone of footsteps and all this. He moved his head upwards a little so that his eyes could see whose present over there. Yash shocked after having a look of Barrack coming over there from upstairs and he is all alone.

Yash mumered, 'Yes....Here he, he came from upside and what he is going to do. Weather he had noticed me over here or there is any other reason', Yash is in entire stress about all this and just became hopeless because even if this time he will try to leave this place then also he was going to be conveniently noticed by Barrack.

Yash become entirely quiet this time but his breathe tone becoming heavier and higher. Barrack came downstairs and just get inside the central space which is three steps downward from where Yash is hiding himself. Now the place where Barrack was been standing is the entire central space of this Tomb which is circularly cover by pillars from all sides. Barrack is standing now amidst surrounded by all the sculptures placed in the circular corridor which is after the pillar. Yash is hiding himself while bending behind the wall in this circular corridor in front of sculptures. Yash hadn't realised that those sculptures are not just in front of him but they are also placed at his backside positioning too.

Yash was perceptional looking towards Barrack because he wants to see that what he's going to do next. Barrack was standing with his folded hands and bend head settle like he is praying this time.

Yash mumured, 'What he's been doing now and his posture settle like he's praying but to whom, it can't be realised by him'.

Barrack continued to stay in his posture for some time as Yash was perceptional looking towards him and seeking to capture all that he is going to do next. Now this is the time for Barrack to take any action. This time Yash is also not spirit well as he is getting feared from the place where he is and also apprehensive about his friends who were waiting for him from so long.

Barrack wrist his eyes faced upwards looking forward. Yash is now too unable to see the face of Barrack as his face was profoundly black and which covered by black hood. Barrack looked in front for one minute and after that what happened.

The thing that happened over there is out of Yash wanders and its being as much worse as Yash could have felt off. Over here Barrack instantly put his arms in both directions as if he is asking someone to come close to him. Then after that from every part of this circular corridor wherever this Sculptures is being kept, a white substance like a spirit eject from those sculptures and started revolving around this corridor. They were many of them so all together started to move round in a circle around Barrack without looking anything else. The place where Yash is being sitting from his back side too there is a emergence of spirit from the sculpture is being observed by him and when he seen that, then this is the most shocking and scaring time for Yash. Now the ultimate fear could be seen conveniently on Yash face. Every spirit is shouting like anything as if they were too happy to do all this. The shouting and screaming of these spirits is also making Yash more fearful and now this place become like where Yash won't be able to resist even a second.

Yash said with stammering tone 'I think these spirit wouldn't have seen me still as they were seem too happy and are busy in just revolving around one another and that's why I think they hadn't given their look towards me'.

Yash was becoming hopeless now after seeing all this awkward happening in front of him. He won't be able to realise anything now and this time just woke up and run towards the door which he kept open still. Yash gone straight away towards the door because he knows that if he is going to make all this late. Then he won't be able to get out of this place as he is not allowed to be here. Yash is worried as if he had seen now the art and activities that Barrack does personally and this is why he took this step to run away from that place.

Barrack sensed Yash spoiling his work by making a sound and running towards the door, Barrack shouted on him. As Barrack could be able to invoked any force till then he had gone out of his place. This time Barrack is unable to collect energies from these all spirits that he is going to do next. All this is happened because of Yash. So as Barrack lost his concentration each and every spirit now started to move randomly over here and there and now they all started crying so badly to each other. Barrack also moved out of his Tomb to catch hold Yash but till that time Yash had gone far off from his reach and this is the thing that meant Barrack to get in extreme anger.

Barrack started shouting himself at the place to kill his anger as this thing was very much deficient for him, which he can't resist. As Barrack was shouting because he lost his whole concentration and much of his power got wasted because of this. Then after looking the Barrack anger his own spirits got distracted from there way and started following infrequent tracks. Barrack was really wanted to know about this person who made him disturbed from his meditation and spoiled everything in his surrounds. This is because Barrack a fragrance in his air which is also meant by him at his place. This is because of the presence of pure soul person at that place. Barrack wandered about Yash that he is not a normal person who came here like others because the mutation that he meant over here at Barrack place can be not be made by any ordinary being. This is why Barrack uncovered his face that covered by the hood and said with extreme anger. So this time when Barrack uncovered his hood, it looks like there are just eyes on his face and nothing else because they are only shinning and everything else is just covered with dark. Now barrack shouted to say to his spirits that; 'Who this person is, his soul is too pure and he mutate my surrounding. I would like to know about him. You all have to inform about him to me as soon as feasible', Barrack said all this to his spirits around that place as no one else is present over there.

Barrack said, 'This person didn't settle to be a normal one and how did came here. I would like to go in brief of this guy as such a pure soul that he consists and develops when a person took birth not for his needs but for others on his land. I wont to know about him, are you all listening to me', Barrack was saying all this to his spirits only as this time with him no one exists. Barrack settle to get much about Yash and now as he wouldn't able to continue what he's been doing. He makes him to go down on the floor on his knees and made his head to face down towards the floor as he want's to realise that what happened and why.

Barrack said, 'I would like to know about this person from where did he came and why he had been brought up over here. As he could be the person that I can utilise for my tasks because he is the soul that I want so, as he is the person after Adrita on this place who have this kind of functionality. I surely want to know about him anyhow and anyway'.

Barrack replied to air all around his sides, looking towards every where. 'I think whatever I said is explicit to every instinct of air that I meant myself on this place'.

After looking to Barrack anger every spirit all around that place has gone back to there respective sculptures. The climate of the Barrack place is becoming normal and inside his place too as there is entire silence spread all apart. Barrack after this just stood up and started walking back upstairs from where he came and where he have his space to meditate and have ease in peace. Barrack crack to utilise his everyday as much as he could but this time he is not able to make it feasible and that too because of an forth person. This time while walking back to his place, Barrack was not that much stressed as he should be because he felt something at his place which he hadn't felt before. Barrack wandering this in his favour this time that's only the reason how Barrack is controlling himself from worst reactions. Barrack felt a natural pure and well refined blood smell at his place and that is just because of the person who came over there. This is the thing he wants to utilise by knowing about the person and joining him with himself then using his blood and soul, which can impulse his power. As after some time Barrack also got misplaced as he get into his room where as soon as he get in he becomes invisible and out of bound.

Sunny saw Yash running too shuffled towards them as if he is seeking to save himself from someone. Sunny felt something wrong in this thing he diverted Ankit attention towards Yash who is running far from them.

'What had happened to him? I think something wrong had occurred inside with him that's why he's remarks like that. Come Sunny lets go towards him and ask about it', Ankit said to Sunny.

Sunny said immediately, 'Ankit notice that climate is getting normal again and started adherenceing Heaven's Hell beauty now. Would Yash have met Barrack or what had happened? Yes we should go and ask him about it'.

They both moved in the way from where Yash is coming towards them and they also get inside of this place of Barrack. Yash seen his friends coming inside, he made his step faster to reach them and take them also out of this place. Yash shouted on his friends as he seen them too coming inside this place.

Yash shouted '*Hey*....Don't be tensed about me. I am ok......you must go back, don't get into this place'. Yash said it all but it settle like they hadn't listened to whatever he said because they were still getting inside this place.

Yash tried harder to get him and his friends out of this place and said 'Come.....just come out....come out with me don't stay at this place it's not safe'.

Yash said this to his friends and hold their hands with both of his palm to take them out with him. Yash felt cure when he succeeded in making him and his friends to get away of this place.

'*Hey*....Yash now what.........why are you acting like that. Tell me first that Ankit says it been right for you. We are just coming to help you out and to probe if you were stuck in any hossile and you had put us back this place with you'.

Yash replied, 'You all consists a base for my love and I don't want you to be wrecked because of me'.

Ankit said, 'Yash halt talking like all this. I think you both are the same. You both are just talking about things that are worthless. Main concern is to be about what you had faced inside not about what you did, you are getting my point Sunny'.

Ankit replied again insistently 'Yash you should tell me first are you ok?......and what you faced inside and somebody is following you for which you are running like that.'

Yash said with a tired and fatigue on his face, 'My dear please don't be in stress first of all. I am going to tell you all about the situations I had faced inside. But for now..........please lets us all leave this place as it could led us in trouble if someone seen us'.

Ankit said, 'Ok.....relax first. Yash......we'll get out of this area and going to move towards residence. You just relax yourself'.

There has seen a bit discomfort and stress on his face which can conveniently measured on Yash face.

They all reached to their room where Soni and Gaurav are being waiting for their arrival from that place. Soni saw these three of them coming towards the door.

Soni said loudly, 'Where......where were you all been. You didn't inform that it would be going to take that much time. Do you even know how much apprehensive we are about you all. Ankit I don't think that you can do like that', Soni said this as he and Gaurav clucthing there feet and palm for them and about their absence for a long time.

Yash get inside the room first and again he clubs hand of Ankit and Sunny in his both palm and put them inside as if he is in hurry to do something.

Yash said, 'I don't want any disturbance or forth subsidy to come and disturb us in whatever I am just going to tell you'.

Yash replied again, 'Soni and Gaurav I do know that you are also tensed while being thinking of us as we came so late. I would like to tell you both also that all this happened just because of me only. Now I am going to share with you all whatever unnatural and mysterious thing I had faced over that place for which even Ankit and Sunny were apprehensive'.

Ankit said, 'Ok......dear feel easy first you can tell us after wards also because I don't feel that you are profoundly ok to do so'.

Yash said, 'No my dear, I am profoundly alright this time and the thing that I am going to tell you all should be known to that'.

Yash replied again, 'I need a favour from you all that till that I get finished up with whatever I want to inform you all. Nobody is going to hamper me in amidst and that's explicit I think'.

Everyone now very much desperate to know all that Yash faced at that place, so they upholded a complete silence and no disturbance created all around. Yash started to explain everyone whatever he faced at that chance because he wanted his friends to realise and make picture in their mind that what this man Barrack is all about. Yash crack to tell them the whole sea-bang and make them realise that how hyper this is getting to Yash at that present time and how he dealt with all that. It took a lot time for Yash to describe all that he faced over that place and his friends were to adherence to listen that all as it settle they all were profoundly lost in the words said by Yash. Every one of them is realising this thing very explicitly. Ultimately Yash got finished off with everything that he wants to instruct his friends and gone towards a corner of this room and sat on a chair lying there.

Soon Ankit replied, 'I am too happy today'.

Everyone shocked to listen that from Ankit. Yash also started looking Ankit with his open and questionable eyes. As if how a person could be happy about it.

Ankit replied '.....I am happy because today my dear friend Yash had told me everything explicitly that he hadn't done before anytime'.

Yash said, 'Is it like that'.

Ankit said, 'Yes my dear'.

Ankit replied to made reaction of everyone normal and worriers as after had been listening to whatever Yash told them. Ankit said;

'I feel you all should not be thinking about all this much as we all know that if we are not going to indulge in anything nothing could wreck us. So just relax now and I think everyone should relax as we all got tired after this whole long tiring day'.

Ankit replied again, 'Yash I think you too should come and relax now'.

Yash this time had come close to the window and was memorising all that he faced at this place. Yash is also wondering about all those things that he faced in this short span of time. As Yash had met with a lot incidences and also started getting attached and mixed to this place because everything over here attracts him. Every creature over here starts getting somehow mixed or attached to him. When Ankit said him to relax, he didn't listened to him first as he was lost somewhere.

So Soni replied, Yash is you listening to us and where were you lost. We got the point that you faced with an abnormal accident but leave that all now as this is not a normal place. May be we had bear things more in the forthcoming days'.

Yash came profoundly inside their residence so that they all can take ease together and make them relief from the stress and anxiety. Yash didn't said anything now and started to take ease with his Friend's. After having all these conversations they all said in their room at there respective place.

Yash Rythms—

"The lights have become so avouch, that I started believing on whatever they said at this unveiling breeze.

Now I start believing on them even if they say to trust a slough.

This surround is so isolated but what can I say as it overhauled me with staking beauty blunders.

Viscous spirits with necklaced sorrow encouraged me to enlighten my mount peak with those flower of happiness that never borrows.

I started managing to walk on a way but that is very Ahead of me and presented as an indispensable way, which I need to follow without any pray.

They adorn it so in a way, which is according to yours feel that evokes from your inside, in yours intellectual way.

This wakes my spirit of love which I had buried much deeper in the crust as if I won't be able to hear even a single sound of my love birds.

This place acquired those love spirit so close to me in a very merry way, as if I had to clasp it in my arms with a face of calm in my shiny day.

I started swiveling those track which I never even realised. This started making to get over those paths which I had never worth and never priced.

These all were seeming less heading me with all sorts of power and a crown heading on me, for which I need to pay love bribe.

I am not alone to verge at this place, as if I am having my helpful hands of boys in my way. Some foots are over shadowing my pleasure for which my boys ever crack to shun me.

My vacant life had never sensed that I would get all this in adhesion cover, which stayed with me every time and I didn't realised as if before, now I am not its believer.

Love too hadn't shut his door for me, it is just being who leg all this in his way and then too he dispraised me.

This is just being this place that evoke my consciousness to believe that I am not been a left corner, as I am having a life which is being precisely obdurate by God.

So I am not miserable about my life as if Heaven's hell is the only place that had make me feel about my life very stimulus and pride.

I am glad to be here for this as if it helped my silence stuck inside the eyes to compete with tempestuous heavy tides. For which I thanks to heaven's hell for coming to me as my power Bride".

5

Gracious Cover

"Skeleton of every person still smiles after everything ruins off, so apart from this what could be the best example of God desire of happiness towards his slaves (Human being)".

19

Last night was too dark as Yash not able to sleep for a long time after getting back to his bed. Yash friends were too implication about the last day scene that Yash faced. They were in last night because apart from Ankit everyone wants to know it all whatever Yash faced and scene both in Prison and Barrack estate but they couldn't as Ankit didn't allowed them to ask much from Yash. Ankit was also correct in his concept as he don't want Yash to think much about whatever he faced, as if Ankit Knows about Yash's intention and spirit the most. Ankit knows that if Yash is going to think about a particular thing so much then he started tempting towards the same and work accordingly. Ankit didn't said that but he also knows that one issue of Yash created over here is also not explicit that's of priest girl because Ankit came to realise that now Yash attracted towards priest girl. Ankit knows that Yash concerned about priest girl. Yash desperation conveniently measurable by Ankit at the time he told them about the night meet with priest girl 'Adrita'. When Yash told them about her there was a glory of happiness and wreck on his face, which Ankit noticed as one who is with Yash since birth.

The next morning time and the forth look was incredibly awesome as every day. As no one soy last night in a good mood and that's why no one wants to leave there bed first. This time Sunny and Soni wake up earlier than others and were just looking towards each other as if they were also asking question from each others about wonders to be seen in this place next. They both doesn't wants to leave there bed and wake up others as if they are also spirit restless still. Soon Yash realised that sun was shining forth and this was the peak time for him to wake up. Yash left his bed moved towards door and started looking forth again but this time he was having a smile on his face. Sunny saw Yash standing and laughing at the door. Sunny felt a bit awkward and speedily left his bed gone towards Yash and commencing stairing him as he is smiling still. Yash even doesn't felt that Sunny is rising just close to him.

Sunny asked, '*Hey* for what you are being smiling like that....?'.

Yash replied while stabilising and smiling in the same status '....See whose there on the door'.

Sunny asked, '......what is this...why Ankit is sleeping over here forth the door and that too on chair....what and why all this...?'.

Yash said, 'You are not going to know him. I had been with him since my infancy and knows that why he's been over here for the whole night'.

Sunny, 'What......ok then tell me too that what he is doing here'

Yash said, 'Sunny... you had also seen Ankit's caring nature that how he cares about everyone. He makes every measure to cure us whenever he feels like we are in difficulty. I think this time he's doing the same'.

Sunny, '*Hey*...really Yash I didn't get a single thing whatever you said, could you please tell me all this explicitly'.

This time Ankit is being sleeping on chair which is just lying near at the doorstep of their room and one thing more is over there that is Ronu also present whose liking Ankit's foot and he's not even realising that.

Yash giggled and said, 'My dear....The thing is that because of yesterday as everything that happened with us was not a normal one. So I am sure that Ankit would be thinking all that till late night sitting forth and then sleept on this same chair. As soy last night. Wait I'll wake him up'.

Yash prompted again '*Hey* Sunny I am getting everything else but what is this Ronu has been doing near Ankit's foot and how his devotion towards him'.

Sunny replied,'Oh!......this....he's the same dog we met the first morning of ours over here. He came daily in the morning at the field just in front of ours room. You know that from past many days we all were being familiar to him and he's being to us as if we all loves him, plays with him every morning. You know even Ankit commence liking him and that too a lot, which you can conveniently measure by the love that he's giving to him. *Hey*...Yash but I didn't get this why had you called this dog as Ronu'.

Yash listened to all this and felt too good about all and said that 'nice...to see that with me. Everyone is also too familiar with Ronu' after thinking Yash replied to Sunny.

Yash, 'Yes...dear I called him Ronu as this is his name and you would be thinking that how do I came to know his name. So I would inform you that he came into prison where I had been kept and there I met him and got to know about his name and all. I also loved him and spared some time with him that day when he came in my prison'.

Sunny in confusion asked, 'But how could he came over there as no one is allowed to came inside prison, Figo informed us'.

Yash said, 'I think we should not talk on this now.

Yash came close to Ankit and looked towards Ronu. Ronu identified Yash as they met before and Yash devoted his love towards him so soon after realization of this entirely. He stood excitingly into Yash arms as if he knows him from a long time. Yash left Ankit and started rubbing Ronu's head as if Yash also loves him a lot. They both seems to be very happy to get each other company but abruptly a sound of hammering metal came and Ronu got too attentive. Ronu without thinking anything else just ran too far away from Yash settle like this sound is a call for Ronu.

Yash saw Ronu till he got vanished from his eyes.

'Ankit...........Ankit my brother wake up.......see where are you sleeping.........Ankit...wake up dear', Yash called Ankit two three times by rubbing his hands and head. So do thereafter Ankit get in consciousness. Ankit realised the place where he is been sleeping for the whole night.

Ankit said, '*Hey* I had been sleeping here for the whole night........afraid. I didn't even felt that....and you all wake up'.

Yash said, 'No so....Me and Sunny are here and others are sleeping yet. I had seen you lying like this over here and started smiling on that'.

Sunny said, 'They both also wake up and just lying like a napkin on their bed'.

Yash while surge inside in the room as he wants to talk everyone about the days they spend over here when Yash was in the prison. He said, 'Ankit you too come in.......Gaurav and Soni leave your bed now, I want to talk all of you'.

Yash replied, 'I feel that you all had blistered every moment over here in my absence too'.

Sunny said, 'What...you are saying man........in your absence that was a much critical time for all of us as you were not over there who is our beam strength' Sunny replied.

Ankit said 'Yash do you know the reason why we are brought up over here at this place'.

Yash replied very conveniently, 'Yes......just to be punished and get aware about the fact behind God norms'.

Ankit said, 'what kind of punishing thing we had beard over here say'.

Yash said, 'Apart from me I don't think so that you all had beard anything wrong over here and I do also punished for my rules breakage at this place'.

Ankit said, 'Yes that's what I tried to inform you. Now you should know that the reason being we had brought up over here is to guide humanitarian norms and about the actual role of human beings in making God meant world like a heaven. So these all things to be taught to us and that are the soul motive of them to call us on this place. You know that we all has attending classes of the same by Mr. Christoper sir in the town hall with all beings present at this place, since you were not here and today you do need to come with us for the same'.

Yash said, '....But......I can't think what these classes are going to be all about and I don't feel it's been required for me to go there'.

Ankit said, 'Why....Why you are not going to come with us but if we are going for that how can you deny for it'.

Yash laughed, '....*hey* I am just kidding. As you asked in a manner you are being worried about my decision to go or not. So I just wanted to look your expression for my concern'.

Yash replied, 'So say when we need to go...........and firstly these two crocodiles should wake up then only we all would liveried up and go for that', Yash said about Soni and Gaurav in his this text.

Ankit said, 'Yes they'll wake up and don't tensed because they know that to reach late over there would be going to bear a punishment'.

Sunny laughed, 'Yes...who can forget that guy last days punishment as being late to class room. He was kept like noose in the sky without any balance for the whole day till the class goes on'.

Yash said, 'Oh!....is it like that. Ok my dear let we all just get inclined for it and move towards this town hall because I don't want to come in hit list of punishments every time'.

After this morning stuff they all get well liveried up to go towards Town hall. This is the place that not known to Yash as he never listened about it over here nor visited that place. Yash was silently curious to know about this place so he asked Ankit before leaving there room.

Yash asked, 'Ankit...dear please guide me a little about Town hall. What is this place looks like and its features'.

Ankit said, 'I know....And expected that curiosity about that place in you. I was just wondering that from the time when I'd informed you about the place you hadn't asked me a single thing about it. Ok......listen I'll tell you that this place is a space which is profoundly meant for all of us slaves, who being brought up over here. This is the place that do consist everything that we want. Town hall place is where God's worship in different manners being done and classes like we had in school also goes on over there at the upper zone. There were several class rooms and several teachers for that, who come and guide us the concepts of human being and living life'.

Ankit replied, 'Apart from all that this is a place nearby which you have a big market area spread up in a long distance and where you can have everything up to your desire. This is the place meant for relaxation and blissful concerning all of us. Here you can see and have those things that you even didn't listened about because this is the market meant for all of us being come from apart planets with differentiate needs. You would be amazed to see everything over there. That said to me by Figo as we had also didn't visited that market place. As we all just attend classes and come back to our room and nothing else'.

Yash was amazed about listening for a place like that over here and as he become desperate to see anything he leg extra ordinary, so same in his reaction to be seen for Town hall.

Soni said, 'Aren't we getting late now......because this doesn't seem good to me when you all talk at the doorstep so much while going somewhere'.

Smile evokes on everyone face after listen to Soni as he said this just because to show them that he is also punctual and can get liveried up in time. Soni was seeking to get a chance to blame his friends as if his friends taunt him every time whenever he did wrong. Soni smiled after he got to know that his friends catch the thing he tried to say.

Sunny said, 'If Soni is becoming punctual we need to adherence him in that', and laughed on it.

Ankit said, 'Ok....ok lets be concerned and go to the class it's been high time'.

They all started to move towards Town hall and as Yash didn't know about the way to reach that place he was following Ankit and others. After some time they came close to the place and Yash saw that a big crowd of beings living at Heaven's Hell were surge towards the same. So he asked Ankit;

'Is it like that we are going to attend classes with all of them and they are going for that only'.

This time the crowd that Yash had seen much creature he didn't even seen at the time of prayer too.

Ankit replied, 'Yes you inferenced right this time, these all are our classmates'.

Yash said, 'See all these creature structure, no one is similar to anyone. Everyone is profoundly apart; it looks like we are going to study in Zoo with apart varieties of animals'.

Ankit said, 'I don't feel that and expect from you Yash to talk like that, do you know if anyone from them is going to look around. We all too, what do you feel if he is going to feel the same as you do'.

Yash felt guilty, 'Dear afraid...extremely afraid and you know that I just said it in the sense to pass smile to others not to heart anyone emotion. Still I am afraid as we are not allow to say comic things to anyone's creation. I do understand that'.

Everyone were again in efficacy as the person Soni who everyone has to guide every time, he was guiding others today.

They all get in and gone to the top floor of the Town hall building where today's lecture is going to occur. Everyone took their specific seats and Yash didn't get any seat vacant nearby his friends, so he had to sit at the back near glass window. Everybody started waiting for Mr. Cristofer who is going to take their today's class. Yash was seeking to adjust himself in this aura like everyone. As this was his first lecture and everyone over here is profoundly apart creature.

Yash wake up from his place gone towards Sunny and said very slowly in his ears 'Where is Figo over here, he is nowhere to be seen'.

Sunny said slowly in his ears, 'He is not in our class and you please don't come and speak like that now as all this is not allowed here'.

Yash moved his head in the sense to say yes to Sunny and gone back to his place. There stood entire silence in the room and Mr. Cristofer hadn't came yet. Everybody is just waiting for his arrival and reading out the thoughts that he had given to them all day before yesterday when they had last lecture. Yash was not present that day and his friends too didn't took that material along with them. So Yash can't borrow that from his friends too and this is very tough for Yash to sit like this ideally. Yash is seeking to make him calm and sit over there without uttering anything. Suddenly Yash seen an old man walking through the door of his class room, he leg him someone whom do he knows but could realise immediately. Yash lost his pat ions that he uphold and ran towards the door to find out who had just crossed the door. Yash said;

'Sir......listen.......sir'. After this, person whom he's calling turned backward and Yash felt happy there is a smile on his face as he realised the person now.

Yash replied again, 'Hello.......sir....You are here, as I know that you didn't came with us inside and we felt that your duty belongs to outside of this Heaven's hell. I had crack to met you also because I want to ask several things from you but you are nowhere to be seen inside'.

Yash said all this as this time he met the priest who brought all of them over here, he is so excited that he left his classroom door and gone towards the priest.

Priest said, '.......yes my child, I think you didn't get that and felt wrong about it. I go to "Earth surface" only to receive the people whom do God wants. But don't feel that I don't stay here. Whenever there is my need I come and perform my work as per you all. Anyhow I am also a slave of God and work accordingly to him. I think you should go back to your class as Mr. Cristofer is just going to arrive. I am also going for take lecture in other classroom'.

Yash said, 'I am just going but sir I want to ask something's from you about my being at this place. I am feeling those emotions and devotion's in me that I hadn't felt anytime in me over there at "Earth surface" but here they were coming and making me weaker. My friends are very much easy going over here but why did I do and concern those things over here that I never matter anytime at "Earth surface". Priest if it's happening with you there would be a reason. Anyhow and I feel that won't be able to tell you more about it.

Priest looked towards Yash face and tried to make him feel easy by revealing him that 'Dear boy....You just have to know about yourself that you are the savior in this world and you have to purify everything that you see. This is your world and please don't think that much about anything else'.

Priest added in his words 'everything is a phase of life like you are going to participate in the sketch making Art that would be going to organised tomorrow'.

'What.......is the Art about pencil sketch and why did you tell me about that'.

Priest said, '......I am leaving now dear and I told you because I know you are a solemn sketch maker. You should take part in that. Feel that it's a new Phase of life and I had told you before only that everything is previously decided'.

Yash couldn't get whatever he said but he just understood that priest was saying him to be normal to every situation. priest left that place and said Yash to go back soon to attend his class. Yash came back to the class and as soon as he seated on his bench immediately Mr. Cristofer came inside the classroom and pointed towards Yash.

Mr. Cristofer said to Yash '*Hey* you......You are new to this class, am I rigorous'.

Yash hesitatingly said, 'Yes...I am new one'.

Mr. Cristofer, 'Ok...today you are not going to sit on bench else. You are going to perceptional look at the point that I am making over here at this corner of the board. I think it's ok to you'.

Yash wouldn't able to realise that what did he had done and why all this is happening with him even his friends are in dilemma. Mr. Cristofer said all this in a manner which is too swift and too simple. There settle to be energy spreading up in this aura because of his arrival and that's why this climate also started acting in a way to adherence him. This is the reason why Yash doesn't have any words to say him and he just said, 'Ok...I will'. Yash friends were wondering that why didn't Yash asked anything from him as Yash never listen to anyone without any concern.

Mr. Cristofer greeting his all students, 'So children, today I am going to tell you about your internal energies through which you could make your soul calm and cure which would indirectly going to increase your power with which you all could help others. All this I am saying to you because whenever your soul is safe then no bad things can come in touch with it and your ultimate goal belongs to uplifting humanity if you want too. So children as per your actions for which you all were pitch fork into up over here. I would say that you want to help humanity. Am I rigrous'.

Everyone present over there said in one tone 'Yes.....sir'.

Mr. Cristofer 'difficult to listen from you all. Well let's start this lesson today which will plough a seed in each one of yours planet in the form of you, who will be going to work against in human nature'.

Yash was perceptional seeking to make his concentration towards the point. Yash came to realise something internally when he is performing all this. An extreme power inside him being evoking and hitting his top head point after being generated from his foot. Yash had faced this thing five times in an hour. Now his concentration is becoming too fortifier as time passes. Mr. Cristofer is happy to see all this about Yash.

Mr. Cristofer said to class, 'I am today going to tell you all about 'Aura (a hidden curve around human skull)' and 'Chakras' these covers were the salient part and comes under the integrated internal energy fields which we have to control and work accordingly'.

Mr. Cristofer said—

'Humans are a Body, Mind and Soul, or Spiritual Being;

And parts are run by energy fields all together.

We have an Integrated Energy Field often profiled as The Aura.

The Integrated Energy Field known as the surrounding. A number of layers that not only surround us, they also circulate our body and cells. The apart layers or fields within our Auras each have apart purposes. To understand the emphasis of the surrounding. Our Mind is made up of mainly two parts our Brain the conscious part. This in computer terms, could be profiled as "The Hardware" and parts of our surrounding which would be equivalent of the "Software", work together. The Aura also has a retentions of everything that has ever happened to us, not just in this life. It is also the most emphasis part of our immune system. The correct function is vital for good health and well being. Disturbances of those Energy Fields are a precursor to all disease, illness and problems with our mental and physical well being'.

All creatures present in the class were too silent as they are seeking to grasp whatever being said by Mr. Cristofer.

Mr. Cristofer added 'Now let me tell you about 'Chakras' which is very emphasis for you all to know about–

We also have seven salient Internal Energy Fields often known as Chakras.

The seven salient Internal Energy Fields control the function of all our organs and everything else in our physical bodies.

These are:

1. Base Chakra (base of spine)
2. Sacral or Sex Chakra (Groin Area)
3. Solar Plexus Chakra,
4. Heart Chakra,
5. Throat Chakra,
6. Brow Chakra (Forehead)
7. Crown Chakra (Top of the Head)'.

This time as class was going too smoothly and Yash was too lost in looking towards the point mentioned by Mr. Cristofer. Yash this time spirit too smooth and energised in doing all this but suddenly Yash came to listen tone of some children that was coming from downward direction. As Yash being standing close to the window so that voice was coming straight away directly to him. Yash being too close to children's because he likes them the most in this world, it was becoming a bit difficult for him to make him doing the work that he was supposed to. Yash was listening to this tone repeatedly after every second which was making his task more difficult but he is still performing that with full grace. Ultimately a tone of a girl came to Yash ears, who had been playing with those children and guiding them about some drawing sketch purpose. Yash wont be able to get what this tone was all about but this time he wouldn't able to control his concentration to get violated. There seems to be a smile came on Yash face this time as he listened the tone. This is the peak time for him as he was unable to control himself to see whats going over there downwards. So lastly Yash attention diverted to see downward from the window glass which was extremely close to him. As Yash moved his head down to see that all, he stuck to see that whatever he's felt it's been that only.

Yash listened the tone of a girl, his mind said him that she is Adrita over there but he wandered that may be its not truth as his emotions are too fortified for Adrita that's why his mind felt that. So to avoid his wooliness he just had a look and saw that anyhow. He wasrigorous and happy for that which dispersed smile on his face. Looking those entire Yash immediately came back to stand in the same position looking towards that point as he was doing before. Yash was spirit scared about his this act and also don't know the reason behind his fear that why he was too feared from Mr. Cristofer as he hadn't feared from anyone before. Yash now stood in the same look and feel but there was smile on his face still after looking forth. Everything is going normal and lecture was also going in the same way. Yash took a relaxing breath when he realised that no one had seen him looking forth. Yash was happy and wanted to know what was going on ground street over there as he saw Adrita too at this place.

Mr. Cristofer while facing towards the board as he was writing something on it said to Yash 'Yash get out of this class I can't bear you more'.

Yash got extremely afraid after listening to what he said.

Mr. Cristofer turned back and said again, 'Yash I didn't wandered, that today whatever I am teaching all of your class member. I should teach you also and do you know why I felt that'.

Yash said, 'No...I don't know anything like that sir'.

Mr. Cristofer said, 'I didn't concerned you for all this because you have everything inclined inbuilt inside you and the need is just to realise it. This is why I crack to give you a practice so that you could know who you are and what all internal energies you have. I am afraid now I don't want you in my classes'.

Mr. Cristofer 'Afraid my dear don't speak up anything now and just get out soon. Now I don't want to see you in the class'.

Yash won't be able to say anything about all this and he just left his place and gone out of the class without disturbing anyone else. Class started again in its usual manner when Yash left the class. Yash was standing just forth the door of his class only. Yash was spirit like it is been going to happen as in childhood days that Mr. Cristofer would see him stressed and with dull face standing forth and call him inside again. This didn't happened as Mr. Cristofer didn't even cared for Yash being standing there. So at last Yash wandered that he is wasting his time and he should be down-steps this time with all those kids and Adrita. Yash ran to reach that place where he saw her with childern's. Yash reached over there and saw that she is nowhere to be seen all around as there is just children's who are making drawing and sketch at that place. Yash had gone towards that person standing nearby and seems to be care taker of all these children's.

Yash asked, '*Hey*....Hello...could you listen to me, I have a question could you please answer', Yash said this to the person and he didn't replied.

So Yash asked again, '...could you listen to me...please tell me whats going over here at this place as I can see everywhere around its been art of these childrens spread apart'. This person who is busy doing children small stuff and helping them out responded to Yash;

'Yes...say...and let me tell you first, I have a name that is frank. So could you further proceed by taking my name? And as such you are asking that what is being going on over here. So let me tell you that these all are practicing for tomorrow as there is a drawing competition'.

Yash asked, 'Ok... I am going to take your name now...is this ok. You said about competition, what kind of competition is all about....?'

Frank said, 'Actually this competition is not for these children's. It's a competition that occurs after every season over here in which no. of artist and solemn painters participate. You know that in this competition who ever is going to make the perfect and auspicious art then that person is awarded in the sense that whatever is his will that comes true'.

Yash said, 'Ok I see, but could you tell me where that girl had gone, who being standing over here with all these children's and guiding them'.

Frank asked, 'For whom you are talking about.....that pretty girl, head of all priest girl 'Adrita'.

20

Yash went toward the Art field of Children's to meet and play with them as children's were a part in Yash's life who makes him happy and brings a smile on his face. You can assume that by knowing he was foster of many childrens on "Earth surface". Yash started playing with those children and allotted his funny feelings with them to make them smile. Suddenly someone kept his hand on Yash shoulder and as Yash hadn't seen anyone at its back, he became scared of it. Yash asked himself that who used come like this without any sound and can put hand on his shoulder. He wants to know this, instantly he looked backside lightened.

'*Hey* why were you asking about me from Frank, and what did you said him too.', Adrita said as she listened to Yash when he was aking about her from Frank.

Adrita said to Yash, 'I had seen you coming from a long distenace and that's why I moved away from this place as if somebody would see both of us together. This is ultimately going to blame me anyhow as I am the member of this place.

Adrita replied again, 'But can I ask you why you were asking about me when you came here. What was been so urgent for you to ask for me from someone else. I think we know very much about each other so why did you asked any other person about me. Do you know if he felt this thing in any different manner then it would be a lot critical for me? It doesn't matter its's your place "Earth surface" or my place Heaven's Hell rules are rules and that remains same for everyone and need to be followed'.

Yash was listening to Adrita perception big speech which he never did anytime with anyone else.

'Don't you think that you are revealing me all those things that are exclusively out of bound? I think you memorises a lot about every single incidence or your it may be like you are following all these rules here and you doesn't like to follow them that's why you are liberating your frustration on me'.

Adrita stammeringly to Yash, 'No...What are you saying about...and...what did you try to say', She wont be able to contact her eyes with Yash while saying all this.

Yash said, 'I don't want to say anything I got my answer...... Thank you'.

Adrita getting esteemed and said, 'You were right and know about my place but I don't want to think about it as I know that wont be able to go there. So there is no need to make a shallow wall that would fall one day'.

Yash said, 'This aid you loves "Earth" place......yes'

Adrita said, Speaking Yes I do...'. She said this and got lost somewhere settle like she started thinking about the place and there was a bit smile on her face too.

Adrita replied being in the same mood with a little smile continued glowing her face and thinking deep about something 'My parents stay there still......', She said all this and get back into consciousness, felt what she said.

Yash started asking bundle of questions from her as he listened the last line she said and Yash replied as 'What...did you said about your Parent.......do they alive and you know about them, tell me..Tell me may I could help you out'.

Adrita felt uncosy as Yash said all this. Adrita replied to Yash, 'Why are you getting into all this I don't understand. I am just leaving now if you want to ask anything else you could because I think when you came first over here, there are some questions going in your mind'.

Yash said, 'Ok...if you don't want to tell then it ok. Yes tell me that is there any competition would be conducted tomorrow. I want to know about it if there any'.

Adrita replied, 'Yes...as in every season there is one sketch and drawing competition being conducted over here and whomever have the best art awarded with his one wish and it could be anything even if he wants to go from here he could'.

'So....I see...then it could be a majestic one I am going to participate in it for sure', Yash said this and as he said this thing Adrita smiled on him and asked 'Do you know...this sort of art'.

Soon from Yash right side a tone came calling 'Yash'... 'Yash'. '...Yash'.

Yash looked towards his right. It was Pojo calling him with a smile. Pojo also started admiring Yash now as his nature is to humble and caring like a right humanitarian person. So as Pojo called Yash, He faced towards him as Yash felt this tone to relevant and known. Yash faced Pojo, Adrita moved away from that place because of which after facing back towards Adrita Yash couldn't find her anywhere around that place. Reaction of Yash was not good to see this as Yash wants to share many more things with her.

Yash said, 'Hay Pojo, you are over here. Afraid I didn't seen you and my dear please don't think wrong about the thing'.

Pojo said, 'For what dear and why are you saying like that'.

Pojo replied again, 'Yash where were you....Had you come here to attend classes or just muffling songs in this weather?'

Yash said, 'Dear the spirit that you have for me being felt by me same for you that's why as I just realised that you said me to meet you as I come out of prison, I didn't felt good but it. So this is why I asked for afraid my dear'.

Pojo said, 'Don't think like that my dear, I even didn't thought about that concern. So you say, you were attending classes over here in Town hall or something else. I had seen you with Adrita and your face define yours happiness after it very explicitly.'

Yash said, 'My dear nothing is like that, its just I had seen children over here and that's why I came at this place. Yes you were rigorous in one concern that today is my first day of lecture and my first throwout from classroom by Mr. Cristofer'.

Pojo said, 'You were send out by him. *Hey* you are like me only as my class is too going there at the first floor see.....and I think my teacher also doesn't wants me to be in class for so long'. Both laughed loudly.

Pojo said, 'You know these children's are brought from every planet and they are not ordinary kids. These all consists of super power in them and God made them take birth on there respective planet and then brought back at this place. So that from there childhood days they can realise the means of humanity and know about there internal power too. So that they become elder and allowed to use them in there respective planets. When they are going to be adults, they will go back to there planet and work for uplifting humanity and spread peace and happiness all around in there space'.

Yash got excited to know all this and said 'Really if it is so then these children's would be much possible and perfect than all of us in every aid'.

Yash waited for certain seconds and replied 'Yes, I think you were profoundly right see....what a kind of energy source being felt over here while standing close to them'.

Pojo is implication and said, 'Energy....What...but I didn't felt that....I know about these children but what about energy you were saying, I didn't realised that. You are also doesn't settle to be normal anytime as if that time in prison you were the only one who didn't faced climatic torcher inside and now you are spirit something that is not being said by anyone before'.

Pojo replied again, 'As you felt this.......then what would I say much about it. Ok Yash tell me that do you know about the competition that is going to be held tomorrow'.

Yash excitingly said, 'Oh!... about that sketch and painting competition. Yes I do know about it and I am going to participate in that too. As Adrita told me everything about it', Yash become silent and lost somewhere as he said the last line where he took Adrita name.

Pojo replied, '....I see, so this is what...about which you and Adrita were talking when I just came but why didn't you told me this before when I had asked you', As Pojo said all this Yash reaction as he become too implication now. Pojo measured reaction of Yash this time and said;

'Ok Park......I am not going to talk in this concern as it doesn't settle by your face that you are going to talk anything about it', after this Pojo change the topic and said;

'Yash do you know that I am also taking part in that, it would be a tough combat amidst you and me. Yash I don't know about your art but don't know why I started believing a lot on you'.

Yash said, 'Lets see dear, but yes the combat would be tough for every person over there I feel so'.

Yash said, 'Pojo I think my friend's class had left off. Dear I need to go now with them as they were finding me. Ok then see you back in the competition tomorrow come prepared'.

Yash said this to Pojo, But he is also not confident about his art because he hadn't came in touch with it since long time, when he started following the track because of which he had to come here. But now Yash feels him lucky to come here and meet everyone executive. Adrita who had evoked that power of love happiness inside him about which he being unaware from a long time. Pojo and Yash both took there way and gone back to there respective place.

Sunny said, 'Yash is over there see. What had he got over there, as he settle to be very much happier while being surge towards them'?

Soni said, 'God known about him he is profoundly apart'.

Sunny said 'who knows last time he was coming from the bus stop in the same style as of today and when I asked he told me that an old lady slapped him that's why he felt good and was happy about it. I got implication to judge what he crack to say. Then I asked him that why he remarks like that on such a thing which shows a bad impression. Yash told me a thing you all don't even realise about that. Listen he said, 'That old lady slapped me as I am unknowingly not allowing her to get inside the bus after that we both are unable to get up on the bus. She slapped me on the bus stop. The time she slapped me her face is looking like my grandmother whom I loved the most. So after that when she left then. There is a smile left on my face remembering my past days' this is what he said, see'...

Sunny replied again to all laughing loudly, 'See... now how can you think about his happiness'.

So as Yash came close Ankit asked, 'Yash why you did like that with Mr. Cristofer and you can even ask for escusing you from him, so that he would allowed you to sit in the class'.

Gaurav said, 'Ok...may be you all feel that I am the biggest irresponsible person in all of us but Yash I do know this, that over here we have peoples from several other space. We need to react in a decent and good manner so that others can also admire our place occurence as it is admirable'.

Yash said, 'I think you all were too serious to take classes over here. Ok........listen I feel that........you all were blissful it as your school. I don't know till this studies trait of you all'.

Ankit said, 'Ok...I feel we had wasted a lot of time over here. We were at this place since a solemn time and because of Yash too we had got very late to go back residence'.

Yash said, 'Thats what just I do want to say you all, Ok come...on guy lets go towards residence'. While walking Sunny said something to himself consisting delight smile on his face that 'just like now, like this Yash does every time whenever he stuck up in some annoyance and don't want to continue any topic. Oh!... god he is a ultimate person, I own all these.'

Yash said, '*Hey* what you all were doing over here, go out and get in touch with this enhancing weather at this place. Why you all are wasting your time by doing a thing that is no use of you all'?

Gaurav replied, 'Yash we have to do the work given by Mr. Cristofer because he will be going to take our lecture tomorrow also'.

Yash said, 'I think you all don't know about tomorrow drawing competition and the whole event. Boys......the best part is that I am participating in this competition.'

Yash added more, 'You don't get shocked about it. The competition is regarding sketch making and I feel Ankit you can tell all these guys my sketch making capabilities', Yash said his last line in full attitude as he is boasting himself.

Ankit laughed when he listened all this from Yash and said' ok my dear.......I will tell them all and anything else you want me to tell them you can say it to me'.

The day passed of slowly and everything around get covered in dark night. Weather was making everyone to get fall in love with it and that's why Yash friends started blissful all that while standing on the door and facing forth, but Yash was busy doing something inside. As this time Yash was busy in practicing for the competition. Yash was designing sketches and everyone was giggling while looking at him and his desperation to do that work. As he was throwing sheet of paper one after the other on the floor because sketches he being practicing were not getting to the mark as he wants. It's been a cold weather this night not like the night before that was warmer. This was why there was a born fire burning inside their room and Yash was sitting close to it, practicing apart sketches on different sheet of papers.

After some time......Yash, mamorised, 'what you all are looking at me......I am really stressful as I am not able to create the thing on paper which I wish too......

Dear I need to practice that as Adrita would also be there and I need to present myself'.

Soni came inside from the door and said, 'What who Adrita. She is that girl about whom you told us before you had gone to the prison. Who she is tell us too about her', Ankit knows about Yash propensity towards Adrita.

Ankit said, 'Soni what had you started now. Leave everything and don't talk about unutilitarian concerns and you all come along with me, leave him stay alone and practice what he wants to'. Soni said, 'But you listened, he just said her name'.

Ankit said, 'Soni leave all this I am saying not.'

Soni said, 'Then...Yash continue with it but brother we will get efficacy when we are going to listen appreciation and applaud tomorrow after the completion'.

Yash said, with a dull face 'ok...just leave me alone for now..... I will try my best for it'.

Soon the night got lost in the Eclipse and everything else become to quite. Everyone were on their bed this time to have ease but trepidation of tomorrow can be seen on their face. After night the competition day had come to rung the bells of Yash room. Today Yash was the first one who wakes up too earlier in the morning and started getting poised for the day. Noise that Yash created in his whole room while getting dressed up had wakes up his all other friends too.

Ankit while being lying on the bed stood upward a little with his one hand 'what happened Yash......don't you think that it's been too early to get dressed up'.

Yash said, 'You know ... today is my exam'.

Ankit said, '..... I know that dear, but it's too early. I feel it would not going to be started at this time'.

Yash said, 'No...you don't know about it and how could you know that as you also don't even know about today's event. Dear I asked them and I got to know that it would be going to be started early in the morning.'

Ankit said, 'Is it so. Then wait for a while let we also come along with you'.

Yash insisted 'No....don't... I am not going to wait for so long as I need to get prepared also mentally after reaching there. Ok...do one thing that you all come over there after me, but come soon and don't be too late to come......ok'.

Yash just told about his departure to the place where this event being going and he said 'yes...I am just leaving ill leg out the place as I know about it a little and I do have some time to reach Town Hall and search for it. You all should ask Pee about that place before coming because I don't want you all to waste your time for finding that place.'

As Yash reached Town Hall it's been early morning and that's why there was fog to be seen spread all apart in the space. Every morning all birds in Heaven's Hell comes to Town Hall and today also they being coming one after the other and getting settled up in the Garden of Town Hall. These all birds collect all together at this place in the morning because priest deliver rice grains for all these birds and he set aside a corner of the garden to watch their activities and there spirit, gesture.

21

Priest was being sitting at the corner of that ground of Town hall and just looking towards those birds who peck those seeds from there tiny master. It seems like priest was too happy while looking to those. Yash came at that place and he also stood still at one side of that ground when he saw a collection of unique looking birds all together at one place feeding them all together and that too in a very decent manner. Yash was carrying his pencil with papers and a big board. priest didn't realised the presence of one more person at that place who was being noticing him and as there was nothing happening still for which Yash came in a rush. So he also gone towards the priest and sat close to him after wishing him 'Good Morning sir'...

Yash asked him, 'These birds do come here everyday and this is your daily routine'.

'To feed them or any other hungry animal is like feeding our soul'. priest said.

Priest said pointing his hand towards the wall which was present at one side corner of that ground, 'don't sit over here the event for which you had came being happening just back of that wall..........and you must go there soon I feel'.

Yash felt happy as he told the way without being asking him where Yash wants to go and he said, '......wonders find of you sir thanks. I just wanted to know this but how could you had known my wanders', Yash said and started surge towards the way priest told him but he was still facing towards priest as if he facet a last nice reply from his side. Yash got to know that everything being prepared over there and competition was just on its edge to begin. Yash make his steps to move faster towards it reach inside. Yash hadn't seen any door or something from where he could enter into that place so he started to crown it all from upside and get into the place as he feels now that he stood late over here. So as Yash reached at the top of the wall. Persons that were inside that field area where this event was conducted stood quite to see that unlawful and ill logical act of Yash as he could come inside by the door meant at just opposite to the place where Yash was seeking to jumping the wall.

At last, Yash get into that park and saw everyone was being present over there, whom all had come to participate and some audience too. This time eyes of everyone was just on Yash as he came to this leave of Town Hall in an untolerable manner like he being unaware of everything and his face was saying the same. Yash explicitly shows that he was not realising that he did a mistake of not opting door to come inside as he came by jumping the wall. Soon a tone being heard from the people that were present over there which says 'Yash...... hey... Yash'. It being Pojo who coming out of the fields towards Yash excitingly.

Pojo said, 'Yes dear you come. You know I am also getting bored here as event is not going to start right now only as there would be some screenings and after that everything is going to happen'.

Yash said, 'Ok.....that's why I see they had done a lot of decoration at this place. This is making me implication and difficult to understand the whole scene. I am getting afraid of all this because see how everyone staring me as I did a big crime'.

Pojo said, 'The way you entered is a big indigestible for everyone. First of all you tell me that how come you had crossed this long heighten wall'.

Yash said, 'This is not the point of discussion Pojo, ... But yes whatever they had done this place is looking so pretty after all this'.

Pojo said, '.....I feel that I had asked something from you and you crack to divert my concern somewhere else. It's ok if you don't want to talk on this topic more but let me show you the exact door so that at the time of passing thought you would go by that. See......at that place where my finger being pointed that's the incoming and outgoing way. Yes...other thing is like that these arrangement were being done in every event over here and you were new that's why you feel so executive and others are in habitual to see all these. Don't ask more question regarding this place just tell me whats your mentality to perform here today'.

Yash said, 'No....dear no such kind of preparation for today. Lets see what would be going to happen next and I do feel that we shouldn't talk about it now lets just go over there where everyone being seated. We should look at all this which is being happening over here so that there is a bit of relaxation before event'.

Pojo said about priest girls to Yash as he want to measure the colour of Yash face after listening about priest girls. He was also sensed about Yash and Adrita and wants to know that. Last time he being unable to gather anything from Yash about it, as he didn't disclosed it off.

The classy atmospheric fragrances was dispersed slightly as time passed off. Yash is becoming excited now as all these cultural screenings that were going around him were very empowering to him, since his infancy days. Yash was handling sketch board captured tightly by his both hands and looking everywhere in his aura. Pojo was sitting next to Yash and he was also looking towards Yash as the craze seen on his face with a sweet smile sleaveling after every second. Pojo also started spirit happier as these all things were not new to him. He had seen all that happening over here many times before. But a comfort coming on Yash face was making him to feel this air once more and flow in the spirit which was running in Yash blood.

Pojo crack to distract Yash attention by making his hand to be on Yash shoulder and said '*Hey,* Yash listen... listen dear'.

Yash facing towards Pojo, 'Yes....*Hey* Pojo I am thinking that, I should come with my friends over here.'

So that they could also come earlier and can capture every moment at this place which were going too wonderful. As if all these things were never seen before and I hope not going to be shown in our further life also'.

Yash replied, 'Pojo don't make that awkward looks. Its just like I am saying this because of the bonding everyone being having with other person over here.

Pojo asked, 'why are you talking like that'.

Yash, 'I am not amazed by the beauty of this place but yes I am really stuck on this thing that I told you just. This is because dear, I don't know about your planet but from mine these all things are getting diminished as the generation passes from one stage to another. Regarding to the beauty I would like to conclude you that our place is also dashing not compatible to this place but Yes its not that much far low than this place'.

Pojo said, 'If you want to say like that, then I must say you dear that in terms of bonding my place is very fine as if anyone over there is connected to someone. He is going to show his pure bonding towards the other person without having any hidden conspiracy in there soul about others'.

This time Yash Friends had come into this confined space that is reserved for this event today.

'Musical sounds are distinguished from noises in that they are composed of frequent, uniform vibration which are meant to give us delight. While noise are infrequent and disordered vibrations. Composers, however uses noises as well as musical sounds, one musical tone is distinguished from another on the basis of pitch, intensity, loudness or quality and timbre.

Quality is dependent on the number and relative intensity of overtones produced by vibrating body and these in turn depend upon the nature of vibrating body'. Yash said to Pojo.

By all these things I just want to tell you about the power of music and that's why it work in both ends and secure his lover's by dug up them out of there sadness. Everything in this world is not easier but music that friend of ours which stand up with us whenever we go close to it and never leave our hand till then we are free from our stress. In our happiness too it doubles up the effect.

Yash said, '*Hey*....who are they and see what they had wore up. Its entire yellowish in colour and see its sleaveling because of falling shine of sun from these top, its really amazing Pojo. I had seen number of dress coats on my land apart count crack and culture but this is something that have meant me speechless'.

'Floor around them also being covered with there dress that is in curly sphere. *Hey* Pojo who are they, why are you not dispersing to me about it, can't you see my excitement to know about them'.

'Is it so, my dear, I am just talking about it and informing you just that......this is the time for priest girls and they are just going to arrive at this place so...My dear these are priest girls only. Then also you are asking me about it', Pojo said.

Yash replied in anxiety, 'How could you say them as priest girl because as much I know they doesn't hide themselves in that posture like a bride. Then tell me that why did they had covered there head and face'.

Yash said slowly to his heart 'Like this how could I am going to identify that who is Adrita'.

Pojo gathered to his heart instant about whatever Yash said to himself, he smiled and said 'Look the girl that is in amidst and holding small umbrella in her hand is Adrita. Now it's ok'.

Yash starring Pojo as he doesn't want him to listen what he said last. Now numbers of small heighten persons like Pojo were standing at the boundary side of that place and they all together instantly get hold of a spray that they were having in there coats pocket. Everyone took out the spray and sprayed it into the atmosphere and made the whole climate full of foggy smoke in the air.

Yash asked Pojo, '*Hey* dear, you are just making me unconscious'.

Pojo faced towards Yash and replied, 'You are a daring guy. I don't feel that you can also feel nervous. Ok my dear listen.....you can see now that the climate is waver now as the spray that being spread by all those Creatures over there is making climate get filled with smoke and this shows the start of today Competition.'

After listening to this Yash and Pojo both faced towards the main stage where all priest girls were present and this time there is a desperation and question in Yash eyes. This is not because of the competition but he wants to see that Adrita is present over there or not as said by Pojo. Till now he's not able to see all that because priest girls face being hidden still. Ultimately after everything that is happening in the surrounding being finished like every game and other parties amidst small groups of people. A gleam of hope is there in his heart, time came for priest girls to remove this '*Hijab*' from their face.

Pojo facing towards Yash face as he also knows about Yash attraction towards priest girls and he wants to see that glow as priest girls uncover there face. Yash expressions tells that there is no comparison of his excitement. Pojo is also happy to see that but he didn't tried to ask much from Yash and also about the name of the girl with whom he got attached so much.

After unveiling face Adrita came two step forward and attracted everyone attention towards herself. She shouted at first and said;

'A warm welcome to all Creatures present over here, come to participate and celebrate this event from my and all the members of Heavens Hell who upholds the integrity of making life standard much higher in all your hearts', Adrita said.

Yash became auspitiously still and started listening to every single word that she is going to spread apart in the air. The crumbling heart of Yash that never halts and relaxes anytime from thinking about some thoughts became still too and he left everything and sat down on the bench lying nearby without surge his eyes from her face.

Adrita continued and said, 'Today is the day, when all of us comes together and does several activities that make all of us close to each other. I feel most of the people from all of you are those who have seen number of events like this before and blissed that too. So I feel other ones also can bliss the same while taking some guidance from you about all the classy spirit that is felt over here', Adrita was differentiating the old people from the new one because she knows this very well that only Yash is the new Creature at this place. So indirectly she is seeking to gather Yash presence at this place and Adrita eyes also settle to do the same, as she is looking sidewise every second while speaking her speech.

Yash friends also came close of this place and certainly Yash came into notice by Gaurav. This time they all were relaxing under terrace where some wooden benches were laying veiling wooden antique tables.

Gaurav said, 'Ankit look Yash is there, we were finding him from a long time and see his presence over there. Look how he is getting entertained by all this'. Ankit faced towards the side where Gaurav is pointing and he said;

What he is doing with that small heighten creature at that place'.

Sunny said, 'Ankit why are you listening to all this nonsense through Gaurav. I think that maybe he had gone off with the competition or that hadn't started yet'.

Ankit responded 'Yes, Sunny I do know that wait...lets go close to him and listen to all that is going on over there. You all come along with me'. Ankit even called Yash many times while coming closer to him but he didn't listened even once. So as they came close to Yash at the place that is deliberately dipped in silence as over here only Adrita is speaking this time. They all came close to Yash calling him by his name. A creature standing there said them not to shout at this place and instantly Pee also came near to them after listening to their tone calling Yash.

Pee said, 'Listen my dear...you all can't talk so loudly over here as there is a speech going on. So do one thing, just be seated over here quietly and after-wards you can talk to Yash. If you want then you can also sit at the back bench of Yash'.

Adrita was speaking about the celebration and event, as she was revealing every person about the mean of organising this sort of event.

This time Adrita eyes were searching Yash presence as up till now. Only Yash knows about her presence but Adrita doesn't knows that Yash is at this place in her front only. After revealing everyone about today event Adrita took a second break and faced towards her left side bench where she left her Ronu last. She came to see that Yash being sitting on the same bench and Ronu is adjusting himself amidst his two foots.

Adrita mumered 'How they both remarks to each other as they were small kids and helping each other to sit comfortably', there was sense of joy on her face now whom she was finding from the start of her speech. Yash was looking perceptional towards Adrita as his dedication towards her was so much desperate. He was lost somewhere looking towards her as he hadn't realised or mutate his expression even then when she was looking towards him.

Adrita started speaking to the crowd 'Now this is the time for competition and let's see who the best is to capture nature's beauty on paper'.

Adrita said looking towards Yash, 'Lets see whose going to trace themselves today and who is the person whom God had praised with divine creativity, swiftness in there wandereds', Adrita said as she came to know about this information that Yash is also participating in this competition.

Adrita added 'Let's see that new forthcoming airs can empower old heavy breeze or they are going to diminish in there first assault', this line of Adrita is profoundly for Yash as she is looking towards him while speaking and smiling a little too.

Yash listening to Adrita's every piece of word very concisely. So as Adrita finished of with her speech Yash stood up from his bench and shouted;

'We all will try to make the new refreshing air to empower old breeze'.

Adrita didn't replied to him as this was against rule and the thing that Yash did just was also against rule. Every Creature over there started staring towards him. Adrita said, 'Ok....Now it's the time for all of you to take your material with you and come down at the opposite end of stairs from where you entire your Art and other crowd is going to settle down opposite to you on the other corner of Stairs. So I feel anyone should not waste the time and cover up there places so that we can start all this with a bell sound'.

Yash friends also covered there area on stairs.

Yash also became attentive and started surge towards the place where other's were going, carrying wooden board and there material in there hands. Everyone settle to be seated after some point of time. Mr. Cristofer arrived at that place to share some words with his children's. There was smile on everyone face while looking towards him which settle like everyone was very happy to see him at this competitive place. But there was one person who was not happy. Yash impression on him was not good that's why he was a bit scared. He could be a lot necklacing for him.

Adrita Conveyed, 'Mr. Cristofer has come here so that he could distribute prizes to the winner's.

Coordinator 'So all of you who are going to participate today sit on your seats. Take out your using material and then start working accordingly your expectation and creative thoughts and all your time starts now...'

Mr. Cristofer realised something instantly and wanted to share that first so he said, 'Wait.....wait everyone your time didn't started now. I wanted to say you something first then you all start working. There is a thought in my mind that I would like to share with you all that it would be much creative if anyone can make the live personality or situation in the Art as that person will surely going to take merit. So this much I would like to share with you all before you all start your natural sketches.'

Yash started thinking as he listened those words from Mr. Cristofer about what live could he make. What is there which he can make without looking towards it. Whose picture is so explicit in his soul that he is not going to fail in this exam.

The time is now passing off every body else started making whatever they know the best. Yash also took his pencil in his hand adjusted himself on the stairs (meant of rocks). Yash seems to be lost when he started sketching and his friends were looking him attentively. They also want to know that what Yash is going to make down.

Ankit said, 'Lets hope for the best, but I am even not having any clue that what would he's going to make there'.

Soni replied, 'I think Yash a number of things going in his mind, may be he would be confused this time'.

Sunny said, 'I feel you both are tensed worthlessly because Yash is to well in decision making that till now he had set his mind for a piece of thing and started working towards it. You all also know that no one can understand and utilise time in a much more furious way as Yash does every-time. That is other thing what he does and how he reacts on things. He is very much concerned to listen what his heart says. Ankit I am saying correct I guess.'

Adrita and other priest girls were there and every person is just waiting for the result as everyone wants to see the creation that all participants were drawing down on the piece of paper.

Yash is profoundly mixed in whatever sketch he is drawing this time and it looks like he didn't even realise now that he being noticed by all Creatures and members of this place. Yash is surge in a circle around his sketch to make it as rigorous as he could.

Soon time passed off now this is the time for Mr. Cristofer to go close to every contestant and have a look over it whatever they meant in that span of time. This time after buzzer is ranged up Yash halted working and it settle from his face that he did what he wants too. Other contestant also dropped there drawing equipments and set inclined to face the results.

Mr. Cristofer started coming close to everyone over there one by one so that he could make a good and concise decision regarding the strategically organised event.

Mr. Cristofer said, 'Now I feel all of you had completed with what you tried to make down. So let finish of this event with announcing the name of winner and for that I need to come at everyone's place and probe out your work in this span of time', Mr. Cristofer said.

Yash said to himself, 'Ok.....this could be helpful to me as I would be from the last one whose creation would be seen by Mr. Cristofer'.

One by one Mr. Cristofer started looking at art and imagination of his contestant that they had performed and he was marking them according to that sidewise. Mr. Cristofer doesn't seem to be happy from his heart to see all this because the thing that he said in the commencing no one worked accordingly to that. He was crossing one by one coming close to Yash and heartbeats of Yash were rising accordingly. At last, after veiling up everyone Mr. Cristofer reached close to Yash. He picked up the art he made and this time Mr. Cristofer smiled, from the time he started judging everyone sketches. He was happy as if the joy that was coming on his face is directly through his soul and it explicitly shows that he is happy to see whatever Yash assaulted to make.

Mr, Cristofer saw that it's been a human sketch which is meant by Yash and that too so well finished, which gives us the actualization of the person standing in front of you. As Mr. Cristofer told everyone in the beginning about his expectations from the entire contestant. He wants an art which would evoke our hidden spirit and emotions. He expects a kind of art that consist of real life image in it and can explain a lot without asking of anyone. Yash was exactly in the desired direction that he expects.

Mr. Cristofer 'I am happy to share this thing with you all and inform you about this creation that is with me right now. I am totally amazed to see whatever he meant over here. This is not just the portrait but it's revealing a whole story behind it. The thing I am revealing you all if you are going to find out on your own after looking to it, this would be fascinate about it'.

Yash was standing close to Mr. Cristofer this time and was remarks like a child, when he being applauded by somebody. Yash friends were also very much happy to hear all this about Yash's creation from Mr. Cristofer as if they are there in the crowd listening to all that being said by Mr. Cristofer. Ankit after listening to all this had even stand up from his seat because of excitement and that too because he expect it from Yash.

Adrita stood at the corner with other priest girls and was smiling too sweetly as if she is also happy to hear all that applaud from Mr. Cristofer about Yash.

Mr. Cristofer said, 'I think this is the time to share all this with all of you present over here so that there would be no mean of judgment and you can own your own announce the winner. Ok for that I am putting this sketch in the middle this place and you all should have a look over it'.

Ankit was the first one to jump from the crowd to look at the portrait that Yash meant and the style he opt to come to see it. Explicitly profiled his anticipation and appetite in all that. Everybody had not even left their benches and Ankit is there on the spot where Mr. Cristofer had placed Yash sketch for exhibiting everyone there. Ankit stood silent and there is no expression left on his face and this is because Yash had meant that portrait sketch of Adrita but yes that's looking too real.

Ankit after looking towards that sketch became speechless till then other peoples also come at that place to look probe out Yash assault. This time even Adrita with her other girls also come to have a look over what Yash meant and being applauded by Mr. Cristofer a lot. As Adrita saw her own sketch over the portrait. This time Ankit was also facing towards Adrita to see her reaction after that Adrita was just looking towards sketch one time and than to Yash, she two folded this mechanism many times which explicitly shows that she lost her hope. Every slaves creature present there saw this sketch and they were all looks efficacy by Yash but suddenly a voice stood 'This is the picture of a priest girl. Sketch looks exactly like her'. as Mr. Cristofer listened to what that creature said he also make himself attentive a little to look this sketch again and accure who she is! Adrita after listening to these words, she didn't have said anything and moved backward, left that place as something being going on in her mind from past long time.

Mr. Cristofer '.......Yes he is right, this is the sketch of one of the priest girl. So yes......Yash you tell me about whose sketch you had made this time'.

Yash said, 'Sir I don't know about her name because I had just seen her once or twice at this place. So......'.

Mr. Cristofer said 'Ok........I feel it doesn't matter, so you all get inclined to handle today's price to the winner'.

Yash was not in a mood to receive prize from anyone as he was profoundly worrried about Adrita unnoticed departure from this place. Yash wanted to find out the reason for all that and that's why he wants to follow her. Yash replied.

'Sir please it could be so nice for me, if you all go on with your party and about my award, I will come and receive it further'.

Mr. Cristofer, 'then Yash....Ok as you wish. Then come-on you all present over here let's start the party again and you all should just bliss this'.

Yash directly run towards the place where Adrita was standing with her well known friend Eelly, Yash reached at that place and started surfing where Adrita had gone as he wants to follow her. Yash asked her friend Eelly about Adrita and she responded;

'I don't know where she went and even she didn't informed me before leaving, but yes through her expression it being seen that she is implication and depressed after she had seen your sketch in which you meant her portrait. I feel she had gone to the snake yard this time because wherever she reacts like this and go to that' Eelly said.

Yash asked, 'Snake Yard where is it and what is it all about'.

Eelly replied 'Snake yard is a place reserved for the apart type of snakes that being leg over the universe are kept over here to show the sign that even the most poisonous animal could also react like non hazardous. As these are kept here for some sort of guidance, person for the people brought over here because priest perform some sort of tactics on them to make Creature believe the functionality of living'.

'Eelly pinched.....what I started to tell you about the place. I think that would be enough for you to know and I would haven't told you that much too if Adrita didn't informed me about you', Eelly said while putting her arms on his head as she started revealing him something that is not even required to tell him. All this is because Adrita started showing appetite towards Yash now a days that is explicitly observed by her friend Eelly from her face. This is why Eelly too got excited and told him some thing that is not to be known by the slaves over here.

Yash listen to Eelly's word prompted soon and asked her 'Are you saying that...Adrita had talked about my concern with you.... is that truth'.

Eelly replied *'Hey* now you are taking thing for granted if I had told you some thing and answered your question then you should finish all this. As If...I am leaving now I think everything is explicit to you', It could because of the reason that Yash is from Planet "Earth" the same from where Adrita is.

Yash said, 'Ok......but thanks for revealing me all these things too.' After walking for a distance Yash reached at the place which being informed to him by Eelly, The Snake yard. Here Yash started seeking to find out Adrita's presence but unable to recover her at that place for a long time.

Yash said, 'Where I am going to find out Adrita at this place because apart from the thing that being said by Eelly about this place, as it is not hazardous. I am spirit it hazardous a bit while looking at all these large and heavy snakes. Are these not poisonous? how it can be feasible. Snakes have there trait as of being poisonous and if they don't do so then why God is like that with all of these Snakes. I don't feel that whatever Eelly said to me about this place is correct and I think she even told me the wrong place of Adrita persistence'.

Yash got voice on ears, 'Yes these all snakes are very much friendly, don't go on there texture and the big part is that they don't consists of poison in them.' Yash immediately turned back and see that Adrita is standing at his backside, covered with three big snakes veiling her from top to bottom. The thing of concern is that she don't even have a bit of tensed or stress on her face of being with such a hazardous animal of the universe.

Yash said, 'So you were here I was just seeking to find your place of presence over here'.

Adrita said, 'But could I ask you for what reason you being so concerned about my presence ever.'

'How can the combinations of both can occur like one side a heavenly beauty and the other one with it a deadly creation of God. Think that impervious to see is there collaboration with one another', Yash said.

Adrita replied, 'Why you were looking like that towards me. Everything over here is natural and I don't feel that you need to laugh or make erotic reaction on this thing'.

Adrita replied again, 'Firstly you say.....tell me that who had asked you to come at this place. As this place is too sacred and mine I am the only one who do come over here. No one else is allowed to visit this place', Adrita can fused this time about that weather she happy of Yash existence over here or afraid because of getting disturbed by him in her privacy.

Yash interrupted again, '*Hey* if it is so then why did your friend "Elley" informed me about this place and told about your presence over here'.

'Well I came to know that you had shared conversation regarding me with her. May be this would be the reason why she dispersed this info of the place and about your presence to me', Yash replied.

Yash added, '*Hey* don't think anything else about it, that I started impulsion on your silent zone and your game with serpents'.

Adrita said, 'I don't even have the time to think that much about anyone else thoughts.'

Yash said, 'Ok...that's why you shared a lot about my concern with Eelly', Yash just wants to see colour of true heart spirit on her face by his last few words.

Adrita started spirit scared because this time someone is there to play with her those emotions, which she on her own never felt before. Everything in her surrounds also started remarks to her in an unusual manner.

Yash said, 'I am seeking to make you feel normal about everything and you are getting more scared. *Hey* everything is ok or if my presence is so awefull and disastrous then tell me I would go away from here. These reactions should be mine while looking to you in that kind of furious posture'.

Adrita breathing healthy and setting her fallen hairs on her face upwards and said, 'Ok.....that's all right but I do feel that you should be present at the event because now you are going to be honoured over there for your that amazing creation'.

'Do you like that. I think Yes as you just said', Yash asked.

Adrita said, 'Yes...I do but that is not because of the thing you meant but for your magical touch that you gave to it, which makes it full of life'.

Adrita replied 'I think that's enough of conversation, now you should go over there and receive, what you deserve...

Go......'

Yash said, 'Its too heart evoking to listen that last word from your side..."Go.." it shows a lot concern about me', Yash said this and run from this place as he don't want to face those violent reaction that Adrita going to show after whatever he said her. But he doesn't know exactly about her reaction.

Adrita stood quite after this and was just looking Yash running speedily out of this place with her numb face.

Yash reached at event place and was happy with a smile on his face not because he being honored and applauded for whatever he made but because of Adrita and his meet with her. Yash came all the way running and just thinking about Adrita with her sober face image around his mind every second.

Yash come to see that this place Yash portrait being kept in the middle and all eyes of Heavens hell slaves were stuck on the case and life that is so truly being shown in that picture.

Yash seen that everybody is just looking at his creation and seeking to gather something from it as if he had written a story inside it and they were just realising that.

Yash said 'Hello......everyone....Can I too be a part of all this'.

All creatures listened to Yash first, turned back and stated clapping and calling his name. Yash saw towards his friends that were standing with that crowd of creature's and were passing smiling towards Yash as if they were also happy about the reaction. They received from the creature for Yash but Yash is not aware about all this till this time. Yash got to know now that he being given a royal remedy by everyone and a sense of being executive. Soon Mr. Cristofer called a name from the stage. Everyone faced towards Mr. Cristofer as the sound was not explicit to anyone ears because of the sound over there. As Mr. Cristofer two folded the name and said so loudly this time as 'Yash......'.

Mr. Cristofer replied, 'Yash....Wherever you are, come on stage and receive the most enhancing and ever lasting memento of Heaven's Hell that you deserve.

Yash excitingly gone all through the place and reached at the stage where Mr. Cristofer is standing with memento in his hand. Mr. Cristofer handled this momento to Yash and big sound of clapping started in that area as if everyone is too happy to see Yash receiving this honour. Apart from everyone Yash is not that much happy this time because he wants Adrita to be here at this place. See him being so much graced by others on the datum or just because of her? This is because she had mixed up so much in his through as if everything being shown in the sketch he meant.

Mr. Cristofer, 'I am too glad to honour you with this as really this sort of thing you did I hadn't seen before at this place. This is making a humbling tone in our ears that is equivalent to the throbbing sound in the church. A kind of magic that it's been creating here is just because of wonder you created with your sketch'. It's not like that Yash hadn't felt that much executive before as in his past life from infancy. He is remedy as a executive person because of his creativity and innovations. Yash hadn't thought of that much love and respect over here.

Mr. Cristofer said, 'This is not all, as you have one more thing as a prize or you can say it as a wish. This is like whenever someone wins in this kind of event I appraise him with some sort of present according to his comfort but this time I want to give you a chance to lead and to make some things get mutate as per your wish in this place'.

'I think you got confused to listen all these things I just said to you, wait my dear till explain everything out to you. As being the achiever of today and for making me thrilled of your art, I would like you to wish whatever you want to for one day', Mr. Cristofer said.

Yash hesitatingly 'But......but sir...'.

Mr. Cristofer '*Hey* my child just say, it's been all yours for today'.

Now everything in Yash control but he is still being nervous to see all this which he hadn't expected for a while. This is the time for him to demand, this is the time for him to explode and this is the time for him to mutation a lot if he wants to.

Yash said 'I am so pleasured to get this much respect and honour over here but I am not going to wish anything or demand for a mis coordinating thing that would destabilize this beauty architecture of this place of God'.

After listening to this Mr. Cristofer laughed 'I just aspected you my dear with precious talent you have a clean soul also. That is why I given you this destructive responsibility to you toward Haven's Hell functionality because I know that too as you don't dare to do that so'.

Yash replied instinctly, 'But afraid sir that doesn't means that I am not going to demand anything from you now. I was thinking that there is one part of this Heaven's Hell that stays for our help and adherence every time every place. Who also impart us the joy and sufficiency of material as I our life'.

'I am talking about the priest girls, who were there in adherence and guidance to us in every situation and I feel this is not just from today but being followed from past many years. So I would request you to please allow me to organise a party for there everlasting adherence to every slaves, so that they can feel grateful and continue there service with more grace', Yash replied again.

'Yes......is it so.....this time I didn't realised that you are going to ask for such kind of unsoiled thing. I can't even deny for that Cristofer replied and smiled.

Yash with cursive reaction, 'Yard..........Yard Oh!....afraid I didn't understand your point', as Cristofer said about space in yard Yash got quite shocked as he wandered that Cristofer knows about Yash presence over the Snake Yard with Adrita and that's why he smiled.

Mr. Cristofer 'My child doesn't think that much about my words. Ok I announce now the party as your wish which is going to be held in the Auditorium of town hall. I feel this would be explicit to all of you present over here. In this Party we are going to honour every priest girls for all that they served to our Heaven's Hell since a past long decade. This would be a first time organised concern at the Heaven's Hell that is just for its own members which are priest girls'.

Yash said, 'At the Auditorium........and that too of town hall. Sir as I know this Auditorium is at 80th floor of the solemn Town Hall. That much height is it ok'.

Mr. Cristofer, 'Don't tensed about that my child this is not only the executive thing that we were doing but the most executive thing over here is that for which you just demanded. So don't think anything else and other thing will going to happen according to our pattern'.

Mr. Cristofer colleague Mr. Zylo is just standing next to him and he is also afraid of whatever Mr. Cristofer said so he asked him;

'At so much height and that too over the tempest floor. This could be reliable to everyone do you feel so'.

'Don't ask a silly thing from me and I am concerned about everyone and there would be no stress for anyone at that place. I am going to make climate normal over there. I said all this just because as Yash asked for all priest girls to be there. Now we all knows about Barrack and his attraction towards our Princess girl Adrita. He wants to make her his part and can do anything to make it feasible. If they both would be there at the Party spot. Everyone knows about the strength of Barrack. so we can't leave our any end unsafe. So this is the reason for Party to be aligned at the Auditorium. As Barrcak is not going to go at that much height because that is not safe for him and his powers get diminished too at that place, so I set all in this affinity. I think you now understood everything so explicitly', Mr. Cristofer replied to Zylo slowly so that no body could listen apart from them but as Yash was standing too close to him and his ears starts working 10 times after listening to the name Adrita. So this is what happened as Yash came to notice that this talk being for her he crack to grasp every sort of words of Cristofer and he succeeded doing that so and came to know everything from them.

Mr. Zylo, 'No dilemma now...all is clear'.

Mr. Cristofer, 'Now you all can go back to your place and get inclined for tomorrow's Party'.

Ankit shouted from the crowd, 'Yash...come now dear let's go back. Come soon we are waiting'.

There are many questions on Yash face this time and his eyes are speaking to a lot from Mr. Cristofer, he faced once to him and then started walking towards his friend.

Yash while walking said, 'That is it like everybody over here knows about Barrack and Adrita's one sided chemistry of his attraction towards her. I couldn't gather still exactly what he wants from her. How could he is able to increase his power and standard with all that. It's too confusing'.

Gaurav said, 'So... Mr. Yash...winner of the day how would you feel now after all this, feel anything but don't be overwhelmed as this is boss not our place we can just play here not win'.

'*Hey*....what he has started now...Look Ankit what he is saying and make him to shut his mouth now as I am not in a mood to talk lets get back to our place', Yash said.

'We'll go dear but tell that why did you asked for a erotic and out of bound wish....I don't feel that could help you and us in any way. You can even demand for all of us liberty so that they could have free us from here. You asked something after listen to which there is a silence in the crowd too...', Sunny said, too sensitivity all that and laughed on it.

Yash said, 'Yes I could ask for that I do but I don't know how this thing stuck my mind and I am helpless to think anything else'.

'You don't know, but I know the whole story behind the scene... my non looking sober brother', Ankit said this slowly and smile on it.

Yash said, 'I think everyone question and answer round had finished now, we are allowed to go or not'.

'*Hey* sure brother.....lets go', Sunny said.

Time passed off and this is the time for everyone to get into there covers and wait for the new day to come. Which can bring any sort of happiness, delight or....a big irresistible discomfort in there life. The aura are complete different now for him with lot of vague back stage storied and wonders that are crumbling his bed and not allowing him to even sleep in night. As Yash and his friend were all together with a difficult bond between theirs hearts of feel and sorrow which make them all to stand in a one single row and in a single category. This is why whatever unusual situations are stuck up with Yash they would directly embolden his all friends together with him. That's because of his heart too as if this spirit of love he didn't even felt before and he Is so conscious about his dear one happiness. This is why situations doesn't settle to be in shell of grievance.

This time Yash on his bed with folded pillow under his head covered by his left hand was looking upward towards his residence terrace while being thinking about all these sort of things. Yash is just wondering about the phase of life that his friend would go to face ahead because of any sort of tragic action he'll opt now. Things are getting harder for him now to perform.

Night had gone darker with silence started going much deeper at Heaven's Hell and slowly steadily Yash eyes also became heavier as he too gone for sleep.....

6

Back to Concrete

"Plan is major of performance ever, as best plan make result enhanced to exciting peaks."

22

Sunlight was over the top with crawling birds those were jumping on there doorstep like a hop. Seems like everybody had come to know about Yash weather it was a human or an animal. Everyone started expecting a lot from him calling him a magician and wanted him to make them get away of there grief. Now silence was no where as everyone at Heaven's Hell even a single leaf had started to breath. Some small white mice gone into the door of Yash residence and get over everyone bed to wake them up for the day as today everything was going to start with joy and party all around that Yash demanded Yesterday. Soon everyone came to realise that something is there inside their sheet and Ankit was the first one to realise that this is nothing else than white mice. Ankit get happy to see all this Heavenly small white crawling mice in there bed to wake them up which is a sign of something good to happen.

Ankit said, 'See......Yash wake up....see who had came to wake up us......This is just because of you my dear that our day is commencing with such a good sign....see...I know you had waked up and knows about all this too. So leave your bed and speak up dear'.

'Yes...my dear I had awaken up too early today and I am also just measuring the joy of all these mice, jumping over all of us. I am blissful there motions from the time they entered our room', Yash replied.

'Ok so you both are not sleeping now...well good to see as if I am also sleeping guys just on my bed and same watching the craze and happiness of these mice while being jumping on our bed', Soni said.

Ankit said, 'Ok... Soni that's good but do one thing. It's really late now so wake both Sunny and Gaurav. So that we all can start getting inclined for today's get together. You know that today it's not just about all of us slaves but it's been like that. All members of Heaven's Hell are also going to come all together in this Party with us. So this is also a nice place to meet everyone over there. So let's get liveried up Buddy...'.

Everyone started being liveried up for today's happening and fun blasting. After all they stepped towards Town Hall Auditorium........

Every sort of thing at the Town Hall was incredibly executive for Yash and his belongings from the base of the Town Hall to the top of it till the 80th floor.

Everyone over there was present with a greeting that was delivered to Yash for his success.

After all this Soni said, 'Yash we should get in now as you can receive all this inside too'.

Yash replied, 'Yes Soni.......even I want to go inside as soon as feasible'.

Sunny said, 'See........we are just waiting for him to get free and he's saying like this......what we can do about him'.

'Sunny don't be afraid or feel about any other though, I know you want to continue standing over here as from here you can have a good look on those far forthcoming priest girls. Whatever Yash is saying is accurate as standing over here for too long would be going to diminish our respect'. Ankit giggled laudly while replying.

Yash instantly replied, 'What...Priest girls are they coming from our backside', Yash said and faced backward with an auspicious smile on his face showing his craze.

Ankit said, 'Yash... you. Don't make me annoyed now, leave everything lets get in'.

Yash with his friends get inside the Town Hall Tower and they moved as everyone was going but that's not the stairs nor any lift something which being never seen before.

There were certain birds over there at the ground floor that were as large as an big giant amphibian and there gesture, feathers, face, peak everything was 100 times bigger than a small bird. Slaves that were coming over there and had to go upwards just sit at the back of the bird in pairs and these birds open there feather wider and drop them out at the top floor gate. Yash and his friends after having a look over it were amazed but nothing was much hyper as they knows uncertain things happen over here. So they also took the same way to go for the party by sitting on birds backside and flying to reach there chance. As they reached over there. There being a executive entry gate meant for Yash at this place with a hording over it which being noticed by Gaurav at the first.

Gaurav shouted with so anxiety to show his happiness and said, '*Hey*....see what's they. Now at this place Yash name is being seen on hoardings too....ha!......'

'Yes you were right my dear see over there you all..............I feel everyone is too efficacy by him and that's why they meant a executive door entry for him. It's been written too over there as "The king of today is the man in gray. So he is the only one to enter this shaft as of his pride and his pure soul Pray" and see Yash had also wear the same. Settle like all is set before, something is not going ok dear......' Sunny said.

'Wait let me see what's over there............' Ankit said.

'Yes, Yash it's been just meant for you. I think everyone here starting loving you a lot as there is something in you my boy........even I feel that from many years', Ankit said to Yash in grumbling the foggy world where he could see just Adrita all around. With a spirit that is coming close to Yash day by day and being burned up by Yash fire of his desire. Yash was lost at the towers ground floor where he heard from Ankit about priest girl.

Ankit replied again 'Where the hell you were looking........whats there at the back......dear listen and see what all these heavenly creatures had set for you and meant you today's actual star of the sky', Yash realised and heard what Ankit said but he settle to be prosaic about all and concentration was too diverted.

'We shouldn't speak to him now as this party is set by him and he's remarks like this, sometimes I get phobic because of him', Ankit said.

'You have to go by that way...look that door is just meant for you and your appraisal. We will surge by this common one door...ok then.... Go', Ankit shouted on Yash this time and they all moved inside the party hall.

Yash........standing with certain spiny dreams, which have to be with a soul for whom his heart neither defend nor necklace. Yash heart was getting fragmented...and tackle with saccharine. He just not getting the reason behind his uneasy behaviour but air came running from his front end slashed him away as if it wants to show a way. Yash make him reliable and easy to see into the eyes of forthcoming air and realise the brazing words it wants to seek of him. Yash faced at its front and saw the beauty and divinity washed away with spiritless sorrow and shinning like a auspicious pearl was just present in front of his eyes. The one whom he was waiting for as she was behind them being standing in front of him now and taking the pleasure of the tribe meet. So this time Yash saw Adrita hanging with other girls in the Party hall.

Yash meant himself get inclined to go towards Adrita today and spray down the spirit which stuck him never before and because of which his life was viersioning after and after every step. Yash gesture were becoming out of his control for which he needs to compress down his expression and emotions all together like before. For which he needed to express his feel towards Adrita. Yash knows that he commencing fining around now a days which shouldn't happen for which he need to sort out his conspicuous verbalism of life. All this according to Yash could happen just when he'll fetch out his thoughts to her. This was what because of which he run from his place get inside the door that being meant for his honour. He didn't even responded to the all fabulous arrangement done for his arrival at the door, just stood inside and followed his way to the center of the room where Adrita was present.

'This is the way you block others without being aware about the fact behind there act', Yash said to Figo shouted which he never done with anyone, ever with his closed one never.

'*Hey* dear don't feel bad enough. Ah!.....I feel that you are being worried about something. Dear say anything to me, you would feel better', Figo replied.

'Afraid Figo my reaction in a way that I can't even feel to do with you, as I am this time shuffled in gathering my own previous identity. *Hey* Figo you say don't you feel that I had been mutated', Yash said.

'I don't feel so....My dear and that's surely not a truth. How could you feel that buck of thing, somebody said you something', Figo replied.

Yash said, 'Figo leave all that frankly speaking to you I am not inventer in this party.......I know that on my wish it's been organised but I had done that for some other reason and please don't ask me about that. So if you wanted to make me in curve just tell me that how could I meet Adrita....Yes that priest girl whom I said you before too'.

'You are not going to tell me the reason but I think I get that.

As I had helped you before in this same concern I am surely gonna inform you again. So you can meet her at the time of priest lecture start off in the last. As lecture would be too long you would get the enough time to convey your wanders and expression' Figo informed in a guiding manner.

'Thanks for that... and now I am just looking for the time to pass of quickly so that I could go and meet her. Yes..... dear you say that you are inclined to come with us to "Earth Surface" because I had promised you that I am going to take you but that's depend on your wish. You must come dear as you like our place girls a lot...ha', Yash said.

The shafting beats and throbbing music has started all around which was making these all surround acrid like a ocean inside as there was not much light over there and environment was profoundly cool with chilled breeze flowing all around. White and snuffs fumes had covered that area and surge side by. People who belong to Heaven's Hell had come wearing suits with nod attached in there neck and this dressing being seen to be wear by after Slaves from various place like Yash and his friends.

Gauarv, 'who had provided them those stuff of dresses.......and if it is provided to them at this place then why don't they provided us the same', Yash whispered in Ankit's ear.

Ankit said, 'Be easy my dear and please don't get hyper on these sort of things, you also knows that this is our first get together like this, so may be they oversighten to impart us all that.'

They all were sitting in the bar, that being organised at the corner of this hall for all of these Slaves. So that there blissful could reach the height that they love at there place too with every sort of comforts and sac standing element to make there excitement consolidated.

Deep blue sky over the top with those fantastic rainbow in right colours that not seen usually and settle like it was also in a mood to break down the grief of any slave. If there was any hidden inside someone soul. Today at this place animals residing at Heaven's Hell were also invited who veiling the corner of that hall and spread in all around according to there reliability. Screenings were started to occur at the stage where some songs and collective activities were going on to entertain creatures. Yash while being seated on today's Guest Cooch being looking after every second towards Adrita as if he's just waiting her to get free. Yash emotions now was getting irresistible that could be conveniently seen by his face and because of which Ankit also implication while being looking him from a distenace as they all were not with Yash right now. These all animal species were sitting too silently as if no one is much obedient and serious about whatever screening is going on the stage. Pheasants, monkey, tortoise, and cats these all the animals that were present with sweet little face just waiting to catch Yash presence over there, so everyone over there wanted to see this sophisticated Yash. All these animal creatures excitement level is on peak for that reason too as they all belongs from the planet "Earth" which resembles Yash. This is the reason making there anxiety level to increase higher and higher.

After screenings get curled down and the show reached its last phase when from priest girls Eelly came down on the stage and announced the occurrence of the biggest honorable justice of Heaven's Hell named 'Pop Jesus'.

Eelly 'Hope you all were blissful the night which being spelled out in your bowl just because of a guy from a planet of spirits and love that's "Earth surface". I feel you all do know about him a little and I am sure everyone is desperate to know about him more because of his story full art'.

Eelly replied, 'So now giving a last emphasis throw to our today's get together. I will like to invite a person on stage whom we all admire and in front of his wisdom we all are just like Haze spelled out in air. As its been a biggest pleasure to hear him and his thoughts of binding the whole universe all together. Next tone would be of our deliberately honoured chief Pop Jesus. I request you to please end our today's meet by your fragrant words and majestic sense of spirits'.

Pop Jesus spoke after coming to the stage 'Good and foremost happy eve to all of you present here in a big giant alignment. This is ours and God step to make everyone over here believe that they are the only one who can protect there nation, there world and there planet. This is why we had called some selected people's like you all from every planet so that while being over here they can realise there power and work accordingly after going back to there planet. Today I saw an enhanced bonding between you all and the best part is that too no one from you all is impious. Which makes all of you executive from others and a beam part of Heaven's Hell incredibility. Today I would go to dig a silent emotion for which we all plead our own soul but it never felt while being alone. This is not that much complicated my children because this thing is much pure than diamond and meant by God in peace, Yes that's Love.... And its behaviours which I feel you all had crossed or going to...'

Pop Jesus added, 'To be compressed in my thoughts and elaborate to you the world largest and majestic beauty of classifying happiness and there deliberate spirit with there whole six senses. As there are seven colour of nature, seven of rainbow. I am going to put away just seven points to make you all concise regarding my expressing concern towards all of you and those were related to the spirit of love as:

1. World begins from the love; through love it grows; Love is the strength in the world; Love senses joy for all; Love

is life; and Loss of love is ultimate death; Love is the skill that builds the House of Heaven in the Island of Hell; Real Love is best manifested in the everyday happening of our lives; Love is a magical wand working according to the wonders; Where there is love, there is every thing; The sweetest life a man can live is that which is keyed to love towards man and god; Love is our act of faith, as faith is reverse to love.

2. Love also means, the love that flows in the form of a river, the river to perform service; Love is to serve the poor, the need, and the distressed. Women love men for wanting to be motherhood. Lovers live longer.
3. Romance starts amidst boys and girls, who have mutual appetite in each other; this mutual appetite leads to companionship that leads to mutual affection, compatibility. and marriage.
4. Biologically, love is like hunger to die for someone's smile, only more permanent. We talk about love being blind or unconditional, in the sense that we have no control over it. But then, that is not so surprising since love is basically chemistry, love can be viewed as a survival tool – a mechanism we evolved to make long-term relationships, mutual defense and parental adherence of children and to promote spirits of safety and shelter.
5. Unlike us, the ancients peoples had several variations, including:

   Love is all of the above. But it is possibly unrealistic to expect to experience all seven types with only one person.
6. Love for parents, comrades, children, country, neighbour, God and so on all have apart qualities. Each has its variants – blind, one-sided, tragic, steadfast, fickle, reciprocated, misguided, unconditional. At its best, however, all love is a kind a passionate commitment that we nurture and develop, even though it usually arrives in our lives unbidden.
7. Love is conveniently experienced apart from being defined. As a theological virtue, by which we love God above all things and our neighbours as ourselves for his sake, it settle remote before its arrival another – in acts of kindness,

> generosity and self-sacrifice. Love's the one thing that can never hurt anyone. It can just teach you, It may cost you. The paradox of love is that it is supremely free yet attaches us with bonds fortifier than death. It can not be served in a toy, it have to be feel in heart; love is life's solemnest blessing'.

This was the time when Pop Jesus had gone cure as he expressed the thing so explicitly that would had touched those hearts whom he wants to affinity. Pop Jesus said everyone to have there specific quality food that they have at there place because all sort of comforts with apart flavour being served today. He ended with all this and left the stages as getting disappeared from the whole surroundings. No one felt it that much shabby as everyone knows about these styles of rescue as these usually occurs and everyone vanishes of from that part of place as an spirit.

Yash spirit had evoked this time to a level that doesn't consist any other height. His spirits and enthusiasm are dipped inside the well of his own love well. Again that air clashed with him and the direction this time is towards the church gate. Everyone was too fine at this place and blissful the severity and seldom night beauty with excitement and as Pop Jesus announced this was the time of food being taken by all, so everyone was going to there specific place to have there sliced food. Yash was even not get into the mood of party still after having such screenings, Pop Jesus speech. Now he was not scary to have food as if clashing maid is not inclined to leave his soul free and mixing in his blood an instinctive spirit of love. Yash faced towards the way that being shown to him by the flowing air. His eyes couldn't see anything explicitly as the mist was spread there in air and not allowing him to look clear as much as he tried and rubbed his eyes twice. Yash was away from anyone else notice even from his friends too as all were busy to have there food. As these mist in the air fallen down and he's being able to look beyond that. Yash saw that Adrita was there standing in the floor's balcony all alone facing towards the church. This meant Yash feel cure as if according to him this time is given to him by God to vacant out his heart spirit to her and get a one way to follow and rid of this bifurcating way he is facing.

Yash stood from his bench and run towards the nearest counter of food towards the balcony so that he doesn't get noticed while doing anything. After reaching there Yash wrapped himself in the noose cloth over the balcony entrance door and covered his whole body with it. He gets into the balcony at last with silent paddle feet so that Adrita doesn't get noticed about his presence till he wants to do so.

Yash while being hidden from all at that party hall was standing now backside of the balcony where Adrita is staring out at the church gate with her folded hands on balcony railing. Yash stood still this time just seeking to get some thing from her gestures. After some minutes he gone close to her and stood same like her with his folded hand on balcony on her right side with full of emotion of expressing himself. Yash with intentions to let her realise some truth faits.

Yash while facing towards the church as if he doesn't wants to see her shocking reaction and want to concentrate what he wants to say and he said 'Adrita...'

Adrita get back from her thoughts and faced towards the voice flow.

'You......you are here........ but how...or I must say why......', Adrita said as she got so....hopeless after looking towards Yash.

She moved towards the door of balcony and started looking out from that and said, 'Had anybody seen you getting out over here because my girls knows about my presence over here................. hey why are you silent please speak up...speak up...this thing you don't know is not easy for me'.

'*Hey*........Adrita listen come here...please come here till be silent you just come', Yash said this to calm her. Yash embrace her both hand on his shoulder and took her near the railing again and told her to be calm.

Adrita stood very quite as the calmness and craze in Yash eyes which is covered with gracious spirit meant her heart beats to slow down. This time Adrita hearts emotions of reliability towards someone were evoking and she is also seeking to walk slowly on this steep way of his heart so that she can guide her heart on her way.

Yash approached 'See.........dear I am going to share with you a fact of my life and try to make you realise some of yours.

Adrita do you know that when my guys were not with me like Ankit, Gaurav, Soni, Sunny, that time. I am all alone. Those times I do steal precious things of my land all alone from various place's but that's not for me to sell them out and help needy people. That datum behind this thing was whenever during the period of my robbery any cop catches me out red handed. That time I set fear in his eyes and get free by just spelling out few words too confidently with a slight proof.

Yash continued 'Those words that I do say him were like "Ok...you leg me guilty that's ok. Now we should do one thing that I can share my per cent of profit with you and you let me free. As life didn't matters to me because if I will die I have the power to rebirth within 24 hours in the same state in the same locality and then you can understand what could I do the next" it just these words I do say him and all get fine for me thing start working in my favour so rapidly waver reaction tone quality and my outstanding confident work that critically fine. So this is the entire story I would like to tell you'.

Yash added, 'Don't make those kind of reaction; I do know that you were wondering that why I had spelled out this one to you what would I try to say. So from all this I just want to concern on the fear of people like you have a hidden everlasting fear in your heart which you never even disclose anytime. Adrita that time those cops leave me from there capture just because of they tensed about there future mis happening or we can also say them as a dumb fool. There is one thing in this world that only those person are being scared of future who does wrong and they only control there spirits accordingly'.

After this Yash shouted and said, 'But now here is the sort of concern that why are you...a difficult, rigorous, decent girl is scared of doing everything that she feels like love to do so. Ok don't say that I am wrong this time. I had seen on your face every time that sort of infrequent discomfort and functionality for which you shouldn't care anytime. You are respectful over here. You being praised and you have the responsibilities that doesn't aid you don't have the license to express your spirits out or live normally and breath that refreshing relationship air that others do. There could be some reason to avoid all these spirit for certain point of time but every time what is it. I don't feel that it would be going to help you anytime in your life to be cure and easy going'.

As Adrita was listening to Yash harsh and truth facts about her life and see this time he hadn't even halted him in amidst and nor even denied to what he said. As he picked all those points that are point of concern for Adrita too. All these deep wanders about Adrita said by Yash without being informed by anyone made her a bit more close to Yash. As such spirits were built in Adrita for Yash before too but now there is an empowering relation that started building up.

Adrita said, 'Everything is not that much easy as we feel. It to be that have a large and deep understanding story beyond it and without knowing that if you say such things then that's not a justice also', Adrita is partially agreed with what Yash said but she said these line in the sense just to show him that she is not in his favour.

Yash said, 'I think that you know everything much well than me and whatever I said you know how much that is true and if in a sense to empower yourself on me you want to say some words you can do so but you actually know the case. But Let me tell you that you can control and handle your heart soft corner spirits but these were too hard for me to do so ever since my childhood'.

Adrta laughed when Yash talked about his childhood because she felt a person who talks such a big words is concerned about his childhood in his words. She laughed and immediately as realised Yash words tear came to her eyes. Yash see those hearties tears of past memories in her eyes with which she is dealing for a long time but neither shared them with anybody.

Immediately Yash asked her about it as its becoming too cumbersome for Yash to see that in her eyes. Yash said, '*Hey*....dear whats happened...afraid if I had said anything wrong to you....*Hey* I didn't mean anything else apart from your happiness'.

'You don't need to be afraid...these just came because of my past memories of my family...not because of you', Adrita said, while rubbing her tears away from her face.

Adrita said, 'It's not like that I hide my spirits or not to be happy. Even I want to go away and fly of with all these spirit that stuck my heart certainly and that do say me to move away with them. This is because I am the superior most priest girl at this place who can't deny with even a single rule granted here for us. So that's why I do need to uphold this identity'.

Adrita replied with a craze and sleave in her eyes, 'Do you know my parent are also from "Earth" as my mother is a priest girl and my father is a slave like you. They left out this place after breaking its rule and after that God demanded there first girl child from them and they had send me back on Heaven's Hell. Now they were alive or not at "Earth surface" I don't know but really I am also fond of going to "Earth surface" and find them out if they do exist now also, I want to meet them, feel them, touch them and have there love and blessings. But sometimes what you want you can't do that because of your helplessness and I am helpless about it'.

Yash replied with desperation on his face '*Hey*...don't be...so dear...if this is your sort of happiness then I make you meet them all take you down to the "Earth surface"........Yes I will'.

'Who are......you and how can you say like that, why would I go with you and for your information. I think you know that we are not allowed to move out of this place', Adrita said this to Yash.

Yash said, 'Who am I....how can you say that...Ok listen now the time came for me to express what I want to because if I didn't it, would be going to spoil out a lot inside me'.

Yash took a minute after it meant his head to go down for some seconds and after that his head stood up like a blond with his eyes consisting trust and comfort asking for reliability and he said 'Dear.......I don't know what I am seeking to say is standby over here or whatever it is but there are certain senses of your body with which you are helpless and never negotiates with them. There is a part of heart that just knows about roses and just wants to flow in that fragrance. My heart never believed and felt about it in my life till now but I couldn't understood that why did this wandered impulses over here made me to realise those things that are too dashing and I am unable to find them out till now in my life. May be because of not having the wisdom about this spirit or any suspicious person for whom my heart beats up would be the reason behind that. This thought, spirit and expression is of love my dear and which is felt by me after meeting you and making my soul the realization of seldom spirit of heart that I never realised before'.

Yash took a break after it and stand still while looking into her eyes with a blank face full of spirit of being loved. He said, 'These all spirits and mutate are just because of you, my heart never says lie to me and this time it doesn't feel anything else much emphasise than you... and at last I just say that "I LOVE YOU ADRITA" and my ocean is getting filled by just your love spirit water and nothing else'.

Adrita crack to speak up and halt him saying all this but he halted her and said 'Don't....Please don't deny this fact as I knows about people eyes and read your eyes a lot every time, everywhere I see you and whenever we meet through. I just request you to make your spirit very much enhancing on your thoughts so that you can also listen to your heart spirits and can know that you too wants to love and breath out all sorrow from life with love'.

Yash said all these words and just left that place. He conveyed his feelings and left else over to Adrita. Adrita stood at that place totally blank looking Yash going towards the out yard in a tensed face as if he wanted something to be said by Adrita in a positive way to him. But she hadn't realised her spirit Yet how could she say something to him now. This is why Adrita remained still, quite and implication at that place and Yash left as he didn't get any response from her side that he wants. So after giving her realisation about silent solemnity of her life, he left everything else on her. The bundles of emotion with a spirit of loved were going on in Yash heart which he crack but not able to express those to the height they flow in his blood. The power to chase is diminishing in his soul as he is unable to fill his soft corner heart vacant holes. He crack to make himself filled with power and boosting craze again but his helplessness here doesn't allowed him to feel the same. He is just walking away from Adrita as if he won't be able to face her silence again with her bowed head facing downward and eyes getting wet because of the spirit to stay without that auspicious thing for which he loved and tried again to breathe.

Adrita's condition was also not in functionality by any manner as if she also stood renounce her hope and wearing a band which can't drop even if she crack to live. The spirit that do run in her breathe and in front of whom she too get knees down with lost hopes as what she wants, no matter but she can't try it to be. These sudden exhausted spirit are striking her and she was getting realised that from having powers no one knows how dried and vacant she feels.

Time get passed, sudden and pickling sound of birds started getting spread up in the whole surrounding's of Heaven Hell as this time party is finished and everyone relaxing at there place. All surrounding started getting covered in the darkness as if nature is asking the twinkling and forthcoming new stars to spread there majestic twinkling light in all the aura. So that it gives us the realization of something in nature is going on every time.

Yash was in his room lying over his bed and same facing the terrace while being stressed about the day and his broken up and left apart conversation with Adrita that have its no commencing point left to start again. Yash friends also wanted to know the reason behind his infrequent behaviour after the party as he seem to be confusing because of which he is shuffling things around without of any reason. As if Yash was not looking normal and his activities were being defining all that so. This is what that Ankit had never seen Yash facing all that in past 20 Years from the time he's with him. The reason of confusion is also getting hyper for his friends as if Yash never hides anything from anyone and whenever he felt bad about anything he spell that out over there only.

'Ankit as you do also know this thing so....explicitly that sometimes Yash don't want any interference in his life by any additional party apart from who is involved in that and then too you are asking such questions to me. No I didn't asked him about anything like that and I feel no one should do so this time because Yash and his nature are as difficult to understand as an forthcoming storm', Gaurav replied to Ankit.

Ankit lost somewhere too said slowly that 'No....I know that but....this time... this time its quite apart and as I am not only concerned with Yash present functionality but the surrounding is also seeking to mix a spirit inside environment of getting exotic change. I had read a lot of books regarding God behaviours there functionality, there's expression and features. I had also read that how does a mutation took place when God demands for that and what are the accurate functionality of the nature for that time period and on that because may be, I am spirit something might be getting changed in ours environment', Ankit said all this with a lot concern.

'You both Ankit and Gaurav don't sit near the born fire for a long time otherwise your ideas would going to be more viral... hey my dear brothers nothing erotic is happening so be chill and let others too', Sunny said while sipping cold drink in this cold night with straw.

Night went darker as time passed and everyone after been having a look towards Yash when he got soy off in the same mood as of previous. They all felt that today night something or the other had happened with the shallow boy because he never keep things go on that much silently as of today.

Ankit was close to Yash and as this time Yash is sleeping. There is lack of expressions and features in his body that every time shows a life living bud with spreading fragrance but today nothing is there. So Ankit gone to Yash bed and started starring him for some minutes as if he'll gather any mischief if it would had occurred with him. As time passed Gaurav impulse Ankit and others to sleep for tonight as his eyes had halted adherenceing him and his senses were getting diminished. So Gaurav convinced all too left out there concern about Yash vacant smile and get down to there bed as if they need to face merely morning shaft.

24

Next morning...

Ankit feel awkward about all they were talking about, so he said, 'Listen everyone. What we started doing here, as if we just need to get rid of this uncertainly came troubles. Let's try and make healthy measures regarding it soon. I am right Pee.'

Pee said, 'Yes for sure, Ankit is right and even I have seen this first time but this kind of rainfall and storm. I had seen before but all this are not fulfilled by that coverage nah......'.

Yash asked Pee, '*Hey* about what coverage and whats all you are talking all about.

Pee said, 'My dear Yash this happens when the biggest Chief of Heaven's Hell "Pop Jesus" wants to call any person to talk about any seldom conversation with him. So that time these kind of uncertain mutate occurs. But that time one thing occur that is must in which whomever he calls, number of small white mice were leg in his room crawling on his bed but I don't think this happened today with anyone. As if now everyone is out of there compartment, someone had seen this kind of mutation he could have shouted and it would had reached everyone ears. So that is not the case today'.

This time Ankit and Yash has got to know the thing that the call is for all of them.

Ankit said, Resurge swat from his face as if he is seeking to save him and his friends from all this and said '..... is it like that, then lets see whose going to be the one.

Ultimately lightening started happening at that place as if it looks like string of light is touching land over there like someone playing with sword. After some seconds a spirit came from the back of the church circled in the atmosphere for a while and fallen in front of them and what happened; It meant to be person.

This person remain stood in front of them for a minutes and he just said that 'You being called by Chief 'Pop Jesus' as they need to converse thing with you only. Yash being called up there. Pee listen this they told me to inform you as you need to send him as soon as feasible to 'Pop Jesus' at 'Vanity Hall'.

Pee replied, 'Ok ill do so...that Jokos...'Jokos the spirit had gone back to his place from where it emerged taking the way from backside of the church,

Pee looked in partly towards them. So he asked;

'Why......dear why you all had said lie to me again, White mice would have came to all of yours bed before but why you all didn't told me about it, for what concern you are hiding and sparing yourself from this. I am unable to get all this out', Pee said to everyone.

Ankit said, 'Afraid dear, we didn't know that much about it before and after you told us we got awaken and tried to hide it. As if we think nothing is going fine and if something could harm us from this. So we just tried to spare ourselves and nothing else'.

Pee said, 'This would not worth you all like that anytime and with me never. If you are going to hide your things like that from me after being knowing about my intentions towards you all then it could be difficult for me to dig you out of any miss happening. As then that time I am green handed as I am not having the accurate information regarding your intentions, your need. I think you all were getting my point and isn't I am saying that thing too correctly, too fine'.

Yash said, 'Oh!...my dear Pee...Please...doesn't be disheartened like that and give us chance from now onwards. I confirm you that there would be no gap between your desire and our thoughts.'

Pee said, 'Ok.......leave all that now. I need to perform my act to make all this environment texture get back to its normal posture by sending the deficit person whom our Honorable 'Pop Jesus' required to meet. So dear say to me that the one from all of you who have white mice is scrambling on his bed. Tell me that soon dear'.

'Pee that was me, on whose bed mice came the last day and for all the period of time they stayed on my bed only. Tell me what I have to do about it'. Yash said.

Ankit impeded him in amidst and said 'Why Yash you were saying like that....Wait for a while let me say all about it'.

Yash very decently said, 'No my dear Ankit you need to wait now, let me finish my words with Pee and there is no need to defend this time. As if you also knows that its not just we who are facing this unreliable climatic change as its been felt by and thrashing other slaves too.

Pee replied, 'Yash if it's been you who is the soul of this thing. So you need to go at 'Vanity hall' as soon as feasible because over there only our honorable chief would be waiting for you.

After listening to this Yash stood him tight and poised to move towards the 'Vanity hall' but he realised that he hasn't been at that place before where could he is going to find that so. So like this again Yash had crack to save his boys as he does ever. This time his friends were also meant speechless as Yash diminished all sort of discomfort by his again performed sub vacant act. Lastly Yash asked Pee;

'Pee before leaving give me the actual way to be followed as if you do also know that. We are not familiar to this place and that's why it could be difficult for me'.

Pee laughed and said, '*Hey* Yash I can understand about others but don't say like that you are ignorant and if yes, then somebody would tell me that from where you look ignorant and sober about everything, leave all this just a part to make surrounds feel good. Yes…'.Vanity hall' is a place where I hadn't gone anytime till now because our 'Pop Jesus' never meets everyone over there. You are going to get 'Vanity hall' just at the back side of the biggest third second highest church. I think you had even seen that church. It's that one where you did your first prayer section, so are you getting my point. You are going to know about that place nearer to that church only and the way to it I feel you do know my dear.

Yash replied 'Yes…I know about it and how can I forget that day of mine in the Church. Ok if that is so I will be going to find it out and go through it'.

Yash started to step forward in modesty about all that he faced and about those considerations, whose instincts are not allowing him to stay calm. As Yash do know the way to the Church but after that all he had to leg it out. A heavy clamour is being heard by him nearby in his way and every time he faces in that direction, he finds nothing to be cared off.

Yash said to him, 'I feel don't need to be worried about these freak tones as if they are just in a sense to distract me'.

Yash proceeded himself forward. As Church is being meant on a short cut of Mountain, so it come into Yash visible area this time from where he can see the whole surrounding in the Heaven's Hell. There were fumes drawing out of a portion which is a slope on the right hand side of the Church. This time Yash need to move down hill as if taking that slope at the right hand side of him and Church.

Yash said to himself, 'I feel this would be the way, I need to go downwards on this slope as if the way is being opening up at the back side of Church. This way looks somewhat enigmatic and peculiar apart one. As this is all about everyone Honorable "Pop Jesus" that's why I do feel that this would the way.

Yash said, 'How could I inference that I have to go where, I feel come to a wrong place. I should move from here as soon as feasible'.

Soon after Yash started move stop from that place. He started hearing sound of bats crawling all around him, even though there is no one to be seen like this in his surrounds. Yash tried to gather that from where and why he's facing this sound but at last slaughtered away and frustratingly he shouted to halt this tone. It started looking like all sunlight is condensing itself on this shelf and veiling a rectangular space from its corner. The whole space is being burned by that heat and Yash came to see a palace inside it.

Yash with his sick eyes from heavy sunshine tried to step into this area; as if this time he had aquired this indication so clearly. Yash is convinced with his though that this is the area where does "Pop Jesus" reside. There is excitement in his gesture after looking towards this palace beauty but on the other hand he's also concerned about the datum for being called over here.

Ultimately a person came in front of him with long large scatting sawdust on the floor, which being veiling his hand from shoulder to palms.

Yash saw him and shouted with a stammering voice to say 'You ... is here... but.... But.... how come this is feasible, I felt that this would be the place where only "Pop Jesus" reside as everyone told the same thing to me'.

'So I am also not saying anything wrong to you, this is just the place of "Pop Jesus". Why you look to be in so annoyance', being said to Yash.

'But you are Eugene Sir… whom I had met at the prison. I am saying right…' Yash replied with a shock on his face.

'Oh!… is that so… Ha… My dear Child… let me tell you that the person which is standing in front of you this time is none other than "Pop Jesus". At that time I hadn't shared my actuality with you my boy because that is the need of that time. I feel you can get that. This is just because you are not a normal and simple personality being I came in front of you and that too in different form. So it would be good for you now to forget about all past things and get concerned about your present and future that is going to be so devotional to others, full of conflicts and Power', Pop Jesus said.

'Huh……..you were saying me too overtight that all so conveniently and now accept you as "Pop Jesus", But why all this is being done? Could I have any valid answer for it?'

Pop Jesus replied, 'First of all you need to be calm and quiet over here as this is not the place where you can shout. Second for whatever reason, I had called you over here, you need to concentrate on that, apart from thinking of those idle things that matters nothing. In front of you to give a start to your journey for which you had been called over here Yash'.

Yash said, 'Ok… let me now feel that all is true, whatever you just said, but this thing is indigestible as you said. I came here for some reason. If that is so… then…please you could describe it to me'.

'To know all that my dear you need to know firstly, that the intention behind calling you at this place of mine is just begin a new era of yours and everyone else life connected to your surroundings. This era just starts with your life and that's why you are being its hero. There is no other reason in this. Yash… Listen dear you are a person of pure and heavenly soul with no impurities embedded in you', Pop Jesus replied.

Yash asked, 'Pure, Heavenly soul what that it is… Sir seriously this whole thing is becoming a lot cumbersome for me as everything is shuffled off. I do respect you, I even trust you that whatever you were going to tell me, it will be a truth. So…..sir please I request you to cut off my this hamper'.

Pop Jesus with a high pitch and heavy tone 'So...Yash for that let me tell you the whole thing from its start point. Yash this is yours new birth and in all your previous generation you are the only person who stood all alone in the sake of humanity and fought for them. Your contribution is so enhancing and imposing which evoke the whole lot of crowd to step towards human growth and this is the reason why you were here in this generation. Yash, this generation being yours where you will be the supreme to tackle humanitarian issues in favour of good things. In this generation you are being praised by that amazement which would make you the hero and the savior of humanity from brutality. So for all this your first stage is to be in touch with Adrita and for that only I had been over there at prison'.

Yash getting more implication said, 'This is getting more infected to me sir, as my tacky mind is also failed to solve out this whole query conveniently. Now how Adrita did came in all that'.

Pop Jesus laughed, 'You were being stressed but you have to be strengthen up yourself as yours world being waiting for you'.

Pop Jesus replied again, 'See... my dear... let me tell you some facts about Adrita, that she also doesn't knows still. You know Adrita is the only priest Girl who being from yours planet "Earth surface".

'Yes... I do know that', Yash replied with ease.

'So as she is from "Earth surface" her mother and father were also from "Earth surface". This is being a long story or you can say story of last decade. This story is of Adrita's Mother and Father. Adrita's father had also come to this Heaven's Hell in the form of a slave that time. Adrita's Mother is being the supreme power of priest Girls who is being praised by those powers which are very less people do consist at this place even though, even I don't have those that time. The climate of Heaven's Hell is being started diverting towards love phase that time, as if her father and mother started to love each other. The last scope of their love is to escape away from this place to the "Earth surface" and establish a home over there. This intention of them were being felt by the supreme authorities of Heaven's Hell. Everyone is being harassed by all her exploit.

So, in case as if they can't put any objection on love because this is a finest and auspitious gift given by God. They had to allow her mother to be relieved from Heaven's Hell and can move to her desired place. The point of concern everyone do have is that how could they save and use those powers which are being praised to her mother as being Supreme priest girl. So for all this, they get a conclusion that Adrita's mother first daughter would be going to have all these powers and she would be going to govern after wards. So for this reason they all asked her mother to leave this place but on a signed note and commitment that she would send her first daughter back to this place. So that she could take her place and cover up the imbalance caused by her in Heaven's Hell'.

Yash breaked his silence and asked, 'Oh!... if that is so.... then because of it only now a days there being a ban on priest girls to interact with any slave... and and say...what her mother did after that'.

Pop Jesus said, 'I had said you not to speak in between and break my flow...... you did the same then... leave let me tell you after that. So her mother became agree to do that with her massive heart and she did the same. After being settling up on "Earth surface", she had send Adrita back to Heaven's hell with a note written for me that time. I am the one who way very much close to her. He was saying to evoke Adrita's happiness in future and makes her competent to touch the hearts of all people over here. She had also send Ronu with her wearing that 'amulet' which covers all those power which she wanted to deliver. Adrita still doesn't know about all these things. She is so sober and cute that she didn't even asked me once to liberate more wisdom about her parents, even though she is too desperate to know it. She knows only that which I told her by mould every situation in my way. She is just obeying my said ways. Yash as if over here I am the only parent of her to take care'.

Yash said in grief, 'I am overwhelmed to know all these things and spirit grateful to know that all from you. You make me the one who could be so much assurance full'.

Pop Jesus said, 'Wait... wait My dear don't flow your emotions like that as if you need to know more. Now this time whatever I am revealing to you are just for you. I had told you about the powers of Adrita. Those powers are not being in use to her as if these are being designed by the destiny to be delivered to her comrade.....means to her soulmate'.

Pop Jesus replied again 'Now Yash you hold your breath and let me tell you that, the comrade of Adrita was being you....yes...... You are the one who being designed to use all these powers. These powers being delivered to you at the time of your both alignment'.

Yash being speechless and breathless this time, he crack to say 'Sir...but...tell me...'

Pop Jesus impeded Yash, 'Hope... don't ask me anything my dear now, I feel all those thing that I reveled in front of you were being secret till now and this is the time for you to deal with it'.

Instantly the surrounds air and climate started erupting and settle its waver colour. Seems like it's being crying to give it a reprisal now. Yash prompted and asked;

'Sir......why did this eruption is taking place? Is it have some significance'.

'It's been happening the same as happened when you were being coming over here. This happens when some pure defined creature crack to approach my place', Pop Jesus smiled and said.

Yash asked, 'So who would be coming now. You would know this'.

'Yes... this time it's been Adrita who's coming towards my estate, as I had called her too at the same time of yours. As much I can see from my sight, Adrita is running like anything to reach my place as if she is being late to reach here. Adrita being apprehensive and tensed by her face, running in the corridors with her long loose dress abrading on the floor. She is so in tensed about my call this time; I feel she had measured my covered devotion in my call. Let's just wait for a while and she'll be here on the doorstep', Pop Jesus replied.

'Seems like you were ignoring this sort of rising discomfort over this place. Which is becoming extensive from the mid of our conversation', Yash evoked with a repeatedly striking and itching question in his mind.

'I asked something from you sir and I don't expect this kind of sentiments on your face as do I adore you a lot. I need a reply for it please. Yash replied again after a bit of time his burning slum is not relieved by Pop Jesus still. As Pop Jesus is standing still wandering in vain.

Yash replied again 'seriously now I can't retain all this kind of your ducked silence...please'.

'Wait...' Pop Jesus replied while leveling out his feet around his surroundings with open hand and palm facing upwards. Listening to Pop Jesus and facing his acts Yash face now went for a deep fall.

'So I feel that you would asking me about all these rising black cloudy waves over my back side......', Pop Jesus asked Yash with his widen opened eyes.

'Yes...but I didn't expected this kind of feeling and emotion of your towards all this, as I do expected an answer for it not an reaction like this', Yash replied.

'I need to elaborate this astonishing thing to you. I know that you asked the same. So listen my child we all can't make this whole thing to eradicate from our place. As all this happens just because of that solemn killing person, killer of humanity...Barrack. As he is the one who is not liable to stay over here at Heaven's Hell, but because of God's demand he is being placed here. By all this even I don't know what kind of game does God wants to play', Pop Jesus replied with his numb voice.

'I can't have a look this time of yours because there is one person whom I had seen over this place. Which never gets low and carries all responsibilities of Heaven's Hell on his shoulders and that's you. So, Sir if you are going to be so defeated then this thing will be going to astonish courage of other's as its imposing to me', Yash replied with his enlightening eyes to abolish this upcoming distress on Pop Jesus face.

Pop Jesus replied in grief 'This is thing which can't be abolished but yes you can stop it to reach its tearing pains in future'.

'What..... sort of tearing pain...' Yash said, stepped towards Pop Jesus.

Pop Jesus said, 'I drawn these words because if that at most aim of Barrack got achieved and he reached those ends. Then it would be disastrous for every one of us to control and consolidate our surrounding and beauty back to its virginity'.

'I want you to listen me very carefully before anything else comes and break our concise conversation. I would want you to give your peak concern on all those which I am going to recite you. This needed your exempted powered response'.

'This time you would have known this thing that Barrack wants Adrita to empower his ceasing bad strength. Which would going to help him to be the biggest unbeatable Monster like an "ambimorph", "Therianthrope" which means a creature which is being with wild trustee greedy. He'll be going to ruin all the peace and reliance that is being present in the nature there after. Barrack is going to be the most strengthened "ambimorph" that time. Which would go to consist powers of all other "ambimorph" present in this nature aura since Greek like:

Cyclops = giants, with one round eye in the center of their foreheads

Cerberus = three-headed Cerberus

Sphinx - the Mysterious Riddler=head and chest of a woman, bird wings, lion claws, and a dog's body

Medusa with Snaky Hair= Monster lady

Harpies = monster birds

Minotaur = Half man close bull

Nemean Lion = Monster lion Half women and close serpent

Lernaean Hydra = Monster 100-headed Typhon'.

Yash little frightened and whispered, 'All this would be going to happen and what is the cure lend for that by our God......who knows'.

Pop Jesus stepped close turned back harshly with his green eyes, this time facing Yash as never before. He said, 'All this is being set by my God and I do know that you had felt your role in all that. Then don't let this nature to fall apart as it trusted you my child this time. So God had praised you with ecstatic love and power to be the savior of humanity. Never let, those belief down my son. You have to make reliance and peace maintained in everyone heart and not destroyed by any soul of a beast. As It's been me too who's being there in the line to deserve those enlisting efforts of your towards this symphony'.

'I know the question were bulging one after the other from your soul at this time because this entire present environment would be telling you about the next disaster. Next is your way, design it on your own way how so ever you want to follow', Pop Jesus said all this and pulled his shiny white blanket covering curculered his right hand.

Yash stuck in awe stood silently and bended waistline towards the floor with his right handed finger trying to design something over it. There is a big smile on Yash face this time as if he had praised with lot of joy and striking fun. Pop Jesus is unable to digest all this reaction from Yash apart.

Pop Jesus asked, 'What do I mean by yours these sort of expression...... Am I wrong......to feel your sentiments and intellectuality before........?'

'Sir, please don't take this in a wrong way as this is my tendency to do such thing when something is not easy for me to digest. But it doesn't mean that I lost my courage beneath my shoes. I am like that only sir that you had presumed before. Nothing gone wrong just painting my way forward over the floor'.

Pop Jesus laughed after a long tough conversation 'So I feel that why does this floor colour started changing up. This is just because of your painting my boy..... *Hah*......'

Yash started facing back by turning his neck around and there was still deep silence on his face, as all these things were not so easy for him. Within some seconds there is a force being felt in the surface as if it's being very lump to feel someone's presence at this place. Sound started pushing backward of the way from where Yash stood inside. Instantly that door wrist up which is being close after Yash came into the Palace.

Eugene said, 'The time had come to block this air for a while and we need to bend beneath this out flowing wind so that it could call Adrita at this place as per my wish. This flowing wind do also know about Adrita's power but she didn't till now. I am today going to wear out a veiling shadow which would give me a terrific face to spread out all case of Adrita's life in her front and then to face her questions that could be in grief. These combating intentions of mine inside me of not revealing Adrita about her being and past life still were going to halt today.

As I would be going to display the chart of frightening life and history that her family up before her birth.

I wish she could understand those very well with all embard spirit of mine in these information of not letting her to know about them before. She would going to believe the sweet and sour taste of case and could feel the glowing hands of God which had covered her since she was a baby child'.

Eugene added, 'I feel Yash that it could make her more resistible and tough to know about the back history of her family, who were also not ever the normal being and consisted a pride place in Heaven's Hell'.

After finishing all this Eugene instantly looked towards Yash and said 'And.... I think I am right Yash, do I.'.

Yash getting awake from the wandered and scene that Eugene had meant in his surmounted spirits and said with a fumbling tone '...oops....I feel its truly right sir. Yes...you should tell all this to her and this is so true that she need to know everything somehow. So why not this should do that now'.

Eugene said, 'Ok....now just be quite as I am going to meditate for a while. As I don't meditate anywhere out apart from my shed but this time I need to dictate way to Adrita so I had to do that. You shouldn't make even a single noise between that till she arrives here. Ok now we'll talk after her arrival Mr. Yash'.

Eugene now clubbed his both hand together and made his both elbows to come in contact with his eyes closed. This time as Yash couldn't say anything but he is conspicuous about all this and very sophisticated to see. His reaction was too anonymous. As in all the auras wind started blowing as an throwing solemn power of natural disaster and its becoming difficult for Yash to stand still at a place. Hairs of Eugene were flying in the air and profoundly spread apart in all direction. Curiosity of Yash is rising like anything as if this time everything is for Adrita and her arrival.

Adrita, Before setting her way towards Eugene previously was at cultural room where she being guiding her students little

Girls about classical dance with giving a brief about emphasis of *Sitar* (musical instrument) and how did these both things combine all together and help to make life more expliciter.

Adrita and Eugene were in solemn consolidate bond so she felt the same as if Eugene senses were calling him at the back side of the estate. Adrita moved rapidly and gone behind the stage and she leg nothing behind and she started looking at every corner of it so that she could justify herself that which tone she heard and can identity the significance behind that realization she felt instinctive. The place is profoundly dark as this was being covered with the shadow of long thirsty shower that is bearing the out sunlight and not allowing a single ray to enter that wizard. Adrita is sure about her realization and want to confirm her call by vague power that she felt just. There is a empty shining bowl hidden in the covers and when it realised that Adrita's presence it stood out of it and became visible to her. As Adrita saw it she had known this time that the call had came from Pop Jesus. As soon as she crack to realise anything by her exemplary wrist and starring eyes towards that shining bowl the sleave emerged from it gone straight away to her eyes. She became helpless to think anything else apart from getting move towards the place where she is being called. This instinctive looking conveyer in the form of sleaveling bowl get dispersed after it. Adrita without thinking anything else ran towards the striking fragrance spread till her designation of arrival. Her emotions were now became too ignorant but she knew that it is a big time for her to have a change. As she is getting a meet full of happiness in her thoughts as she is meeting here, *Dada*. The confusion can be felt in her feet as she is running in a manner to chase that sort of spirit as soon as feasible. These reaction strikes to Adrita after a long time because the life she is being living is not up to her expectation even if its being having a chunk of butter rolled around its corner. She didn't have any info regarding her past and future, as she can't even think about it. The Caspar she wants to create in her sorrow spirits is being lot far from her reach. This time when the realization and her wanders were touching heights as the spirit she just felt is not allowing her moral of love and to be loved get down. She got frightened this time like a lighted up lamp. Started running like anything which she never did before as if the delight rid of vacant smile is just waiting for her at the next door.

Adrita ran all across the way to church crossing up the forest area, crushing up the fallen leaves by her feet. Same as she started killing her blank hopes because this time this the spirit and belief that is going inside her soul is lightening up a way of her desire where she could have someone to lend herself on as she wont be able to do till now. She felt now about those flowers getting evoked in her way which never wants to born either. This time they are fluffing and spreading fragrance and prosperity in her way. Adrita is implication while running towards the chance as her desired were making to knock that door as soon as feasible which had blown all these bundle of powerful breaths in her life. She is wearing a long gown that she wore at the pray and its been flying in her way as if it is also blissful the joy and excitement with this flowing breeze with an aspiring day. White scarf that she wearied to cover her face is been hanging on her neck and flying all through her way, falling down to the ground and rising up in the air. She is unaware of everything because of the clumsy spirit that headed her on the way.

25

After been veiling the whole long distance and getting noticed by Creatures fallen in her way about whom she didn't care. As if her dedication to meet her desire meant so exhausted and she couldn't feel now about her position and rules of Heaven's Hell. This enthusiasm of Adrita explicitly shows her need to be in a climate that she wanted to be in and this climate of Heaven's Hell can't be the one to fill all that. Veiling the way and denying to every other thing which came to her way she reached the place behind the church as fragrance that took her up to this place has diminished. The power which captured her mind and soul is not allowing her to think anything else apart from just being over this place also wrecked off. She came back to her consciousness and objective that she is following from her child hood. She stood still at this place and her breath wrenched this time as she crossed a long distance without being halted at any place on her way.

Adrita mark lines getting deeper on her head which were making her unsustainable as if she can't find anyone around this place. Nobody is there but Yes it was shining outlined rectangular part on the mountain wall in her front.

She stepped close to it and said 'what does this mean why its been like this, do it have some relation with my call'.

After that she took a stone and thrown towards it and that neither came back nor fallen nearby, as it had gone straightly inside that wall.

Adrita said, 'Oh!....this is nothing just an illusion and the way is beyond it. I need to get into it as this would only going to chill my ongoing fire and stress'.

She stood inside and felt energised by the energy spread all around, which told him that the presence of Pop Jesus around and then she gone towards the big giant closed door, where she had met Pop Jesus before also because now everything became familiar to her.

Adrita was still not breathing well as her breath is in anxiety and not making her to relax even for a second. She stood inside the door by opening it through her both hands. She became numb as she saw that at her front Pop Jesus is standing holding the stick of wonder that can mutation time as he wants. Which he doesn't carry usually and the frightening this for her was that too as if Yash is standing just nearby to Pop Jesus with his hand folded and facing backside towards her with questionable eyes. Adrita felt a little weird and fearful as the wandered came to her mind the information leaked to Pop Jesus regarding Yash and Adrita meet at this Heaven's Hell which is against the rules. Adrita just making measures to uncover all those thing as heart beats started getting more wild, till Pop Jesus spoke to him. Before that time they all stood facing each other with a blank wandered of expression.

Pop Jesus, 'Come..Adrita....come...its been me who had called you. Come nearby and stand close to him. Listen I would like to make things easier for you today but the depth about which I am going to talk today my dear, You need to listen that very clearly and precisely'.

Adrita asked, 'Things are clear to me then what would you are going to tell me so, before that I would like to know from you as for what reason you had changed your appearance today. I don't feel so that you need to hide anything from me as if I know everything about my Eugene *dada's* pop Jesus confidentiality. Am I right'.

Pop Jesus, 'No my baby you were not..........................as I am going to convey that next but before that I would say..."yes I don't have to hide anything from you but today I am here in the look of Eugene just because of Yash". As if he just know me in the form of that and no other form my dear and I think now this would be explicit'.

Yash was confined to his place as he's the only one at this place whose new and don't know either Eugene (Pop Jesus) in a better way nor Adrita that much apart from what she told to him. Yash reaction's was getting exhausted that time as the number of questions those were amusing out from his heart are blank bucks whom he can't solve on his own. As all this Eugene (Pop Jesus) to woke them out with a better response.

Adrita said, 'Yes that's explicit to me, but confusing blunder from the inspiration you evoked in me to come here is not stabilising and getting queued up in my mind one by one'.

The way that Adrita was talking to the superior most person Eugene (Pop Jesus) was quite in apart to understand as if she being talking to a person who is in solemn touch of her life, a member of her life delight. By these words of Adrita love Eugene (Pop Jesus) expressed towards Adrita were being seen in words spelled out by Adrita in a bit arrogance towards an close one, as if she wants to resolve her dilemmas soon.

Eugene (Pop Jesus) said, 'Today as I said you before that whatever I am going to say to you and I didn't answered in your whole life you need to concise towards those concerns. Park your every sort of trembling questions arising in your heart and listen to the future concepts to curve humanity that God on his own wants to make wandered'.

Eugene (Pop Jesus) replied, 'I feel you know this person whom God send over here, standing just aside you'.

Adrita asked, 'whom.......this....this person Yash'.

Eugene (Pop Jesus) replied, 'Yes...my dear this person curved with God wellness and faith and I feel that you also measured the same in his eyes. This was only the thing which made you to have your further conversation with him and I do know what else happen as you also know that'.

Adrita in a fear of being caught said, 'I think the things are not that much clear to you as they were actually and he just need some help that I delivered to him I feel'.

Eugene (Pop Jesus) said 'and I do feel that you don't have to curve anything like that as I had delivered the best lessons to you and know one knows about by baby Babin (Adrita) more than me. Now I feel I am correct'.

Adrita with her eyes facing downwards as if she don't wants to have eye contact with Eugene now. As her were not up to the mark and she felt that she had dismissed her lesson in some way or the other and she said 'Yes...you were right I think'.

Still having look towards all this Yash is unable to realise anything as his mind is stubbing because everything that he listened were not making a tough nod. Yash now is simply facing them with blinking eye and shuffling wanders and he had nothing to say.

Eugene started chuckling to see the demolishing reaction of Adrita (Babin) after his words so he replied and said, 'There is no need my dear to move your eyes away from this concern and getting shy about anything, You also knows that all members of this Heaven's Hell wanders are also governed by our God and everything moves according to his wish. As if today is the time to answer your questions from me since your infancy for whom I denied every time and diverted you towards your goals'.

Eugene added, 'My dear I had told you everything before but that time your eyes were saying something that I can't even face. So for that reason and your mind comfort I didn't dis closed you. The reason behind all this is that too, as the time was not the rigorous and decisive for you and me both as your gesture and emotion that time would be unestablished and not easy to handle. Before I tell you anything let me introduce you Yash once more but this would be in my views that you were unable to realise and go through'.

Eugene took a break turned backward put his both hands towards the sky to gather some power. After collecting those power for the good spirits surge every time in the air of this place, who all were being governed and emphasised by him. Eugene gathered all that and thrown it towards Yash and this power couldn't make any sort of unresistingly to Yash as he just move one step Back as the bunch of all this strikes his chest but within a second he became easy and reliable. Eugene then seen towards both of them and said dictatingly that;

'So Yash and Adrita have you both seen what happened just, this everlasting and empowering power which is not affordable to any one had meant on effect towards Yash. This is what I want to tell you my dear Adrita and which you were unable to realise about Yash'.

Eugene shouted loudly and make his tone to be heard by the flowing spirits and Adrita that 'He is the man who have those features which can build and severe this diminishing love and humanity over the beautifully meant place of God. He is the only pure soul person who devoted his life for several generations and this time God praised him with a slave to save everyone from a long lasting big damage to be occurred in this period. My dear Adrita, he is not the only person who can do that, as you both being allocated for this task all together. You must know that Yash didn't came because of his characteristics and job that he did at his planet but he is being called by God here to take over the affinity and save the place from forthcoming massacre and blunder on humanity.

He came here in the sense just to meet you and save you from the harsh and bluntly tactics of Barrack against you. Those that were not just going to damage you but harm in bulk the happy humanity over the land.

'This time I can see that everything that I am revealing you both is not so much clear to both of you, as it consist a mysterious case behind it and which I told Yash just a while before and to inform you the same. Adrita dear you do know about Barrack a lot but I should tell you that he doesn't want you to be with her for a good reason. He wants to eject those energies from you that even you don't know and didn't measured in yourself. So today I am going to brief out these things to you as if I meant it late to inform you than this whole world is to sacrifice there souls and then too we can't save the blossom of humanity in this world. '

Adrita's condition was too anonymous and she is getting conspicuous wanders in her mind. Her face is not inclined to accept that Eugene had hidden something very much serious from her which is beneficiary as she trust Eugene a lot and he is the only parents she thought from his childhood days. Yash too stood close to Adrita this time and was analysing Adrita's intimate expressions when she would be going to hear all that as Adrita is shocked after listening about Yash from Eugene.

Eugene said, 'Yash I want you to go apart from this place now as if I told you whatever is desired for you to know and now this time me and my baby Adrita would be going to dealth with the short coming emotion hidden behind the realities. Before you Go Yash I would like to conclude you both to meet all together once our biggest philosopher and Guide of this place Mr. Bares. Then all sort of things that were going to be left by me towards you both would be told you in brief by him as if he have the written records of everything that had occurred here since decades. He is the only sagacious person after me that would be going to inform you both regarding your next step that is to be taken for upholding the prosper climate every where. Now you could leave Yash as this period of mine with Adrita is to precious for both of us'.

Yash bowed his head and said, 'Sure sir as you say as I also feel that this would be the time for you to be just with her,' Yash said this to Eugene and his eyes interacted with Adrita as he also wants to say a lot more things to her and this time She is also looking helpless. She listened which is telling of his histories, which she wanted to know every time but as her age passed off she tried to oversight them all and this time they were standing in her front whom she had to face. The time when Yash reached to the door to went out of it he looked back towards Adrita as he can't see her that much helpless and wants to increase her moral. Adrita also wants to feel Yash once more before he leaves place so she also faced towards him and this time the sense of having each other adherence could seen in both the eyes. This is the start of there unbeatable attachment which governed by nature.

Yash had gone all the way out of this place leaving Eugene and Adrita all alone and then Eugene started surge side wise from one place to the other of that closed curvature brick meant room. Adrita tried to ask every second but she couldn't as she is just waiting for Eugene to start first. After taking time Eugene spoke at last.

Eugene said, 'My dear... I had not told you something about your parent that you asked me since your infancy. I am your victim for that but all these thing doesn't depends on me just because you too know God empowers me for everything I do. You should know that you are not a simple priest girl or I must say that you are not a simple soul as if God had praised you with the power of Miracles which happens wherever you stay. You are the one who consist of those enhancing power which can over rule this world in the favour of humanity and this is why Barrack is following you since your birth and wanted to gain all from you. After that he is going to sweep world happiness a long way and going to cover that with his dark magic and brutality. Your mother is too a priest girl my dear and your father is from the planet "Earth surface" as your mother stay over this place with a solemn respect and power with her to deal with every kind of harm that strikes here as God had praised her with all that. Your father is a slave who had came here from your planet some 22 years before. I don't know what happened and what is the reason your mother and father both started devotion each other. As your mother was the only one whom our last Biggest God saint who taught her and had praised with those immense powers. He have faith on her that she is not going to violate even a single rule of Heaven's hell and not going to use these powers in any negative way. She even didn't misused those powers but the thing that she did is to love someone, which is strictly being denied for every priest girl at this place. She did that and then she is too daring to face any sort of discomfort against it and to protect her love. This is a regard for love which God doesn't denies, so no one over here.

No one, also blamed her or said her to face any discourage and freaking stress for this inconvenience but she is not allowed to stay as a priest girls now. So she was send back to the "Earth surface" with your father to live as she wants, but her powers are being plucked up from her. God only praise with natures enlightening power those whom he felt full of pure soul and that is your mother is all about. While getting away from your mother who is the only one who can take regard of this Heaven's Hell all together on her own. Everyone is dishearten over this place and is being apprehensive about Heaven's Hell for its continuity like the same. There were anxiety about own happiness. Then our respected chief of that time 'Maven Bells' who had assigned all those functionality and responsibilities that your mother do consists with her in that period said to your mother;

Maven Bells to Adrita's mother, 'You should be apologised for what you did but that's not as I am talking about your love. I am saying this because of your stage in which you assaulted to love. I granted you all the veiling shelter to you of this place to make yours and others living better than anything. I graced you to teach lessons to these forthcoming slaves and make them to live more effective and efficiently. These all things I drove in your bucket for building something and not like this that you did. You know that creatures like you are too limited whom I prefer that much so I didn't expected that Grave from you this time. But as all this love and spirits are a dashing gift of God I can't even deny you for it'.

Respected Maven Bells shouted then and added to his wards, 'This mishap you did is not a part of yours easy way as it took a deep turn for you and all of us at Heaven's Hell. You had meant me a slave today who is helpless of his decision that he took to deliver you with the showering' thunder of powers and You are the one who can't afford it. As you need to leave this place now as soon as possible but I am not going to leave you like that. This is because as peoples are brought up to this place for being punished and make them learn something. So that they could become ordered and help others too. This time you are the one who is out of order and that's why you should also need to get the same'.

Adrita's Mother is not scared about any sort of work that she could going to face the next as she was too daring and believe a lot on her decisions. In her means she feels that doing everything that your hearts says you to do without spoiling anyone else happiness is a good thing to go for. At that time yours internal enhancing thefts are also no one to make it taste sour to you. She was standing that time also like the wall of fortified thoughts.

Maven Bells replied fortifier and said to your mother looking towards the sky and re surge his point of attention from her as if he doesn't want to peer in her eyes next;

'Now......as you were blessed at this place and making your all powers to be ruined off but I don't want to do all that. As now your point of punishment is to lend and devote to your first baby child back to Heaven's Hell and that would be a little baby girl. Your powers will get diminished for you as you step down to "Earth surface" but you need to devote and praise your first child baby girl who will nourished, pure and prosperous. Who will going to born as a beam of your inbuilt powers and going to consist all of them like a wall covered with flowering stems. The main thing that comes is your attachment towards her is like a spray of delight for a short span of time and after that you would have to send that baby back to the Heaven's Hell. She should be going to grow and learn here every sort of stuffs as if she needs to fulfill your roles and responsibilities. She will be the power who can only necklace the all invincible power that break natures peaseige and its beauty. She will be the one to uncover the harsh case and save the nature from it'.

Maven Bells added 'Now you both can go back as if whatever I had said you all meant to be too pure and a harsh truth for you'.

Eugene said to Adrita, 'My baby this is the last thing that Maven Bells said to both of your parents and freed them and he to get dispersed from that place and get mixed in air, showing your both parent the way to move out of Heaven's Hell and proceed towards the planet from where your father belongs "Earth Surface". This is the whole story my dear for which I negate your questions you put to me since your childhood as if I severely denied for this to be known to you before today'.

Eugene said, '*Hey* dear... don't be too dull this time as I think this is not my fault as if that time when you came to Heavens Hell and you were dropped in my arms. Your innocence and cute smile didn't allowed me to break this auspicious happiness of yours and some what mine too as you became from that day my child my part of living'.

Adrita moved close to Eugene step by step as she was lost somewhere looking towards Eugene in a perception manner as if she was in a deep thought. She came too close to Eugene and while looking to her eyes dullness Eugene was also get apprehensive. Adrita didn't said anything and whispered any emotion. She just clubbed Eugene in his arms and tears commence flowing from her eyes. She was not able to say anything this time. Eugene was aware that the bluntly heartiest spirit that she had hidden in her soul, just moved out in the form of tears from eyes, so she started wetting up Eugene shoulder.

Eugene said, 'My dear child don't weep out your tears like that. You don't know that what does you mean in Exaltation humanity for the whole. You are the one who is going to curb every sort of blunted wound of mango people that were every time strikes then to work under there limits'.

'There is no end of anything my dear child as if Yash is also at this place who knows everything about you and would be your comrade in saving all that for sake of humanity,' Eugene said and he putted his hand over the Adrita's head and started rubbing it through which he thou give some reliance and empower positive faith in her.

After a long time conversation came to halt with a deep sleek silence on both there face. Eugene started stepping his foot back one by one while being looking towards the crafting waves of emotions emboldening on Adrita's face. This time when Eugene too settle to be braised up as he is unable to her this time. This is the time for Adrita solder herself on her own and make well defined prescription for her way ahead.

Adrita without facing to his sides with her bowed head relaxed herself and moved out steeply. It settle that the whole picture and the scene behind the case had became very familiar to her now. So now she knows what to do next. Yash was too waiting for her just at the doorsteps hidden from everyone behind some bushes across the corner wall of it and just seeking to catch every instinct that could inform him about her escape from it. Yash was gazing from a bit of space between these bushes and all his desperate spirit were very clear from his all these facts assaults with desired intentions.

26

Soon a tone stood Yash ears and Adrita moved out of it. She fastened her steps and moved straight away to her place without facing sideway.

'You haven't told anything like that', Yash asked.

Adrita who is lost in her own the world that being set by Eugene for her after delivering all those stuffs. A equipoise spirit inside her is making her implications as she is not able to understand the conspicuous chemistry of God. Every phase, every moment that she had gone beneath with Yash and seeking to relate everything to know about the depth of this concern. So she replied:

'I think these all things are not a point of concern for you. So that's why I didn't told all that', Adrita said with a sheering flow in her eyes. She fastened her steps to walk away on her way.

Vibrations were getting too vibrant in Yash's compartment which is making him more sagacious as time passes. Yash too put forward and blocked Adrita on her way and tried to stare in her hidden eyes which nevertheless want Yash to go through.

Yash said, '*Hey* my dear I had expressed my sort of feeling towards you before only. By my those affinity you can feel what sort of discomfort is conspiring and evoking inside my heart after looking to these water drops in your eyes', Adrita getting still and listened.

Yash proceeded, 'I am profoundly embarrassed this time dear because all these words you just listened are not mine but were being said by Eugene sir. You are going to do like that and avoid me, then it would be a crime that you were doing. As much I know the biggest thing for a person to do is to work according to the happiness and spirit of those who prefer you foremost. So that they don't make any one disheartful and I think, I am right', Yash with his widely wrist eyes and leaning towards her as he wants to be answered furiously.

Yash two folded again to break her silence this time 'you can't be quite an ignorant at this tedious time as if I am sober and having a big question mark in my mind about this concern. How all this happened and I and you became the only flying birds of this land. I don't know about all this neither I am aware of things to be faced forward'.

Adrita prompted, 'So do you think that I know about all this before or you were thinking as I am from the members of Heaven's hell and aware about all this that's why I avoided you before.

Adrita replied 'If that is so, then I am afraid'.

Yash said 'And you feel that I can even go in that much conspiracy kind of thing about you.

Yash relaxed himself and replied again, 'Dear...I just want to know about you....nothing else. I want to listen those words that you didn't shared with me still. All this is emphasis for me to know if you can measure this drifting shadow of case below me'.

'Hu... do you', Yash replied.

Adrita said, 'Yash I don't know that how much you understood me but if you felt me so deep then you could have seen that colour of this bird which is not seen by anyone still. The colour which says that it wants to live yours planet life, as I am too much impassioned to be in that hemisphere and was bounded to touch that so. If this thing you measured a bit then you would have measured the excitement and courage on my face at that point of time when I crack to tell things about me. Anything valuable that I wandered you should know I had shared that one with you. Now if this thing is about my parent then it is only the left untouched part of my life about which even I am not having a explicit well defined picture in my mind. So you say how I could have shared with you all that'.

'Yes if this is a concern for you that I didn't told you about me. So let me tell you today that all this, I know is just what being told to me by Eugene sir "Pop Jesus". All this that I know before is like a land that have many bushes spread in its greenery. I also hadn't asked that much from him even if I remedy him as my parents. Still as being at apart stages and consisting unique responsibilities there is a slight gap between both of us which I hadn't crack even once to cross through. All he told me before I am just living with a hope in my mind that there would be a day when I can get into touch with my parent and be in the shelter of my mother. So with this hope I never crossed my steps, my speech to know more' Adrita said with full emotions.

Adrita replied again, 'Don't be so shocked about it because if Eugene sir had told you about my past then I am sure that he must have told much more than I do know', Adrita smiled after saying this with tears still flowing from her eyes.

Yash who was lost in her words and not even facing her, rubbed her, head with his hand like seeking to think more and recapitulate everything that he faced here from the day he came to Heaven's Hell.

Adrita replied again, 'Well... so good to listen about you from Eugene sir and the story regarding your pure soul'.

Adrita didn't find that change which she wants to see in Yash from the last line as Yash is lost still. So she said '*Hey*...why you being too shuffled and convicted this time as all that Eugene *baba* said to you is very much impulses which provokes you and your surroundings'.

'Ok....Listen please doesn't say anything now and please....just help me to dig out of this whole. Please make me realise all other things; give me a explicit and concise way to decide further. For all this you just need to answer few questions of mine that I am going to ask you further'.

Adrita's sweet face bowed towards Yash.

Yash took her along with him after the wall nearby where a bench was lying vacant for them to sit. Adrita after realising Yash feel and touch which had started getting dispersed in her soul, started getting spirit numb. This time she was spirit too much relief as if she wants this pleasure and reliable feel from a long time.

Yash kept his both hands on her shoulders and tried to make her sit on the bench. Yash took the place below Adrita and sat near her tows looking upward into her eyes.

Yash asked, 'Now tell me that do you know that the "amulet" that you had tied in Ronu's neck being having the forecasting power that had been embeded by your mother into it at the time she had send you over here'.

Adrita replied, 'What are you saying about that "amulet"... what... I don't know any history and story behind it as it is just wrapped in Ronu's neck to make him secure and free from this nature's abnormality, thief's of life who could wreck him. As everyone knows that Ronu is not a normal creature as he had upholded his physical standard since my birth. This is all that I know'.

Yash said 'Oh!.....even I do know that much before but it's not everything about him as he consists of a deep blue case beyond that scope. If you also don't know about him then listen;

The conceptual case behind Ronu is just aid to protect you and your crust from others. So that you didn't face any discomfort ever and no one could break you and make you to be in grief. He is with you not for any other sake apart from just simply protecting you and your's powers delivered to you by your mother which makes you executive from everyone. He is your best comrade and a mean who secures you from any blunder and set you every time in a curve'.

Adriat said, '*Hey* how come you got to know all these things,......Tell me because really this would be a biggest case for me which stayed behind bars still'.

Yash was shocked to hear all this and he stroked his head over her head as Adrita's reactions were extreme exotic this time showing her desperation regarding all this.

'I think you were saying right before that Eugene sir hadn't told you much and I do know more than you about all this concern', Yash said this and smiled as if he wants to change the shocking mood of Adrita toward a easier one.

'I feel now you and me both knows about the functionality of nature and its mysterious things that had make us both together. I don't know why a boy like me who never consider girl in his life ever had a garden of love in his mind with the flower of severity and delight that started impulsing me to believe on actuality of love and attraction... All this is just because of you and only you my dear Adrita'. Yash soul calmy conveyed all this.

Adrita faced Yash with sleaveing, deliberate and consistent eyes as Yash simply bowed his head to make her realise once more about his heart datums which he had shown earlier too.

The time was getting hailed and every one whether it is nature trees or animals in its surrounds had halted this time as they are also waiting for the next phase to be listened by Adrita's from her lovely, sweet little solitary tone. So that the nature and aura get thrilled with the buds of love hope that are been sown in this surrounding.

Adrita after looking towards Yash without saying anything slashed her face away from Yash and started facing down towards the green grass floor.

Adrita said, 'You know about me a lot now and I feel you started measuring my gestures & motions to predict what a person I would be. You know that too as if I am devoted towards "Earth surface" my parents were also there and my vacant smile talks about that place to me a lot. As it wants to glow. I don't know the history two folding itself once again and why just me and only my life is being focused by God. This time it's in the sense to protect humanity, So I don't feel that it could be some wrong thing to do'.

Adrita too quietly and slowly said, 'And at last I want you to know my dear that it's not just you who is attracted towards me from the first day because I am also the one who started facing the same and getting lost in you day by day from the first day I met you'.

The words that being expressed by Adrita was havenlitious beautiful. This time is incredible not just for both of them but the beauty of sound. Air fragrance is making itself more empowered as is too getting energised by the frequent distributing flow of sweet air that is of love spread all apart. There is a new birth of love occurred at this place after a decade and this will be in the favour of humanity.

Buds of flowers are evoking by stretching their arms out in the sky, so freely as if this explicitly shows the sign of freedom towards humanity. Everything is very much reliable and going too smooth but there was a person who concentrating on every word said by both of them. This is a slave of Heaven's Hell who had hidden himself behind the bushes that were lying in the corner of this place. He was seeking hard to gather everything from Yash and Adrita before anyone could be able to measure, his presence over there.

This was a crucial time for Yash and Adrita, which helped the creature to stay away of the reach of Adrita as her power consist of attraction and measurement which she gained from Heaven's Hell through which she can feel, smell, hear attract anyone more than other's. So apart from all those features in

Adrita then too this beautiful acquisition of world emotion had covered her mind. In case of that she is unable to measure presence of any unwanted thing or creature in its auras. This is why she is letting first time any third creature to know about her secrecy.

The nature is going too demanding for a happy ongoing love to bulge out more and more with a fragrance as quickly as feasible before any other creature could measure this sweet taste of love at this place. Sober and freelancing breeze started in a second to show their contribution in this saffron.

Yash said, 'Your words had evoked that pleasures in my heart which I never seem and assault to feel before. I am sure that If I had tried to get this love feel before I won't be able to get that delight. Adrita, I feel like I am completed my soul request and that too at the accurate time'.

Yash deemed his life with Adrita and replied, 'God plays a game and I feel his best game is "The Game of Love" which is full of 'MIRACLE' in our case'.

Adrita smiled and said, 'Miracle' yes this love being a 'Miracle' since many decades and this time this *'Miracle'* is for a mutation and that too with his arms sheds for his peoples to save them from this harsh, humanity. If this Miracle is competent of serving every person wishes and request for their easy living then I would be blessed. If this Miracle can change the nasty thoughts which every bad human think about the other human being then I am blessed. I am thankful to my God for making me feel executive and realise who am I. While being at the supreme position then the other priest Girls, I hadn't felt grateful ever. This is because the memories of my Parent was being away from me since birth, even I hadn't seen them which is the only part of mine from all other priest girls. This spirit never left me alone and the uncompleted lines and wisdom that do I am having about my parent before which is being flue up by Eugene *Dada,* "Pop Jesus" in my brain. These things never left me to breath freely but yes they had taught me with the best ever lessons that anyone couldn't have in their whole life. Then along all these things from my childhood time everyone over here at this place started to give me remediation like a leader and piece of training every day. Every datum behind all those things I got to know today that I had been poised to host the flag of humanity with giving and taking honours from everyone'.

'Adrita, I am thrilled today. I feel at the top of the mountain over which I am standing and looking the other downside of it, where my mother and father were standing, facing towards me with a smiley face', Adrita looked upward towards the sky facing upward and took a deep breath.

Yash being frightened to listen to the last stanza she said and he whispered slowly 'she is talking about mountains..... height......her parents......what is this I am not getting. What had she wandered in her mind?'

Adrita turned towards Yash and said, 'You were saying something afraid, I didn't listened, come up again', as soon as she finished saying all this to Yash her eyes came togather that mischief creature hiding this time behind a giant trunk of tree at a very far distance from their place listening there conservation. She instantly read the mind of this creature that is profoundly consuming there's most valuable conversation. Adrita eyes started burning with anger. Her postures and emotions were profoundly mutate this time and she is about to burst upon. Yash too got stressed to see her like that and he too faced in the direction she is facing. Adrita run instantly to catch that creature but till the time she reached over the place that mischief working Creature noticed her approach and dispersed from that place. Yash too run after Adrita towards that place as the intention between them had been mutation a lot because of this interception.

Yash asked, 'Adrita........what happened dear......had you seen something at this corner.

Adrita 'Don't be stressed and worried, this person is seeking to listen to our conversation. We also don't know that how much he had grasped from all the talk we did. Ok...but leave you don't be scared about it. I know who's he and what they are concerned about. Yes......I know you too also want to know about him'.

'Yes dear......yes please tell me soon because my pat ions are not that much.' Yash asked from Adrita.

'This work being done not other than Barrack and I do know this is his foremost priority person and very loyal to him named Alasky. I had set my mind to trash him away today by catch him red handed doing all this but I am unable to do so', Adrita replied.

'Alasky...ok....so do we have to do anything now to sort all this out. Tell me if something can happen', Yash asked.

'No.......don't tensed about it as if its upset that I am unable to catch him "with gun in his pocket", Adrita said.

'You seen yourself now as you had changed profoundly in these few minutes. I think Firstly you should relax yourself', Yash expressed.

'You don't need to tensed in that case because my mood fluctuate instantly and its been governed by me. I had said my soul to be cure and smile and you can see now smile getting dispersed on my face', Adrita said with a smile.

'Ok....If that is so then it would be the right time for me to move forward and express me deliberately', Yash said this and put his step ahead.

Adrita just seeking to collect what he's being talking about. She stepped back as Yash stepped ahead towards her after entire his words.

Yash said, '*Hey*....what......I don't feel it's been too hot now, then for what reason sweat being seen on your forehead. *Hey* what is there any problem?'

Yash replied again, Ok.....so this is very crucial and emphasis both for prosperous living. What I am going to say to you, I wouldn't said to you, if I hadn't felt that same emotions in your expressions. This is because the thing I want to say you is not easy but yes that's emphasis for both of us to be happy and that is the thing that even "Pop Jesus" to wanted us to do'.

Adrita furiously asked, 'Now could you please tell me that thing without any delay as my feet are also not spirit resistible to stand here for too long. So Please hurry up, let us go inside now as this place is not safe also for both of us to stay for so long'.

'Yes...I also wants to hurry up and sort out every buck of our life so that we could start a new refreshing living without any anxiety and pressure. So I would request you to come with me all along to my land which I know you also like a lot and please....don't speak negative even a single world', Yash spoke to Adrita and get numb. He stated stepping closer to Adrita as she was being quite after this with clashing thoughts. Yash took the charge this time he knows that he is the only one who have to handle everything that would come in there's way, as he is very much poised for all that. They were too close and compatible to hear breath of each other. This closeness is the need of God because god even wants these both true powers to combine together and pluck off the pain and anxiety from this climate.

Soon as nature's demand small drops of water started to fall over this green grass carpet and colourful flowers spread all around with blooming buds. Emotions of both were in tensed this time with their holding hand each other tightly with closed eyes. Nature was writing up the story of love for them.

Yash whispered slightly in her ears, 'I want try to make your dream true that top of mountains, your parents and the enlisting delight that you would have when you will be in our planet. I pledge to cover you with all this worlds' happiness and not going to allow this vacant whole of sorrow to evoke ever after in your life. Look up....Look into my eyes dear they just want you to be happy. The respect for you is enlightening up my world and my tears are rinse away the depth of silence in my life, which is all just because of you'.

Adrita constantly looking into Yash eyes as he make her chin to move up and stare into her eyes and realise everything on her own while listening to Yash.

Yash impeeded, 'I want you to feel that all sort of imagination that I am creating in my eyes because this time my eyes know that they had met with his soul mate. I had nothing to say more than that my dear as if my crumbling heart just wants to hold you in my arms and give relax to my magnetic blood flow that is tempting to yours'.

This time Adrita didn't say anything as she was still looking into his eyes and after a while she replied, 'This is not felt by me and I never dreamed also because my heart might had set this thing with it that all this is not going to happen anytime in my life. Yash I am speechless to say anything to you and every drop from my eyes that is coming out is being thrilled of joy and happiness that is unmeasurable'.

Adrita confessed, 'Yes...Yash I love you too now from my bottom of heart as all barriers and all milestones in my way had been broken up now. I am all set to live my life. This would be up to my wish and I am not going to allow your wish to come forward in future', Adrita said and smiled a little with tears in her eyes and clubbed Yash in her arms. She started crying loudly as this time her soul is also cure because this is the time being dashingly designed by almighty God.

Both stayed like that and the rain also started falling heavily over them as nature also want to show his desire towards there alignment. Time settle to be halt this time and there is no disturbance for both of them in this aura as everything started to react in favour of all their owance.

Then after a bit of time Yash said, '...now just...move away, these golden drops from your eyes lets think for a brighter world. My dear so you will be coming with me to my land...'

Adrita moved a step back breathed heavily and ejected by speaking, 'Yes... off course I am coming with you. As all my dreams are going to start now only. How could I deny to that my dear?'

Yash going too excited and rubbing of tears from her face like a child said, 'Ok........then you are not going to say anything or not going to do anything so that I am going to set everything for our escape from this place as if I had been told about it by Eugene sir'.

Adrita impeded, '*Hey*... not Eugene sir... says "Pop Jesus" from now onwards. He is my Eugene *Dada*... whom I love a lot', She said and smiled towards Yash.

Yash too smiled and said, 'Ah! I do know that my dear... Ok... I am not going to say that now. He is my one and only "Pop Jesus" is... that....ok now', Yash smiled.

Adrita stood in attitude like a teacher putting both hand on her waist 'Yes now it's been good my child...', Adrita smiled and Yash got a bit easy as if happiness of Adrita's smile is seen on his face explicitly.

Yash said, 'Ok... dear I want to take one Creature from your place to our planet. *Hey* please don't say no for that, I... had promised him'.

Adrita replied, 'So you think that I am going to deny...', Adrita said in a bit cure way.

'You can do anything now my dear, you hadn't listen my words that now I had broken up all the walls and barrier that defend me to cross my line and that do emphasis me to follow rules meant over here. There is nothing for you to be worried about me in all these cases. As this is the time when I am also going to show you my silenced clubby nature that will going to be anonymously apart and not fragile in any circumstances. That is going to change colour with not nature's but my willingness. So who's that creature which had made you so fascinating about him as now you want to take him along? Tell...tell me his name, maybe I do know him', Adrita replied in excitement.

Yash said, 'You... Ha!...you would know... I can't even think like that. Have you seen that what a life you were living over here. Even I don't realise a day in front of me, you had seen any Creature apart from doing your work. So you tell had you?'

Adrita instant reply, '*Hey*... what you were thinking about me that I am ignorant and hopeless. So let me tell you that I do notice everyone who comes up over here and I am very conscious about that. You would be shocked to listen that I do even know the name of that Creature. He is one from the Heaven's Hell slaves and his name is...', Adrita took some second to bliss curious faces made by Yash this time and she replied again.

'That's......"Figo"...am I right', Adrita blissful even sort of second this time.

'Hah! ...you know all that and then too you were acting too innocently. *Hey* this is no way you did', Yash said.

Adrita insisted, 'Dear... My...dear, I easily gather everything happening at this Heaven's Hell anywhere whatever I wish too and if that thing is about someone for whom there are some spirit in me then those things are very explicitly represent able to me. Your every instance on this place from the first day we contacted till today everything automatically came to my notice, whether it is about any of your activity or relations over here'.

Adrita with her big wisted eyes stared towards Yash and said, 'Now I do know everything about you internally and externally or you can say that I know about you more than you know about yourself'.

Yash mind became awe-stuck because the picture that he having about her in his mind which do scares him to come closer to her become profoundly opposite.

Yash replied, 'But if I did know about you all these things before, then I hadn't wasted so much time to meet my heart desire which is being you.'

'Relax... My dear... don't react like that as nothing work according to you. So that's why God had set best time for everything. Like today is only the day for both of us to flow down in the ocean of our love wanders', Adrita said to Yash while her hand on Yash shoulder.

Suddenly the room in the tower where Adrita took classes of girls enlighten up and that too so brightly as it also knows that Adrita is not present at her place so wherever she had gone, she can know about this call for her and head touching Yash cheeks.

'Yash this is becoming darker now and see my class time is up. So I need to leave and this is also not good for you to stay over here for too long, so my dear go back to your resident' Adrita said after measuring the situations.

'Ok...then you must go back but we are going to meet the next day as now, I can't wait for my punishment to get finished and then I am going to take you along with me. As I don't even know will would be the circumstances at that time though we all would be leaving next evening as I need to meet the person whom "Pop Jesus" said me to. As he is the only one that could guide me the way to move out', Yash tried to express his action forward.

Adrita said 'We'll do so everything as you say my dear but move from here before anyone could see or feel your presence it's been high time now. Dear over here apart from "Pop Jesus" there are some more power's that control Heaven's Hell which are not going to allow all this even once so you please go apart'.

'Ok... I am going to set everything and going to deal with all sort of distraction in our way, but you need promise to me that you are going to meet me tomorrow morning...and that would be explicitly at the accurate time when the morning water shaft starts up in the canal. We will be going to meet at that place', Yash said.

'I think there is some problem with you I am revealing you to leave this place and you were still busy in these questions stuff. *Hey* dear I meet you for sure any place you wish too but the thing now suitable for both of us is to go. So I am surge towards my classes as children's are too waiting for that and you should go away too', Adrita said.

The next day would come but they both have to put a big step forward with it in the sense to mutation the way sun looks towards them. Yash gone straight away to his residence and when he reached at the door step of his residence he saw everything in that aura which is being destructed due to that un natural exhausting power of nature. Nobody is being seen out of there Yard.

Yash said, 'Ah!...this is good that's the way. I want nobody is out here as I am scared on my way for the question everyone is going to ask me though. Now I need to just go straight away to my room and have to handle only my boy's queries. Hm......how easy it had been ... but God knows how they are going to trash me. Let me get inside first'.

Yash gone straight away and wrist his door. He leg that Pee is also present over there. His friend looks like talking about his concern only all together with Pee and everyone's attention was now towards him. He was standing on the door with a smiley face facing everyone as they all were facing him only.

Ankit said 'Oh! ..... the gentleman come, now. He was going to sort out anxiety of all with us which we all were dealing since he had gone', Ankit taunted him.

Gaurav said, 'You were asking what from whom, as I don't feel that he is going to tell you anything this time also. Yash... I am saying rigorous naaa......'

Sunny stood up gone close to Yash and make him to come in, closed the door. Sunny tried to make Yash easy and asked him, 'Yash what had happened with you and where were you from last long time. The reaction of everyone like this is because they were waiting for you desperately and you also walked away from this place without informing us about any concern.

Yash took Sunny in a corner and whispered slowly in his ears '*Hey*..... I just come here to describe the whole story to you all but what pee being doing over here'.

Sunny replied, 'Pee...he is making all of us to feel a bit relaxed. As he is adherenceing us why were you talking like this for him'.

Yash replied, 'Ok.......listen now I came up ... so I don't think that Pee's requirement is over here. *Hey*.........my brothers understand, I am going to describe all facts and functionality in front of you but he should leave first. As we all know that he is the member of Heaven's Hell. So that's why I can't disperse anything in front of him. Ok wait...He is going now back to everyone and you are just going to adherence me in sending Pee out from our room....ok'.

Sunny said, '.....ok as you wish dear'.

Yash said loudly facing everyone and coming back in between of his friends. 'Listen you all dear I hadn't faced anything over there... so I feel that you all shouldn't take that much pressure in your mind for knowing about that from me. As there is nothing which I am going to describe you all.'

27

This last line being shocking for all of them as before they didn't feel that he was going to react in such a way. Gaurav replied instantly;

'See... I was saying you all that he's not going to tell you anything even a single word for that and it's been in front of you all'.

'Gaurav I was just saying this because I didn't faced something for which we all have to sit over here and waste our time and do nothing else. So I just want you all to please get back to your work and leave this thing here only'.

Ankit is a lot afraid about all this so he just stood up from his place and shouted on Yash, 'Do you know from how much time everyone is just simply waiting for you, worried about your well being. No body from us had even took food and water from that time. We are waiting for you, so that you are going to come and remedy all of us like this.

Sunny impeded in amidst, '*Hey* Ankit be cool dear don't get so hyper on this. Yash had talked to me about it and believe me there is nothing like that wrong which he had faced. Nothing unnatural also that is why he is asking you all for be normal. This doesn't mean anything else my dear believe me if you can't believe Yash'.

'Pee... what had happened to you now...as I don't feel there is anything to laugh upon as if Yash had make this climate a clumsy one. Say anyone did something...'. Ankit asked.

'Oh!... No... no there is nothing wrong being done by anyone, I am just smiling after having a look at both of their faces that is seeking to hide the ball but their pockets are having a hole', Pee said all this and moved towards the door with the same smile attached on his face.

Soni said '*Hey* Pee......where were you going dear wait over here, as you are also worried for Yash. Pee....And you have to help us too to ask Yash about his past some hours as we don't feel that he'll tell us conveniently'.

'Don't be tensed about that... I said you all don't try to be knowing things happened with Yash last as he is going to tell you all everything. Let me leave now as if this environment is being demanding me to go. Some natural positive points are getting negative for me in others heart'.

Ankit asked, 'What......what did you said last something getting wrong, what all that if I am getting your point then you were saying that someone is over here who don't wants your presence. Is that so......'

Pee said, '*Hey* I didn't expected my words are going to be explicit to you so much as I just said those for Yash to get through'.

Soni stepping forward towards Pee, 'Please...Pee...get in as well as wants you dear this time'.

Yash spirit low after disheartening Pee, '*Hey*.........you all just be silent........give me a minutes......as all this is getting wrong because of me. My lack of wisdom who had oversight the sensing power of Pee and started doing something which even I don't think for him'.

'Yash...so the person whom Pee is talking about is you......' Ankit asked.

'Yes....Ankit....Pee....Please try to understand me as if my intentions were not wrong in this affinity because the thing that I had faced apart from the Heaven's Hell rule. I won't be able to convey all this in front of Pee so that's why I said it all in the sense to avoid Pee in all this conversation. As I am going to put forward all that I faced. Afraid......Pee now I feel guilty but my intentions are not wrong in that regard'.

'Pee.......please believes on Yash words, they all were true. You know Pee previously also in past Yash is only the person who never let you words down as if he praises you the most', Ankit insisted Pee.

'Yes, Pee as you are the only one who had shown me the first stairs of Heaven's Hell. You are my first comrade too of this place and all these things matters me a lot', Yash added to Ankit's word.

Pee stepped towards Yash making his hand to cover up his shoulders, 'How could you feel that I am annoyed or disheartfelt from you and your any acts. I had collected this thing from your mind that there is something which you don't want me to listen though and that's why I wish to leave'.

'But......my dear now you don't have to go anywhere as if you also have to help me out in my annoyance. Hello..........you all guys just come together, I need to tell you all about the way. I had been remedied by "Pop Jesus" as I reached over there. But before that you all had to promise me in sharing and helping hands. Executive you my dear Pee.......I really need your help dear', Yash said.

Pee said, 'Yes dear I'll be going to do all sort of feasible things for you that I could...........I promise for that. Now without asking anything and wasting time just start your story, so that further I could give you any suggestion'.

Yash said, 'Ok.....over here I am with my best buddies of life in which Pee had become one of it. Now I want you all to come together at one place and sit still so that you can get what I faced and how I need all of yours help in that'.

Yash started 'So as I reached the place at that time it's not me only who is being called by "Pop Jesus" but with me he had also called priest Girl "Adrita". I had seen that the person whom I had met in the prison is the only person who is "Pop Jesus". At that time whatever is my condition I couldn't explain you all'.

'*Hey*....Yash this priest girl is that one only whom you had talked before also like after that first volleyball match we had seen. After that you were in prison too because of her', Gaurav said.

'Listen don't hamper in between please Gaurav and I had been in prison but not because of her, that being my fault', Yash replied.

Yash continued, 'So after that "Pop Jesus" started to tell me about my this life and my previous life too. They told me a lot about Adrita also and that time I got to know that why do I feel so much attracted towards her and not to anyone else'.

'"Pop Jesus" conveyed me that Adrita and me were soul mate and we both have to be together in future that would empower us and this nature. How much its worthy I don't know and I don't even to think about it. They told that we both have to secure this world diminishing humanity and love. This is why this generation is going to be ours both together', Yash said and took a glass of water kept sidewise.

Yash put down his glass of water and continued 'So even "Pop Jesus" wanted both of us to move away from this place conspiracy soon and get back to the "Earth surface" as Adrita's origination land is also "Earth surface" only'.

'And this is all, that I wanted to inform all of you. Adrita dreams are just related to our planet "Earth surface" and nowhere else', Yash said all this and ended up leaving left things on his guys.

'Pee......please...I feel you could make this puzzle easier for me....so help me out', Yash asked Pee.

'Before taking any action, I would like to tell you that I am quite aware about all this before', Pee said to Yash.

Yash being exhausted now to hear this and said, 'Pee.......... so you know all these thing that I had told you just and if you know all these thing then why didn't you had told me about it before. This is very unnatural behaviour of yours.'

'Yash I am not saying that I know about all this before but I am saying that I know about your's and Adrita attraction from the beginning, as may be you had forgot but I am the first person from whom you asked about her. That time I had seen all this in your eyes as this energy to analyse is been given to me by God when he had given me responsibilities. Now I think you were explicit with my point', Pee said.

Yash replied, 'If I am going to ask down in brief then it would be a large short of questionnaire to be asked from you because to leave this Heaven's Hell without anyone's wisdom is a solemn thing and I had known that while living over here'.

'Pee...tell me about that person who being said as geographical architect of this place. Afraid Pee... His name is being told to me by "Pop Jesus" but I had forgotten that. I am seeking to memorise but failed to so', Yash said while being lost in his wandered to recapitulate that name.

Pee replied, 'let me tell you the name of that Geographical architect and a big scholar. So he is the solemn "Abraman" who control all the geographical characteristics and he is the only one who knows the exact well defined way inside and forth corners of Heaven's Hell'.

'*Hey* listen and you will leg him inside the church only. As there is a secret entry gate of church inside which no one goes apart from priests and Abraman. Abraman stays over there and remain be seated at his place for many days without even surge a little. His chance is in one corner of the inside room where a giant candle kept and he stays close to that candle every time meditating in his own world and not allowing that candle to halt either', Pee replied.

Yash to be quite cure and enthusiastic in his every words because he had to start a new walk.

Yash set reliance 'Ah......I got the name of that person...........Pee can't realise that how much stress I am spirit on my way when because of my exult and excitement I had forgot the name of this person'.

Pee smiled, '*Ha*........the stress being seen on your face too...ask others', Pee triedto assault him as everyone knows that there is no stress and discomfort to be seen on his face as he reached residence. As the exult of his being with Adrita now had overcome all his pain and anxiety.

Yash said, '......why are you all looking like that towards me........I am saying right dear. As I am being stressed for that and it's been sort it out once again by Pee... *Hey* Pee you are simply a heartiest devotion comrade of mine'.

Yash replied, hope arose in his friend's heart for now to be got known about this context but Yash said, '*Hey*....Pee this is my request you please come along us. Lets all of us together get back to "Earth surface". Pee I am sure you are not going to be bored there, as there is very impulsing technologies that would entertain you and boost your love towards technologies more and more. *Hey*......don't think that much come...along with us'.

Pee said, 'Dear....What you are memorising, I am not getting that....But Yes I would just let you inform about this thing again which I told you before also that I had responsibilities over here and which I can't leave for anyone. Even I left my own planet for fulfilling this requests of the place. So this is worthless talking to me about all these things'.

Yash said 'Oh!.......if that is so then you can say like that even I do admire this dedication of yours and not going to ask this thing again from you. *Hey* but I need to inform one thing to you that I had been taking "Figo" along with us as I had promised him and committed to take him through, as he would be happy there and I know his appetitevery well'.

'What........you are going to take even "Figo" along with you. Could I ask you that who allowed you to do all this', Pee asked after getting annoyed on his last words.

'No one... no one said me or allowed me to do that but it's been "Figo" wish my dear. You don't want him to be happy, and play many more varieties of games at our Planet "Earth". Pee you too also know about Figo's smile and happiness... which is diminishing over here like anything. So...can't I take him along with me to a place where he could have a freedom of expression, freedom of thoughts and the last altogether freedom of living, which he is not able to conceive at his place too', Yash crack to evoke the buried sentiments of Pee, so that he could help him through.

Pee..........replied 'Ah!............ hum ...... these exotic spirit again arose in me that I didn't want in my soul. Ok......close this point and take away Figo too along with you'.

It is very hard for Yash friends to know that who is going from here and how. If even they are not getting the way to get out of this place and for what Yash is including others.

Soni said to his left friends steeply getting away from Yash and Pee *'Hey...* are you all getting the datum behind the whole scene going over here because this is becoming unfavourable for me to listen more both of their talk, while being ignorant about everything word they were spelling apart'.

Yash asked, 'Well...Pee could you please tell me, where could I find "Figo" this time'.

Pee said, 'You were not required to go anywhere as you just need to turn backward and "Figo" is standing just there. He is there in your room now dear'.

Yash turned and replied, *'Hey* "Figo" you had come here...sorry I didn't saw you'.

'Even I didn't realise this thing that I had come to your room and my face is tensed because I am seeking to find the reason for being here at your room this time. Which I am not getting though', Figo said with his widely twist eyes.

Pee said, *'Hey*....You all don't get tensed about this thing. It is like when I had allowed you to take away "Figo" along, at that time only. My attractive forces had gained Figo presence at Heaven's Hell and brought him up over here. This is due to my wish only, so you all are cure'.

'Oh!...so Figo as you had come over here and my friends. So let me brief everything to you all and wind it over', Yash said with excitation.

Ankit said, 'Oh!..... God thanks at last you cared to tell things to us also'.

'Yash...Apart from saying all this you should mobilise me at my stage because this is not easy for me to do? I don't know how you feel like that as I hadn't stepped even a single step without all of yours ignorance', Yash said to vaporise there sort of spirits and condense his own over that.

'Yes we all know this thing very explicitly to a larger extent, you don't need to tell that', Gaurav smiled heavily and said.

'Listen Gaurav, be quite. Let Yash describe himself now and for that only we are being waiting from a while', Ankit stinted Gaurav.

Yash said, 'Yes...now let me tell you all that time had came for all of us to leave this place'.

'Leave this place, what the rubbish? this is not a small place as its been Heaven's Hell.......so mind it before', Sunny replied.

'I mind all that and on that because I am revealing you all as this is being told to me by none other than one of the chief of Heaven's Hell that's "Pop Jesus". He granted to leave this place as no one knows will any other time be accurate for us to leave or not', Yash said.

Yash replied, 'Dear that couldn't be easy for you to understand but let me tell you that both of us Adrita and me met over here because of God's will. This is the time for black power to empower this universe and to make it diminishing us both need to be all together.'

'So...... my dear friends please tighten up your desires belts as if we need to leave this place now and get back to the "Earth surface". Afraid......my dear brothers this time I could explain you all that much only as time is very short for us to leave, that's why I just want to act. I know that there are bundle of tough question arising in your soul but you have to handle them own and just follow my words because we need to move out of here very safely and secure', Yash said.

'But... but...' Figo said.

'*Hey* No if.... No but dear the thing is that you were coming with us as I had promised you and for that reason only I had called you', Yash said this and soon smile sleaveled off from his sweet green cheeks.

'Oh!... I am going then and you still remembered your promise, my pleasure. Thanks my dear, I am excited. Really', Figo said to all.

'Ok... so this is the whole story and you wants all of us to move back to the '"Earth surface"' while being breaking the rules of Heaven's Hell. Ok...' Ankit said and gone in a deep wandered. After that as his other friends were too implication and lost in their wandered because even they are not able to answer anything to Yash still.

Ankit laughed and shouted, 'Hurry!... yes we all go... start the preparation', and as Ankit said this Yash's all friends evoke like a stream and started laughing as they all favouring Ankit being inclined to leave this place without other's warry'.

'*Huh*... thanks my dears for all this for a second even I went numb to see all of you in silence', Yash replied.

Yash replied, 'Now dear the next step is to move towards The solemn "Abraman" of whom I and Pee were just talking before. So Pee had left this place but he had informed me all description and chance about "Abraman". So now I know what I need to do and for that I had to meet Abraman first'.

Gaurav asked, 'You are going to go alone for all this'.

Yash said, 'Yes now we need to meet "Abraman" so that he could give a brief description of what to be followed next to move out and this is a thing that I alone won't be able to do that'.

'Yes we can also inference that the next step of yours would be to meet him. It being only you who had been told about him... by yours... whats that,... yah "Pop Jesus"', Sunny said.

'I agree but first of all you listen dear, he is a old age and very respectful person. He is not just mine as he's all of us the same..."Pop Jesus"... so don't be ignorant about him next. So the thing I was wanting to say all of you is that, I am not going to that person alone as it's been difficult for me grasp all the wisdom from him at once and remember that. So for that reason I am going to take Ankit along me'.

Ankit while getting from his place and being affraidto listen said 'have you even asked me before and without that you had just declared all this. What if I would say no, then ......'

Yash said, 'My sweet Brother... I know you are not going to say that to me ...... that much love meter I do consist in my heart', Yash seeking to butter Ankit.

Sunny said, 'Ankit, I do feel that you should go away with Yash an that's emphasis too'.

'I haven't asked you also, I feel, If you are not going to say that too then also I am going to go with him', Ankit said.

Yash said, 'That's it...'

Figo impeded in between 'I think I should also come along with you Yash. Don't tensed I am not going to get into Abraman room but would be going to help you to find it out conveniently as I do think I had seen that place in church'.

'Ah!.....you also want to come......I am expecting only one with me but I am getting more... Wah.... thats solemn......' Yash said.

'Ok dear.... you can also come along with me as if may need your adherence', Yash said.

'Ok... so your team is being inclined to go... amazing good you haven't asked me because I never quickly change my decisions and if you had asked me then I would have said straight away No...', Pee said after looking to all this.

'So apart from wasting time here you all must go to gather yours utilitarian stuff from him', Pee replied.

So these three of them stepped to move towards the backyard of the church which according to Figo is the frequent way to reach Abraman soon.

Ankit said, 'Figo this scene over here is awaken. This is like a deep blue magical place that being covered by the sky with its foremost delight and fragrance spread gradients all over. I don't think climate have any bar to this place'.

Figo, 'Yes you were rigorous Ankit this place remains as it is every time and no fluctuation and discomfort could even try to exist at this place', Figo replied.

'Yash see...these butterflies here. They are not scared of anyone and sitting over me and elsewhere as they wants. The light that is being slaved by their giant feathers, scene making everything as a dreams. *Hey* speak up Yash why you were standing like a dumb silent creature', Ankit said this and faced Yash in a irritated way.

Yash laugh increases and this is getting higher as he came to notice the increasing erotic reactions of Ankit's face and said, 'My...... my dear you are talking about a thing to me which is a lot familiar from the first day of our Heaven's Hell. The beauty of this place had come across me in my every way. So that's why as you had been shocked to see all this here. I got in a picky mood and smile spelled out from my face. *Hey*... Dear you know me very well'.

'Please be quiet you both now as we had come very close to Abraman estate and he prefer entire silence in his surrounds which could help him to meditate and feel the gesture of flowing wind though', Figo said.

'This is the back side door of Church and I had brought you both up here because if we had gone from the front door then priest had surely impeded us and denied all of us to meet Abraman. But you know that Abraman is not a person who doesn't want others to meet him. He loves to meet all Creatures but his work doesn't allow him to do so. As his powers get deflected when we black soul Creatures meet him. So listen now, we would go straight away reach, to meet chance of Abraman as his room is just behind this door', Figo said.

'Behind this door, to meet him we need this door to be wrist and as per my wisdom this door is not been used by any person. So it remains closed ever', Yash replied.

Figo insisted by stepping forward towards these both, 'My dear there is only a single way that we had to fold our hand in front of this door and Pray Abramans to open this door this time because he is the one who could do this my dear'.

Ankit said, 'So if that is so then lets us all perform this action as soon as possible.

These three stood still in peace and folded their hands in grave to pray Abraman's, so that he could measure their desire and instincts. Everyone stayed in this position for a quite long time, settle like they were too lost in any other world. Passions of Figo is being very low so he had broken up soon and wrist his eyes and shouted;

'*Hey*... you both...listen... my dear... open up your eyes and get back in your consciousness if the door is being change by wrest up....listen you both dear'.

Yash and Ankit started coming back and started opening up their eyes a little bit.

Yash said, 'What is....This? Figo....Why this sleaveling light is to heavily coming to our face as I am not able to open my eyes because of it'.

'Yash you don't need to think about that even I am facing the same as if this light is being coming from Church. The gate has been wrist up and before we would step in this light would make our soul very pure as if this response given by Abraman because of our prayer.' Figo said.

While stepping into church now, Yash presence being felt by Abraman's as he is in a dilemma before about these creatures that were praying for him. He felt that quite tough to know their need from Abraman's but as soon as he sensed Yash presence he came to know about all sorts of things.

With heavy and pitching sound a wave came and spelled off in the aura touching everyone's with an instinct, which do convey message regarding severity and prosperity uphold at Heaven's Hell. This tone was of Abraman who is a scholar and a powerful member of this Heaven's Hell and was seeking to start up his conversation with them through a message.

Abraman message 'Life is a preparation and death is Examination'.

Discomfort for all arose in that place as no one knows from where this tone being spelled off. Yash who informed about Abraman's by "Pop Jesus" knows a little about Abraman's chance and posture of existence at this place. So because of this Yash faced towards every corner of that room so that he could leg Abraman's anywhere out there, as if it is being difficult to view anything here because the aura was foggy inside. Abruptly Yash feel a white cloth flowing in the air with this fog. So Yash analysed that it could be of Abraman and moved close to that place. He leg a young woman at that place scaling her hairs with her long pointed fingers. Even though her appearance was quite apart from the ordinary one but her beauty is too incredible and unmatched.

Yash after having her look and the way she is being pretending of ignorance about their presence, he approached her and asked;

'Miss.........could you hear me. Please tell me about Abraman for whom we had came over here and afraid for disturbing the integrity and rules of Heaven's Hell while enter inside through back side of it'.

She smiled and replied, 'this is my place and for whom you had come over here and whose place is this you should have known first', she said all this but still she is not facing anyone of them as she is busy playing with her hairs still.

Yash asked with a dilemma, 'Afraid I didn't understood what you said'.

This time she left all her forgoing things, stood up and said 'So...dear listen I am the one for whom you had come to this place. Yes...I am.........................I am Abraman'.

Yash said 'Wow......how could this possible as if............... you are a lady and Abraman it would not that so. Figo......tell me about what she is saying. Do someone is kidding with us or what'.

'Relax Yash for a while, let us know everything conveniently', Ankit said.

Figo unconfidentally said, 'Off... Yash.... afraid but I also didn't seen Abraman's before so I don't know exactly that whether it's been a male or female. I just tried to help you', Figo was very apprehensive about all this.

Abraman said, 'Wait you all for a while this is my place, either I had allowed all of you to enter it but still I am very much afraid of this noise that you all had messed over here. Even the shafts of nature never dares to disturb my piece then how could you all were doing that so', Abraman instinct.

'*Hey* my friend Yash......please don't utter a single word now, as we are allowed to enter this room. This is on its own a big thing. Figo assault to make everything normal there.

Abraman's said, 'No you were wrong this is not a pleasure for you all that I had wrest this door for you because your prayer doesn't matters in that. As if I know about your arrival and approach towards me before. As "Pop Jesus" had informed me. If you all hadn't even prayed then also the door is being wrest for you as Yash efforts and sacrifices in his past life's aid a lot to Heaven's Hell. Even I do know about him everything before even "Pop Jesus" told me'.

'The statement that I had stated when you all just entered my place is for Yash only. He praised by God in this generation because of his practices as he did in his past life's', Abraman replied.

Yash said, 'So you do also knows all that... Yes.

'Yes I know all that and from the beginning when you came to this place and I even know that you would be going to come at my place in the last because you had been brought up over here due to a motive and not for any blank theft', Abraman's replied.

'So you were going to ask about the escape', Abraman approached towards them.

'Yes for that part only we had approached you.' Ankit said as other both of them became quite and still after knowing about Abraman.

'Could you tell us all that in brief please......', Yash asked Abraman.

Abraman replied, 'Oh!...off course... because my help is very much efficient for you and I do say that you should not feel it as my help because it's been my duty to do that so in yours case. So you should have to listen all that thoroughly and very profound'.

Abraman stated, 'You are going to leave this place with Adrita and your friends and you need to be safe from the wisdom of other superiors of Heaven's Hell apart from "Pop Jesus". As its been only "Pop Jesus" who is being adherence to you and no one else as they don't know about you my dear Yash and they also don't know the story of yours birth. I feel you are getting whatever I am seeking to say you', Abraman asked Yash.

Yash replied, 'I think I got very much clear about all this by looking into Heaven's Hell aura and facing everything'.

Abraman said, 'Adrita would not go along you alone my dear, as Ronu is also going to go with her. Your attachment with Ronu consists yours being with him in past am I right?'

Yash, 'I would be a lot efficacy to hear that all from you as Ronu is like my good comrade and if he too comes along me then nothing could be solemner than that. I am afraid just that Adrita didn't said me all this', Yash said in excitement like an empty glass become full of water.

Ankit impeded in between 'Now Yash could we talk about the thing that is being very emphasise for Our escape'.

Abraman said, '*Hey*.......you all have not to think about that thing as If this should be told by me to you. But before that I need to inform you about Barrack too Yash'.

'Barrack... Ah... I do know about him very well. But I don't have a good eye for him as if he is a blunty, harshy and fishy person. He is the person who even hampers Adrita in her well being which is the thing that cuts me apart. My love is depressed and dishearten by his actions a lot', Yash informed Abraman's.

'Let it be. Yes Adrita had noticed a creature named Alasky......who is noticing us. He would be the only person who would have informed Barrack. But really Abraman I don't even care about all these things and have power to handle them through', Yash said.

'If that is so then that's been too good and you should don't oversighten that also as if you are the warrior', Abraman applauded Yash with more energy.

Abraman said, 'Now dear listen let me tell you all the exactly well profiled way to move out from this place. As much I can see the way for you to move "Earth surface" from the core of it is not that easier one. You can't go really straight as you came. So for that you need to took way out through the "Milky way Galaxy"'.

'Milky Way Galaxy' what did you mean by that... we need to go through Milky way that is being full of stars and as much I know it's being a disk shaped structure and 100,000-120,000 in diameter then how could it be feasible', Ankit impeded again as his curiosity is being rising as time passes.

Abraman replied, 'Yes through that only you need to go through. I want to say one thing to you dear that I am efficacy by your wisdom about "Milky Way Galaxy" but dear you need to be silent this time till I finish off my everything ok'.

Abraman started again, 'So I was revealing you about "Milky Way Galaxy" from where you need to go through. You all firstly need to move towards our River at the T point junction. There you could take a boat that is being coloured sleaveing "silver". So this boat is being used by just the supreme personal of this place and no one could ride it though. You have to take one in the reference of "Pop Jesus" and as soon as you get into it the boat comes under control of "Pop Jesus" and else he do on his own'.

'So I felt that you would be going to tell us all the way in brief through which we have to proceed but you didn't said that. As you had lend everything on "Pop Jesus"', Figo strikes his comment as he feel the info of Abraman's invariant unfavourable.

'I haven't denied revealing you anything still as I have even didn't finished my last line. So the whole thing is that. Everything is being governed by "Pop Jesus" but you all should know the way to be proceeding through. So "Milky Way Galaxy" is a dim glowing band arching across the night sky in which your naked eyes cannot distinguish the individual stars. This Galaxy as a whole is being surge at a velocity of approx 600 km per sec with extragalactic frame of reference. After traversing through the Milky Way for a enlisting long time you would be going to contact with "Bermuda Triangle" that is a term which is being used at your place to describe that black hole in the Ocean. This triangle is being said as Devils triangle by some of yours "Earth surface" people but it does have its existence. Imagine that there is no making and no natural borders to let people get known about it when they come across that region. You all are going to move out of that giant dark hole and then come into existence of your world'.

Yash amazed about this thing whatever he listened about "Bermuda triangle" and he asked, 'So the existence of Heaven's Hell is beneath this hole. Is that so, because I don't feel that we had come from it when we reached Heaven's hell first time?'

Abraman smiled towards Yash 'I think you all don't need to get into these entire thing and shouldn't matter that too. Whether it lies inside "Bermuda Triangle" or not, you just remember your escape way and that's it'.

Abraman continued to explain further all other sort of things. Bermuda Triangle is a loosely defined region in western part of North Atlantic Ocean. This is the place from where after getting through to your "Earth surface" you would be going to meet a person named "Avnish". Avnish stays all alone at the shore of the ocean and you will meet him as you all reached the corner of shore. He is the person then who will be the one to help you out in your further task', Abraman's then asked, I think all these things are being very much explicit to you all.

Yash insisted to Abraman 'Please... let me know that is this place Heaven's Hell do exist under "Bermuda Triangle". As if my senses were profoundly getting favoured to this. I want to know that all'.

Abraman said, 'It's obvious thing for me to be listened up by you Yash as I do know about your instincts a lot.'

'And now I am not going to answer even a single question of your regarding this Yash', Abraman replied.

'Ok... so the conceptions I am spirit about it were rigorous. Now, Abraman but you hadn't told us about that guy "Avnish" who would be over there to help us further', Yash said.

'You can't say like that, as you haven't given me the chance to do so', Abraman's replied.

Abraman added 'So "Avnish" is a person who is too purified by his heart spirits and expressions. He is a person of God and had visited our Heaven's Hell before. This person had completed his time period of slavery at Heaven's Hell and gone back to the "Earth surface". So he does stay away from human beings with animals and greenery because after reaching back to his planet, he is not able to deal with ongoing cruel human behaviour. That time he decided to leave that place and live along with this nature that is so pure and prosperous'.

'Seems like this person is going to be very helpful to us and the way of ours also would be going to very innovative with him', Figo said.

'Yes Figo....You were correct, this could be an adventurous thing from commencing till the end', Yash replied.

Abraman said, 'No query is there in your soul now. So you all should depart from my place now as I need to work for your escape a bit more.

'Yash... thanks a lot for all that Abraman and yes I feel you were saying it rigorous to leave now. We should go back to our place', Ankit replied.

'Yash....All the golden stuff you had shared with us, the efficiency is being entired and I am thrilled by your adherence dear. Thanks from my side too Abraman. May God bless you with more power, more grace', Yash said to Abraman.

Abraman in a cure and very cool mood said 'This time it's been you all who need to take care of yourself and your loved ones. This is being a biggest exam of yours in terms of devastating nature and combination of two lives, that's of Adrita being on your planet. I hope Yash that you would do it in an enhancing way. So god blesses you all and makes your way easier'.

Yash said, 'Thanks, I didn't felt that I would go to meet a person that is so stable and cooperative in all affinity'.

Ankit said, 'Ok......then let's cut short all this and move towards our residence as I feel Pee would also be there. We would tell him too about this concern as now our lives wave have build a unique way to follow. I just pray God it to be prosperous'.

'It would be prosperous my dear........don't tensed about getting into any annoyance now', Yash smiled and said while being facing towards both of them with. Peace on his face.

Yash replied, 'Ok......Abraman we took leave from here now. Ankit You and Figo now move towards our room and inform others about all this, so that they do also know about the forthcoming picture. I need to move towards the cultural room where Adrita and other priest girls were being playing instruments.'

Yash while looking towards his watch and smiling said 'she would be happy to listen all this and I want to see her happiness so that I can double up my own part of comfort'.

28

On one side all these preparation were going on and on the other end Barrack is getting aware about the solitary consignment between Adrita and Yash. Barrack got to know about all this from his one of the responsible and trusted loyal person Alasky.

Alasky is the only one who is being gathering all sorts of deficit and valuable conversation amidst the both Adrita and Yash which they don't want to let other person know.

Alasky left that place after collecting all info in his mind. He had dispatched every word he listen with their intentions and emotions to Barrack. Today this is not the day and time for him to meet Barrack but he requested Barrack to meet him as if he feels that he would be close to him more after revealing about all that stuff. Barrack had come down from his easeroom to the hall and spirit those he had captured and make his slaves all around that place.

Barrack shouted standing near to his Globe 'This is the time for you all to come though, this is the time for you all to curve me as I am getting weaker, this is the time when I need you to show you colours. So come out from your sculptures for what you all had upheld silence still and save my numerous year efforts which is going to be diminished by a synergic actions of a simple Creature. This is only the time when I didn't got even a single political gesture so that I can assault and make this bulgy thing to be ruined off. Before I need to cave down all my efforts together to cut there way that they mean to follow. Yash now would know everything about me. Now as Adrita would have told him though. I am bounded by this place resources because of which I won't be able to harm or block that person in any regard. The main reason beyond is that too my commitment to stay at this place with God that I am not going to utilise my powers on anyone and if he knows well about me then I can't even think to harm on my own. If I had faced that person, my existence would get diminished. Now I realise that this person is that person only for whom God asked me to take pledge and curl my hands. I want to blame that time for making me so helpless this day that I am not even try to do my will for which I can conveniently work forward'.

Soon Patrick who is the super precious and foremost trustworthy Creature of Barrack. Patrick left his ongoing work there, and sensed that his supreme Barrack is in annoyance, so he took the firelight over Barrack on his shoulders and said;

'You can't do anything and I won't allow anyone to necklace yours efforts so conveniently and go through like this', Patrick replied in care of Barrack.

'You need to order and give a way to yours spirit now. So that can ditch the person and make him away from the entire scene. These spirits can also make him to go away from this time period or to their own world. So you have to put forward and give them a way to drive the whole cycle forward', Patrick suggested Barrack to pull him out of this deck.

Barrack smiled and shouted with angry while being facing towards his foremost Patrick 'Ha!... Same like one more time. My trust on you never goes worthless as if you safeguard me from all sort of diminishing events by flushing them away'.

With a huge heavy sound and facing to every corner of his place of estate, as if now he wants his spirits to work though 'leave your covers soon, tear your blocking limits and empower yourself to awake your long sustained power this time as if they are being required. Come... come out soon and drain my deficit sorrow with the black powers of yours', Barrack said being closing his eyes pulling his hands upwards to cover up the whole surface. He evoke a wave of his intentional so that they could be conveniently heard by all these spirits that started surge out of there sculptures.

Auras of that place had been so much messed up by these black power as Barrack has been utilising it all this time. After making a suspicious kind of environment at his place where now spirits are revolving around in the room like a globe and just waiting for next word to be heard by Barrack.

Barrack was relieved and cure as he saw that he can utilise those suspect of his power which he didn't even though.

Barrack said, 'I can see in my globe that this person is surge in the streets of this place still and I tried to accure his intentions though. His intentions was to meet Adrita and take her along with him towards there departing place'.

Barrack, 'But who do know that what he had to face now at the next door. Let's me show him now......ha!' Barrack said it all while watching in his globe and started laughing loudly.

'So... listen my all bonded spirits now I am going to play a game for which my team would be all of you. So you all should listen to my every word in a very much expliciter way. I can't allow this person Yash to depart this place in a way he wants', Barrack started to state his mentality on his sources.

Barrack replied, 'So... my spirits the way is like that. This person is going towards place of Adrita's existence for his final assignment of this place which he is going to disclose in front of her. This... this is the thing that I don't want to be preceded and to reach Adrita's compartment because if this had been done then nothing could be happen next. I won't be able to force them in blocking their way. As if there's both soul had been mixed up partly into one another and if they had crossed this step though then there's alignment become entire worthy. Everything would be halted then. So we would have to take a quick step to succeed'.

Patrick said, 'Yes now you know that in your hand there is immense power, it's just like that you need to use that and prove your success. I think you know it my entire superior'.

Barrack replied, 'Yes I know it all and that to in a very clear and concise way. Ha!... I can prove my willingness now. So my spirits I need to inform you that in Yash way I am going to make a same virtual monument like that one towards whom Yash is going though. As he wants to meet Adrita over there that would be practicing with musical instruments right now. But I am going to shuffle him in my pyramid and make him realise enter my virtual meant monument. After he'll be going to enter. Then he would straight away move towards its fourth floor where he would feel that Adrita is present. As he is going to reach that floor, he'll find nothing over there and then your work starts. Slowly and steadily that monument starts to get filled of water and the rising water will threaten Yash of his life. This is the time you have to safe guard of not allowing him to leave that monument at any cost and after that when he is going to be so much threaten and scared about his life. All this is going to make his soul get much weaker and you can cover up his soul and him along with you to yours time period'.

'I feel all this is being very much explicit to you all present over here. Now this is the time for all of you to leave out and club my virtual monument from its every end. Now just simply

Depart...', Barrack finished aggressively which explicitly shows his desire behind his act.

All his spirits now started to move out of his estate as to fulfill his desire.

On the other hand Yash is being surge in his same last happy going fashion as if he's a lot excited to tell all those sort of things he grasped from Abraman. Yash on its way come to see the monument in which he wants to meet with Adrita. For a second Yash felt it a little afraid as if he found this monument, he reach over here very soon. Yash don't want to hamper his fabulous going mood this time and though he compromise with his wandered and made it to believe on this monument. He set a realisation that because he is so messed up in memorising and was curious to measure Adrita's expressions. He stepped inside the monument and same as Barrack profiled he had gone all the way directly to fourth floor. Seems like he had lost his senses and he can't even measure the instinctive air in his surrounds. So as Yash reached fourth floor and faced upward with that smile still attached on his face. He said;

'*Hey*... where everyone been lost... does it so because they know that I "Yash" is being coming over here to take there's "Adrita" along with him and because of that they left me and Adrita all alone... ha!...' Yash crack to uphold his same happy mood on his last words.

'Hello... is anybody over there... hello... is someone there...' Yash was getting depressed as nobody presence or commotion is being felt all around that place though which frightened.

Yash expression and emotions are plunged now towards silence as if it's becoming very difficult for him to realise. After some time Yash see that a perception flow of water being started coming inside through the floors balcony. Yash walked through that place to get the point of emergence of this stranger kind of water flow.

Yash prolonged in this stress and was surge here to find out any safe space there. Yash came to know that this waterfall is not just happening on his floor also on every floor of this monument. Now the six senses of Yash gather that this is not a natural thing as if he is being trapped in a well planed game.

Yash immediately crack to escape this place while being walking down from stairs but stairs are being blocked by spirits as he move forward to step on the stair, his foot is being thrown away. Yash two folded this kind of effort many times as if there is no other way to get out of it. Yash mind this time is being fully fledged collapsed as he got to know the whole scene but not getting the way to get out through this. On every step of stairs there is one spirit lying over it so that Yash can't even jump any stairs and cross it. Yash is being lost this time and whenever he comes in situation like this, He close his eyes and asks his God from help... Yash is being covered up from this power of black forces from all around and even this water level is being rising as time passes. This evening getting darker forth. This time is being so tough for Yash to go through as water level had reached a life danger mark.

Suddenly there is a scene astounding of Blue Moon. This is the moon from which all these spirits of Barrack are apprehensive about as if they can't even resist in its light. This Blue moon comes once in a while of the whole month. This is not its day but it had come now. Though soon the light of Blue Moon started following inside the cape yard of monument corridor. This light started sleaveling every corner of this virtually meant monument, in the sense to help Yash to move out of this chance. Water had reached up to Yash mouth. This is the time for him to react though he took a speedily decision of getting towards the window and jumping out of it to save himself.

He did that so only and there is no spirit power left now for blocking him to take his action of survival. These black powers of spirit are being diminished by the light received from the moon that is now straight falling inside that monument to save Yash. Yash jumped from this peak height to the ground and nothing went bad to his body.

Yash said 'Ah!... My God this is a big trap... and I had just been saved from this by blue moon astanding, otherwise anything could happen'.

'I do want to get that person who had done this sort of mischief act but this time it has been very essential for me to reach towards Adrita so that I could deliver here all information before the time passes and we do get more late for that'.

Yash Hastily moved towards his left way towards the place where he could catch Adrita. After surge a little bit more Yash reached the actual monument. This timing is too late everyone from the priest girl had finished their practicing session and were being coming out while carrying instrument in their hand. Yash and Adrita they both captured each other from a far distance place as if stress took place on Adrita'a mind while being looking to Yash, who was not in his normal nature and physical standard. So Adrita too moved toward Yash and asked him the reason of his discomfort. Yash don't want to tell anything to her about the impact he faced just. As they are going to do itself not an easy going task for both. Yash diverted everything and said;

'Yup... Adrita leave... leave everything here only and just come along me. I met Abraman and he adherenced us a lot. He had dictated every sort of thing to us and told us how to curve everything'.

'*Hey*... let move towards the corner as everyone is being staring furiously towards us', Yash said.

'Listen... I am a lot scared about everything and I want to know that all. Do you know what is my physical standard from that time when you left me? I am not able to concentrate on even a single thing. Ok........if you want, lets go at the corner but you need to tell me that all', Adrita said with anxiety as she is losing her never ending pat ions now.

Yash hold her hand and took her at the side of this place. He makes her to sit and relax and then he started describing everything to Adrita that he had gained from Abraman.

'Now I do feel that my dear is spirit cure as I haven't saved anything in my mind and lot of everything to you. Now can I see smile on your face dear', Yash smiled and said.

Adrita smiled and said, 'yes... now you can have a look of my precious smile that is not been seen by everyone'.

'Oh!... grateful dear', Yash asked.

'Aaah... let's leave all this aside and you now tell me that how much time you are going to take to get inclined to go', Yash replied.

'Hm... we were going just now, I feel we must wait for some time', Adrita said.

'Dear please understand me that there is no time for us to wait. So it would be very nice if you could get inclined as soon as feasible. I don't know when these Heaven's Hell power come in action and got to know about our escape', Yash insisted.

'There is nothing emphasise of mine is being left. So not tensed, I will come with you whenever you say. Yash as I think you could realise that I am not going singly and I am going to take Ronu along with me. We both are a part of each other and need each other', Adrita said.

'You know about my attachment towards Ronu. The finest picture of mine and Ronu's bond is very much explicit to you? Yash asked.

Yash replied, 'Make this thing as quick as possible . You and Ronu both reach at the shore directly because from there only we are going to get the ship No as I told you that before too. I feel that it could be more relevant for you to reach that place as you do know the whole architecture'.

Adrita asked, 'But there were two shore one of north and second one in the south. I need to reach out which one?'

'*Hey*... if that is so then it could be a confusing thing for us. This time you had plunged me more towards this confusion. I feel that could be sort out', Yash evoked up in joy.

Yash replied, 'Ok... dear listen...you could be knowing this thing and it is the only that could help us in solving this pole features: As I am going to ask you two questions and answer me those.'

'Yes... do ask', Adrita with conspicuous mind.

'Yes...love so please tell me that soon as:

1. Which pole side you all opt to devote yours pray towards your God?
2. Tell me about the area in which most of yours superior resists? Yash asked these two questions.

'Your both question are relative of South Pole as if our prayer region and superior estate is both towards south of Heaven's Hell. So what do you mean by that or you seeking to say that south shore will be the way of our escape', Adrita replied.

'Listen love, I hadn't shared the last thing with you that Abraman told me. He said, We are going to leave from this place with the help of boat which belongs too of our "Pop

Jesus" and none other than that. As if this boat is being coordinated by its owner and would work according to the mindset of the same person and no one other than that. You know that "Pop Jesus" is being deliberately involved in this affair and had been coordinating with us. He is the only person who had sent me to Abraman. After reaching to Abraman I got to know about this thing that there are several other superior most priest and high official of Heaven's Hell who don't know about our estate and our future trickery. So that why we need to refrain ourselves from their organs so that they can't feel our presence too', Yash focised to set the mentality of Adrita so that she could resist strain and pressure due to any one of these things in future.

Yash said, 'So the last thing that does come out of all this is that you and Ronu should leave towards the south and capture boat of "Pop Jesus". I will be going to get back to that place with the whole crew............ok'.

Adrita pumped oxygen in her throat and said, 'Ok.........My chief... I got to know everything now don't get that much deeper. I will be waiting for you'.

Yash reached at residence and said.

'Look my friends don't taught and torture me with your eyes, as I wouldn't be able to answer anyone of your question this time. I feel you all had grabbed the entire story from Ankit and Figo, which I don't require you to say though. This time everything is being explicit to all of you and I am hiding nothing in my pockets. So... now the time come to get set free from this place, for that give me your hands of relaxation that could console and give comfort to my heart to combat forward. I feel this time you had got to know that also as if you all came to this place just because of me. So there is no tensed for you all being leaving this place without forced your days of punishment, as if none of us had done a comper migation with Heaven's Hell. So.....we leave it though', Yash was not facing anyone while he said all this, as he's being seeking to make everyone feel cosy about whatever is being going though.

Soni come in Yash way, halted him and said, 'You were thinking that we were unaware about your and Adrita's attachment before. My dear all sort of things are being known to us. The reason being is that they were not clear though, but

I felt bad because you haven't shared that clearly with us', Soni giving realization to Yash about the datum.

Yash added, '*Hey*.......brothers you all know me well. I hadn't done anything that could make you all feel disheartful. If you are concerned about this then let me tell you dear, I had disclosed my heart's love blunder to you at the commencing stage of mine but you all didn't bothered that.

'If you all are still in any sort of problem with it, you can straight away ask Ankit about all that', Yash said.

'*Hey*.... What the hell are you saying dear... why wouldn't we are going to believe you. This had not happened before as if you said anything to us and we denied towards it. As we all have a big ladder of faith on you. So please never do say these lines ever', Sunny stood up from his place and crack to change the direction of thoughts that Yash developed just.

'This is why? This is the only reason dear that why I said my first stanza when I just entered the compartment. As I know this very well that nothing is emphasis this time apart from making a consortium, so that we could all tackle everything conveniently and get out of it', Yash answered his friends.

Ankit stood and initiated, 'Yes... I do feel the same as if.........everything is being set and explicit in our skull and we have just to move in its flow. Now I had got to know this thing also that all are efforts at this place is not just for our own as if these are also meant to save the killing humanity and horror hopes of people. To make our planet as blood deficit land. So now I feel we all should join our hands all together to get rid of this place as soon as possible'.

Yash asked, 'Firstly tell me that you all haven't met Pee at ours room when you came back to this place?'

Figo answered 'No dear there is no one present over here apart from all of us. You say what happened, do you want to convey anything to Pee'.

'I was asking about Pee so that we can meet him last before leaving this place as he had a big hand of adherence towards us at this place and nothing apart from that'.

Everyone started surge towards the southern shore of the river at Heaven's Hell where they is going to meet Adrita for the first time. They all were set to leave this place and were started dreaming about the wonders they had to face after reaching their planet. The way is being very much explicit in mind of Yash, Ankit and Figo.

Yash said, 'Yes....Its like we had come across that place. Look around that place would be hereby somewhere'.

Ankit said, 'what are you saying Yash could you even see any water presence all around and then too you are speaking like that'.

'Really I had felt the presence of Adrita around this place and I had send her at this place to wait for all of us', Yash replied.

Figo said, '........even I am not getting what Yash is saying'.

Yash said, 'Ok......you all just follow me.........because I am very much sure about my concern'.

Yash took them along with him and they crack to cross away the green bushes of coconut leafs separating that place from the other one. These leaf are collected all together due bunch of trees present at this place in a close contact to one another. So as they all removed it, huge sound of waves started getting heard by them and everyone believed that this is the place where they need to arrive. The level of excitement by Yash is touching heights as the fragrance of Adrita felt by him is mixing up in his soul now and making him joyful. So they all removed the whole bunches of leafs that were separating these both places and they come in touch with deep blue ocean. Which is at some meters of distance from them? Yash saw Adrita sitting on the shore at that boat which he told her. There is both of them Adrita and Ronu settle like they were waiting for Yash while facing towards the red sun that is being going to set and remain close above the ocean. They both were looking towards it. Yash saw and ran without thinking anything towards her and as he reached there, Adrita blankly faced Yash. After a second she also started smiling towards Yash which explicitly shows her happiness to go towards "Earth" which is one of her dream.

Adrita being thrilled with happiness at this moment and same is the case of Ronu as he's too jumping there. Yash said;

'My all pain and every discomfort get ruin of... when I see you smiling like this. Please this is my request dear that you have to uphold your this kind of smile throughout your life'.

Soon his friends reached that place and Ankit said.

'So she is the one...', Ankit asked while facing Adrita and smiling towards her.

Sunny said, 'I knew that... the girl for which Yash is so cut off from this nature would be one that have none of its presence apart from her in this world'.

Soni said, '*Hey* what would I say now as if my brother's had conveyed everything in just one line'.

Adrita smiled and said slowly in her sweet tone 'I... am honoured to hear all that from you all... and if you all were Yash friend then you would be having one or other feature of him inbuild in you and I can sense you all by that'.

Gaurav said, 'Now it's my turn to speak as I didn't applaud Adrita. I didn't consist that much bigger words to do so but I have a answer about the thing she said. So true as if yes we all do consist one or more kind of similarities. This is the reason of our bond Adrita'.

'Ok and what would I say to you about Ronu as you all have met him before and know him very well. *Hey* Soni you also blissed playing with him a lot na', Yash introduced them all again with Ronu.

Soni said, 'Yes... I bliss a lot but its not just me who shared his infantile with Ronu as other also went to be child in front of him and flirt with him. So there is no need of introduction for Ronu we want'.

Yash '.......that's true. See Adrita there happiness for Ronu being with them'.

'As you all get into it, I will wish to move and then this both will initiate after that whole is carried out by "Pop Jesus" who's boat it is. "Pop Jesus" is also the person who had carried all the responsibilities of Parent for Adrita, so that she never feel lonely', Yash informed his friends while being facing towards Adrita and looking to the tears in her eyes for getting apart from "Pop Jesus". Yash just make his palm to rub her shoulder.

Everyone had board the boat this time and this is for Yash to initiate the boat. Yash closed his eyes and set the command from his inturn auspitious soul for the boat to begin though.

This boat started to stare in the eyes of this clean blue flowing water as it's been seeking to tell him to mold his wave towards the direction where it wants to proceed. This is the way to get apart of this place, which have no connection, no boundary to state further as if no one opts this way before from this place. Now Yash saw that everyone is being stressed to know about the next way to be followed by them. As apart from Adrita and Ronu everyone else started looking deep inside the water to get its wave moves. Yash prompted and said;

'Listen you all why, were you all being so scattered and stressed about all this. Now our way had been started off and it's going to halt on the "Earth" Atlantic Ocean. As everything is very much explicit to you all and then too you all were remarks in a very curious level'.

Adrita smiled after listen to Yash and said, 'Your seat......see sit across me because this is a phase full of anxiety and at this phase you are going to say them to be normal then that's quite be difficult for them. As they also consist of normal being blood that pick up high speed at these stages. They'll be normal give them some time and you come sit across me. The last thing that it's the boat of Eugene *Dada* "Pop Jesus" who will be going to take a better care of all'.

Natural forces had started softening up there way and make them feel that the whole universe mixed up and the collection of stars cluster started to revolve across them. This ocean of Heaven's Hell had dropped everyone inside the white milky fluid that started giving them realization of surge on the milk. The best part of their ride is that no one from all of them is spirit Vertigo and spirit dizzy ride. They were also not detached from their place on the boat even when boat turned upside down while being flowing with waves and natural wind.

Everyone started feeling sleepy now on the boat after looking towards all these natural mutate at once there eye lid start dictating after some seconds. As if it's becoming harder for them to stay active for a long time. At last everyone from them got faint as it became entire black out for them now. All curiosity and all sort of terrible scene faced by them had come to an end as now there consciousness had turned into unconscious behaviours. There boat was smoothly surge in the way that is being dictated to it and its proceeding one step ahead towards the final destination that is "Earth surface". As being said by Abraman that they have to go through the Milkyway galaxy in which they were right now at present no one can feel it though. These bundled stars over here were working as the shelter to all of them and also acting like a track builder because of which there boat is being flowing freely without any unwanted discomfort aligned on its way. After the thunder breeze of Milkyway galaxy come to an end this has aligned them to the next phase that is of ocean of "Earth surface" in which they are being dropped finally. So there is a long way journey left for all of them inside that ocean but they were free from all its realisation at present as if sense had been profoundly lost in vain and being captured by some vague force. Boat consistently moved on his dedicated way in the same fashion. The wonder land "Heaven's Hell" had been left far away as now they had been taken all the way to this Atlantic oceans floor. Which is carpeted with muddy sediment, made up of the remains of tiny plants and animals, that sank to the bottom of the sea after they died, along with volcanic ash and other materials carried from the land by rivers and winds.

The sediment has built up over millions of years, so most of the oceans floor is smothered by it to a depth of hundreds or even thousands of meters.

Large animals move on the floor, churning up the sediment and water currents move it around. The carcasses of large animals from high up in the pile sink to the bottom, producing food hotspots for other creatures.

As these animals are getting in interaction on their way but due to a power liberation from the boat they can't even dare to come close to it as it will deficit them from their existence at this place. Everyone body had got completely loughed wet they had been going on through the ocean from a past some hours. All of them started felling shivered as they started curling, shrinking their bodies without getting into consciousness or spirit and observing anything else. The boat started surge in its high extent as if the time for which it is being scheduled was getting over and before that it had to make them reach the North Atlantic Oceans shore after crossing the giant tempestuous and wild "Bermuda Triangle". That never makes about coming in his wild coverage area to go through, but there is not a tensed for all of them as they need to just draw forth from that and all will be going to be smoother for them afterward. This time the boat is reached its highest mark of flight. As if the time of boat would be finished then there is no one who could make them eject out of the "Bermuda Triangle". They would be in capture of these *wild* birds, mammals, amphibians, reptiles and lion-fish or killer whale that do never allow any being to stay free at the time when there thrust alarms them and evoke there wild behaviour.

So its seems that they had come a lot close to their destination after a number of hours journey with this boat. North Atlantic "Bermuda Triangle" is now too close to this Boat. Boat worked not like a non living thing but it acts like a mind is being attached to it to feel the situation and react accordingly. Same is being done here by this boat, after getting in contact with the coverage area of "Bermuda Triangle" that has no boundaries of it. This boat sensed this far before and as there is a storm kind of behaviour in this trustee looking ocean. Boat stood straight away to the lowest height it can go, so that it could reach just below that Triangular portion of it. After reaching that portion this boat had masked a invisible cup shaped cover over its curvature, so that anything, any force is unable to set them away of it. Through the assault of it is to take safely everyone across the shore of this ocean to finish of his work.

This is the time for that boat to eject itself out of "Bermuda Triangle". It surroundings is same as of below water and above water. As both region of this place is under cover of Squally and the water of ocean is rising many meters up in the sky veiling the whole open space of this black hole from its surrounds due to Pop gun. Boat started to give his last assault and to make everyone present there in the boat to get actualization of their planet arrival. Now boat developed a heavy thrust force below the surface by getting still over there for some minutes and then the last through of it to get away from this stress region of hole to the cool and calm surface of the ocean.

After swirling in this Pop gun while getting ejected through it. They need to cover a solemn height above this black hole too as in the sense to cross it though. At last with a instinctive jump they all reached to the surface of Atlantic ocean that is free, calm and adorable. This river of ocean has become quite adherence to the Boat. All those present inside it after a long time as if its setting a kind of climate for them in which they all could realise the beauty of nature and water to a higher extent.

7

The Final Emergence of Power (The Last Through)

29

The Atlantic Ocean occupies an elongated, S-shaped basin extended longitudinally amidst Eurasia and Africa to the east, and the Americas to the west. As one component of the interconnected global ocean, it is connected in the north to the Arctic Ocean, to the Pacific Ocean in the southwest, the Indian ocean in the southeast, and the Southern Ocean in the south (other definitions describe the Atlantic as extending southward to Antarctica). The equator subdivides it into the North Atlantic Ocean and South Atlantic Ocean.

The Atlantic Ocean is bounded on the west by North and South America. It connects to the Arctic Ocean through the Denmark Strait, Sea, Norwegian and Barents Sea. To the east, the boundaries of the ocean are proper Europe; the Strait of Gibraltar (where it connects with the Mediterranean Sea–one of its marginal sea–and, in turn, the Black Sea, both of which also touch upon Asia) and Africa.

In the southeast, the Atlantic merges into the Indian Ocean. The 20° East meridian running south from Cape Agulhas to Antarctica defines its border. Some authorities show it extending south to Antarctica, while others show it bounded at the 60° parallel by the Southern Ocean.

In the southwest, the Drake Passage connects it to the Pacific Ocean. The man made Panama links the Atlantic and Pacific Ocean. Besides those mentioned, other large bodies of water adjacent to the Atlantic are the Caribbean sea, the Gulf of Mexico, Hudson Bay, the Arctic Ocean, the Mediterranean Sea, the North Sea, the Baltic Sea, and the Celtic Sea.

This is the description of that place and everyone is now on their way over the surface of this Ocean to reach out towards the corner shore. Slowly and steadily everybody started getting sense of empowering nature, which this time playing a role to awake them from there tippled and astonishing kind of behaviour. As this is the time for them to get into the actualisation and face the whole vast natures breeze colours. Colours that had left a delightful and peace devotion life for them, which is needed to be covered now, as if it involves the whole humanity in its affinity. What's being going to happen, what a phase has life left for them to be followed? No one from them is aware about the next scene. Everything is not told to them and just they know is to meet the person named "Avnish" who stays near that ocean shore. He is the only person at present who could narrate any other thing to them. Now the shore of Ocean is just some meters away of this boat. Adrita, Yash and Figo had come away from their last prolonged intoxicated dullness and unconsciousness. Adrita stood up on the boat and saw all around with a sick face as if they are not aware of where were they going to be. So she prompted;

'Busshhh........look.......where we are......tell me anyone about this place as anyone told before', Adrita facing toward the Ocean.

Yash replied, 'Oh!......you were asking about this place and I felt that you got in some annoyance. Ah!.......yes about this place, it's been told to me before by "Pop Jesus" as if this would be the place from where we will going to get down to our actual world and people. So I guess you don't need to tensed about that'.

Figo getting up while rubbing his both eyes by his palm said 'Hm......you were right but see......your side we had came to the corner shore of it. I feel we all should wait to reach there and then make every other person conscious so that there are less questions stuck in there stomach and we need to answer those worthless things. As if our main concern and motive now is to get down there and Find person named "Avnish" somewhere around this place. He is only the narrator and descriptor for all of us'.

Time to drop them at the shore. As if boat also needs to leave to get back towards Heaven's Hell. The time of its interval is being diminishing off. They dropped down by the boat at the ocean end and everyone get down of it as to start there next journey.

Boat said to all of them standing this time away from it 'Now my work is over, you please give me the consent to park'.

'*Hey*.........you could speak also........as if your other extra ordinary functions being known to us. The way and assault you would had meant to get us back to "Earth surface" would not be any easier one', Ankit said.

'Yes I could....speak, I could breath, I could live also as if I am regarded as a living being at Heaven's Hell. Even do I consist of a name', Boat said.

'Oh!...yes if you do have a name then please share that too with us', Yash asked.

'My name is "Fluury" and I am a female. *Hey*...now I can't stay here for even a second as I need to go back. So God bless you all for your life ahead and give me the permit of fly'.

She diminished within few seconds. Everyone perceptional stares to her way because they don't know the next thing and phase to play. All started to move out of this place as they need to find that man who's been blessed to help them all by god will and pray. Surfing and searching started in every direction, though the long lonely land across the river looks like bundle of peace and happiness fall in over here. Each and everyone spread apart in that space, do some one eyes capture that person hidden in any cave.

So this is the hectic most time for all of them as if they don't know how to proceed and not even getting any sign of someone existence on that place so that they could find Avnish.

Adrita said, 'I think we would get nothing apart from being wasting time like this over here. This is obvious that to stay at this coldest place, there would be the requirement of wood and for food purpose also he would require substantial equipments whose availability at this place is in feasible. So he would be living in those forest area, that you all can also see in the east and over there only he would be going to have his home instead'.

Sunny replied, 'Yes... Adrita I feel you were profoundly right. Yash, I do feel the same thing that we are just simply wasting our time by finding him over this vacant land full of ice spread apart instead we should move now to that forest upside on those hills'.

After explication to this sort of thing everybody started to move towards the area in an alignment. So after walking for a while in this forest, in between of numerous green trees.

Soni Said, '*Hey*.... You all listen to me. There is a guy over there that's been cutting branches. I feel he could help us find out, in revealing the way towards Avnish estate. Seems like he would be very familiar with this place'.

Gaurav turned back, 'yes... he is right there is some one. Let me go across to him and ask about Avnish estate Wait...'

Gaurav called him.

'Hello... could you listen....to me..., could you hear me. Look.... I am hear your down stairs'.

That person looked towards them and he is being at 100m height distenace at most from where on the call made by Gaurav.He jumped straight away to the surface in front of Gauarv as if 100 m are nothing emphasis and difficult for him to jump though. He dropped his feet in front of Figo and asked him about his will from him.

Yash came in front and asked while putting his fingers into his chest, 'Look we are looking for Avnish very desperately as if our whole future depends on his words. So please inform us where is he. So that we could feel a bit more cure and go to have conversation to him'.

'Oh!...So you all had been come from Heaven's Hell. Oh!.....I see', person said.

Person replied, 'So my dear the person who is standing in front of you is being Avnish itself and let I explain you all that. this is not a easy place to live though, it's only me and only me who could survive over here, other's not even try to sustain their life's over here. I am surprised to see you all so quickly reaching this place, as if I had received the message of yours arrival, just an hour ago'.

Yash replied, 'Ok...then you are the one whom we want to meet. Ok you live over here but afraid it would be very difficult to do so'.

Avnish replied, 'It's not difficult than killing your soul everyday while facing cruelty and killing of humanity every day. Over here whatever I face but yes this place have no bad thoughts like human beings and is warm welcoming to every new thing. There is no race of success here so no cheating and killing is being done. There are lots of examples with me to say for that but I feel that this is not the time for all of us to talk about these things. As if this is the time for you all to know more about your life ahead'.

'So... just come along me to my estate just nearby there. We can share ourselves with no boundation', Avnish said while curling the cloth over his right hand that he is being having to wipe out his forthcoming perspiration due to hard word he did.

'You are an ultimate hero Yash, I didn't remember my last generations but "Pop Jesus" says that you were my best friend. He also told me some of your previous generation stories at apart levels. Believe me I got to be your fan while being hearing all that. Sometime I do think that too, as why didn't I had done those solemn things like you because if I would have done those, then I would be the hero of this generation as of you now', Avnish smiled and faced backward towards Yash to receive his reply on his comments.

The mark of innocence and the glory of power around Yash face made everything explicit to Avnish as if he didn't said any word to him.

Adrita put forward and said, 'Now we are not getting late. As if you had started some stuff over here'.

Avnish smiled and said, 'Miss... nothing to say. afraid for that we are just some steps away from my place'.

Hut made of broken rocks and covered by big green leafs to give it shelter. It is being meant very architecturally fortified and profoundly of mixed temperature with the refreshing clean river flowing over the rocks lying in the front door of his place. Everybody get inside into it.

Yash before taking his place asked, Avnish 'Now it's the time for you to help us and liberate all sort of wisdom that you do consists and that "Pop Jesus" had said you to tell us'.

Adrita started spirit warmer in that climate as if sun directly shines over that place. Her facial reactions was getting wild as now. It's becoming difficult for her to resist all this. Everyone remarks were towards Avnish at this time as they were being evacuated by Avnish to this place in the mean to know some depth. Ronu felt some abnormality in Adrita which he had felt never before, he started barking with anxiety so that everyone could probe out what had happened with her. They all gather that the condition of Adrita is not being in a proper as she is unable to breath conveniently. She was spirit a lot discomfort at this place which could be conveniently measured by her body and eyes movements. Yash leave his place run towards Adrita, bend his feet, made his both palm to pull Adrita chin up so that he can see the pain that she is seeking to hide from everyone. Tears are there in her eyes and she is being breathing heavily.

Yash asked in a grief and tone;

'What being happening to you dear tell me please as if I can't see for even a single second'.

Everyone is too shocked and wanted to know about her pressurising pain so that they could arrange the ultimate help. Adrita replied in discomfort;

'It's becoming difficult for me to breath in this air because my body is not able to bear all this heat at this place. It is being felt by me from a long time but before temperature is a normal one, that could be beard but now it had evoked as a rising fire inside me'.

Yash shouted for help and said, 'Which thing is over here that is creating all that. What is the mean of secure towards all this......' Yash cry and said, there any way who could help us out.

The increasing pain of Adrita is tearing emotions of Yash apart. He is just nneeded Adrita to be normal anyhow now, as his eyes are not allowing water to stop flowing. This situations had become too worst, I and everyone just seeking to make Adrita feel reliable whether it is by dragging one by one pale filled with water over Adrita, that is being done by his friends.

Yash becoming helpless this time and he has been holding her in his arms while bending on his toes and screaming loudly. When Adrita shouted due to her pain Yash broken up internally and he clasped her tightly in his both arms.

Adrita said, 'It's becoming harder for me to breath'.

Avnish impinched after observing this whole situation and put forward to say '*Hey*....You all listen I thing I do have the solution to all this as I got to know the reason being its happening. You all just help me out. So firstly Ankit bring that big giant Pitcher lying at the right corner of my room. You..... Sunny do one thing takes this empty pail from my room and fill it profoundly through the flowing water just forth the door. You both do this thing soon and come back'.

Avnish on his own moved towards his cup board wreste that and started finding an small bin of glass which he had kept somewhere around in his top most shelf. Ultimately he found that though. Ankit and Sunny also reached there. Yash was still clasping Adrita in his arms as he is not getting any way to sort it out. Avnish took that small bin close to Yash face and crack to take Yash tears drop in that bin. At last Avnish got those tear drops in that bin. Then he took a glass of water from the Pitcher that Ankit carried and dropped that too in the pail of water that Sunny carried. He mixed those Yash tears drop too with it. Now he being all set inclined for his assault and for that, he said.

'You all help me out to take Yash away from Adrita for a while as I need to drag down this whole water on Adrita because this is the only one that is going to help her out'. They took Yash away from Adrita and he dragged all that water on her who started showing its ease and cure as if Adrita intimate and erotic expressions were becoming normal now and she is being relief from all sort of her pain. Yash was sit with his waist attached with front wall facing towards her. Yash was reliefed after looking towards Adrita peace and cure face. Smile dispersed from his face with his eyes getting wet. Yash desire, desperation and his pain all that demonstrate everything in a clearer way.

Soon Yash wake up from his place gone close to Avnish get hold of his both hand by his palm and asked, 'How did you solved this thing, your hands worked like a god to me.'

Ankit said, 'Yes please tell these things to us soon, as if this thing had ruined all of our vain'.

Avnish said, 'All this saviour thing is not happened because of me. Yash as it had been happened because of you. Firstly when Adrita started spirit awkward, I crack to measure her pain and then I gathered that there is no direct sunlight heat comes to the Heaven's Hell and Adrita hadn't faced this anytime at her place. So it is surely because of those wrecking instincts that do grow in this sunlight and try to harm her pure and refreshing power. This is not the only case. There are number of cases that would come across her in future. So this time I grabbed this thing that you and Adrita are being meant for each other to complete your comrade by both of yours measures. This is why I did all that with holy water. This thing of mine worked as I did expected. So there are no of others measure also to be taken at "Earth surface" which could wreck Adrita by several means'.

'This is a very serious concern though Avnish. Doesn't it have any way to sort this thing out, so that Adrita would be safe from all anxiety and stress? This thing should be cured anyhow', Ankit asked to Avnish.

'Yes... I had been informed about all these things before also but I was ordered that I am going to liberate all that to you when this is been required and I had never felt that this will come so soon', Avnish moved around his room and said all this to them.

Adrita after getting relieved from her pain asked, 'If you do know about everything then you would know about my parent too. If that is so then please give way their place to me. I had suffered a lot while being staying far from them for my whole past life. Please......I do want to see them. As you can ask Yash that how much I'd been desperate to meet them since my birth'.

Avnish replied, 'Adrita.... You were saying like that I am vague about your desperation towards your parent. I know that over here, I am the only one to tell you these entire things and help you to meet your belongings, but before that we should solve some salient things. If we didn't solved them and moved forward towards our other wills then this would be a crime because it is not just going to harm you only. If this time I had started to tell you the whole impact that humanity can face, then these things would be going to make you all very complicated. So lets us procedstep after the other in an ordered manner to freak out every problem in our way'.

Yash stood close to implication, shuffled Adrita and said while putting his hand across her shoulder '*Hey...* dear now please wipe out your tears from your eyes. There are enlightening powers over here that just knows capture and necklace, so you need to be known about that all dear and work accordingly. So don't hesitate and panic let's make a castle but with severity bricks whose frigidity can be feel by others eyes too'.

'So can I feel that... you are getting my point dear', Yash replied.

'Yash....!!!.......you don't need to be tensed about that. We will follow the way that Avnish is going to set for us', Adrita replied.

'Oh!... Thanks, thanks a lot for understand my points. *Hey* dear I do know that I am nothing in front of you both. You both are the power required by this nation and who will be the forthcoming saviours and natures hero. I just want to say that after coming back from Heaven's Hell I had dealt this whole world from the depth and that's not because of me. This everything is just because of you both, so that I can help you out afterward when you both will be going to come to me', Avnish insisted his heart true spirit towards them.

'What did you said just...say, you had also come from Heaven's Hell. You are also being called to Heaven's hell like us before and had drawn your period over there. Is it that so?', Sunny asked as he became to furious to know about it.

'Yes.....!!.......you were getting it right now, as I had also being called to Heaven's Hell like you only. I done some faults for which god feels I need to be punished at his place. So for that reason I had been over there. I do know about Adrita a lot as I had noticed her over there and at last time when I was leaving that place I had been told everything in deep about her. Dear believe that everything that we are going through is being set up by the God. That is why at the time of my departure from Heaven's Hell I had been given this soul responsibility to remedy you at the "Earth surface" and make ways expliciter to this world. So that new super power can take place and balance world's imbalanced pure forces', Avnish set for a relief that his identity is being profoundly explicit to all of them.

Yash asked, 'Avnish, this is the past whole story of yours. You could have told this to us before also, so that we started believing on your things from the commencing but now it is also not been late so, it doesn't matter. You could express anything now as we all our just waiting for you to speak up'.

As all this is going on Gaurav said to him 'Seriously whatever is being going on doesn't settle to be less than a super natural power story. Ok.... I feels we have to wait a bit more, let's see what's going to happen'.

'Yes Avnish, doesn't get tensed about anything now, as if with me all of us believe you now and this gives you the freedom of Expression', Adrita added in Yash words to make the aura easy for Avnish to proceed.

'Say Avnish... say we all are just waiting for your words', Ankit said to Avnish while coming close to him.

Avnish moved towards the door facing forth and said, 'Yash you and Adrita have to play a salient role in developing and decorating our nature. You both have to build a humanitarian world by spreading humanitarian beliefs that no one know more than you both. You have to utilise your power to save humans from erroneous damages by any black force or power. You both need to do a lot, but before that you both have to align yourself all together. You both need to become each others power', Avnish said these words and left the door, come in close to Yash.

Avnish added, 'Yash you both have to save this nature from not only internal damages but the external damages also, that any forth black source crack to impulse on them. Yash I feel that I don't need to tell you much about Adrita as "Pop Jesus" sir had informed you all about her past life and her powers that she do consist but had never used and that's why she doesn't knows about them', Avnish replied again to make both of them go inside the truth as quickly as feasible because anything could happen in the next phase.

Yash lost somewhere 'Yes... you were right as I had been informed about all sorts of things before by our respected "Pop Jesus" and he is the one who told me about Adrita and her parent. Yash shared his entire wisdom about this thing with Avnish.

'Ok...all this things are true and alright, but do you know what had happened after it. How did Adrita came back to Heaven's Hell', Avnish asked Yash.

Yash replied instantly in a loud tone 'Yes I do know... as if Adrita came back to Heaven's hell due to the demand of that time authorities from her mother in case of her punishment', Yash said and faced towards Avnish who is still facing blank.

So Avnish replied, '*Hey* Yash.... You hadn't reached to the accurate point. The point is that what do the mother's of Adrita had send all along with her. That is the thing which is emphasis'.

'Yes "Pop Jesus" had told me about it that there are two things with Adrita one is Ronu and the other one is that "Amulet" which is their in his neck and stores Adrita powers safely, so that no one could wreck her and her power', Yash informed Avnish.

Avnish replied, 'Now in picture there are three character you, Adrita and Ronu. So there are you three of them who need to stay together in a collective manner. So Yash "Pop Jesus" would have informed you that so, as if Adrita's power was being kept in that "amulet" that do stay in Ronu's neck and this power of her is worthless till that time she deliver that to her comrade. This power of Adrita can't be used on her own. As if it would be going to delivered to a person of pure soul, who would be going to become Adrita's comrade'.

Adrita shocked after listening to all this because of her ignorance about all this. Since childhood no one told her and even Yash didn't conveyed to her when he was revealing her those words he faced with "Pop Jesus".

'Yes I do know that... "Pop Jesus"... informed about this thing to me that time and I didn't shared with Adrita as I don't want to give her stress and crumble her smooth going life by knowing those things', Yash said to Avnish.

Yash said, '*Hey* Adrita please don't look over me like that. It's just because don't want to give you mind more pressure of wanders and emotions that's why I didn't shared this thing with you. As I though I will tell you all that whenever required', Yash said to Adrita after measuring her discomfort by listening to Yash words to Avnish.

Avnish said, 'I don't feel that you both need to flow in emotions this time, as if the time is very much crucial and to take action though'.

'So Yash as you had profiled everything to be so. I can feel that you know it all and you don't tensed now. I am over here to guide you what to do the next', Avnish replied.

'You all need to be concise in everything and every task from now onwards. I am saying all this not for just Yash and Adrita it's being said for all of you. As Yash would be the super hero after getting his actualization and he have to face many deficit powers thereafter. You all also needed to be poised for that', Avnish added.

Yash asked Avnish, 'so....Could you tell us about the next step to be followed? '

'Yash, Sure as for this thing only I had been over here, but Yes now. I got your functionality that make you more superior and extraordinary than me. As if at the point of work you just want to talk about it and nothing else. This is what you did for this nation and its people in your previous life. I am not like that in my past generation also and in this too, I lack in those functionality', Avnish replied and applauded Yash for his characteristics.

'But I think you are not getting the point. *Hey* say... can't you see my internal insist to know about the next step of ours as you are just circling around those thing that are being said to me by "Pop Jesus"', Yash said with an hesitating tone.

'Now I am not going to argue with you on all this, as if you also know that I am just seeking to help you out in the best feasible way, I could. Yash so you just want to listen about the track to be followed to save Adrita from viral nature effect that her body is not competent to bear, so I disclose you that', Avnish got a bit upset by hearing the last words of Yash.

Avnish took a break of some second gone towards his right hand side wall, bend a little and sat down on the wooden chair lying across his bed. He looked upward then and said 'the way to solve all these is just both of yours alignment. You both Yash and Adrita need to tie a nod of relationship with one another so that you could make each other entire and secure. As Adrita gets in relational bond with you all those powers which are non utilitarian to her could be used by you and with those you can be the next super natural power Hero to save humanity. Because of this power only Barrack at heaven's Hell was following Adrita from last many years and not allowing anyone to come in contact with her. Barrack is insecure to see whenever Adrita comes in contact with anyone and he does everything to make that person stay away from him', Avnish informed them.

'Yes I do.......know about these things before as "Pop Jesus" informed about this to me but I never felt that all this is going to happen like this. Regarding Barrack also I do know everything and at the time of our escape. He had crack to halt me too, but he became unable to do so', Yash replied.

Adrita prompted heavily, 'What he came in your way when we were leaving Heaven's Hell and you didn't even attempted tell me this entire still. This thing is really embarrassing Yash'.

Yash replied, He is not able to harm even a single scratch on my body. I broken up his pyramid conveniently and God also helped me in that. I feel all this thing occurred because of that faithful person of him which is being listening to our words. What is his name?...'

'Alasky...', Adrita replied.

'Yes Alasky very accurately', Yash added.

Ankit said, 'Its been ok for this time but for next time you would have to tell us the whole story I brief... is it ok for you dear'.

Yash laughed, '*Hah*...yes brother'.

Avnish approached everyone now with his heavy tone 'So listen you all this time as if this should be known to you all. Yash you had to go Church not alone but with Adrita. Take her along with you and protect her from the sunburn and don't allow her to get in directly contact with it because if that happened then this could be very devastating for everyone. You need to be so conscious about it'.

'But at least tell me the reason for which I need to go there', Yash asked.

'Ah!......I haven't told you about the priest first and I was thinking that I had told you', Avnish said and slapped his head.

'Ok let me tell you about our honorable priest named "Osheen". He is the foremost priest who had sacrificed his whole life in sake of humanity. He had survived with an unoriginal life style without building his family and enemies. You would feel grateful to meet him there as his face calmness will fill your soul with power of delight. Over there you will meet him early morning at 7 am. After that everything is being governed by him. Then you and Adrita would be tied in an unbreakable bond for your whole life that is the bond of Marriage', Avnish ended as liberating wisdom to them is being finished now.

Yash came more closer to Avnish and asked, 'What marriage... we need to do marriage in the sense to protect Adrita and others. How could it will be going to work? Tell everything in brief Avnish don't cut short things and say one after the other'.

There had been happiness seen on Adrita's face when she heard about there both alignments as she wanted that only and she said 'Sometimes God desires matches exactly my desire of thought. May be God read it all from my mind first?'

'Yes... everything will be going to work automatically after you both get aligned. After you both are going too tied up in a nod then honorable "Osheen" sir will describe all natures wonder things for you. Now I request you all not to ask anything more form me as I don't know even a single block more than that. All other things would be going to get explicit to you both at the church'.

Adrita, 'If that is all so....................then I am excited about it. I hadn't got time to express my whole sort of love towards Yash before all this happened because after this we would be all together'.

Yash smiled and said, '*Hey* don't tensed my dear you can express your love to me for the whole life. I didn't said anything for that', Yash tried to tease Adrita as he loves to see every reaction of her.

Gaurav said in Soni's ear 'all this things is getting filmy out over here, with *kadak masala* and magic dear. This happens in actual life too, I'd realised it today only'.

Soni said, 'Agreed... I am profoundly agreed said as me too thinking that so, some time before'.

Avnish now pinched in this romantic kind of environment set amidst Yash and Adrita. He said, 'Ok... cut it off all this dear... everything is being explicit to all of you. You all need to face the actual life of "Earth surface". Where you do know what different kind of people resides. It could be difficult for Adrita to understand them at first but afterwards she would be going to mixed up in all this culture'.

Adrita's anxiety started increasing about the "Earth surface" as smile is dispersing from her cheeks which clearly shows her overwhelming happiness about knowing these thing from Yash.

Adrita said, 'Means all this would be going to be a lot adventurous to me. Surely... I am going to love that all to peaks'.

'Afraid to hamper you all, as if I am standing in the corner listening all sorts of things. I reached to a conclusion that you all can follow if you like that. It's been a long journey that we did after that we climbed rocks to reach at Avnish place and now we are standing over our respective place since hours. I think everything is clear now whatever we have to do next, would be going to done tomorrow as if this place is not Heaven's Hell. This is our "Earth surface" where day light shuts down soon. I think you all understand what I need to say', Sunny said it all and started looking to everyone face.

Now this time Sunny had make everyone so implication in his words that they shouted all together and said 'So....what you are seeking to say then......'

Sunny stepped back and said 'So... I wanted to say that it's been dark now and we all had covered a long distance with lots of stress. Shall we have rest now... ', Sunny said that in a very helpless face.

Sunny furious expressions which make all of them to laugh a lot. The happiness is being now spread all over on every tensed face. This is how these all ended their first day back on "Earth surface" with Avnish. After all this everyone took their respective place in the room of Avnish and covered up surface of his room. Everyone sleep that night very peacefully. Yash and Adrita were lying all together with their hand curling each other and Adrita's head being on his Bows. They both dreamed for a bright future ahead and in this entire thing Yash is quite a bit afraid also about. As if he would be competent with providing happiness on every face and building humanity when he'll be the power owner. With all these wanders and happiness this night started getting darker, Everyone soy in wondering bundle of smile at their next door in near future.

30

Clock...Clock...this is the beginning of a new day and the day of Yash & Adrita.

Heavy sound of crawling birds, chipmunk's ground squirrel that all were bursting around the tree nearby to their place. As these sounds are very familiar to Adrita in Heaven's Hell. It is a usual thing for her to wake up through their tone. Adrita even plays with these small creatures and try to gather there sound to communicate with them. She knows a lot about their gesture and emotions. Within some second as she looked out from the window, one squirrel came and sat on the forth stand of window. Then they both started talking to each other. It settle like Adrita is giving the accurate response of every word said by the squirrel which shows she understand their language of expression. Both their communication is being making the aura quite exciting. Soon Yash heard something from vising sound in the surround, he wake up slowly as if he don't want to disturb Adrita. Which according to him is still sleeping. Yash see that this quisling sound is being produced by Adrita while facing out of window towards top of the tree where a cuckoo is sitting and they both were allotted words. Yash won't be able to remove his eyes from this scene as he is being overhauled to see all this act of Adrita.

Yash said, 'Oh!... how cute she looks while being doing all this'.

Adrita distracted towards Yash and said 'Yash...you waked, are you saying something'

Yash smiled and said, '*Nah*...nothing'

'Then see, what this cuckoo is saying me two fold. She is saying me to sing, same as the cuckoo of Heaven's hell says to me. I felt nothing apart over here dear everything is the same over here and animals are also sober of this place, with just a dull deflection of climate', Adrita said to Yash.

Yash smiled, '*Hah*... this you are saying just for my happiness and not because things are same over here. As there is a big natural difference between the both'.

Figo is not being seen over there on his place where he had soy because of which Yash got so much apprehensive as he is new to his planet. Yash started getting mad on this thing while being finding him all around that place and as Yash reached the shore; he had seen a creature very far from his eyes jogging near that shore. He couldn't see that person explicitly for which Yash moved little nearer to him in his direction.

Yash said, 'Ah! that is our Figo I got so much worried about him and he's busy doing his daily routine to jog in early morning'.

'Figo......... come dear', Yash shouted to call him up.

As Figo reached back to Yash. He is being gasping for breath Yash smiled on him, '*Hey*....My dear you have any alarm set inside you that awake you exactly at your right time and pressurise you also to perform those. Hm... is that so...'

Figo while being painting still, smiled and said 'Na... Yash that's not the thing it's like whenever I do perform my all daily activities properly then whatever it would be the place I am profoundly cozy over there. So as if "Earth surface" is being new to me, so I am seeking to get familiar with it as soon as feasible'.

'Oh!......my buddy!!!.......that is the scene......felt good to listen your wandereds of living which are apart from others same as mine', Yash replied.

This is the time when everyone had been awaken up but still lying on bed. Soon Soni asked Gaurav;

'Dear........see Avnish is doing something over there, while being sitting down with his curled legs and facing the wall. You are close to that place see what he is been doing.' After that Gaurav stood partly upwards to notice Avnish activity and he found;

'Ah!.........he is making tea........for all of us......... Morning tea', Gaurav replied to Soni.

'Oh!..........sweet,......he is going to boost our day with morning tea, really it's been a long time I didn't tasted morning tea. Now this is the first spirit that makes me feel as if I am back on the "Earth surface"', Soni replied happily.

So Yash took along Figo back to their room, Avnish Said;

'Hot and sizzling morning tea is been inclined for you all my friends'.

Yash said, 'Oh!...You make tea, my one of the best lonely comrade. You make tea but how and from where did you get all its ingredients?'

'*Hey*....listen I do know that I live in a forest kind of place but I am not away with any of my daily needs, as if I make it available to me anyhow. If that is not feasible then I develop another similar dish to my older one. So you got my point, I feel', Avnish answered.

Ankit, soon wake up from his bed after listening about tea, he rubbed his eyes and said, 'Yash I am not going to listen anything from you as I am also going to Church with you today. My dear may be you did not know that for every marriage there is a requirement of a witness and you would require that'.

After saying with a sober and requiter face. Everyone felt that, Ankit slept last night or not. May be he would be thinking for the same thing his whole night, that's why he started his day by ejecting those words out of his stomach.

Yash have no words to answer him now as he is just laughing perceptional on this thing like others, holding cup of tea in his hand. Soon after getting all this Avnish said;

'I feel Yash, I would have said you wrong that you and Adrita had to go alone at the church today. So you must take down Ankit too with you as if he must act as a helping hand', Avnish smiled for a second.

Adrita asked, 'That's ok......and what about Ronu as he is the one very emphasised creature to go along with us........yes I am right'.

'Yes.................you are correct my miss. How could you can be wrong anytime. Ronu have to go along with you, both as he is the only one who kept you safe from others and carried this "amulet" full of power in his neck since years', Avnish replied.

Soon after having a look on tea, Adrita asked 'What this thing is being called and why you all are drinking this like taking one nip at a time and then waiting for some second to take the other one' this become a point of fun and laughter for everyone.

Yash said, 'My dear......this thing being a heritage in our planet. Whoever we are everyone loves to have this and its name is "Tea". In our place at "India" this is being regarded a lot by people. I give you a look of it as we move ahead towards India'.

So the conversation remained like that but Adrita and Yash were not being involved in it now, as if they both started getting refreshing up to move towards the church.

Avnish said, 'You both..............would require my "Zuby" to get out of this place and move to the city area where you need to travel on other convinces. *Hey* over there you would require currency but I don't have that, as if it is not required by me anytime over here and I don't travel to that place also'.

Yash said, '*Hey* you don't tensed about that we'll manage but yes you said about some "Zuby" where it is and how it's going to help us out in reaching over there'.

'"Zuby" is just standing at yours back said see', Avnish said, as Zuby is an big giant Eagle of Avnish with whom help he took a ride of the whole forest and area nearby to it. Sometime Avnish do go to cities also but he really hate cities and human selfish nature so he try to stay apart from that.

Yash and Adrita both turned to see Zuby. Yash said, '... It's been a giant Eagle, this is yours Zuby. Whatever it is but yes I must say it's been a very appetite personality'.

Adrita said, 'Zuby... Wow... she looks like my "Harry" at Heaven's hell, as you don't know Yash I am also having the same over there. The difference is just that she is in is in brown colour and my Harry is in entire white colour, but both have same innocence on their face.'

'Seems....you both loved that...that's fine then my pleasure, but where is Ankit and Ronu as they also need to go with you', Avnish said and within a second tone came from inside that 'I am coming', this is said by Ankit. After this Ronu also come out running towards so that Yash could clasp him in his arms and give his love.

Everyone came this time and now it's been a time for them sit on Zuby's waist and fly down to the city area from where they can board to the church. Everyone had been set to take their flight over Zuby which started within some seconds. All four of them were blissful about the ride and the height on which they are at present while being on ride. As time passed, they had reached the border of the city land area. Zuby dropped all of them nearby to the road from where they could conveniently go through towards the Church as said by Avnish. Zuby went off from that place soon so that no one notice her over there as she is not a normal creature in wildlife.

This time all four of them are standing across the road waiting for any Taxi to cross that road and complete their journey.

Yash said to them, 'You all can take a corner of the road and I'll try to halt any taxi or someone else who could take us forward, so that we could reach the Church as soon as feasible. As time is also being passing through speedily. Wait......I'll try'.

Yash said, Everyone to stay out of it and him on his own, started seeking to take lift from any car or to halt any Taxi. After a long struggle there was no one who had was a good poured a hand of charity to them and everyone had just rushed away. Yash was astonished by these things.

Adrita said to Ankit while standing at the corner, 'How many arrogant and unreal people do resides over here, as of now no one halted to help us. See how Yash is been seeking to make things work but no gain, this is seriously not good'.

Yash now stood in the mid of the road to ask for lift from anyone as there are only limited taxi's crossing this place. This is the morning time and every other person is too engaged and occupied in his work that they don't even think to help anyone. After some time Yash stopped a car and started persuading him to drop them at church as if this person is also going through that way. After a long conversation that man didn't agreed to took them along with him, so Adrita stood close to Yash now and she bend to gaze this person through his open window. Adrita Gazed he perceptional with her eyes for a minute and when she removed her eye contact that person agreed to take them along anywhere. Yash got sick after looking all this. He asked Adrita.

'How did you make this true dear? As if I do have measured this person and he is a entire negative one. He wouldn't have allowed coming along with him in any cost, but you made it?'

'I just used my eyes for that', Adrita said fluently.

Soon after a little time they reached to the Church and get down it. Yash thanked the person and that person replied with a smile towards him.

Yash said while stretching his arms in the both direction 'This is not at much distance from that place where Zuby had dropped us. Even then too no one is being agreed to come over here. How do we teach all these things to people?'

Adrita said, 'Yes.... that's so true... See these are your people and how did they react'.

Ankit impeded in amidst and said, 'Ok... then let us halt all this and move towards the Church as we need not to waste any time more standing over here'.

'How could I forget that........as the timing is 7.00 am and we being late still', Yash ran and picked his small bag that he's carrying with him. Yash bit Adrita's hand tightly and faced started hoping step by step on the stairs. This time he is being facing towards the cross mark held at the top of the Church, as if this is being tempting him towards itself. So as Yash started climbing stairs of Church, he started spirit some sort of stamina being developing inside his intellects which being emphasising him and evoking extra ordinary juice inside his body. Yash faced Adrita once while there both being hoping stairs. This look of Yash is entirely apart this time as Adrita felt him profoundly filled of might on his face and valor is seen conveniently by her on his features and expressions. Adrita settle to come to know about and air of this place that is making flow of their blood particles to attain its natural empowering colour. Ankit and Ronu were following both of them and really this time Ankit was also having a look of unconscious Yash which he had never seen before. This time the floppy flow of air do have some intrigue hidden behind it which wants some positive mutation to occur. This mutation they do want to wipe out some never ending tears in others eyes.

So at last Yash, Adrita and all others reached at the foot step of Church door, which is been closed. Yash with his flame of passion wreste the big door and soon he received sight of Jesus exactly in front of him that blessed him loads. They all stepped inside after Yash. No prayer, No lectures are being going on at this place now. The whole church world is squeezed in deep silence as if it is being waiting for this. Soon a heavy tone come from the corners;

'Welcome.......you all come......My Gentleman; you being blessed by the paramount energy in this generation which can combat with all the bad datums and black energy at once. The thing that is just making you away from it still is because you don't know about that and you haven't gained your comrade', This tone had came from the four sided corner of the church and nobody is being seen too over there so it's hard to inference that who said all these.

Abruptly a reflection started getting into the church from the sides and this increased till they could realise about whose reflection. This shadow is of priest "Osheen" who came out from the back side of the giant bible carrying effigy of our loved God "Jesus". He came out of it with a smiley face and he said;

'What.....why you all are being sick for. Yes this is being my tone at the commencing time. So no need to make your faces like this, as I just want Yash to know one thing again that this is the time for responsibility. This is a responsibility attached to the power which Yash have to utilise in the best natures effective way. I want to make this thing clear to you all that after you all are going to get out of this church your life starts its third phase. This third phase could be difficult for you all. It depends how you all manage', priest Osheen said all this while coming close in contact with all of them.

So as Osheen came close in contact with them, He put his hand on Adrita eyes and closed them though. Osheen said then;

'I wish before I do anything let me give a look of future to our all devotion and very pure tenet following girl because of whom all this is happening today', Osheen said all this to Adrita as if this time he wants her to see something beyond this time period.

Adrita stood calm and quiet for a while and then her expression started modulating, her breaths were started becoming heavier. All others are the same remarks and worried to know the scenes seen by Adrita. In the last Adrita became happy and that happiness of her stayed for a long time. She started breathing normally and peacefully. After some seconds, Osheen put his hand away from Adrita and the memories of all that she saw were still in her mind at that present time. So because of her last emotion was happiness. She had uncovered her bad part that she saw, as if "End is well then all is well".

She started facing everyone now as to realise those scenes she had seen before and seeking to relate them. She is getting implication and tensed as if it's becoming difficult for her. The past bad scenes were also started coming again to her thoughts. . Osheen felt that this needs to be finished now as if whatever he wants to do, he had done that.

Now Osheen took a step close to her again did the same... closed her eyes, but this time it is for some seconds and he moved his hand away.

Yash asked with anxiety 'Sir... what is this and why were you playing like that with Adrita... if it do consist some reason then you can share with me too'.

'Though if you are not even going to ask that then too. I am going to answer your question dear. This I did to give way a look of your future life to Adrita. As she is the one purest in soul than you all, so she could sense everything very conveniently so I had given her that phase close to her eyes for a while. Now...before you all ask me the next question that what did I done second time. So let me tell you my child, second time I had ruined and abolished all the memories that had been developed in Adrita's intellect after looking of future suspects. As all this is being said to me before', Osheen replied with a smiley face.

Osheen said, 'Afraid my child you all need to deal with it as I can't do anything in that'.

'That's I can understand sir from your helpless face' Yash said while kissing Adrita's head, as if she had been scared after both these acts to her and she don't know anything about these.

Osheen said, 'Now I feel you both apart from Yash and Adrita could take your seats as if I am going to start their Marriage ceremony... So You both my child inclined for that'.

Yash and Adrita with their clubbed hands and looking in each other eyes with a bit of sleave in those said 'Yes, Sir', with a smile.

'I am not going to ask you both those number of questions as if both your story is very much explicit-er in my eyes. So come children lets finish tiding this band in both of your hand to make a bond between you both', Osheen said and he started;

'So you've decided to get married in a Catholic church. Congratulations on the sacramental journey you are about to begin. Indeed, the ceremony you will be planning is more than just an event, it is a sacrament, a sign of your union together legged upon the love of Christ. It is not a sign like a halt that says one thing plainly and simply. Rather it is a sign to the world of the covenant (sacred and permanent) relationship into which God has called the two of you. Because your marriage is that kind of sign, it will have an effect on everything about you. Likewise, it will have varying effects on everyone you know. In short, you do not marry in private'; Osheen said these things to inform them about Marriage first. After hearing this they both again faced each other and smiled as if they are overwhelmed to marry each other.

Osheen asked then from Yash, 'Do you regard Adrita as your wife for whole life'.

Yash agreed. 'Yes'

Osheen asked Adrita, 'Do you regard Yash as your husband for whole life'.

Adrita confidently said, 'Yes'.

As soon they both agreed for it, everyone as if Ankit, Ronu and Osheen became too happy. All others started clapping to express their excitement and craze towards all this.

Adrita and Yash face now settle to be easing in peace, as if they are perceptional looking into each other eyes by overtightened the whole world.

Osheen said 'Now my child you both can kiss each other……'

There is no response by both of them to what Osheen said as if they were still lost in one another. Osheen smiled and said loudly this time;

'Now… my child you both can kiss each other… are you listening'.

Then climatic excitement without saying anything, Yash and Adrita went to have a smooth long sizzling kiss. This scene is becoming memorable as did anyone could measure there desperation towards each other and there's last-longing love.

So Osheen scratch his through a bit in order to make a popping sound to get both of them back to this world, as if now Osheen need to talk with them on a serious concern.

After listen to Osheen they both came back from their love in the actualization and Osheen said;

So if you both had come back into this world then now we can talk on the main and serious concern. On which I had talked with you all at first. Now as you Yash had been married to Adrita and become the owner of that whole power which can combat with any devastating creature's power. So let us talk about it a bit.

'Yash as you had uncovered everything and become the Super natural power bearing hectic superior now. So there is no need for Ronu to carry this amulet in his neck now onwards. These powers being delivered to you for helping humanity and needy people. Yash you need to follow every principles that all were being meant to help and cure beings from the astonishing disastrous effects. Yash this is the time for you to come up in action as if to hide your desire and fulfill others. You have to be present for every human being whenever he is going to be in your need. The main motive of yours is to protect this declining humanity from our surrounds because if you are being able to teach others in building that so, your work could lessen up. Yash you have to make People feel that they could stay happily while following humanity by being humanitarian to every single person. Osheen given a big brief speech to Yash about his upcoming future strength wonders and the deed he needs to follow with it.

Yash stood quite at this time over his place as he's realising all that is being said by Osheen sir.

Surrounding of that period is too vacant with any emotion as do its waiting for Yash to evoke world from his generous spirit now that will make the next move to the out flowing air. As this is the time of Yash to realise himself.

'Sorry dear...Sorry through your fascinate doesn't provoke me still, I feel it would going to take time for your insight lightening waves in your body too sense all that in you. As if you can't act as an saviour of humanity and strength of universe till your soul vacant spirit is not going to get filled with truth blood that had started from this period to encover the whole land', Osheen replied after his measures.

Osheen replied, 'Yes...little hamster Yash its been true that you were unable to make your soul instincts to reliably accept this major turning concern. This will be going to take time for you to realise all that'.

Yash make a move and said, 'The first thought you expressed is hard to digest by my fluctuating wanders and you had through a new ball'.

Osheen replied, 'You can't move away from anything my innocent walker as you are the only one who is clubbed and approached by God to handle the flag of saffron beauty of this world beyond with whatever you were praised at present'.

'I don't know while living onwards how much time it would be taken up by your surrounded positive aura to make your senses work in an efficient way towards your upcoming strength. But this is true that they will make your robust internally and externally soon to relief all those sort of upcoming disastrous faced by the world', Osheen continued to give Yash thoughts a shape of future figure that he have to modulate and design further.

Adrita standing still with her same innocence and sweet little cheeks just waiting for relieved thought now after all this hard fight. So that they could soften up this tough surrounding a bit with there laugh. Seems like she had lend all her responsibilities and even her dependency on Yash. She also becoming relied on Yash now for the next phase lead. Seems she knows and too confident about the datum that "Those trusty eyes of her are enough for Yash to fight with anything".

Osheen now just turned around took a Handcart in his hand and came back in front of Yash. 'Yash......take this my child'.

Yash with his titter tone, 'What is there in it'.

Osheen said, 'It do contain your dress my dear boy as you are going to be the next super major curing power, who is going to uplift humanity and save it. These would act as your power dress which increment your energy and protect you too in your tasks.

You are a super hero now my child... as soon as you get my point that would be good for you'.

Yash replied, 'No.... No sir doesn't think like that, I am very much cozy with all this now... but you also know this is a big way and I need to make it expliciter'.

Osheen said, 'Yes... very true dear, it's been the time of prayer at church. Every person will be going to come over here and I don't want them to see you like this over here so.........you all this time should leave from here and Yash you should start performing your duties with yours Heavenly unbeatable Powers'.

Adrita said, 'Yes sir, we leave for now and you bless us for our well being. As you just said that we are going to start our third phase, we are going to move out of the Church'.

'Yes my dear and you don't even need to say that either as my blesses are all with you my childcare's... every time'.

Now every one of them turned towards the door even Ronu is remarks in so intelligent way this time as if it settle like he is getting everything that is going on over here. Numb is there on everyone face. Yash is wondering about the thing that do he is able to manage all these powers in an accurate way. Yash shuffled in his bundled wanders this time. There is only Adrita from all of them who is very confident and started blissful everything again as if nothing had happened to them. She doesn't settle to be cared of future then too as she had seen it from her eyes. Whether those scenes were being removed from her retentions but they could come back if she would try a bit.

So they all stepped out of the Church Yash straight away looked towards the Sky as he is asking something from his God. His stress is being declared by his forthcoming lines on forehead. Adrita saw Yash came across him and said;

'Yash... what is this what are you thinking dear... Ok if you don't trust yourself that you would be going to manage all this very conveniently, I give you that trust and confident of mine. This is because my dear I do know you very profound now and that's also true as if no one other person is being competent to have these powers also apart from you. You have to do that my dear and you will be going to believe me that am true', Adrita said this while keeping her hand on his shoulder to give him reliability and strength.

Soon heavy rain started at that place to drain the whole area in the spirit of love and prosperity. Every one of them was walking this time on their track to get back to their other friends. abruptly rain started happening very heavily so need to take shelter of nearby Mall across that road. They all get into it. Adrita dress was too unique and quite similar to a princess, so every other girl is being afraid to see her like this. Adrita was not cared about all, as this rain is making her so amazed about it that she couldn't able to halt her steps. They all were standing this time on ground floor, an area separated by glass from forth. They all were looking towards rain and lost in their wandered. Adrita is getting too queasy this time as if she wants to dance in rain and she did that so. Adrita ran towards forth while Yash being blocking her with his hand in her way, then too she hadn't listened. She had gone out and ran with her hands wreste up in the sky to touch its every drop. She started swiveling in a circle out there on the road with her closed eyes full of dream facing towards the sky.

The other parts of Creatures of this story were being over the forest areas that were also being waiting for the arrival of them all. Everybody over here is stressed and circling around the room as they had took a lot time to come back to the place. All were apprehensive about the happening they would have faced at church.

Avnish said '*Hey*... I think you all need to ease in peace apart for being so apprehensive about them. Yash is not a normal person and Adrita is on her own can handle the whole situation. So this belief of ours towards them for getting into any annoyance should not be even felt by us'.

Sunny replied, 'Yes I feel you were saying rigorous-pro'.

Avnish waited for some time closed his eyes and lay down on his bed. Avnish said;

'There is lot more things to be done as if Adrita would have to meet her parents and then I am also apprehensive about the Barrack,' Yash said.

As if Barrack would also not going to let be relieved everything. He is going to come and hamper Yash in his life and task. Many things to be seen my boys... Many things to be seen... Many things to be seen... Many things to be seen'.

So Avnish said his last words and he soy off after revealing all that.